Also by Josie Silver
Available from Random House
Large Print

The Two Lives of Lydia Bird

ONE NIGHT on the ISLAND

ONE NIGHT
on the
ISLAND

a novel

Josie Silver

RANDOM HOUSE
LARGE PRINT

Copyright © 2022 by Josie Silver

All rights reserved.
Published in the United States of America by Random House Large Print in association with Ballantine Books, an imprint of Random House, a division of Penguin Random House LLC, New York.

Originally published in the United Kindgom by Penguin Books UK, part of the Penguin Random House group of companies.

Cover design: Sarah Horgan

The Library of Congress has established a Cataloging-in-Publication record for this title.

ISBN: 978-0-593-55874-4

www.penguinrandomhouse.com/large-print-format-books

FIRST LARGE PRINT EDITION

Printed in the United States of America

1st Printing

This Large Print edition published in accord with the standards of the N.A.V.H.

For the completely marvelous Katy Loftus

ONE NIGHT on the ISLAND

Cleo, September 28, London

Finding my flamingo

You genuinely want to send me to a remote island to marry myself?"

A warm flush creeps up my neck as I sit across the desk from Ali, my terrifyingly enigmatic boss at **Women Today**. She's asked me to do some fairly out-there things over the years, but this one tops the lot.

"It's not legally binding," she says, as if that makes it better.

"Look." I pinch the bridge of my nose, choosing my words carefully. "It's one thing for an A-lister to declare she's 'self-coupling' for an interview in **Vogue**, Ali. It's altogether different for an almost thirty-year-old dating columnist to claim she's doing it too."

I stumble as I say my age; the number sticks like glue in my mouth. Thirty felt like just another year until I was twenty-nine and three-quarters, but now that my landmark birthday is a few weeks away, I've started to experience all kinds of unexpected and unwelcome anxieties. I was, I **am**, determined not to be someone who makes a big drama out of it, but with every passing day it's as if someone adds an extra weight onto my shoulders—one of those mini cast-iron ones you see in old-fashioned kitchen scales. I'm disappearing under tiny, invisible kitchen weights, and Ali has noticed my diminishment because Ali notices everything. She didn't get to be the editor of one of the UK's leading online women's lifestyle magazines by resting on her laurels; her meteoric rise is well documented in the industry with both green-eyed envy and huge respect. I consider myself lucky to work for her; I'd even go so far as to count her as a friend. A laser-eyed, ball-of-energy friend who terrifies me and makes me do things I don't want to, such as decamping to a remote Irish island I've never heard of to marry myself.

"Honestly, Clee, I came across that old Emma Watson interview again over the weekend and all I could think about was you." She gets up from her chair to pace, too excited by her own idea to sit. "A string of dating failures and disasters, about to turn thirty"—she ticks the list off on her fingers as she speaks—"trying to define her place in the world as a single woman, pressured by the media and the expectations of others."

"I feel sick with sorrow for her, I really do," I say. "It must be a shocker having to snog R-Patz for a living." He made a lasting impression on teenage me—all that immortal glittering. Is it any wonder I've struggled to find love after being set such unrealistic expectations? There's a whole other column for another day.

"She's never had to snog R-Patz. Don't minimize Emma's contribution to make yourself feel better, you know I'm onto something here."

I pick at a loose thread on the arm of the office chair. "It's not strictly fair to say I've had a string of dating disasters. It **is** my job."

"I know, I know. We pay you to swipe right and wear your big, beautiful heart on your sleeve. We love you for your optimism and your faith in finding your flamingo."

Finding My Flamingo is the name of my online column, so called because flamingos mate for life. We experimented with other animals that mate for life too, but Finding My Gibbon suggested red bums and picking each other's ears, and Finding My Beaver lowered the tone in a most unstylish way. Finding My Flamingo felt appropriate, but as time has gone on I've become somewhat less invested, in no small part because I've been gifted so much flamingo-related shite that I could open a flamingo-related shite shop.

"Look, Clee, you need to do something to mark turning thirty. It's a seismic moment in a woman's life." Ali pauses in that specific way she does when something bad is coming next. "It's this or the tattoo."

I sigh; I really should have seen that coming. The tattoo has become a bit of an in-joke at team meetings. Any time I'm struggling for column content, someone gives me the side-eye and then suggests I get a flamingo inked indelibly on my skin, preferably in a place it can't easily be concealed.

"Okay. Look, I always kind of liked what Emma said about self-coupling," I say cautiously. "I get it. She was saying she's enough already, alone but not lonely."

Ali nods. She doesn't interrupt me; I know she's hoping I'm going to talk myself into it. She's excellent at deploying silence to get what she wants.

"She's a vibrant, independent woman who understands that there's more than one way to achieve a fulfilled life," I say. "She isn't a failure because she doesn't have a partner and a bunch of kids, and **she** doesn't let the fact that both of her sisters and her brother are married with their own broods pressure her, or feel forced to defend her singledom at every family gathering, even if she is drowning in an ocean of wedding and baby shower invitations— I mean, I'm genuinely happy for them all, but do they really need to wave it in my face in gold italics, for God's sake?"

I stop, realizing my voice has grown loud and somewhere in there I'd switched from talking about Emma Watson to talking about myself. Besides, it was unfair of me to include my brother, Tom, in my list of grievances— he's the only member of my family who never mentions my waning egg supply or lack of a significant other. Of my three siblings, he's furthest in age from me, seven years to be precise, yet we're closest in every other way. It'd be easy to cast him as a father figure in my life, given that I was a baby when our father died, but Tom was the one slipping teenage me an illicit cigarette under the table and covering for me when I stayed out late at night. We both take after my dad, apparently, dark hair and eyes full of trouble, if Mum is to be believed.

Ali sits back down, absolutely unfazed by my speech, her fingers steepled in a way that suggests she's either thinking or praying. "Exactly my point," she finally says. "This is the perfect opportunity to get away from the pressure of the huge surprise party your family is planning for your birthday, a valid reason to politely duck out of any impending weddings and baby showers, and the chance to catch your breath for the first time in three years."

"My family is planning a surprise party?"

Ali nods. "Your mum emailed me last week to check if you'd be able to take some time off and to ask for a list of all of your 'London friends.' I use air quotes because she used actual quotes. She also mentioned looking up your old schoolmates on Facebook. Old boyfriends. Your funeral without you dying, basically."

My fingers itch to text Tom for the low-down. I love my family dearly, but surely they know me well enough to know that the ghosts of my past jumping out at me in a darkened room would be my personal hell? I'd rather get that flamingo tattoo. On my face.

"So basically, it's a huge birthday party, or I accept your proposal that I self-couple alone on a remote island no one's ever heard of off the Irish coast," I say, summarizing the meeting.

"Salvation Island," Ali says. Her satisfied expression tells me how pleased she is by the serendipitous name of the aforementioned remote island. She probably changed it herself by petition, or whatever it is you have to do to change the name of an island. It's the kind of stunt she'd pull if she thought it would boost readership.

"All expenses paid," she adds, as if that's going to be the clincher.

"Can't I self-couple in my flat?"

"No."

"The Maldives?"

"Not all expenses paid, no."

"Will it be cold?"

Ali's face contorts with the effort of trying to turn a grimace into a smile. "Come on now. Who ever wrote their best work under a beach umbrella? Think inspirational log fires and steaming cups of ambition."

"You totally stole that line from Dolly Parton," I grouch, not at all happy with the situation.

Ali's eyes gleam. "No nine-to-five on Salvation Island," she says, slowly reeling me in.

I weigh up my options. Just thinking about turning thirty spikes my anxiety levels again; marking it with a huge party surrounded by people I no longer know, who will no doubt be sporting wedding bands like medals, has my heart reaching for its suitcase.

"I do love Ireland," I say quietly, feeling Ali's web closing around me. As it was always going to.

She nods. "The lodge is so beautiful, totally off-grid." She pauses. "A writer's dream."

She's saying words she knows will speak straight to my heart. I may be a dating columnist right now, but thanks to wine-fueled confessions, she knows about the secret novelist hiding out inside me, the fragile teen dreams all but buried under London life. I begrudgingly admire the way she says just enough to trigger a flare of tender hope. "How do you even know about this place?" I say, wavering.

Ali sighs. "Carole sent me the details. One of her hippie friends used it as a Reiki retreat, or for rechanneling her negative energy, something like that. You know what she's like, always thinks I'm on the edge of a breakdown." Ali's sister-in-law, Carole, expresses her concern through birthday and Christmas gifts: cupping vouchers, life-decluttering manuals, a Tibetan gong Ali sometimes whacks when she wants everyone's attention. "Think of it as a honeymoon," she says, getting the discussion back on track. "Or a . . . unimoon." She doesn't even try to hide how thrilled she is with herself at that.

"Is there Wi-Fi?" I ask, clutching at straws. I can't go if I can't file my column.

"Technically no, but would I send you somewhere without it?" She shudders. "They have it in the village—it's just a ten-minute stroll away, apparently."

Great. Cold, damp, and no checking Insta while I'm on the loo. "You've already booked it, haven't you?" I say, resigned.

She hums the bridal march as she reaches into her drawer and slides a red pom-pom hat across the desk. "You fly on Friday."

Cleo, four days later, somewhere on the Atlantic Ocean

Forecast: High chance of unsolicited advice

I'm about to die and it's Emma Watson's fault.

If I had any phone reception I'd call Ali and swear like a sailor, which would be entirely appropriate, given I'm on board a rickety tugboat out in the middle of the unforgiving Atlantic Ocean. It's like being on the pirate ship at an amusement park, except without any sense of safety or fun.

Salvation Island, or that's the English translation, in any case; it's actually called Slánú, but Ali tells me most people use Salvation, probably so they can maximize on WELCOME TO SALVATION tea towels and other tourist shite. If I had the strength, I'd find the name ironic. Instead, I grip the slippery railings beside my bench seat and mutter a made-up prayer for safe harbor. I shiver inside my inadequate coat as ice-cold sea spray smacks me right in the face, and I fervently wish I had a hood on rather than the drenched scarlet woolen pom-pom hat Ali gave me.

"Fix your eyes on the horizon, it helps with seasickness."

I squint at the only other passenger on board the boat, unappreciative of his unsolicited advice. I can't understand how I'm being flung around like a rag doll, yet he's managing to stay stuck to the opposite bench as if he's strapped himself down. He might have. He looks like someone who never leaves the house without a spare carabiner clip in his pocket. He probably goes on outdoor adventure holidays for fun.

"I'm fine, thank you," I shout to make myself heard.

"Okay, it's just you look a little . . . green," he shouts back. I can't quite place his accent—American, maybe?

I feel that he's made a snap judgment about me; he considers me wimpy and unfit for high seas. And I may well be both of those things, but I've had enough of people making assumptions about me.

He shrugs when I don't reply. "Just trying to help. If you're gonna hurl, aim over the side. That's all I'm saying."

And there we go. Jane refuses Tarzan's offer to hitch a ride on his rope swing; Tarzan gets his grump on.

"I'll do my best," I yell over the racket of the engine. "Apologies in advance if I miss and throw up in your face."

God, that was a bit gross, even for me; I'm grouchy in the way only being fearful for your life can make you. And also because he's wearing a parka that looks as if a million geese died to insulate him. The hood is bigger than the tent Rubes and I took to Glastonbury a few summers ago. I can barely see through the blowing salt-sting. At least my feet are dry, though, which is more than I can say for the rest of me. I shake with terror every time we bounce off the crest of a wave. I did not sign up to drown with a Stay-Puft American in the middle of the Atlantic.

I don't fall to my knees and kiss the sand as I clamber off the boat and wade the last few feet onto Salvation Island, but I sure feel like I should.

"You know where you're headed?" The skipper peers at me through a long tangle of gray hair. "Only I need to make it back to the mainland before dark."

I, of course, have absolutely no clue where

I'm headed, but in that same way that you don't tell the hairdresser you hate the fringe he's just hacked into your hair, I nod and say I'm fine. He lingers for a moment, watching me.

"Only one way to go anyway, really."

He nods to the right, into the quickly gathering gloom. I can just about make out the figure of the other passenger from the boat, already striking out into the mists in his massive red coat. No dallying around for him, probably a local who knows the place like the back of his hand.

"Follow your nose, you'll come to Brianne's shop soon enough."

And just like that, he leaves me, raising his hand in a parting gesture as he jogs back down the rocky beach toward his boat.

And now I'm here, alone, at what feels like the end of the world. All I can see is a deserted beach in front of me and boggy fields sloping up and away into the mist-hung distance behind me. I'm not as scared as I probably should be, but perhaps that's because my life was in actual, genuine peril ten minutes ago. I breathe in a deep lungful of cold gray Irish air and find myself quite excited.

I've had a creeping feeling over recent months, a nagging sense that it might be time for something new. I was twenty-six when I signed up to share the search for my flamingo with the nation, and back then it was a lark, a brilliant way to earn money. I had arrived in London a couple of years before, fresh off the train from northern suburbia with champagne dreams and lemonade money, and somehow, someway, I managed to dig my claws in deep enough to not have to buy a return ticket home. I flung myself at every available opportunity and shoved my foot in any open doorway, buoyed by youth and an unshakable certainty that I was hurtling in the right direction. And little by little, sofa by studio, crummy job by slightly less crummy job, I finally hurtled into the laser eyeline of Alison Stone, a woman who looked at me and saw ambition and grit where others, my family included, saw naïveté and recklessness. In truth, she probably needed a dating columnist and I flew through her door at the opportune moment, but it didn't matter, because I'd found a nest and I made sure to feather it well enough for no passing magpie to oust me. For the next three and a half years, Cleo Wilder became a woman in search of her flamingo, and I've had some truly brilliant times; I've met people who've become close friends, been to places I'd never have otherwise discovered, and laughed until tears have rolled down my face. I've cried sometimes too, of course, because occasionally, someone has appeared flamingo-like for a while but turned out to be nothing more than a passing pigeon. If I had to pin a word on my feelings about my life at this very moment, though, I'd choose **exhausted**. I'm tired down to my internal organs, and there is a bed somewhere on this island with my name on it.

My most pressing priority right now is to find Brianne's shop (which Ali's printout reliably informs me is just inland), collect the keys, and head to my temporary new home. Otter Lodge. It sounds like the kind of place that might have nice pillows, so I put one determined foot in front of the other and set off in search of civilization.

Civilization turns out to be closed. The sign on the door of the small white shiplap shop tells me that it opens for a couple of hours every day. But thankfully there is also an envelope tacked to the door with **Key to Otter** written across it in blue marker pen. Okay. **Wow.** If I tried that in London, someone else would move in and start a marijuana farm within the hour. Pulling the envelope down from the door, I turn it over and see that someone has scrawled a message on the back.

Hello! Sorry I missed you. Here's the front door key to Otter Lodge, you'll

find the backdoor key under the snail.
Follow this road until it runs out, go
up over the hill, and you'll be able to
see the roof down by the beach. It's a
bit of a scramble. I've put a few things
in the fridge to start you off. Sure I'll
see you around soon enough. Brianne x

I shake the contents of the envelope out
onto my palm: a silver key on a yellow plastic
sun key ring. There's optimism for you. From
what I've read, the sun is a fairly infrequent
visitor around here, but the guide said that
when it does come out, this and the neigh-
boring islands transform into blue-and-green
jewels strung out across the ocean like beads
from a broken necklace. No chance of any
sunshine for the foreseeable future, though;
I checked the forecast this morning, and it's
gray, cold, and windy for as far ahead as they
can reliably predict. That's okay. I haven't come
to Salvation for a suntan.

Brianne failed to mention it was a very, very
long road. Or maybe it wasn't, but dragging
an unwieldy suitcase in lead-heavy damp jeans
and high winds made it seem so, and the less
said about my ascent up the hill (aka massive

mountain) the better. Brianne was very much under-exaggerating when she said it was a "bit of a scramble." But none of that matters now, because I'm standing at the crest looking down, and even on this gloomy midafternoon it's pure, top-of-the-world magic. Rolling, rock-strewn green slopes stretch out toward the horizon crisscrossed with low, uneven stone walls, the occasional abandoned hut on distant hillsides in one direction, the downward slide of the land toward a small, sand-fringed cove on the other. And there it is, Otter Lodge, a small shingle-roofed building nestling in between the rocks. There's a deep wooden porch wrapped around it, the kind you see in American movies. If there isn't a chair on it, I'm dragging one out.

In the course of my work I've described many things as breathtaking over the years, but this place genuinely snatches the air from my lungs. I settle my bum on a conveniently placed boulder, trying to get my breath back and take it all in. It's spectacular. My eyes are assaulted by the majestic, solitary beauty. I feel engulfed, as if I've just walked into the open arms of Salvation Island. I listen to the harsh sound of my unsteady breathing as the wind circles tight around me, and then a strange, unexpected thing happens. I start to cry.

Mack, October 2, Salvation Island

You think I'm your bellhop?

The key isn't here. Three flights, two boats, and three thousand miles, and at the final hurdle I'm crawling around on my hands and knees in the dirt looking for a damn door key. I'm sure Barney said it was here. "Under a rock by the door" were his exact words. I straighten, taking the worn, wide wooden steps up on to the wraparound porch to rattle the door handle. It's locked. Just like it was when I tried it two minutes ago. I sigh and lean on the porch railing, looking out across the bay as I weigh my options. I could break in. I'm entitled to be here, and the repair cost for one of the small panes of glass in the door wouldn't be huge. More inconvenient than anything—the population of Salvation Island hovers somewhere around a hundred, and I seriously doubt there's a window guy among them. I table the idea in favor of a look around the building. Maybe one of the windows will be unlocked. If not, well, it's probably too late to go off in search of civilization; I can't guarantee making it back before dark.

Not for the first time today, I'm glad I let the sales guy back home talk me into this stupid jacket—if it comes down to it, I can hunker down on the porch. I've slept in worse places; a few years back, a spell on the streets of New York City doing a project on homelessness made me frighteningly aware of the luxury of a roof and four walls. I produced some of my best work during those bone-cold nights, but heavy rocks lodge in my stomach every time I look at the images of those gaunt, hungry faces. I learned how fine the line can be between success and failure, how a few wrong turns of the wheel can spiral into all of your possessions in a single plastic bag and a bed on a store stoop. I've heard that a couple of the people I met have since passed on, and I know for a fact that every last one of them would switch places with me right now, missing keys or not. The wheel of fortune has spun and dropped me here on the porch of Otter Lodge, and I need to make the best of it.

I walk around to the side, taking a moment

to admire the bravery of whoever decided to build this little outpost in the middle of nowhere. The building has been hewn from austere gray stone, probably gathered from its surroundings, nothing like the log cabin we rented on Lake Michigan a couple of years ago. The boys run through my head: Nate's skinny legs in his faded red cargo shorts, Leo taller by a head and quieter by a mile. Joyful as they clambered from the car to pelt full speed toward the lake, shafts of sunlight illuminating their blond heads. Freewheeling with them down shaded forest trails. Susie calling after us to slow down. And now I'm here alone, closing the door on those memories.

Concentrate on the now. Find a way in.

The heavy clouds overhead have just burst their seams, the rain sharp in the wind. I hurry from window to window, but they're all securely closed, unresponsive to my rattles. I sigh, the beginnings of a plan already formulating in my head: my backpack for a pillow; the corner of the porch out front for a bed, which will give me the most shelter from the elements. The back door is locked too. **Wait, there's a back door.** And there it is: a glint of silver beneath a stone snail just to the left of the door. I kick it aside and almost laugh out loud with relief. I was looking by the wrong door, that was all. All thoughts of roughing it slide from my shoulders as I slip the key into the lock and feel a satisfying click as it turns. I'm in.

I don't know what I expected; I haven't looked at any photos online, and Barney didn't send through any specifics. For me Otter Lodge is a place to eat, sleep, and work. Somewhere to get my head together. But as I swing the door wide and step inside, I find myself pleasantly surprised. It's one of those all-in-one-room type places: kitchenette in one corner, a deep sofa in front of an open slate fireplace taking up most of the space. There's an old brass bed frame at the back, the fur throws and plaid blankets lending it a homey touch.

I strip off my wet jacket and duck through the only interior door to find a small but decent bathroom—no shower, but a deep copper tub with my name on it. First, though, something to eat. Susie always liked to say I'm a man who needs a plan in order to function. There's probably some truth behind her wry assessment of my character, and my plan right now is food, bath, early bed. Maybe a beer in there somewhere, I think, rolling my aching shoulders as I head out of the bathroom. The back door swings on its hinges, reminding me to grab my stuff from the porch and batten down the hatches for the stormy night ahead.

There's a loud scream and I stand still, rendered momentarily stupid by surprise. There's a woman in my lodge.

"Sorry, you made me jump," the woman says, her hand over her heart. Then when I don't manage to form any words: "Um . . . Hi."

"Where did **you** come from?" Because I've seen this woman before.

She pulls off her damp red wool hat and stares at me. "London."

"No, I mean—"

"Wait," she says, interrupting me as she narrows her eyes. "Weren't you on the boat earlier?" She switches from her own accent to a terrible, fake American one. "**If you're gonna hurl, aim over the side?**"

"Ah. And you're the sweet girl who offered to throw up in my face," I reply, and fake a smile.

She sighs. "I'm not in the mood to be patronized by . . ." She waves her hand toward my headlamp, a sharp slash of air. "A cyclops."

And I'm not in the mood for company, I think, pulling the elastic from around my skull. Why is she even here? Is she lost?

She looks at me for a few beats and then unzips her unsuitably thin jacket. "Look, I'm grateful for you coming to check on things, but I'm all set. I've dragged my own suitcase over the mountain, I'm perfectly capable of lighting a fire, and I can find my way around the electrics. I don't need the welcome tour."

"You think I'm your bellhop?"

She smiles determinedly, clearly stuck between trying to be polite and wanting to tell me to fuck off. "Caretaker? Friend of Brianne's?"

"Lady, I was on the same boat as you. Ask me where I've come from."

"I don't need to know."

Jeez, she's obtuse. "Boston."

"I didn't ask."

"Well, now you know anyway, which means we both know I've traveled much farther than you to be here, and you'll be relieved to hear I don't need the welcome tour either." I watch understanding begin to seep into the edges of her exasperation.

We stare at each other across the room, silent aside from the rain pelting the window, and then her stance softens. "This is Otter Lodge."

I nod. "I know that."

"And I've rented it from today."

"Me too," I say.

She rubs the heel of her palm up and down on her forehead, hard and fast, as if she's massaging my words to make them mean something she likes the sound of better. "You can't have."

"I absolutely promise you I did."

She bends down and opens her bag, riffling around until she produces a handful of neatly folded paperwork.

"Here. It's right here in black and white." She smooths the sheets out on the end of the wooden kitchen counter, running her finger down the page as she picks out salient details. "Otter Lodge, reserved from October second. Paid. From Brianne, the property manager. And also, I have the key."

There's a triumphant glint in her eye as she dangles a key from her fingertips.

"I don't need a piece of paper," I say. "This is my lodge. And here is my key." I dangle mine right back at her.

"Your lodge," she says, deadpan. I can tell she doesn't believe me.

I swallow. "My cousin's place, to be exact." Even that's a stretch; Barney is my second cousin twice removed, or something like that. We've never even met in person. The lodge belonged to his aunt, my mum's cousin, and is now jointly owned by Barney and his sister, who lives in Canada. He did mention something about renting it out sometimes, but I have no idea who Brianne is. "I have emails, but the battery on my phone died."

"Well, isn't that convenient."

I'm not sure how to play this. It's after five in the afternoon, already dark, and it's obvious neither of us knows the geography of Salvation Island at all. It isn't safe to head out, especially in this weather. The store is the nearest building to here, no doubt long closed, and beyond that the only proper habitation on the island is up in the north. Otter Lodge sits some distance away on Salvation's most southerly edge.

"Maybe," I say. "But it's true."

We lapse into tense silence. My beer, bath, and bed plan is disintegrating in front of my eyes, and I don't like it one bit. She pulls her phone from her pocket and stabs at it for a few seconds, then raises her eyes to the ceiling. I'd say she's counting under her breath, the way you might when you don't want to explode with absolute rage.

"I'm not going back over that mountain today," she says, shoulders squared.

"I don't blame you," I say. "Me neither. Though technically, it's a hill."

She screws her wide mouth into a tight line, the exact same way Nate does when things aren't going his way.

"We can't both be right," she says. "And I know I am."

Man, she's infuriating. She's still having a hissy fit, while I'm over here working out how we're going to get through this. "We're both going to have to stay here tonight."

She makes an uncute choking noise. "Oh, no. I don't think so."

"Okay." I fold my arms across my chest. "You know where the door is." For the record, I don't actually expect her to leave in this weather. I just need her to understand that it isn't an option for me either.

She flicks her eyes toward the door. "And I'll lock it, right after you leave."

I wait a couple beats. "I'm not leaving."

"But . . . you have to!" It bursts from her like a child.

I sigh and rub my hand over my eyes. I know this must be tougher for her than it is for me. I'm not such an ass that I can't see that any woman would be wary about spending the night with a guy she doesn't have any reason to trust.

"I'm married, if it helps." I pull my wallet from my back pocket and flip it open to the photo of Susie and the kids. "My wife and my sons."

"Why the hell would that help?" she snaps.

"Someone thought I was a decent enough human to marry me?"

She looks pointedly around the lodge. "Well, she isn't here to vouch for you now, is she? If she even exists."

"She exists," I mutter, pissed. She exists . . . she's just three thousand miles away with my kids.

"I can't do this," she says. "You're a stranger, and a man, and"—she waves her arm—"big."

I shrug. Not much I can do about that.

She presses her fingers against her brow. "Just so you know," she says, "I do krav maga."

I don't smirk, but I highly doubt she's telling the truth. "Okay."

"I could totally take you down if I need to."

"You honestly won't need to," I say. I think of Susie and how I'd want someone to act around her if she ever found herself in this position. "Look, I'll sleep out on the porch tonight. I'm not saying you're right or that I'm leaving, just that I get that it's dark and we don't know each other. We can sort it out in the daylight."

She stares at me, indecision all over her face. "I need to think," she mutters, opening the door to step outside. There's a rumble of distant thunder as the wind tries to yank the door from her grip. The weather is really ramping up out there. Within seconds, she slams it shut again. She leans her back against the door and swallows hard. "Where's the bathroom?"

I step aside so she can pass and breathe a sigh of relief when she's out of sight. Christ, I could really use that beer.

Cleo, October 2, Salvation Island

Holed up at the end of the world with Han Solo

I don't know what to do. I mean, I do. I know I've got no choice but to share Otter Lodge with a random American. Having seen how wild the weather is just now, he'll probably do something dramatic like die if I take him up on his offer to sleep on the porch. And now here I am, hiding in the bathroom, sitting on the loo with my horrible wet jeans bunched around my chafed ankles, wishing with all my heart to be back in my flat in London. So much for solitary beauty.

I fight my boots off and kick the ball of wet denim across the room in a temper. God, that bath looks inviting. The lodge may be remote, but someone with a flair for interior design has worked some serious magic here. I couldn't properly take the main room in because of the six-foot American standing in the middle of it, but sitting here now, I appreciate the calming neutrals, the roll-top copper bathtub, the expensive bath products, the fat church candle and jar of long matches. The slate floor is blessedly warm under my feet, and a pile of snow-white towels sits on an uneven wooden shelf that looks as if it might have washed up on the beach. If I was going to search for something like this on Pinterest, I'd type in "rustic luxe." It's proper cottagecore, and I can't wait until I can enjoy it without a stranger in my peripheral vision.

"Can you please pass me my suitcase?" I shout, hoping he doesn't try to score any more points by refusing or something.

"By the door."

I crack the door open enough to make sure he's not lurking, but he's out of sight, so I haul my case inside and flip the lid open on the floor.

I'm married, if it helps. I roll my eyes as I remember his words. I mean, what did he think was going through my head to make him say that? Are all murderers unmarried? I don't think so. For that matter, how does he know **I** won't murder **him**? I triple-check I've locked the door and tip a little of the luxurious bath oil into the running water, my shredded nerves soothed by the scent of exclusive spas and far-flung, sun-soaked shores.

"I'm taking a bath," I yell, dragging my jumper over my head. Every layer that comes off feels like a weight leaving me. I'm not a winter person; I don't understand anyone who says they prefer snow to the dog days of summer. I'm a woman made for flip-flops and places where you never need a jacket. The opposite of here, basically. When I light the candle and slide into the bone-deep heat of the water, it's so nourishing I could cry. I won't, though—I've already chalked up my out-of-nowhere crying incident for the day. God, that was bizarre. I didn't feel driven to tears by the horror hike up the mountain. If anything, I was elated to have reached the summit, and then sideswiped out of the blue by this almighty gulp of emotion.

I hold my breath and duck my head beneath the bathwater, immersed. This place is definitely getting the better of me. Or more likely it's just been the longest of days, the journey to get here full of peril, and my much-anticipated time alone has been punctured by an unwelcome intrusion. I try, on the whole, to be an adaptable person, someone who makes the best of a situation, but I can't shake the feeling that I've fallen at the first hurdle.

• • •

"There's coffee on the stove."

I nod, unable to squeeze words of gratitude out of my lips, even though I feel marginally more human now that I'm bundled in my pj's with my hair in a towel.

"And bread for toast. I've had some, you should probably do the same."

"I don't need reminding to eat."

"Whatever," he mutters, heading for the bathroom. "I'm going to take a bath."

Is it wrong of me to hope there isn't quite enough hot water left in the tank for him to have a really good wallow?

I glance at the rain lashing the windows and sigh, because it's time for me to act like a grown-up. "You can stay inside tonight."

"Thanks." He turns to me in the bathroom doorway. "You can too."

"Are you always this annoying?"

"Apparently so," he says after a beat. He looks at me, and for a moment he reminds me of someone, but I can't think who. "Take the bed, I'll use the sofa."

Once he's gone, I help myself to coffee and sit at the small, square dining table, warming my hands around the mug. I feel as if I'm trapped in the opening scene of a cliché old movie, him a young Robert Redford, me the dewy-eyed Jane Fonda waiting to fall head over heels in love with him after our classic meet-cute. Except I'm not. I may make a living writing about love, but I'm no wet-behind-the-ears romantic, and there's nothing cute about this encounter. The American is abrasive. Beardy. And then it comes to me who he reminds me of, and I close my eyes and sigh. My brother is a massive **Star Wars** geek, he watched those movies on a near loop when we were younger. I can't say I shared his enthusiasm, but there's no denying that a young Harrison Ford looked like he ate pure charisma for breakfast and could save the world before lunch. I'm holed up at the end of the world with Han Solo. I can only hope that Darth Vader comes over the ~~mountain~~ hill and takes his head off with a lightsaber.

I haven't been to bed at seven o'clock since I was old enough to choose my own bedtime. I've always been more night owl than early bird, and there have been a few too many mad Saturday nights with Rubes when I haven't been to bed at all, or else I've woken up in places I don't remember falling asleep in. But after the day I've had, my eyes keep drifting shut of their own accord.

I've just poured myself a second cup of coffee in an attempt to stay awake, and I'm perched on the edge of the bed. The American is still in the bath; I've heard the water running every now and then, so I know he hasn't nodded off and drowned.

Oh my God, the bed is **divine**. Suede-backed furs and heavy knitted throws all contribute to the hygge vibe. I relax back against the pillows in the low lamplight and close my eyes, and it's easily the most blissful moment of my day. I'm not sleeping here, though, regretfully. I'll take the sofa, thank you very much, and the higher ground that goes with it. I'll claim the bed tomorrow, once he's hightailed it out of here.

The high ground doesn't stop me from stealing a couple of pillows and a thick blanket to make myself up a nest on the sofa, though; it's kind of cozy. I settle in and finish my coffee in peace, basking in the warmth from the fire he must have lit while I was in the bath. Heaviness slides through my bones as I put my empty cup down and close my eyes, but then I jolt straight back up again because the bathroom door flies open and I'm no longer alone.

"I'm taking the sofa," I say primly, pulling the blanket up to my chin.

He glances from the sofa to the bed, and for a moment it feels as if he's going to argue the toss, but he just shrugs. "Up to you."

I shrug too, like kids caught in an **I'm less bothered than you** competition, as he roots around in his massive bag.

"I'm gonna have a beer."

"Suit yourself."

"That's what I'm here for."

"I'm sorry?"

He digs out a four-pack of Budweiser, cracking one open before stashing the rest in the fridge. "That's what I came here for. To suit myself."

I nearly engage, then take a deep breath. I don't need to know. "You can stay in here tonight, but come tomorrow you need to suit yourself somewhere else."

He stares out the dark kitchen window and takes a long drink, huffing under his breath. "It's been a hell of a day."

I don't appreciate that he's swerved the conversation, but I'm too weary to have this battle now. It'll keep until morning. I flick the table lamp out and plunge the lodge into sudden darkness, and I don't know if it makes me a terrible person, but I get a small flush of satisfaction when he bangs into the table as he navigates the unfamiliar space for the bed. I wait as he swears and jostles around: the sounds of clothes coming off, blankets being pulled up, pillows being punched.

"Do you need the lamp back on for a sec?" I say once he's gone quiet. He doesn't dignify it with a response.

Cleo, October 3, Salvation Island

I need to evict the alien

You know those mornings when you wake up slowly, as if you're drifting up through layers of mist toward the surface, fragments of your dreams floating around you, trying to lure you back in? This isn't one of those mornings. I wake up and jerk bolt upright because I can smell fire.

"You're awake."

Everything slots back into place as my heartrate slowly returns to normal. The burning smell is just newly laid logs in the fireplace.

"And you're still here." I flop back on my pillows, unrested and freshly disgruntled. This isn't really the kind of sofa you want to do more than nap on.

"Did you think it was all a bad dream?"

His tone is too chipper, as if the situation is

slightly amusing rather than massively bloody inconvenient. He's already dressed and ready for the day, probably just to get one up on me.

"There's bacon in the fridge if you're interested?" he adds. "And, weirdly, champagne. Bacon, milk, and champagne."

I look at the ceiling. Actually, I really do want bacon, now that he's said it. I weigh up my options. It's quarter to eight in the morning, barely even light outside. My plan, such as it is, is that we should head to the shop as soon as it opens and find a human being who actually knows the island. There must be other accommodation options for the American. I'll stock up on provisions while I'm over there, and then I'm going to come back here and properly claim the space. Bounce on the bed as if I'm the heroine in a road trip movie, wipe yesterday from my mental slate, and start again. There's no need for me to be unnecessarily grouchy in the meantime.

"You know, I think I will make bacon," I say, getting up, glad of my plain black jersey pajamas. "Want some?"

He glances my way as if I've asked a trick question. "Sure."

"At least the weather seems to have calmed down," I continue, making conversation, gazing out the kitchen window as I flick the kettle on. Christ, that view is something else. The window looks out over the curve of the tiny bay. The lodge is set back from the shore, far enough for safety, but near enough for the damp, dark silvery beach to be your front garden. This is the kind of place worn-down artists might visit to reconnect with their creative soul.

"It was pretty damn amazing out there this morning," he says. "I went out to watch the sunrise from the beach."

Of course he did.

My London flat doesn't even have a garden; the difference between here and there is the difference between Jupiter and Mars. Perhaps that's the way I need to look at things—as if I'm an alien on a reconnaissance visit to consider if this new planet is preferable to my old one. So far it's not, but I've yet to give it a fair crack of the whip. I need to evict the other alien who's landed here first, because it doesn't look as if Darth Vader's going to turn up and lop his head off. I sigh under my breath at the whole stupid analogy—my writer's brain is always doing that—as I dig through the cupboards for a pan and breakfast crockery. The cupboards aren't heaving, just nicely stocked with plain, decent things. My cup collection at home is what you might kindly term **eclectic**, mostly made up of mismatched mugs gifted to me over the years. BEST AUNT from one of my sister's children. A Pug Hug Mug from the office secret Santa, even though I'm not particularly a pug fan. A National Trust squirrel cup and saucer from my mother. A hand-splotched tankard I made a few summers ago with my brother's kids at one of those artsy make-and-take café places.

"I was thinking we should head to the store this morning, sort this mix-up out," I say, sitting opposite the American at the dining table a few minutes later. I'm doing my best to be polite.

"Sounds reasonable," he says, raising his bacon sandwich at me. "Thanks for this, it's good."

"No, thank you for not making a fuss about leaving," I say, watching him over my coffee cup, testing how difficult he's going to make things.

He finishes his food and reaches for his mug. "Yeah, about that . . ."

I don't say a word, trying out Ali's trick of using silence to make other people do what you want them to.

"I know this isn't what you want to hear, but I'm not going anywhere." He pulls his phone out of his pocket and flips it toward me. "My emails." I don't take the phone, but

I can make out recent dates and headers like "Stay as long as you like" and "You're going to love Salvation" and "Say hi to Raff for me."

I swallow. "It's not exactly the same thing as a reservation, though, is it? I've paid actual money to be here."

"Barney, the owner, **my cousin,** personally offered it to me."

"That would be the same owner who's taken my money?"

"Via this Brianne woman, who clearly made a mistake. I'll make sure you get every cent back."

"Penny," I correct grouchily. "I don't want the money back. I'm here now and I want what I've paid for."

We stare at each other.

"Can you get this Barney on the phone and see what he has to say for himself?" I spit.

"I can't find any reception." It's the first genuine note of angst I've heard in his voice.

"My phone got some at the top of the hill yesterday," I say. I know this because as I was sobbing on the boulder like a baby, I got a "call me soon and tell me everything" message from Ruby—a cosmic nudge to pull myself together.

He widens his eyes, and I see that he has two different-colored pupils, one warm hazel, one translucent green. It catches me out, and he notices me staring.

"Heterochromia," he says, obviously used to people asking.

"I've only ever seen that once before, on a dog." I speak without thinking as I fold away my makeshift bed. "Our neighbor when I was a kid had a husky with odd eyes. One sky blue, one brown. And it was vicious too, took a chunk out of my brother's shin when it escaped into our garden one summer. He got a tattoo to cover the scar as soon as he was old enough, a howling husky. He thought it was ironic. My mum went nuts."

The American stares at me with those odd eyes, taken aback, and then he half laughs, incredulous.

"Fine, I'll try up on the hill in a while." His gaze shifts toward the sofa. "Mind if I sit on your bed?"

"Knock yourself out," I say, standing up to reach for my coat. "I'm going to go and have a nose round outside." I shove my feet into a pair of yellow-and-white-striped wellies beside the door. There are hats, scarves, and umbrellas in a basket too. I drag a blue woolen hat down over my ears and leave him to it.

• • •

London has a particular smell: diesel fumes choked out by early-morning bin trucks and late-night buses, office workers' shirts damp with sweat, anticipation, dread, and ambition. It throbs and twists, the heat of the Underground beneath your feet, the symphony of sirens, a sense of confidence and threat, a pulse, a rush, a beating drum.

Salvation Island is not at all like London. I pick my way along the uneven shoreline and listen to the sound of the ocean rushing over pebbles, gulping down air as clean as a cold glass of spring water. Yesterday the sand appeared like a solid gray mass, but the morning light reveals it now as pale silver and powdery as it dries. A seabird wheels across the sky and lands on a nearby rock to observe me, gray with a black feathered cap, its bright orange beak pointed toward me, a guest in its living room. "Morning," I say, feeling slightly foolish.

I shouldn't think I look up to the job of wintering here, pale and fragile as I am. Waiflike, one of my sisters once said; like a Brontë heroine, my other sister replied. Both older than me and blond-haired to my blue black. They've always looked upon me as their beloved doll-child, someone to indulge and coddle. But unlike doll babies, this one grew up into someone who felt suffocated by her position as the baby of the family. Don't get me wrong, it was a wholly pleasant tenure; I was pampered and loved. And I loved my siblings equally in return. But I can still recall the sensation of their cocoon pressing my teenage wings too close against my sides, of the pressure building inside me to be released. I meet the bird's eye and respectfully ask that it reserve its judgment; it doesn't know me yet.

I've spent my life being underestimated, and I've learned for the most part to either ignore it or use it to my advantage. One of the many reasons I appreciate working for Ali is that she has never once made assumptions about me based on my enjoyment of a glamorous dress or the pleasure I take from a well-applied smoky eye. She doesn't find me waiflike or imagine me roaming the moors in search of my Heathcliff. I was a blank page, and she has allowed me to write myself onto it.

I'll admit it—it might not be the Maldives, but it's its own kind of eye-wateringly beautiful here. I can only imagine how spectacular it would be on a brighter day. Maybe I'll even love my time here so much that I'll return to see it bathed in midsummer sunlight. First things first, though. I need to secure my tenancy at Otter Lodge.

Mack, October 3, Salvation Island

What time is the next boat?

I couldn't get a hold of Barney."

It's not a lie; I did attempt to get in touch with my second cousin twice removed, but without success. I don't tell her that I didn't hold much hope of catching him, because I'm aware he's off traveling, and my experience of him to date would peg him as elusive, to say the least. I also don't tell her that I've spent the majority of the last half hour pacing around on the top of the hill trying to text the boys, even though it's the early hours where they are. If I close my eyes and try really hard, I can almost summon the scent of Nate's shampoo when I bend to kiss him good night, the squeeze of Leo's slender fingers in the dark when I turn out his lamp. I miss them down to my core, pieces of me left behind on another landmass.

"Oh, for God's sake," she says, chucking her beanie into the basket by the door with unnecessary force. "How hard did you try?"

I'm not in the mood to be told off by a stranger. "Hard enough, okay?" I hear my own abruptness but don't apologize. I'm getting tired of her sense of entitlement.

"The store opens at eleven," she says neutrally. For a moment she reminds me of Nate's old kindergarten teacher, an angelic-faced woman who always seemed on the verge of losing her shit. "Shall we head there, see if we can make sense of things? I think Brianne owns it, and hopefully she can get hold of Barney for us."

"Fine."

She shoots me a look. "Fine."

If I had a book, I'd pull it out now and read it for dramatic effect, because I've been waiting outside the store for ten minutes and I've only just now caught sight of her huge red beanie coming toward me. We'd set out from the lodge together, but it wasn't what you might call a pleasant walk. She was in a bad mood because her brand-new boots have rubbed the skin off her ankles, and I was preoccupied with getting there and with thoughts of Susie and the boys. At one point I offered to give her a ride on my back, because I'm not wholly without a heart, and to be honest I was sick of her whining, but she just stomped off, so I left her to her own devices.

"You made it," I say. If looks could kill, I'd be dead. I nod toward the door. "After you?"

I expect she was planning to go in first anyway, but it makes me feel better to think I had a choice. I'm not sure, but as she passes I think I hear her mutter "bloody fucking mountain" under her breath.

Inside, the store reminds me of the one at the lake campsite I went to every summer as a kid, random stuff piled next to each other on the shelves: flashlights next to canned soup, shower gel beside pet food, a cardboard sheet of hair combs hanging above a rack of birthday cards. It seems like there's no one in the place until we approach the cash register, then an elfin-faced, pixie-cropped woman bounces out from behind a beaded curtain with a sandwich in her hand. She radiates energy like a lightbulb at full brightness.

"Oh, hi." She dips her hand behind the curtain to lose the food, brushing her hands on her jeans to get rid of the crumbs. "I'm so sorry, I expected you to be someone else."

I instantly warm to her; if there's a more

welcoming accent than the Irish one, I have yet to hear it.

Her smile widens, a gleam of anticipation in her clear blue eyes as she looks at each of us in turn. "You must be our honeymooners."

"Honeymooners?" I say.

"Over at Otter?" she says. "Sorry I couldn't stay yesterday to meet you with the key. I usually do as a rule, but it was my husband's birthday."

"We're not honeymooners," we both say at the same time.

"I don't even know him."

"And I don't know her."

The woman behind the counter narrows her eyes, confused. "Oh, okay. Well, I'll start, will I? I'm Brianne," she says, bright and breezy as a kids' TV show host. "And you are . . . ?"

Brianne shifts her gaze between us, waiting for one of us to speak. For a moment neither of us breaks cover, probably for similar reasons. I deliberately haven't asked her her name, and she hasn't asked for mine either. It's not easy to analyze why knowing something as simple as her name feels like too much information. I guess she'll become somebody rather than nobody, and I'd prefer her to stay a nobody, however harsh that may sound.

I sigh, about to speak, but she whips her

paperwork out of her inside jacket pocket and pushes it across the counter to Brianne, who scans it and looks up.

"So you're Cleo?"

Cleo. And there you go. I sigh and shake my head, because just like that, she's somebody.

Brianne's gaze shifts to me, uncertain, no doubt picking up on the weird energy between us. "And . . . you are?"

I clear my throat, unwilling, feeling like I'm thirteen and in trouble in middle school. "Mack," I mutter.

I feel her, **Cleo,** bristle beside me, and I deliberately don't glance her way.

"Look," Brianne says, bringing a black planner up from beneath the counter. "I've no clue what's happening here, so you're going to have to help me out." She flips the book open as she speaks, riffling through the pages. "Let's see what I have written down in here . . ."

I hold my breath. **Please, Barney, come through for me.**

"Cleo Wilder," she says. "But whoever made the booking ticked the honeymoon champagne package, so I kind of assumed there'd be two of you?"

Even I'm confused now. I turn to look at Cleo. "**Are** you on your honeymoon?"

"Oh, shut up," she snaps, irritated. "You

know perfectly well I'm not on bloody honeymoon. It's probably my boss's idea of a joke."

Concentration furrows Brianne's brow. I'm not surprised she's having a hard time keeping up. So am I.

Cleo's exaggerated sigh shudders up from her boots, a clear **can everyone please just stop speaking and listen to me?** I don't think so. I need to get a word in here.

"My cousin Barney owns Otter Lodge," I say.

Brianne's face breaks into an easy, relieved smile. "Oh, so you're Barney Doyle's cousin? We were in school together. In fact, he was my secret crush when I was about six years old."

She's grinning, pink-cheeked, and so am I, because here it is, bona fide proof of my claim. The only person not loving this trip down memory lane is Cleo.

"That's so sweet." I laugh for a few seconds too long. "Anyway, Barney has offered me the lodge until New Year's, so Cleo's looking for someplace else on the island to stay."

"Hang on a minute." Cleo yanks her beanie off and thumps it down hard on the counter. "I'm not the one who needs a new place to stay."

"You might not realize this," I say, "but you express a lot of your anger through hats.

Jamming them on, pulling them off, slamming them down."

"Oh, just piss right off," she says, unable to mask her annoyance.

"My family owns Otter Lodge," I say, pressing my advantage. "You heard Brianne. She has a crush on my cousin."

"**Had** a crush," Brianne jumps in. "I haven't seen Barney in at least fifteen years."

"He doesn't live on the island, then?" Cleo says, homing in.

"Not for a good few years now." Brianne's eyes flick toward me, as if I might want to take over the story. "His mother moved them across to Donegal after her father died, if I recall correctly?"

I nod noncommittally, not wanting to let it be known that I'm hazy on the finer details.

"So how do you know who's letting the lodge?" Cleo asks, cutting to the point, uninterested by my family history.

"Alice usually emails me, Barney's sister. She came back for a while when they first inherited Otter Lodge. These days she just sends me the name of who's arriving so I can make sure the lodge is ready, hand out keys, that kind of stuff. I don't really handle"—she pauses delicately—"disputes."

"But my name is in your book," Cleo says.

Brianne nods, troubled. "It is."

"And my cousin owns the lodge," I say.

"He does." Brianne shrugs her shoulders, unwilling to make the call. "It's a fine mess, for sure."

"Okay. So **one** of us"—I throw a look at Cleo—"needs somewhere else to stay tonight."

"**You** do," Cleo shoots back, then turns to Brianne. "Can you point us in the direction of other lodgings, please?"

Brianne scrunches her face into a grimace that tells me she doesn't want to say the thing she's about to.

"I'm afraid there isn't anywhere else on the island."

"It doesn't need to be fancy," Cleo presses on. "Anything will do."

Speak for yourself, I think, but don't say.

"We're just not set up for tourists here," Brianne says, regretful. "Never have been. Your family caused a fair bit of controversy opening Otter Lodge up to strangers, truth be told," she adds, glancing at me. "Not everyone approved, even though it's mostly been used by artists and professionals."

"There must be somewhere," I say, because it's sinking in that this situation might not actually be resolved. Up to now I've felt relatively confident that when it comes down to it, my family connection trumps her piece of paper, but in the absence of anywhere else to stay, things could get territorial. "An empty place? Someone with a guest room, even?"

Brianne thinks but shakes her head slowly. "Honestly nothing, we just don't get unexpected visitors out here. We aren't the kind of folk who keep a spare room ready just in case," Brianne says. "You'll get luckier on one of the bigger islands, or there are places over on the mainland, obviously."

"I don't want to stay on one of the bigger islands," Cleo says, bright-eyed and stubborn. "I've paid to stay at Otter Lodge, and that's what I'm going to do."

"Is your husband coming to join you soon?" Brianne asks.

Cleo turns her head slowly. Under different circumstances, I'd mention how the move reminds me of one of the raptors from **Jurassic Park**.

"I think we've established that I'm not on my honeymoon," she says through gritted teeth.

"Oh, right. Are **you** on honeymoon?" Brianne asks, to me this time. "Maybe that's where the confusion has come in?"

Okay. Not so funny. "Neither of us are on honeymoon."

Time to finish this. If there's genuinely nowhere else on the island, one of us needs to leave Salvation, and I don't plan on it being me.

"What time is the next boat?"

Brianne closes the planner slowly, bracing both palms flat on the cover. "Eleven o'clock."

Cleo looks at the clock behind Brianne and sighs theatrically. It's almost midday. "Great."

"On Friday," Brianne adds. I couldn't say for sure, but I think she held that back for dramatic effect.

"Friday?" Cleo says, too loud in the small store. "As in not today, or tomorrow, or even the next day, because today is only Saturday?"

Brianne takes a small step back. "We only have the boat once a week, unless there's an emergency. Medical. Um, a death or something."

Kudos, Brianne, I think. She absolutely mentioned death to prevent Cleo from declaring our situation emergency worthy.

"And there's really nowhere else on the island to stay?" Cleo sounds like she wants to cry.

"No, I'm really sorry. I'd offer you my sofa, but the cats sleep on it and one of them is arthritic, so, you know . . ."

Cleo eyes me. "You look as if you could swim to the next island," she says, desperate as she turns back to Brianne. "Is it far?"

Brianne's eyebrows shoot up. "He'd die for sure."

"Okay," I say, flipping into practical mode. **Make a plan, Mack. Think ahead.** "We're going to need some stuff to get us through to Friday."

Same as yesterday, Cleo folds her arms and refuses to accept the truth that's biting her on the ass.

"We need food, and I don't know about you, but I'm gonna need more beer," I say.

"I can have your shopping dropped at the lodge later, if you like," Brianne offers. "My husband delivers around the island after we close up for the afternoon."

"That's helpful, thank you, Brianne," I say, on autopilot manners, shooting Cleo a **be more grateful** glare. She just glares right back.

"Why don't you go grab some chocolate, see if it sweetens your mood?" I mutter, sick of her pigheadedness as I grab cheese, milk, other basics. "Are you vegetarian?" I ask as I stand in front of the produce.

"You literally watched me eat bacon this morning," she says, picking up chicken and tomatoes. We fill the basket in uncompanionable silence: pâté, eggs, lamb chops, and potatoes. Brianne rings us up, and I search for my wallet. This damn coat has too many pockets, I know it's here somewhere.

"I've got these," Cleo says, adding wine to the haul and whipping a bunch of bills out of her coat pocket.

"No way." I shoot Brianne a **do not take her money** look as I'm patting myself down. "I'm buying. Or we can split it, if you want."

Cleo glances at the total on the till and pushes her money into Brianne's hand, leaving her little choice but to accept. I know it's not fair to expect a total stranger to step in as referee, but all the same . . . I thought we had a rapport going, but apparently not. I can't help but feel as if Cleo has somehow scored a point over me.

"Where's the nearest place on the island that has a reliable cell signal?" I ask. "It's nonexistent at the lodge."

"Only in the village, really," she says. "There's Wi-Fi at the pub and the café—you can usually get the password at the till. Delta has a computer set up in there if you need one; you can book it by the hour."

I'd probably find such antiquated systems charming if I were here on vacation, but right now it's another thing to add to my growing list of irritations.

I pick Cleo's red hat up and hand it to her. "Here, put this on, see if it cheers you up. I'm going for a walk."

Cleo, October 3, Salvation Island

I don't like rice pudding

There's someone sitting on the boulder on top of the hill.

I've puffed my way up here to check my emails. My ankles are killing me, and now someone has beaten me to the spot. The good news is it isn't the American and his ridiculous coat.

I loiter a little way from the boulder, out of earshot of the woman sitting there with her denim-jacket-clad back turned to me. I can't tell if she's on the phone from here or if she's just taking the air. Taking the air—get me using ladylike phrases! That's what you get when you binge-watch period dramas when you should be working. I tell myself it's research, even though my life has very little in the way of corsets or sidesaddle horse rides. Although, at a push, I guess it could be said that we're all just looking for our flamingo, aren't we?

God, is this woman going to be much longer? I feel a bit ridiculous queuing for the boulder as if it's a bloody telephone box.

I can't hear her talking, and she's very still. Then she suddenly cups her hands to her face and shouts. Or screams, to be accurate, a proper blood curdler. I wince and take a few steps farther back, intending to edge quietly away, but my phone beeps loudly in my pocket, finally picking up the elusive signal.

I pat my coat down in search of it, panicked, as the woman on the rock swings round. A few things strike me all at once: she's younger than I thought—my age or thereabouts—her eyes are as green as Salvation grass, and she's really quite pregnant. A lot to take in, along with the massive rainbow-striped knitted scarf around her neck and the many silver earrings poking beneath the rim of her pom-pom hat.

"Were you sneaking up on me?"

She scowls, suspicious, and then just as I start to mutter an apology—"No, I . . ."—she cracks up laughing.

"You're staying at Otter," she says. It's not that great a leap, given that, as I now well know, Otter is the only accommodation on the island, and I'm clearly not a resident.

"I am," I say. "Are you, er, okay?"

She looks confused, and then her face clears. "Oh, you mean the primal screaming thing? Just letting out a bit of frustration at my mother. She does my head in. Good for the baby, a bit of wailing, or so I'm told." She rests her hands on her bump and grins. "I'm Delta, by the way, wayward daughter of Slánú, back with a bun in the oven to bring shame on the family."

"Cleo," I say. She's the first local I've heard pronounce the island's Irish name. "Slánú?" I say, hesitant as I attempt to pronounce it. "Did I say it right?"

She shrugs. "Not bad. Stick to Salvation, though, only the old guard use Slánú."

"And you," I say.

"Only when I'm being pissy about my delicate situation," she replies with a grin.

I feel a zing of female connection when we smile at each other. I guess it could just be that we're a similar age, but something about her registers in my psyche. It might be that she reminds me a little of Ruby—she's colorful and sparks with a similar energy—but I get the sense that she's someone who knows herself well, and I feel a pang of unexpected envy. I often feel like a child playing at being a grown-up and hoping no one will notice, whereas she gives off the impression she knows where she's headed in life. She looks as if she's about to say something when my phone pings again, a volley of queued voicemail messages clamoring for attention.

"Work," I say, glancing at Ali's name on the screen. Ruby's too.

She nods slowly. "Are you a writer?"

"Yes," I say, wondering what led her to the assumption.

"Thought so," she says. "I can see it in your aura. You've the look about you of someone who writes sweeping romances."

It's on the tip of my tongue to tell her I'm not a romance writer, but then . . . am I not? Not in the conventional sense, perhaps, but I write about love, so maybe I kind of am. Or perhaps it's more than that. Maybe it's destiny that I met this green-eyed woman here today, maybe she's my cosmic nudge to grasp the mantle and finally finish the novel I've been writing forever. To be honest, I'm a bit embarrassed about it—a journalist wanting to be a novelist, so cliché—but secretly I have been wondering whether this trip might be a way to explore that long-held dream.

"Something like that," I mumble, at odds with myself.

Delta looks away, out toward the sea. "It's

always been one of my favorite spots on the island," she says, standing up to stretch her back out. "I better get down the hill, leave you to your work."

"Don't feel you have to leave on my account," I say.

"Oh, I'm all yelled out for today," she says. "You should give it a go, no one will hear you up here."

Except for Mack, I think, watching her as she walks away. She isn't the kind of person I expected to find here. No Fair Isle sweater and ruddy complexion for starters, which I realize is my own terrible stereotyping.

I sit on the boulder as I press play on my first message. Ali's voice bubbles into the air, demanding the full warts-and-all lowdown, of course. I'll call her on Monday. I could try now—the woman doesn't know the meaning of **weekend**—but I don't really want to because I feel as if I'm still decompressing, a London-weary accordion unsqueezing.

Ali and I made a Salvation bucket list before I came here, mostly my ideas with a few of Ali's additions, stuff she thinks our readers would love to read about. I open my Notes app now and scan it, wondering which of the items I'll be able to tick off first.

Swim in the sea—that one was mine. I

love to swim in places other than chlorinated swimming pools but rarely get the chance, so I'm hoping the sea will be calm enough at some point to swim in without dying.

Spend twenty-four hours naked. I was reluctant to add this. Not because I'm especially prudish or have any major body hang-ups. It just felt a bit shoehorned in for entertainment value. But Ali argued it on to the list as a way to connect with nature in the most elemental way, which I guess I can get behind. Not something to contemplate while Mack's still around, though. I slide my fingertip down the screen.

Build a fire on the beach.
Eat a meal you've foraged yourself.
Make a life-changing decision.
Sleep outdoors.

I strike that one off the list. I hadn't taken the inclement weather into account.

Write a poem or maybe a song.
Make something with your hands.
The self-coupling ceremony.

I pause, tapping my finger lightly against the words. It's still a work in progress, a brain-sketch more than a solid plan. The ceremony will be on my birthday because I want to do something to mark the day I turn thirty, a symbolic celebration of me. Ali is insistent on billing it as "marrying myself" because it's headline grabbing, hence the ironic honeymoon booking. I prefer to think of it as a self-commitment ceremony, a pause to acknowledge that I'm secure in who I am as a single woman. A champagne send-off for my twenties; a welcome to my thirties. I bought a balsa wood bowl off eBay with unformed ideas of putting things in it and floating it out to sea. Or setting fire to it on the beach. I don't really know yet, I'm still thinking about it. My eyes scan back up the list and pause on "Make a life-changing decision." Ali didn't see that one; I added it after I'd left London. It's something I've been mulling over in my quiet moments. What do I want the shape of the next few years of my life to look like? Who am I without a flamingo? I blow out a long, slow breath. **Come on, Salvation Island, live up to your name. Save me. Or help me save myself at least.**

I stare at Ali's name in my voicemail for a few seconds, and then, resigned, I tap her name to dial. I'm duty-bound to at least let her know what's happening here, check in and see how she wants me to play things. I hear the clicks and pips of the numbers as my phone attempts to connect, hillside to capital, but just as it makes the link a fierce whip of wind unbalances me and I stumble forward and lose the connection. Shit. I try again, holding really still, but all I get is voicemail. I can feel myself coiling back up with the familiar stress of it all, and I roll my shoulders and tell myself to step back from the feelings and leave it for now. I sigh and hang up without speaking, gritting my teeth against the urge to drop-kick the phone out into the Atlantic.

I tap Ruby's voicemail next, her recorded voice erupting from my phone like hot lava.

"Cleo babes!"

I raise the phone to my ear, because wherever she called me from is noisy—a din of music and background voices.

"I'm at that place—you know, the one with the blue neon lights and the waiters in rubber trousers? And you'll never guess who I think is over at the bar. That guy . . . ah, fuck, what's his name, the one from last summer? Remember he had that part as an extra in **Hunger Games** and told us he'd met Prince Harry?"

Someone shouts something to Ruby, a harsh sound, and I hold the phone a little away from my ear.

"Sorry, Clee, that was Helena—you know, the temp from my work? Someone spilled his drink down her dress and he's bought us all shots to say sorry. Don't think it'll cover the cost of getting that dress cleaned, though, 'cause whatever he was drinking was sick orange. At least she's pissed enough not to care."

Someone in the background is counting, loudly and excitedly. I grimace at the sound of drunk people egging one another on.

"Better go, Clee," Ruby shouts. "I'll down an extra one for you."

And then she's gone, sudden silence, and I breathe out slowly. I watch my breath drift away down the cold Irish hillside, and not a single part of me regrets not being in that bar last night drinking shots of something that would have given me a headache this morning. I think back over Ruby's message. She didn't ask me how things were going or even if I'd arrived safely. It felt more like a **look what you're missing** call than an **I'm missing you** call. Not intentionally unkind, just a reminder of how breakneck London life can be, and how you can so easily get wrapped up in blue neon lights and rubber trousers.

It's strange. I spent most of my teen years fixated on the idea of making the well-trodden pilgrimage to London, of living cheek by jowl among writers and publishers, of going to sophisticated parties where brogue-wearing literary agents laughed at my wit. But dreams change, or else people do. I know now that there are people who find the pace of the city suits their bones. Rubes, for instance. Then there are others who stay for a while and slowly realize it isn't their forever. Am I one of these? It's a difficult realization to accept. If I am, where will I go? What will I be next?

I pocket my phone and check around me to make sure Mack isn't in the vicinity, and then I cup my hands around my mouth and have a go at primal screaming. It's feeble. I'm embarrassed. Clearing my throat, I swallow hard and give it another go. This time I really try to give it some oomph, and the sound that leaves my body is part strangled cat, part Hulk with a throat infection. It's not what I was going for. I get to my feet. Limber up. And then I roar, feeling the air around me displace with shock. Wow, that felt good. I roar again, a mountain (fine, large hill) lioness, throwing all of my frustrations behind the sound until my voice is hoarse and my shoulders ache with the effort.

Primal screaming isn't on my Salvation bucket list, but it turns out it should have been.

As I walk slowly back down the hill, I

resolve to be more positive. It's only a week
until Mack can bugger off. Because obviously
he is the one who has to go—I'm here to literally figure out my life. He's just here on some
tourist trip. So until then I am going to be
polite, maybe even nice, so I can bring him
over to my way of thinking.

I'll pretend I'm spending a week with a
slightly annoying random roommate, like they
get assigned at American universities.

It's raining again. I'm not even going to
bother noting the weather anymore, people
should just assume it's raining unless I say
otherwise. I've had the lodge to myself for the
last couple of hours, a glorious taste of what
it's going to be like all the time when Mack
leaves. I've lounged in the bath and tried out
the red velvet armchair beside the fireplace, a
perfect reading spot or planning-the-future-
with-a-glass-of-wine spot. There's a loaded
bookcase I'm looking forward to exploring
in detail, and a poke around in the cupboard
beneath the TV offered up a few games like
Monopoly, a deck of cards, a box of chalk.
There are spirits too—tequila and a couple
of different whiskies. The TV doesn't actually
work; there's a note in the handbook that it's

really more of a monitor for the DVDs that are in a box on the bookcase. Actual DVDs! I didn't look at them; I'm spacing the moments of discovery out for delayed gratification.

Brianne's husband dropped off the food an hour or so ago. He looks as if he's been carved from Salvation rock, a great slab of a man with a huge beard and an even bigger grin. He made me think of those men who wear Lycra and pull lorries for fun. I'm sitting with a glass of wine, trying to make myself relax. Mack looked equally wound up; I spotted him pacing the shoreline when I glanced out the window while I opened the wine. His movements suggested agitation, simultaneously placing me on alert for trouble and pissing me off because I don't want to have to deal with someone else's shit. So I don't get up when the door opens and he rumbles in, scowling, his big coat drenched. And I don't say a word as he sheds his outdoor paraphernalia, slants a strange look my way, and grabs a beer before coming to sit on the edge of the coffee table directly in front of me.

It's an unexpected move, leaving me no choice but to listen to whatever he's about to say. I mean, I could uncurl my legs from under my bum and walk away, but that kind of open hostility just isn't in me. So I swirl what's left of the wine in the bottom of my glass and wait, studiously focusing on it.

"I'm sorry if I've been short with you," he says eventually. "This isn't your fault."

Oh. That was unexpected. I meet his eyes, caught off guard, and for a few frank moments we're just two normal people caught up in a genuinely difficult situation.

"Why don't we start over? I'm Mack Sullivan, thirty-five, photographer from Boston. Two boys, Nate and Leo. I like cold beer, the Red Sox, camping out." He pauses to think. "I'd take summer over winter, and lobster rolls and cheesecake would be my death row dinner." I notice the flush on his neck when he takes a long drag of his beer.

It's such a turnaround that I'm left floundering. I found it difficult just learning his name earlier; I don't know what I'm supposed to do with all these new details. He isn't just the American anymore, he's a photographer and a father and a cheesecake lover.

"Well, it's good to meet you, Mack." I half smile, telling myself this is what I wanted—to make nice. Only **slightly** annoyed he's done it first.

He touches his bottle to my glass. "Good to meet you too, Cleo Wilder."

I don't think I've heard my name spoken in

an American accent before. It sounds a whole lot different, as if I'm someone far cooler and more daring. What I'm feeling right this minute, though, is peer pressure. He's shared, and now it's my turn. He made it sound so easy, but then he has that innate assured articulation Americans seem to be born with. I, on the other hand, am a buttoned-up Brit.

"So as you know, I'm Cleo, twenty-nine, and I'm, er, a writer from London."

His eyebrow does a thing, and I pause.

"What?"

He shrugs. "Nothing, continue."

"You thought I was older?" I guess. "Younger?"

Mack shakes his head.

"You're surprised I'm a writer, then?"

He drinks his beer and rests his elbows on his knees. "No. Go on, tell me more things."

God, this is hard. I wish there were still wine in my glass. "I'm not sure what to tell you, really. I don't have any hobbies besides writing. No animals, no kids. Horses scare me, and . . . I don't like rice pudding."

I don't like rice pudding?

"That sounds like a whole lot of negatives," he says. "Why do horses scare you, Cleo?"

His mismatched eyes hold mine for a few heavy seconds, and I feel bizarrely self-conscious about answering. I think he realizes, because he gets up and grabs himself a fresh beer. I breathe slowly into the space he's vacated.

"More wine?"

"A little," I say stiffly, as he brings it over and pours for me. I feel slightly foolish and out of my depth. I can't even slink off to my room, because this is my room. And it's his room. Gah.

"Good walk?" I ask, glad when he drops into the corner of the sofa this time, instead of back on the table.

He nods. "This island is so much more than I expected, and I expected a lot."

I'm almost ashamed to admit that I didn't research Salvation in any great detail before I set off. Coming here was more about me than about here, which sounds pretty shallow now that I think about it.

"Salvation is the childhood home my grandmother talked about, the place where my mother set bedtime stories," he says. "I was always going to come here someday."

Fine, I get it. He wants me to understand his connection to the island, to realize how much he needs to be here. But I can't, I won't, tell him my own stories. They're too private, and I'm still figuring out myself why being here means more with every passing hour.

"I can't leave on Friday," he says. "I know you want me to, and I get that you've paid and you have a piece of paper to prove it, but I need to stay."

And **that's** where all this sharing has been heading.

"I see." I sigh. "And now, because I know you're a Red Sox fan, you love cheesecake, and your mother told you stories about this place, I'm supposed to feel as if I know you and put your worthy circumstances ahead of my own?"

He looks down and sighs as well. "So what are your worthy circumstances? How would I know? I know you're scared of horses and you don't like rice pudding. That's all I've got. Go home and meet people, Cleo. It's too lonely here for someone like you."

His words hit a nerve.

"**Someone like me?** You don't have the first clue about who I am or what I need in my life."

"So tell me," he says, raising his hands, beer and all. "Convince me you need the lodge more than I do."

"No," I say, pissed off. "Look, Mack." I scoot forward to perch on the edge of my seat, wine in hand. "You've come a long way to be here, I see that. You have family connections you want to explore, I see that too. But you know what? You can do that just as easily from the next island across. Go and meet people. Eat steak, drink Guinness, and talk about your ancestors. They'll have Wi-Fi too."

And there we are, back in our respective corners of the ring. Our eyes clash, and I down the rest of my wine, and he heads for the bathroom, taking his beer with him. I hear the bath taps turn and breathe a sigh of relief.

The atmosphere's too frosty between us to share a meal or any further conversation. He boots up his laptop sitting on the bed, and I do the same on the sofa. The only sound over the course of the evening is the tapping of keys; he's disconcertingly fast. Probably just typing random letters to psyche me out, I think, deleting the words I've misspelled in my haste to sound efficient. I give up and try to get into a book I grabbed at random from the bookshelf as he was coming out of the bathroom, a war thriller drier than Saharan sand.

Mack heads outside at around eleven and stomps around the porch with his phone held aloft, and I feel a hollow thrill of territorial victory that he clearly hasn't had any success working out where the boulder telephone box is. A more generous person would probably show him exactly the right spot and how to hold his phone in exactly the right way, but I'm not feeling all that generous right now.

I can't sleep. I've done my best to compensate for the sofa lumps with strategically placed pillows, but I'm not holding out much hope for a more comfortable night. It's bugging me that he offered me more insights into who he is than I did. I feel the need to share similarly weighted snippets in order to even the scales, but I resent this game of emotional show-and-tell, so I'm trying to dredge up three random snippets that won't give too much away.

"My first boyfriend, Lewis Llewelleyn, was a Goth who wrote terrible horror scripts. He was sixteen, I was fifteen. He asked me for my honest opinion on his masterpiece and then dumped me unceremoniously for not blowing smoke up his ass. My gran taught me to knit, and horses scare me because I fell off one when I was eight years old," I say into the late-night, pitch-black lodge as I shift into a different position on the sofa.

"Did he make it as a screenwriter?" Mack asks after a long pause.

"Hot tub salesman, last I heard."

I hear him snort.

"You didn't mention your wife," I say, before he can ask any more intrusive questions. "You said you have two boys and that you love lobster rolls and camping, but you didn't mention your wife."

He sighs. "It's complicated."

"Is that your Facebook status?"

"No, Cleo, it's my fuckin' life," he says.

Fine. Despite his carefully orchestrated getting-to-know-you session earlier, it's clear I'm not the only one playing the cards that matter close to my chest. Keep your secrets, Mack Sullivan. You're entitled to them, just as I'm entitled to mine. And I'm entitled to the keys to Otter Lodge too.

Mack, October 4, Salvation Island

Every loosened thread

I haven't unpacked my cameras yet. I'm itching to, but this ridiculous situation with Cleo is hanging over my head like a goddamn guillotine. Coming here is once-in-a-lifetime stuff for me. There's no space in my head to accommodate an obstinate British woman looking over my shoulder or chewing my ear off. Being here is an intensely personal thing, and when it comes down to it, I'm a pretty private man.

You didn't mention your wife. Cleo's voice grates in my head from last night, and I slam the teakettle down harder than necessary on the stove. **No, I didn't mention my wife, because here's the thing: it's none of your damn business. I told you a bunch of other stuff in the hope that you might try to understand that this is more than just a vacation for**

me, that this island is in my DNA, and that whether you like it or not, that does give me priority. I glance across the lodge to where she's still sleeping, passed out with her dark hair spilled across the white linen pillow. The woman perpetually looks as if she's on the set of a Snow White movie. Again, my fingers ache to close around the familiar form of my Leica; I can't look at anyone or any place without assessing the shot, mentally adjusting the lens, choosing the precise moment to capture it exactly as I see it. The thrill never gets old. I took more shots on my wedding day than the guy we paid to take photographs for us, images that have been pulled out far more often over the years than the official white leather album with our names embossed in gold letters on the front, because they catch the people we love in their most unguarded moments. Susie's mother, cupping her beloved daughter's face in her hands. Daryl, my best friend and best man, casting a longing first look across the sunlit church toward Charlotte, Susie's colleague, now the mother of his daughters. I swear you can almost see threads of love arc their way over the heads of the congregation from his eyes to her profile. A second later she turned and met his gaze—I captured that too. It hangs on their bedroom wall.

I've walked through every important moment of my life with my camera around my
neck, and I've always known there would be a
time in my life when I'd come to Salvation to
capture the landscape and meet its people,
to create a visual record of the place that runs
in the blood of my grandmother, my mother,
and me. A few days before I left, Susie referred
to my coming here as a vanity project—harsh-
edged words chosen to cut me, to diminish me,
to underscore how far apart we've grown. She
knows me better than anyone. She's listened to
me tell our kids stories of this faraway island as
their eyes fluttered to sleep, the same stories my
mother used to tell me. She knows full well this
runs soul-deep for me. Vanity project? Right
now, it's more like a fucking sanity project.

I've followed the trail that leads to Salvation's
northernmost point. My first glimpse of the
island's simple stone church and the grave-
yard beyond it—a collection of white granite
crosses scattered across the cliff top, strikingly
simple, their words turned out to face the
sea. I walk among them, hands shoved in my
pockets, my shoulders bunched against the
harsh wind. Jeez, the weather here is a daily
struggle. The last names carved into the granite

are unknown to me yet familiar: Macfarlane, Campbell, Sweeney, Macdonald. They echo my grandmother's stories, faces in faded black-and-white photographs stored in an old cookie tin in the back of her kitchen cabinet. I wish I'd found the time in years gone by to ask more about them, to make notes on the back before the early stages of dementia started to throw dustcovers over her memories. And then I find a cross inscribed with ELIZABETH DOYLE, DECEMBER 1907, beside her husband's, HENRY DOYLE, MARCH 1909. I study the scant information, hungry to know more about these long-passed relatives of Barney's. Of mine. Elizabeth died when she was seventy-nine, Henry just fifteen months later, aged eighty-four. They clocked fifty-six years together. I stand behind their graves and look out to sea, a hand braced on either stone. **Fifty-six years, folks,** I think. **That's a damn fine number.** Life couldn't have been easy for them out here on the island, especially back then without modern comforts. Or maybe I'm wrong and it was bucolic and romantic, far from the madding crowds and all the better for it. **Less complicated, anyway,** I muse, thinking of my own tangled marriage, faltering before we even reached double figures. Day by day, week by week, and month by month, Susie has systematically untied every knot that bound us together, and with every loosened thread she drifts further from me. She said there wasn't anyone else, just that she needed something different. She said it hurts like hell that she isn't sure if we'd make better friends than lovers. It doesn't seem like we're either at the moment. And that, Elizabeth, Henry, is why I'm here, three thousand miles from the people I love most in the world. I hear a creak—wind in the trees, or perhaps it's Henry turning in his grave at the thought of a Doyle man being so remiss as to let his family slip through his fingers.

"Morning."

I turn at the sound of a voice and find a woman behind me, early sixties at a guess, though that's a game I never play because it only ever ends one way. She's a cool kind of sixty-something, in any case. Blue hair pokes from beneath a wool hat with huge flowers stitched to the side of it, her coat made up of bold slices of color and textures. My fingers ache for my camera.

"You must be our honeymooner," she says, but the glint in her brown eyes confirm that news of the mix-up has reached her ears, and probably every other ear on the island.

"It came as news to me too," I say, and she laughs, pleased.

She glances at the cross in front of me. "It's been awhile since we've had any Doyles on the island."

I make a mental note not to tell Brianne any secrets. "I'm a Sullivan by name, but yeah, my mother has a cousin named Lauren Doyle."

"I remember Lauren leaving with the little ones," she says, sticking her gloved hand out. "Ailsa Campbell."

I pull my hand from my pocket and hold it out. "Good to meet you."

"You too," she says. "So what brings you to Slánú?"

I savor her use of the old name; it reminds me of my grandmother's stories.

"Oh, it's okay if you'd prefer not to say," she says when I don't reply straightaway. "It's just that few folk choose to come to a place like this without a story. We've had flashy, exhausted city types, the occasional novelist trying to blow writer's block away. Sarah, the doctor's receptionist up in the village, came to get away from her revolting husband about twenty years ago and never bothered going home. Staying long?"

There isn't a particularly straightforward answer to her question.

"That's up in the air," I say. "Planning to. A

couple of months or so, maybe even until the holidays."

She stands back and crosses her arms over her chest, assessing me. "Intrepid reporter hoping to land the scoop of your life?"

I think she's having a little fun at my expense. I shake my head, even though there will hopefully be an element of interviewing and documenting to go along with the photography project, as long as I can get the islanders to trust me enough to talk to me, that is.

"You're not one of those explorer types are you, set on walking all of the isles? We've had a few of those over the years."

"No," I say. "This is the only island I'm interested in."

Ailsa narrows her eyes for a few seconds, then shrugs. "Okay, Doyle, you win. What brings you out here?"

I offer a few details, aware that by telling one islander, I'm telling them all. **He's a photographer,** she'll say, next time she's in the store. **Here to capture the home of his ancestors, the people, and the flora and fauna, he said,** she'll explain, raising her eyebrows as she nurses a drink in the tiny village pub. **A slice of history, his and ours, for an exhibition in Boston next summer,** she'll tell a neighbor while walking her dog on the beach.

"You should come to the pub. It's open most evenings, weather permitting," she says, looking out at the clouds on the horizon. "A good place to get to know some of the locals."

"I'll definitely do that," I say. I'd been loosely planning to anyway—much easier to get people talking over a whiskey than a gravestone.

"And the girl? What's she doing on an island like this?"

"Cleo?" I say. "God knows. Sleeping in my lodge, wallowing in my bath, and . . ."

"Eating all your porridge?" Ailsa suggests, smiling.

I smile, aware how ridiculous it sounds. "I honestly don't have any idea what she's doing here. I just hope she'll get on that boat on Friday."

Ailsa's eyebrows slide up into her blue bangs. "Way I heard it, she's fair set on staying for the duration too."

Wow, they really do keep one another up to date in this place.

I'm ready to stop talking about Cleo, because the uncertainty around her is driving me a little crazy. "I better hit the trail," I say, glancing at the flowers in her hand. "Leave you in peace."

"That's one thing that's never in short supply around these parts," she says, her smile easy.

I nod a goodbye as I head back.

Cleo, October 5, Salvation Island

What if he doesn't get on the boat?

Cleo, is that you?"

I know it sounds dramatic, but I could cry at the familiarity of Ali's voice.

"Yes," I say loudly over the wind. "Listen, this will probably cut out because I'm sitting on the top of a hill and the reception is shite, but I've got a real problem here."

I managed to text her last night to give her a sketchy outline of the issue and probably the impression that it would be resolved within a day or so, but now I give her the full lowdown; she needs to know that my whole project here is potentially compromised. She's commissioned me to come to Salvation to document my self-coupling experience, which is pretty damn difficult to do when you're not actually on your own.

"And now he won't leave," I half shout. "He just won't, so I think I'm going to have to."

"No! Cleo, you absolutely can't. How's that going to look to our readers? You know ninety-five percent of reader loyalty is based on trust. Once you lose it, you can't get it back. Just stay there and play chicken. He'll walk first."

I knew she was likely to say all of those things. "Mack Sullivan is as stubborn as an ox."

"So be as stubborn as a whole goddamn herd if you need to! Come on, Clee, where's my most tenacious writer? Where's the girl I know I can rely on to get the job done no matter what?"

"Stop flattering me to get what you want, it's unseemly."

Her laughter is balm. I miss it. "Just sit tight and get the story in."

That's the power of Ali—she can laugh while simultaneously delivering an ultimatum.

"What if he doesn't get on the boat?"

"Then he has bigger balls than we thought," she says. "Stay cool. He'll get on that boat."

I hang up, wishing I could move through life with even half of Ali's certainty that things will always go her way.

Cleo, October 8, Salvation Island

Yikes! One day until the boat comes

"Can we talk?"

I look up from my laptop when Mack breaks the silence in the lodge. It's three in the afternoon, and we're both inside because the wind is blowing something fierce, sheeting rain hard against the windows. In a different context with other people, the inclement weather and the log fire would be cozy. But not here, though we have fallen into a pattern of strained civility. **Would you like coffee? I'm putting the kettle on. Do you want to use the bathroom first, or shall I go on in?** The kind of things that don't really qualify as talking. It's been more a case of ignoring the elephant in the room in the hope that the other one will admit defeat. It's Thursday now. Just one more day.

"Sure," I say. "Let me just finish this up first."

He closes the book he was reading. "What is it you're doing?"

I flounder. I don't want to tell him that I'm working on my next Flamingo post. "Keeping a diary of things, I guess you could call it."

"Am I in it?"

I've decided that the only thing I can do is be honest with our readers about the hiccup. Or is he more of a burp? An American burp. I laugh inwardly as I type a note to refer to him as such in my next column.

I level eyes with him across the room. "You're the annoying American who makes a fleeting appearance."

"Chiseled jaw?"

I pretend to check my screen and then shake my head slowly. "No mention of it."

"Remiss of you," he says.

"Is that what you want to talk about?"

He has his elbows balanced on the arms of his chair, and he leans his head into his hands, pushing his fingers into his hair. It's a gesture that makes me think he's anxious about whatever it is he's about to say. "I've been wondering what really brought you here."

Oh.

"Otter-watching?" I say, attempting to

channel Ali's lightheartedness. Besides, I **have** been entertained every morning by the family of otters who roll around the slippery rocks close to the lodge, a tumble of slick silver-brown fur. Otters really do sleep holding hands so they don't lose one another, it's not just a story. Maybe that's where I've been going wrong—I should have been searching for my otter, not my flamingo.

Mack waits, watching me steadily. I'm realizing that, like Ali, he's one of those people who employs silence to get what they want. And that's really frustrating, because I'm one of those people who feels the need to fill silence with nervous, garbled words.

"I'm on a sabbatical? Recuperating from an operation on my, er, knees?" I close my eyes and feel really, really stupid.

"Both of them?" he says.

I sigh. "Look, we both know I haven't had double knee surgery, okay? You made me nervous, it just came out of my mouth. I might not have an Irish surname or any distant relatives knocking around, but that doesn't make my time here less important."

"I make you nervous?"

"I don't like having to justify myself."

"I wasn't asking you to," he says. "It was just conversation. Someone asked me about you the other morning and I didn't know what to say."

"Who?"

"Ailsa, a woman I met out on a walk."

I haven't ventured far beyond the beach and hill around Otter Lodge since arriving. I'm aware there's a village up at the top end—I don't think I'd have felt able to come here without the security of other people, even if they're not close by. I'll get my boots on and explore, once this week is over and I'm finally alone.

"We need to talk about tomorrow," I say, because I know that's the real purpose of this conversation he's trying to have.

"We do," he says, getting up from the armchair and pacing to the back window.

I mentally square up, formulating my counter.

"Cleo, I'm . . ." He stops midsentence, hands braced against the windowsill as he leans forward to peer out. "There's someone coming this way, over the hill."

I'm surprised enough to get up and join him, and I see he's right, someone is heading toward us at some speed.

"It's Cameron, I think, Brianne's husband," I say, because I can't imagine there are many other men on Salvation who pack out a parka with quite such stature. We both head to the porch, as Cameron steps up to shelter from the worst of the weather, water slicking from the bottom of his coat as he sticks his thumb down at us in greeting.

"Bad news, guys," he says, coming straight to the point.

I wrap my long cardigan more tightly around my ribs, my arms crossed as my stomach flips over. "Come inside?"

He shakes his head. "I won't if it's all the same to you. Best to keep moving and get on home." He pauses, and neither Mack nor I say a word. "Storm shows no sign of knocking off. In fact, it's going to get worse before it gets better," Cameron half shouts, loud enough to be heard over the weather. "Boat's canceled tomorrow."

Mack runs his hand round the back of his neck. "I caught the forecast earlier, thought that might be the case."

I fling him a filthy **you did what now?** look, wishing I'd had the forethought to check it too.

"Too rough," Cameron says. "Not a prayer of safe crossing." He shrugs. "Fairly regular at this time of year."

I take the conversation in and try not to let my feelings erupt all over my face. I expect common sense should have sowed seeds of doubt in my mind too, although I haven't had the benefit of a shipping forecast to alert me. Or the benefit of a roommate who shares important information.

"Might it be safe at some point over the weekend?" I say, subtly crossing my fingers.

Cameron swipes away the rain running down his hairline. "Shouldn't think so. We can wait until next week, unless there's an emergency or the like."

"Such as death," Mack reminds me under his breath.

"Right," I say. "Well. Thanks so much for coming all the way down here to let us know. It was kind of you."

Mack slides a look my way and then steps forward and claps Cameron's wet shoulder. "Yeah, thanks, man. You sure about not coming in for coffee? A beer for the road?"

Cameron adjusts his hood. "Bree will be clock-watching until I'm home," he says. "I'll be on my way."

And with that, he's off up the hill, leaving us alone again. I back into the lodge, and Mack follows, throwing the bolts on the door to stop the wind from rattling its hinges.

"Did you really already know?" I think about how we've both spent all afternoon in the lodge and he hasn't said a thing.

"I was just about to tell you," he says. "I wasn't sure, but I for one wouldn't want to get on a boat in this weather. Would you?"

Of course I wouldn't. But I guess I hadn't really considered the perils of the crossing, because I wasn't planning to be the person doing it. It was, I see now, a rookie error in a place as beholden to the elements as this.

I look at him, and he looks at me, and a steady spiral of fury rises in my gut. "Goddamn it," I say viciously at the fucking weather. I scrub my hands over my face.

He fills the kettle and sets it to boil as I sink down onto a dining chair, my face in my hands.

"It's like a conspiracy," I say. "They're all colluding to stop the boat from coming."

"Unless someone dies," Mack reminds me again.

"I might," I say.

"You probably won't."

"Can you?"

He shoots me a look. "Unlikely."

"I can't work with you here," I say. "I want to be alone." If I were watching myself from the outside, I'd scoff at such Greta Garbo melodrama, but I genuinely feel as if my very reason for coming to Salvation is negated by Mack's presence.

"You know what, Cleo? I don't find you easy either," he says. "Frankly, you complain too much."

I raise my face slowly from my hands and stare at him as he opens the cupboard.

"Coffee?" he asks, as if he didn't insult me two seconds earlier.

"I complain too much?" I say, opening my eyes wide. "I **complain too much**?"

He shrugs, filling two cups even though I didn't say I want one. "I don't want you here, you don't want me here. I get it. Trust me, no one wishes that boat was coming tomorrow more than I do."

"Because you think I'd have been on it?"

"Cleo, I'd have put your bags on it myself." He reaches into a low cupboard and pulls out a bottle of whiskey, then splashes a good measure into his cup. He glances at me as he hovers the bottle over my cup, and I nod, grouchy.

I know for sure now—Ali is wrong. Mack Sullivan is never getting on that boat, storm or millpond, which means I'll be the one forced to make the choice to stay or leave.

I don't say thank you when he bangs the mug down in front of me, but I don't refuse it either, because I'm stuck in a cabin off the Irish coast in a storm, and that warrants whiskey.

• • •

"Have you ever been to Boston?"

I dig around inside the contents of my whiskey-confused brain for the answer. "No," I say. "New York, but not Boston."

Mack rolls his shoulders, his hands around his glass on the dining table. We've dispensed with the need for coffee in favor of drinking the whiskey neat.

"You know one of the best things about Boston?" he says. "We have this huge frickin' tower with a light on top that tells everyone the weather forecast."

I frown. "A tower?"

He nods. "Blue for clear, red for storms."

"No need for massive men to climb mountains to deliver the forecast in person then," I say.

He tips his glass toward me. "Exactly." He shakes his head. "You know it's not a mountain, right?"

I flick my eyes at the ceiling. "You should have realized by now that sometimes, occasionally, I exaggerate when I'm stressed."

He puts the back of his hand against his forehead. "**I want to be alone,**" he says, dramatic, taking the piss.

I shoot him a glare, and he laughs into his whiskey.

Over the last hour or so, we've sat at the dining table sinking whiskey and trying to come to terms with the fact that we're interned here together for another week, and then only if the boat comes. Or someone dies. We've moodily concluded that it would be better if neither of us does that.

"Want to know something else Boston has that nowhere else does?" he asks. "My two fuckin' amazing kids."

It's a sharp conversational turn from light to heavy, the kind of confidence we haven't shared up to now.

"You must miss them a lot," I say, kind of a question and kind of a statement, because his boys are his phone screensaver and his laptop background. He picks his phone up and flicks through it, sliding it over the table toward me.

"Nate's eight, Leo's twelve going on seventeen." His half laugh doesn't get anywhere near his eyes.

I look at his family, so healthy and alive they're practically climbing out of the phone screen; Mack and his youngest are bent almost double with laughter, and a woman, his wife I presume, has her arm around their eldest son's shoulders.

"You have a beautiful family," I say, handing his phone back.

He swills his whiskey around in his glass. "Had," he says. "I **had** a beautiful family."

An awful feeling of dread creeps over my skin. Has something tragic happened to his wife? Have those boys had to endure losing the mother they clearly adore? God, I hope not. If so, I'll willingly get on that boat. He can have the lodge.

He sighs, a bone-deep rattler that heaves through his body as he finishes his drink and slides the empty glass onto the table. "And now I get to see my boys only when Susie allows it, and every now and then she lets me help them with their homework over FaceTime. The rest of the time I live in a condo alone, and the silence is so damn loud I can't hear myself think."

So on the upside, I don't think anything terrible has happened to his wife. On the downside, he's clearly unhappy both at home and not at home, apart from the people he loves.

"So . . . why here, why now? If you miss them so much, I mean?" I ask, because from everything he's said, I can't understand why he'd sign up to be three thousand miles away from the sons he adores, or why, if things were so dire, he didn't use our little issue as a reason, an excuse even, to go home again.

He sighs again heavily and slumps back in

his chair, a defeated sag to his body. "Look, being a good dad is everything to me, but the situation with Susie . . . I kind of reached a point where I felt like I was doing them more harm than good."

"What did you do that made you feel that way?" I'm unsure of what else to say. My dad died when I was a baby—my only experience of my father is missing him.

He shakes his head. "Why do you assume it was me? Susie holds all the cards, and I have an empty hand. My whole life was perfect, and then boom, she drops this huge fuckin' bomb in the middle of it." He makes air explosions with his hands. "I'd been home less than a week after my last assignment, and she tells me she isn't happy, she needs something different, asks me to step out of the picture for a while so she can think straight. And I do it, because this guy"—he jerks his thumbs to his chest—"this guy decided that the only way to hang on to the life he loves is to back the hell off."

"Had you been away long? On assignment, I mean."

"Two months that time, I guess? It's unpredictable—that's the nature of the job. I'm home as much as I can be." He sets his jaw hard. "I'm not an office kind of guy."

I can tell it's a sore point. My eldest sister married a soldier, and their marriage almost broke up over the fact that she felt like a single parent a lot of the time.

"Can't be easy on either of you," I say.

"It isn't," he says. "She asked for space and I gave it to her. But now Susie calls the shots and I wait around hoping to be let in, always on hand in case she decides she needs me. So, yeah. That's how it is. My relationship with my kids has taken an awful hit, and with Susie, I . . ." He rolls his head to one side as if he's trying to massage out old, nagging pain. "When my parents split, I was Nate's age," he says. "For me, that meant years of feeling guilty about whichever one of them I wasn't with. They weren't good at keeping their animosity from me. I was the ball in their game of emotional tennis, you know? I can still remember the chill in my gut whenever they were around each other."

He swallows, looking somewhere over my shoulder. "I shudder at the idea my kids might ever feel that way, so I laugh and joke around as much as I can with them, and I smile at Susie, and my kids are doing fine, mostly, I hope, because they think I'm fine." He stares at the table.

It's clear that life has taken some pretty

vicious chunks out of him. Despite our differences, it's obvious that he's an intrinsically decent human to the people he loves. Abstractly, I envy the depth of love necessary for a breakup to cut this deep. He's in a very different place in his life from where I am, for sure, surrounded by complications and ties and demands, while I'm spinning slowly in the same lonely spot. Two opposing problems with the same solution: Otter Lodge.

"It's strange," Mack says. "I never fully appreciated the impact my parents' divorce left on me until I became a father myself. I knew I wanted to be hands-on—well, as much as I could, given the demands of my job. So this last year has been the struggle of my life. I'm so thirsty for time with them, but still, I can't resist turning the conversation toward Susie whenever I'm with them, digging for details, using their answers to assess the state of things. But they can see right through my casual questions. Echoes of my own childhood." He looks at me across the table, his eyes bleak. "So I guess that's why I'm really here. I'm removing myself because it's the only way I can see to be a good dad right now. I don't know if walking away shows strength or weakness, if it's a risk I shouldn't have taken, but at least my kids get a couple of months of not being in the middle of whatever's happening with me and Susie. They get to talk to me on the phone and hear news about Salvation, and I get to hear about their days in Boston and not ask so much as a single question about their mother." He pauses to sigh deeply. "It was a real low point to realize that the best thing I can do for them is be somewhere else."

Wow, he's a talker when he's had a drink. I feel completely unequipped to respond in a helpful way. I wasn't expecting him to open up to me like this, to be vulnerable. I wish I knew the right things to say. I don't want to offer meaningless platitudes, but my experience of parenting is limited to high days and holidays with my nieces and nephews, and even then never as the responsible adult. My siblings see me as the baby of the family, so they don't look to me for childcare.

"Yikes," I say. It's the best my whiskey-softened brain can come up with. I'm not proud of myself right now.

"Yikes?" Mack stares at me, silent for a few seconds, and then he starts to laugh, as sudden as if someone pulled a stopper from a bottle. "Fucking **yikes**?"

I stare back at him, a little bit horrified, and then whiskey-tipsy laughter bubbles up my windpipe too, until I need to wipe tears from the corners of my eyes. It's like a dam burst, the tension over which of us will leave swept temporarily away and replaced by a slice of giddy elation. Neither of us knows what the hell we are going to do, now that we're not set urgently against each other.

"I'm sorry things are so tough for you back home," I say, when we've both calmed down. "And that I don't have anything more useful to say."

"**Yikes** was pretty seismic," he says. "I might start to use it back home."

Mention of home centers my mind back on my more immediate problem. "I can't spend another week here waiting," I say. "This time is too precious to let slip away."

"What are you waiting for, Cleo?"

Things have shifted between us tonight, a fragile truce of sorts. He's given me a window into his world, so I don't bat his question away. I reach for my glass, more for something to do with my hands, and I can't quite meet his mismatched eyes as I speak.

"I write for **Women Today**." His neutral expression tells me he hasn't heard of it. I'm not offended; he's from another continent and he's hardly our demographic. "It's an online magazine," I say. "The most popular in the UK by miles," I add. If I really drill down into why I said that, it's because I want him to be impressed or at least not dismissive. I don't want to drill down even further to work out why his opinion matters to me. "I write a column about being single in London, and more specifically about searching for love." I flick my eyes up to his to check if I see derision. I don't, so I carry on. "And I don't know if I'm just looking in all the wrong places, but I've been hitting dead ends and going round in circles for a few years now. It's become . . ." I search for an appropriate way to express it. "Monotonous. And wearying, and shallow. I feel as if I'm fading away."

I raise my eyes and find him studying me. I notice warmth there, like he's really listening.

"I'm thirty soon, and the closer it gets the more anxious I get. I've been trying to understand why I feel so increasingly conflicted, because I'm not consciously worried about the number itself, or even about being single and not having kids yet."

"Well," he says after a pause. "This sure is the wrong place, as you say, to come looking for love."

I smile, saddened. "But a really good place to know for certain I'm not going to find it, which was kind of the point."

He nods slowly. "So you're what, an

anti-love columnist now? Because you've ended up stranded with the right person to help you on that score. I can give you a million reasons to call off the search right now, Cleo. Love fucks you up."

An unexpected laugh escapes me. "I might just file that," I say. "It's pleasingly succinct."

"You're welcome," he says, raising the bottle at me as he tops up our glasses. "Buckle up, there's plenty more where that came from."

"Are you going to tell me I'm better off alone? You wouldn't be the first to trot out that old chestnut."

"The old ones are the best, as they say," he says. "I'm not here to warn you off love. You might still find someone who wants you for- ever." He rolls his glass between his palms. "But I'm probably not the best person to dole out romantic advice." He looks into his whiskey. "Turns out forever is too long for some people."

I've had enough to drink to let the words in my head fall out of my mouth unchecked. "But forever love can't just stop, can it?"

Mack takes his time to answer. "Not sud- denly, no. But a grinding, gradual halt? Yeah, maybe it can do that." He holds my gaze. "I don't fuckin' know, Cleo, I honestly don't. I guess it's the difference between what you say and what you do."

I don't say anything, because he looks as if he needs to carry on, when he can find the words.

"I probably should have said no to some of the assignments, prioritized family time over money, but . . ." He shrugs. "Susie's a real live wire, you know? Thrives on company, naturally the center of attention in any room she's in. I don't think two kids under five and an endless diet of **Peppa Pig** fulfilled her emotional needs long term. And that's not to say she's not a good mom. She's phenomenal. Just that maybe forever love fades if you don't feel seen, or if you don't spend enough time together in the same place."

"Susie sounds quite like my friend Rubes," I say. "She's a proper firefly, always burns brightest in a crowd."

Mack raises a finger at me, telling me the description feels familiar to him too.

"It's funny," I say, thinking back to the first time I saw Ruby. Or found her, to be more exact, sitting on the step outside my flat at two in the morning because she'd lost her front door key—arms around her patchily fake-tanned knees, shoes in her hands, her blood-red hair in a high ponytail. She lives on the top floor, I'm at the bottom. I've lost count of the number of times she's lowered a plant pot on a string down in search of an emergency cigarette or gin. I keep a box of cigarettes on the windowsill in readiness of a distress text even though I'm not really a smoker.

"When she and I met, we seemed like two peas in a pod, always up for anything: a night out, a shiny adventure, the newest nightclub," I tell Mack. "But now . . . God, I don't know. If she's a firefly, I'm more of a . . ." I break off to think. "A glowworm."

He laughs despite himself. "You're definitely not a worm."

"That's probably the nicest thing anyone's ever said to me," I say, and then I laugh too, because we're definitely drunk and it feels good not to be angry with him for a while.

We lapse into silence, and I wonder if it's a bad idea to drink any more whiskey.

"I think what I'm really scared of is that I've fallen out of love with love," I say, and then I huff all the air out of my lungs like a deflated balloon, because that's the thing that's been gnawing away at the back of my mind. "I tell everyone I'm a big old romantic, that I cry at movies and at weddings and at love stories, and all of those things have been true—but I'm not sure they are anymore. So now I'm here, attempting to focus on me, to love my thirty-year-old self instead of some nebulous other, and I'm worried that either I'm not going to be enough, or I **will** be enough and I'll be alone forever."

"Jeez, Cleo, that was a lot of words to say to someone who's drunk as much whiskey as I have," he says, frowning. "If I could remember them all I'd try to say something helpful."

I nod. "It's all right. I can't remember what I just said either, which is a bummer, actually, because I think it might have been important."

He looks at his phone. "How can it only be six o'clock?" he says. "It feels like midnight."

"It's the bloody weather," I say.

"Should I cook something?" he asks.

I cooked last night, so I guess it's technically his turn. "We should have a rota," I say, "to save arguments."

"A rota?" He frowns.

"You know," I say. "A plan? You do the dinner on Monday, I clean the kitchen on Tuesday. That kind of thing."

His expression clears. "Ah, a schedule."

I blink. "I say rota, you say schedule."

"Let's call the whole thing off?"

I make ironic jazz hands, and he leans his elbows on the table. "You do your **rota**," he says, drink-decisive. "You do that, Cleo."

"It might help if we think of ourselves less as roommates and more as neighbors," I suggest. "As in you live over there"—I wave toward the bed—"and I live over there." I flop my arm out in the direction of the sofa. "And this"—I knock my knuckles on the tabletop—"this right here is the town square."

Mack throws his hands out. "Works for me," he says. "You're a little messy, to be honest."

"Messy? I'm bloody not," I say.

We both gaze around the room, and it's fair to say my things are unevenly distributed.

"Fine," I say, getting up. "I can sort that in a . . . thingy. A jiffy."

Gosh, whiskey. Right.

He gets up too, and after a second he stands with his back braced against the door and his outstretched hands in front of him, palms together, pointing like a compass. I don't tell him that he's never looked more like Han Solo. "There," he says. "There's your line."

I follow it with my eyes.

"Your suitcase is in my half," he says.

I wheel it across the flagstones toward the sofa. "And your boots are in mine," I say, kicking them over the imaginary line.

"I don't think so," he says, looking down the line of his arm as if he's sighting a gun.

"Well, I know so," I say.

"Border dispute," he says.

"Already?" I say. "Are you going to be one of those pedantic neighbors who measures the length of the grass?"

"Are you going to be one of those inconsiderate neighbors who lets their dog pee on my perfect lawn?"

I shake my head. "I'm disappointed in you," I say. "I thought you were a little more . . . easygoing."

"Hey, I'm easygoing," he says. "I just like order."

"Order," I mutter, trying to visualize where the line is. "All right, hang on," I say, laughing under my breath as I cross the room.

"Hey, you just walked through my house," he says. "And you didn't knock."

"I have an idea," I say, rooting through the cupboard beneath the TV. "Here we go."

I cross to stand beside him by the door, showing him what's in my hand.

"Chalk?" he says, accepting the small blue box.

"Draw the border," I say. "But be warned, I'm watching you like a hawk." I point two fingers toward my eyes and then toward his, pausing for a second because I'm struck by those different colors again. I don't think it's something I'd ever not notice.

He shakes a stick of chalk out of the box.

"You can trust me. I'm a scrupulously fair man," he says, bending to mark the floor.

I watch as a stark white line appears down the center of the lodge, and I don't make any land grab attempts because, true to his word, he makes a fair job of it.

"There." He straightens, leaning a hand on the dining table to steady himself. "Your place and my place."

I take my seat back at the dining table, now designated common ground.

"I like it," I say, and bizarrely enough, I really do. I now have space that is mine, and I feel I know Mack just well enough to believe he won't violate it. I'll return the favor, and maybe, just maybe, this coming week won't be as mentally draining as the last one.

He clears his throat, and my eyes open in the darkness, my head still slightly spinning from the whiskey.

"I'm a cat guy, not a dog guy," he says. "I drink tequila if I need to get drunk fast, and I'll always argue the case for **The Wire** over **The Sopranos**."

I don't tell him that I've never watched either, because I kind of love that he's picked up the three-random-things-in-the-dark baton. It tells me a lot in a shorthand way.

"My family clubbed together to buy me a secondhand lime-green iBook for my fourteenth birthday, remember the clamshell kind? It was the stuff my teenage dreams were made of. I've started so many novels since then. I want to finish one," I say. I don't tell him about the longing to feel my book in my hands or about my secret dreams of red carpet screenings when my book becomes a smash-hit movie. "I always pick the killer beans out of chili, and Helvetica is the only sane font choice."

"Killer beans?"

"Kidney beans can poison you if they're not cooked properly. How can you not know that and still be alive? I never touch them, just in case."

I hear him laugh as I close my eyes, and for the first time since I arrived, I don't wish he was somewhere else.

Mack, October 9, Salvation Island

~~The boat arrives today!~~
Seven days until the boat comes

They were right about that storm," I say. It's almost eight in the morning, and neither Cleo nor I have felt the inclination to leave our respective beds yet; it's barely light thanks to the stormy skies, and the wind rattles the windows of the lodge. Cleo looks up and sighs, her face illuminated by the light from her laptop screen. I don't know how she can focus to work; last night's whiskey has given me a pounding headache right behind my eyes.

"My eldest sister is terrified of thunder," Cleo says. "She used to hide under the kitchen table when we were kids."

"I'll never understand that fear," I say. I'm a fan of big weather. Scorch my eyeballs out or snow me in, just don't bore me with endless gray days. My life has felt like a series of endless gray days since I moved into that damn condo. "How's your head?"

She tips it from side to side, testing it before she answers. "Clear as a bell. I don't usually get hangovers."

"Wow. You're already my most annoying neighbor."

Her eyes flicker along the bold white chalk line that seemed like such a good idea last night. "I know you might think it's stupid, now that we're both sober, but I want to keep it."

I won't lie; in the cold light of day I think it's impractical and untenable, but the subtle rise of her chin suggests determination, and it's not a battle worth fighting as long as she leaves next week.

"Fine," I say.

"And I'd like to suggest a few other house rules too," she says, watching me through narrowed eyes. It feels as if she's pushing against the edges of my patience to see if she can get a rise.

"Go for it."

Her shoulders slide down and she clears her throat, like someone stepping onstage to give a TED Talk.

"Okay," she says. "So, as you know, I've come here to be on my own, and you being here makes that almost impossible." She pauses, and I don't interrupt. "But I have to at least try to make it feel authentic for work, if nothing else, and to that end I'd appreciate it if we could imagine the chalk line as more of a . . . well, more of a brick wall."

"A brick wall?"

She nods. "Rock solid."

I think about it, trying to decide if she's serious, if it matters enough for me to care.

"So," she says, "if I'm on my side, no chatting, no **Can you pass me this?** or **Fancy a coffee?** That kind of thing."

And there she goes again, pushing at my patience, the look on her face somewhere between apologetic and confrontational. I wonder if it's the case that while she doesn't get hangovers, she does get super-fucking cranky.

"And the bathroom?" I deadpan. "Would you prefer some kind of booking system?"

"Are you poking fun at me?"

And now she sounds hurt and I feel like a dick. "Cleo, this is hard work with a headache," I sigh. "Just write your rules on a sheet of paper and stick it up on the fridge. I'll give it my best shot. I'll be out of the lodge working most of the time anyway, so you'll get it pretty much to yourself."

She narrows her eyes again, looking for a catch. At some point I might tell her that she wears her emotions too close to the surface, that she'd make a terrible poker player. I'm not used to it; Susie is adept at keeping me in the dark, especially lately. She'd probably say something similar about me, to be fair. We're not exactly at the **talk to my lawyer** stage yet, but we're not enough steps away from it either. It breaks my heart just thinking about it. I mentally write the next few hours off and drag the quilt up over my shoulders, turning my back as I work out what time it is in Boston. Early hours. The kids will be sleeping: Leo spread-eagle in the full-size bed we upgraded him to a year back after a monumental growth spurt, Nate curled into a tight ball around Stripes, his beloved and bedraggled tiger from a birthday trip to Franklin Park Zoo years ago. I can still see his chubby little hand reaching out from his stroller to snag it from the store display, refusing to give it up even for candy. Jeez, I'm in even worse shape than I thought if I'm having sentimental thoughts about a stuffed animal. I shove my head under my pillow to block out the storm and close my eyes, hoping for both a clearer head and clearer skies by the time I wake up.

I think I might have been too hasty when I said to just stick the rules to the fridge. It seemed like the fastest way out of the conversation at the time, but I'm standing here now reading through Cleo's list, and it feels as if I've handed the cards over to someone else again. I've been following Susie's rules for the last year. I didn't come here to play someone else's games. One, no idle chatting. Two, no possessions across the line. Three, no judging. Judging? What's she planning on doing that I might get judgmental about? I see from the list that I can at least use the bathroom as required without a booking system and that chatting is permitted as long as we're both in the shared kitchen space. Well, whoop-dee-fucking-do, Cleo. I pull a thermos out of the cupboard and fill it with coffee, swallow a couple of ibuprofen. It's stopped raining at least. I'll head out for a walk, see if the wind can blow the cobwebs away.

"Is talking allowed outside?"

Cleo looks up from her perch on the wooden porch steps as I exit the lodge. She's bundled up in a huge blue-and-green plaid blanket. She ignores my spiked question, and there's something vulnerable in her eyes that makes me wish I'd been a little kinder.

"It feels like the last outpost of civilization,

doesn't it?" she says, turning her face back toward the beach.

I follow her gaze out to sea: nothing on the horizon but blackened clouds and a heaving body of water, churned by a chilly wind blowing in across the Atlantic. "Mind if I sit?"

She nods at the empty space alongside her, silent as I pour coffee into the thermos cup. I hold the thermos out toward the mug she's cradling between her hands. She hesitates, then throws the dregs of her drink away and accepts a refill.

"Keep swimming in that direction and you'll hit New York," I say.

She nods, reflective as she sips her coffee and then shudders. "No sugar?"

"I like it bitter," I say.

"I like it sweet," she says.

We fall silent, and I wonder if that's a reflection of how different we are.

She slants a look at me. "You saw the rules, then?"

"Yeah, I saw."

"Are you okay with it?"

"Do I have a choice?"

"Of course you do." She turns to look at me. "I'm not trying to tell you what to do, Mack, just that I really need to do the things I've come here for. Say if it's too much."

I sigh and take a swig of strong, scalding coffee. She isn't insisting or deliberately throwing roadblocks in my way to spite me—this is about her work and her personal needs. Besides, I have stuff to get on with too; it might even help me concentrate.

"No, it's cool," I say, the heat taken out of my annoyance. She's just trying to salvage the best from this crazy situation we've found ourselves in. "You do you, I'll do me."

She smiles at me, and I feel a flush of satisfaction at how easily resolved it was. No drama. It's refreshing.

"Cheers," she says, holding her mug out.

I touch my plastic cup against it.

She takes a sip of coffee and then flings the rest of it on the ground at the base of the steps.

"I can't drink that," she says, sucking her cheeks in with distaste. "Tastes like cat piss."

I laugh under my breath and make a mental note that she takes sugar in her coffee.

We didn't eat together this evening. I think we both wanted space after last night. Neither of us needs a nightly whiskey-and-confidences habit.

"I could use a whiskey," she says, joining me at the kitchen table just after ten. "Want one?"

Well, okay. That went out the window fast. I close my work down and shut the laptop. "Sure. As long as it's within the rules and all."

She doesn't take offense, running her finger down the list on the fridge as she takes a couple of glasses down from the cupboard. "Nope, I think we're good. We're in the common space."

"Cool."

I watch her set the glasses on the table and pull the whiskey from among the bottles on the countertop. I feel familiar with her already, and truth be told I kind of like the idea of an evening drinking partner. It's less lonely.

"Common space, huh?"

"Like at uni," she says. "Work all day, and then let loose in the kitchen in the evening."

"What did you study?"

She pours decent measures into both glasses. "English."

"Figures."

"Does it?" she says, sliding into the chair opposite mine. "Am I so predictable?"

"God, no." I laugh. "Women are a particular mystery to me, Cleo. I'm just going on your work, and the fact that you . . . well, you just kind of scream English major."

She rocks back in her chair and looks at me, amused. "I'm not sure how to take that."

I look at her, unsure what I even mean

myself. "You have this . . . I don't know, this English **thing** going on."

"**English thing?**" she says. "Just so you know, I'm leaving the table if you use the word **waif** in your next sentence, so tread carefully."

"You get that a lot, then?" I can't say it's a word I'd apply to her. Sure, she's slight in build, but she takes up a lot of physical space with her extravagant arm gestures, and she crackles with emotion like one of those plasma spheres you see at science exhibitions. You sure know when she's in the room.

"It's my sisters' go-to way to describe me," she says.

"Are you the youngest?"

She nods. "Of four. I have a brother too, Tom. He's the eldest, not that you'd know it; he's the biggest kid of all of us. Our parents had three babies in three years, and then I came along four years later."

"Ah, so you're very much the baby of the family."

She sighs, resigned. "Even now, when I'm about to turn thirty."

She doesn't look thirty tonight. She could pass for one of those college students she talked about, sitting in our communal kitchen with her dark hair twisted up on top of her head and no makeup.

"I was married with two kids by the time I turned thirty." We'd just moved out of the apartment into a real house, somewhere for our family to grow, a forever roots kind of place for the boys. I try to push aside the memory of staggering over the threshold carrying Susie, pretending she was too heavy when in fact I'd never held anyone who fit so perfectly in my arms, or my life.

Cleo's mouth twists, and I realize I've said the wrong thing.

"Isn't everyone?" She takes too big a slug of whiskey, coughing when it hits her windpipe.

"Not everyone," I reason. "I wasn't saying it's better or worse, just that it was my life." I stare at the table, following the grain of the wood for something to concentrate on. "Is my life."

We sit at the table in the quiet of the lodge, nursing our whiskey, lost in our own thoughts. I could ask what she's thinking about, but I don't, because I'm too caught up in my own melancholy.

"I think I might call it a night," I say, because the whiskey has turned bitter on my tongue.

"Yeah," she says, downing the last of hers as she stands up and glances toward the sofa. "Time for me to head home."

"Night, neighbor." I raise my almost empty glass in salute.

"Good night, Mack," she says, rearranging the cushions on the sofa. There's an unexpected intimacy to how she says my name in her tired, late-night whiskey voice.

I drop our glasses in the sink. "It sounds different when you say it." I glance her way. "My name, I mean."

She pauses, a cushion in her hands. "Mine sounds different when you say it too."

"Cleo," I say.

Her mouth curves, soft, and her eyes linger on mine for a few seconds. Man. It's late and I've had too much whiskey. We spent the first few days under the same roof picking fights with each other. Not fighting anymore is better for both of us, obviously, but without anger we have to find a way to be around each other, twenty-four seven. I pick up the whiskey bottle and turn away, placing it back with the bottles on the kitchen counter.

It's been silent in the lodge for a while; the weather outside has calmed enough now that I can hear the sea. It's a soothing noise to fall asleep to.

"One, I can eat a bigger burger than any

man I know. Two, I collected snow globes as a kid." She pauses. "Thirty-seven of them in all, no doubt still in a box somewhere in my mum's loft."

In my head, I see a slight, dark-haired child turning the globes over in her hands.

"And my dad died when I was two years old," Cleo says. "I don't have any real memories of him."

My heart cracks for her. I see my own father next to never, but there's some comfort in knowing he's out there in California with his fourth or maybe fifth wife. He's a flaky kind of guy who dyes his hair rather than let anyone know he's going gray, and he finds it impossible to put anything above his personal happiness. He sends Christmas cards, and he FaceTimes my boys on their birthdays. He seems to find being a grandfather, albeit a mostly absent one, a whole lot easier than being a father. No responsibilities, I guess. Anyway, I have all of those things, and Cleo's revelation that she doesn't makes me appreciate them in a way I don't generally take the time to.

"I'm so sorry, Cleo."

"Tell me yours?" she says quietly.

I stare at the ceiling and dig through my memories to pull out three things that might send her to sleep smiling.

"I had a Maine coon called Blink as a little kid, pure white with one blue eye and the other orange," I say. "My mom found her at a shelter and brought her home because her odd eyes matched mine."

Cleo doesn't say anything, just listens for the rest of my list.

"I got my ass wedged in a bucket when I was five, almost ended up in the emergency room . . . And I always wanted a brother."

I don't know where that last one even came from. All her talk about her siblings maybe? And thinking about the loneliness of being an only child caught between warring parents. I close my eyes and think about my sons, glad they'll always have each other.

Cleo, October 12, Salvation Island

Remember **The Truman Show?**

When I made my bucket list of things to do while I'm here, it didn't include "refresh the chalk line down the middle of the lodge," but that's what I've just done as I wait for the kettle to boil.

Mack left early. I heard him get up, trying to be quiet as he moved around and gathered his camera gear. How can anyone need so much clunky equipment when the cameras on our phones are so damn sophisticated? My sister Sadie sends me pictures of her kids all the time; you'd think she has a professional photographer following her around twenty-four seven. I've taken loads of shots since I arrived here too, and I know it sounds like I'm blowing my own trumpet, but some of them look good enough to be published. I might just send them to Ali along with the next piece.

I've set my bucket list aside today in favor of striking out and following my nose. I've been here for ten days now, and I've yet to see much beyond the island shop. It isn't that I'm disinterested in my surroundings; for the first few days I was too wound up by the un-expected complication (aka Mack), and since then I've felt like a diver decompressing slowly through the fathoms in order to not get the bends. London is breakneck; here you move to a different beat. I think I'm finally ready now, acclimatized and keen to see what the rest of the island has to offer. A village, I know, and a church, quiet paths and views across the ocean. I've never lived in close proximity to the sea. Back home it's easy to forget that we're an island nation, especially living in London, but the ebb and flow of the tide is intrinsic to life here. It sets the island rhythm, dictates who leaves and who stays. We're beholden and dependent on it, and I find that reliance on something so out of our control soothing.

Even the mountain feels like less of an ob-stacle today. The wind has dropped and I'm not soaked to the skin, and it's really not all that awful now that I'm taking it at my own pace. All the same, I'm glad to reach the boulder at the summit. I park my bum for a few minutes to take stock. God, the air here tastes clean. It's like drinking diamonds. I gulp it down, imagining the purity party happening in my lungs right now.

My phone pips in my pocket, reminding me I've reached the only decent reception spot. Ruby's voicemail blares out unnaturally loud when I autopilot click the screen. "Seriously, girl, no messages? No how you doin'? Rubes, don't forget your keys because I'm not around to buzz you in?" She pauses and then starts again, fast and laughing. "I borrowed your blue top from your wardrobe—you know, the one with the red buttons down the back? I have a date tonight. Well, not a date. More of a hookup, but you get the picture. It's Damien, so, you know. Other news—your yucca died. I forgot to water it, it's beyond saving, soz. Oh, and get this! You know Lauren, that girl from—"

I click the message off without listening to the rest. I don't know who Lauren is. Rubes has a social circle bigger than the Arctic Circle, and I can't retain all the names. I've had that yucca plant for bloody yonks, it was in the flat when I got there, all parched and sorry for itself. I know it was only a plant, but I'd grown to enjoy the ritual of wiping its glossy leaves after I revived it. And she knows perfectly well

I love that top—it's vintage from a market we stumbled through a few summers ago. I don't like the idea of it crumpled on Ruby's bedroom floor. I've met Damien a couple of times, usually when I'm running out to work and he's ambling out of Ruby's to do whatever he does with his days. He seems all right, a tall, angular man with unruly Harry Styles hair and half-buttoned shirts that cling to his body. They have a relationship that involves few words and a lot of action.

I loosen my grip on my phone. My emails are undoubtedly stacking up, but I'm not in the mood for further intrusion. I'm not as addicted to my phone as a lot of people I know, but I've certainly allowed it to become a necessary part of my life. My morning alarm, my distraction on the loo, music for the shower, my train journey companion. It keeps me up to date with my family too: a like for the gold star Sadie's eldest received for her project last week, heart-eye emoji for the tooth fairy's visit to my youngest nephew. TV stars and celeb gossip. Colleagues and my mum. It drops me momentarily into their lives, a like or quick comment so they won't feel offended if we haven't spoken in a while. I turn it over in my hands, my portal to the rest of the world. To Ali, chasing my words. To Ruby, wearing my clothes. To scads of email marketing campaigns I won't read. I hold my finger down on the side button until it switches off.

You know in **The Truman Show,** that movie with Jim Carrey where he discovers his world isn't the whole world after all? I'm walking through the main street of Salvation village experiencing one of those moments. Otter Lodge feels as if it's floating in a bubble at one end of the island, detached and unaware of the village barely an hour's walk away. There's a handful of shops, a bakery, a butcher, even a veterinarian. The buildings are made from the same weather-beaten gray stone as Otter Lodge—low, sturdy places made to withstand the tempers of even the fiercest storm—curls of smoke rising from their chimneys. Should I go and buy a loaf, introduce myself? A few splats of rain land on my face as I stand and ruminate. Honestly, this island must be the wettest place on the bloody planet, it rains every five minutes. Glancing up now, I see the sky is black as a bag. I think of the basketful of umbrellas back at the lodge and wish I'd had the forethought to bring one with me. Island woman fail.

There's a long, hunkered-in building on

my left with SLÁNÚ VILLAGE HALL etched into the stone lintel over its faded yellow wooden doors. One stands slightly ajar, a few notices on the board fixed to the wall beside it: yoga classes on Friday mornings, coffee and crafts on Wednesdays, knitting circle every Monday. Someone in the **Truman** control room turns the rain dial up, and it's enough to push me through the daffodil-yellow doors in search of shelter.

Several pairs of eyes swivel toward me as I stand there dripping rainwater. I'd expected a deserted village hall, the kind with a bouncy wooden floor worn by skidding kids' knees, old floor-to-ceiling red velvet curtains with dust creases because they're never closed, stacks of chairs dragged around the edges. I was a long way off the mark. Floral wall lights cast a welcome glow across the boarded wood ceiling. It isn't overly big, and in place of piled-up plastic chairs there's a loose circle of mismatched armchairs: rosy chintz, buttercup-yellow cotton, faded blue linen. There's a sofa too, and a huge low coffee table covered in knitting paraphernalia: a jug of tall knitting needles, various yarns, patterns, and scraps of material. The room smells of coffee and it's toast warm, making me realize how cold I am. I take in all these details in an abstract way as I blink rainwater from my lashes and pull my red pom-pom hat off.

"Um . . . hello." I aim for confident and end up half shouting. "Hello," I say again, a little quieter to show I understand the concept of inside voices.

"Cleo, hi! Come in!"

Brianne bounces up out of an armchair and across to me, and I smile, relieved to see a familiar face.

"It was raining, and I . . ." I glance back toward the exit.

She takes my damp hat from my hands. "I'll put it on the radiator to dry," she says. "Here, give me your coat too."

I do as I'm told, glad not to be thrown back out in the rain.

"Ladies, we have a visitor." Brianne draws me across the room toward a group of women like I'm a prize specimen. "This is Cleo. Remember I told you she's staying down at Otter?"

A slight woman with jet-black Jackie Kennedy hair looks up from her knitting. "The honeymooner?"

Brianne steers me into an empty corner of the sofa before dropping back into her own armchair alongside me.

"No, Dolores, the **non**-honeymooner, remember?" Brianne says. "The mix-up we talked about at the lodge?"

Dolores is mid-sixties, and I'd say from the look in her eyes she remembers perfectly well about the mix-up. The gold buttons on her tweed Chanel-style jacket gleam like soldier's medals when she fixes her gaze on me.

"Let me introduce you round," Brianne says. "This is Erin." The woman to Brianne's other side smiles at me and reaches across to squeeze my knee. Her pale blue eyes are welcoming, the smatter of freckles across her nose reassuringly similar to my eldest sister's.

"I'm Doctor Lowry's wife," she says, "so you know whose door to knock on if you need anything medical."

The small, elderly woman beside Erin clears her throat. "And I'm Carmen, officially the oldest resident on Slánú."

I notice Dolores's slight nostril flare; whether it's because Carmen always trots out the same line or because she disputes it, I don't know. No one else missed it either.

"Ailsa." The next woman round in the circle raises her mug in my direction. I'd say she's about sixty or so, and her tie-dyed top and blue-tipped hair lends her a festival vibe. "I met that man you're not married to a week ago. If I wasn't a lesbian I'd take him off your hands, let me tell you that for nothing. A fine piece of ass, and the kind of face that could get you into all kinds of trouble."

She catches me off guard and a snort of laughter escapes my throat. The other women around the circle all try not to laugh too, except for Dolores, who looks pained.

"I think I need to see this man I've heard so much about for myself," says the only woman left to speak. We've already met—it's Delta, the pregnant girl I spoke to on top of the hill. She raises her glass of water to me in greeting, and I notice the delicate floral tattoo dancing across the back of her hand and around her forearm. I notice other things about her too, now that she isn't bundled up in rainbow stripes. Like how outrageously pretty she is: luminous green eyes and slightly out-of-control jet-black curls pulled up in a messy bun on top of her head.

"I don't think you need any more trouble in your life," Dolores says, earning herself a sharp look from Brianne.

"Thank you, Mam." Delta laughs, unfazed. Looking between the two women, I see a strong family resemblance, despite their opposite styles. Same dark hair, same startlingly green eyes. "I won't get up in case I give birth."

I'm instantly drawn to Delta; I like her

couldn't-give-a-damn attitude. I could use some of that.

"Do you knit?" Dolores tips her head to one side and stares at me. Everyone falls quiet.

"Actually, yes. Not for a while now, but yes, I do. My gran taught me." **Thank you, Gran,** I think.

I almost see everyone's shoulders relax. I get the distinct feeling that I've just passed Dolores's initiation test; I'd have been putting my damp jacket on again and heading back out into the rain if I didn't know my way around a pair of knitting needles.

Brianne has a look of genuine surprise on her face. "Cleo, that's so great! We don't get many new knitters on the island."

"The last one turned out to be a crocheter," Dolores mutters, as dark as if she'd said **murderer**.

"The audacity!" Delta's green eyes dance. "Ma, you should have shoved her crochet hook right up her—"

"It was a real shame she had to leave for the mainland, so it was," Brianne cuts in. "I miss Heather, she was great craic."

"Told filthy jokes too," Ailsa says. "I'll see if I can remember any."

I'm grappling to understand the dynamics

of the group. From what I can gather, Dolores is the straight one, and her daughter, Delta, doesn't miss a chance to wind her up. Brianne is the peacemaker; Ailsa, the free spirit; Erin, the capable doctor's wife; Carmen, the oldest, and rebellious with it.

"Let me get you some coffee," Erin says, unfolding her tall, slender frame from her armchair. "Sugar?"

"Please," I say, wondering if she disapproves as the doctor's wife. "Just half a spoon."

"Sure?" She pushes her pale red hair behind her ears, grinning. "I take two."

"Go on then," I say, sensing an ally.

I sit for a few moments, acclimatizing to the sound of voices around me again after ten quiet days. It's nothing like the drama or pace of the office, more a low-level hubbub, the soft lilt of their accents music in itself. Brianne picks up the brightly painted needles jug and holds it toward me. "Help yourself," she says. "To the wool too."

I falter. I can't really recall how things go with needle sizes, and the jug seems to have just about anything you could want.

"I'm making a scarf." Delta holds up the sea-green and gray color-blocked length on her needles. "Easiest not to stuff up." She riffles through Brianne's jug and picks out a pair of needles, handing them to me without comment. I appreciate the unfussy help.

Carmen nods toward a bowl of gray woolen yarn. "Use that." She shoots Dolores a sly look. "It's from my sheep. Best on the island."

Dolores couldn't look more as if she's sucking a lemon than if she was sucking an actual lemon. I slowly reach out and pick up a ball of Carmen's wool.

"Oh, wow, it's so soft," I say before I can stop myself, not even daring to look at Dolores, because the wool does genuinely feel like holding clouds in my hand. On closer inspection, it's storm gray marled with subtle flecks of natural colors—marine greens and topaz brown. It reminds me of the colors of the Salvation landscape. "Thank you, it's pretty," I say.

"So you have wool and you have needles," Brianne says, keen to make me feel included.

"And now you have coffee too." Erin returns, resting her hand on my shoulder briefly as she passes me a mug. "You're all set."

Gosh, I'm feeling a spot of performance anxiety now. I don't know if I can even remember how to cast on. **Under, over, through. Under, over, through.** I can hear my gran's voice in my ear as clear as when I was eight years old. I take a gulp of coffee, my eyes skittering around the various knitting projects the women are working on. Brianne has a complicated white shawl on the go, and Erin is making a silver-gray pom-pom, presumably to finish off a hat. I drink slowly, using the cover of their chat as a shield while I try to remember what to do. Dolores lowers the sleeve she's working on every so often to shoot me a watchful look. I wish she wouldn't, she's not helping my brain fog. Ailsa tucks her blue hair behind her ears and reaches into a bag at her feet, pulling out fresh needles and some bright yellow yarn.

"Almost forgot," she says. "I need to make another new patch for that stool Julia insists on not chucking away." She looks at me. "My wife has this stool as old as God's dog in her painting studio, won't sit on anything else."

"Another patch?" Brianne says, surprised. "Sure it must be more patches than cloth by now."

Ailsa shrugs, throwing me a discreet wink as she picks up the fresh needles and yarn. And then I get it, and I pick up my needles and yarn too, mirroring her movements until my hands remember the moves for themselves again. Dolores glances up and I smile, proud of the storm-gray row of stitches that have appeared on my needles. Ailsa shoots me a smile as she ducks to shove the beginnings of the

yellow patch back into her bag. I don't think
Julia's stool needed patching at all.

"Scarf?" Delta nods toward my needles.

I hadn't got that far. "Um, yes," I say.
"Think so."

"Good," Carmen says. "My wool is the
warmest on the island."

Now I'm 100 percent certain she's deliberately winding Dolores up.

"Or we have a squares basket here," Brianne
says, pointing to a wicker basket on the floor.
"We all make a square every now and then
and throw it in, and when we have enough,
we make them up into a blanket." She picks
out a couple to show me.

"Oh, cool idea," I say. And what a cool
circle of women, I think, so varied in age and
life experience and attitude. I hadn't given
much thought to the islanders, but I guess
I'd lazily imagined that the residents would
fit into a certain type. Farmer-ish. Hearty. I
hadn't expected Delta's tattoos or Brianne's
on-point cat-eye or Ailsa's blue-tipped hair. I
hadn't planned on knitting either.

"Do you do yoga?" Erin asks. "I run classes,
if you fancy coming along."

"I might, thank you," I say, warmed by the
coffee and sense of inclusion.

"Will you be staying long?" Carmen asks, peering at me over her glasses.

My mouth twists. "I don't know, really. I'm booked for a month, but it's all a bit up in the air with Mack over at the lodge too."

"Must be cozy," Delta says, coy. "You and Luke Skywalker squashed up together in that tiny place."

"Luke Skywalker?" I say.

"Bree said he looks like him." Delta laughs, poking Brianne, who turns pink.

"I did not," she says hotly.

"You definitely did," Delta insists. "In the pub the other night."

"I think you mean Han Solo," I say, realizing the villagers have been discussing us over a pint.

"Do I now?" Delta's lively green eyes flash. "Then I definitely need to call over and see you guys soon."

"You'll do no such thing," Dolores chips in. "No grandchild of mine is being born on Wailing Hill."

"Is that the name of the hill by Otter Lodge?" I ask. I glance at Delta, remembering the first time we met.

Erin, the doctor's wife, looks up from counting stitches. "There used to be a woman here called Clara who'd shout herself hoarse up there every morning, some kind of wailing therapy she'd been taught in the Middle East."

"She died a while back," Delta says mildly. "She was pretty ancient, though, so maybe there was something in all that wailing after all." I get the feeling that she keeps her own visits to the hill to herself.

"Not as old as me," Carmen sniffs. "And I've never felt inclined to wail in my life."

"Yes, but your books keep you young, Carmen," Erin says.

"Carmen writes erotic thrillers," Ailsa fake whispers, lifting her eyebrows. "I've learned a thing or two reading them."

I glance at Carmen, surprised to hear she's a novelist.

"Cleo's a writer too," Delta says. "Romance books."

I open my mouth to correct her, but different words emerge. "More general fiction than romance, really. That's what I'm working on, anyhow. Among other things." Even to my own ears I sound flaky.

Brianne sighs. "I love a good romance."

"Not enough murder for me." Carmen curls her lip. "I prefer a man with an ax buried in the back of his skull."

"Explains why you've always been single," Dolores says under her breath.

I look down and pretend to count my stitches to hide my laugh. Farmer-ish and hearty? These women refuse to fit in boxes. Good for them. We all fall silent and concentrate on our work for a couple of minutes, lost in thought.

"Just so I'm clear, you're **not** married to Han Solo, then?" Brianne says eventually, and they all start laughing. And I do too, adding stitches to my needles rather than be drawn further on the subject.

Mack, October 12, Salvation Island

Can you stand on one leg without falling over?

I hold my breath waiting for the phone to connect. "Nate?"

"Dad!" Nate shouts so loud it's as if he's sitting beside me on the boulder. "Leo! It's Dad! Come on!"

"Hey, buddy," I say, laughing even though the sound of his voice so far away breaks me. He sounds even younger than his eight years, high-pitched and exuberant.

"Dad?" Relief loosens my shoulders when Leo joins his brother on the other phone. They're both here.

"There's my guy," I say. "How are things going back home?"

I listen to them tell me about their days, my eyes screwed closed, my cell tucked into my hood so the wind on the top of the hill doesn't steal their voices from me. It's nine in the evening and pitch-black for me, end of the school day for them. Nate aced his spelling test, Leo made the baseball team. Big things and small things I'm missing; it turns my heart heavy in my chest not being there to high-five them. I'd give everything there is to be where they are right now. I hugged them right before flying out, and it struck me how narrow Leo's shoulders still are, how fragile his frame is. So much growing still to do. I had so much shit dumped on my shoulders at his age, it's a wonder I ever stood straight again. Whatever happens between Susie and me, my boys will stand tall and unencumbered.

"Mom said we need to go get ice cream now," Nate says, his voice edged with worry. That kid loves ice cream more than just about anything in the world. I do him the favor of not making him choose.

"Then go get it, kid. Tell Mom I said you can have extra sprinkles."

I trust Susie to give him the extra sprinkles. She won't withhold them to score a hollow victory over me that I won't see anyway. Nate blows kisses through the line, laughing as he hangs up, his mind already on ice cream.

"You sure you're okay, Dad?" Leo asks, so grown-up my heart fractures.

No, my lovely boy, I'm not, I think. I'm lonely and blue without you, and I miss your mom.

"I'm doing great," I tell him, forcing a smile so he can hear it. "I've taken some pretty cool photographs, and I've made a couple of friends too."

"Will you send me a photo so I know where you are?" he says, and I rock inside my coat, because I think he might be trying not to let on that he's crying.

"Soon as I get off," I say. "Promise. Love you, bud." I hear Susie calling him in the background. "Now go get your ice cream before it melts."

I sit for a while after he's gone, wondering if he's okay. It pains me to hear him down when he should be bouncing off the walls with excitement about making the team. Maybe I'll get in touch with Susie, make sure there isn't anything underlying we need to keep an eye on. It's a cold, clear Salvation night. I look west out over the ocean toward where they are, eating ice cream, three instead of four. And then I look down toward Otter Lodge, the welcome light on the porch switched on to guide me home. Except it isn't home. Nowhere really is right now.

• • •

Cleo has her huge headphones jammed on when I head back inside. Her fingers fly over her laptop, a sure sign that my neighbor wants to be left alone. That's okay, I'm not in the mood to talk either. I'd kill for a long shower, the powerful kind that feels somewhere between a sports massage and being beaten up. A soak in the bath just doesn't cut it. I do it anyway, but I don't enjoy being alone with my thoughts so I pull the plug, restless. I've made a decent start workwise at last—that's something positive. It was therapeutic unpacking all my gear, turning it over in my hands, working out how to best capture the first light this morning. The familiarity of the frayed leather strap was like an old friend's hand resting on the back of my neck this afternoon as I snapped the otters emerging from their den, the blue-black gleam of a seabird's wing, the comedic scuttle of a hermit crab that had outgrown its shell. It'll find another that fits it better soon enough; life is definitely more straightforward for crabs than humans.

Beer in hand, I lean against the kitchen counter and idly watch Cleo work. She's been out most of the day. I'm guessing that's what has her typing so vigorously tonight. My fingers reach for my camera on the kitchen table, operating on impulse to capture the moment:

the low flames in the hearth, the warmth of the lamplight, Cleo lost in her work. Have I turned into a creepy stalker-neighbor spying on the girl next door through an invisible window? I lower my camera, and it's good timing because she closes her laptop and pushes her headphones off.

I don't say anything, because the first rule on the fridge list is staring me right in the face. No chatting. I watch her throw her blanket aside and get to her feet, stretching. Is she balancing on one leg? From the way she's swaying, I'd say she is.

She turns and catches me watching her and gives me a small, embarrassed wave, the kind you might give your neighbor who just caught you doing something weird.

"Yoga?" I guess, when she comes over to the kitchen and pulls the wine from the fridge.

"Something like that," she mutters, reaching for a glass. "Can you stand on one leg with your eyes closed?"

I can't say I've ever tried. "Of course."

"Go on then." She sounds a lot like a teenager issuing a challenge.

"Now?"

She nods toward my half of the lodge. "Over there in the clear space in case you fall."

I scoff. As if. I've never been one to back

down from a challenge, and because this admittedly bizarre one is momentarily pushing the rest of my crap to the back of my mind, I go with it to distract myself.

"I will if you will." I put my beer down. "You on your side of the line, me on mine."

We cross to the space behind the sofa and stand opposite each other, a couple of feet behind the line.

Cleo ties her hair up securely and rolls her shoulders like a fighter.

"Someone's been watching too much **Rocky**," I say.

She ignores my jab. "Don't forget to close your eyes, that's important."

"Why?"

She frowns. "Because I say so."

I sniff. "Bossy."

"My game, my rules," she says.

"Eyes open, eyes closed, it makes no difference to me," I say.

"Oh, it will."

I allow myself a tiny eye roll. "I'll close my eyes."

"On three," she says, über-confident.

"One, two, three," I say, then raise one leg and stretch my arms out to the sides.

Cleo lays one foot flat against her other calf and steadies herself, her arms spread too.

"Eyes shut!" she barks through clenched teeth, closing hers.

I do as I'm told, and shit, it's actually harder than I thought. Much harder. I squint through one eye, struggling, while she's still bolt upright. I'm about to fall, and oh . . . there I go.

"Goddamn it," I say, as I hit the floor.

She has her eyes open now, still standing upright on one leg as if to make a point.

I could let her claim victory right now, but I don't. I wait it out and hold her gaze. She's red-faced with the effort, and then she suddenly starts to sway like a palm tree in high wind and face-plants to the ground.

"You're over the line. Five-second penalty," I say. "Which I think you'll find makes me the winner."

She sits up and retracts her foot back over into her own half, rubbing her ankle. "Er, I don't think so. I was standing for a good ten seconds longer than you."

"Best of three?"

She puffs. "I would but I think I've twisted my ankle. I need you to pass me my wine to numb the pain."

"A likely story," I say, but I get the wine anyway. I snag my beer too, never one to let someone drink alone. I sit on my side of the line again, my back turned to her.

"What are you doing?" she says.

"Leaning against the boundary wall," I say.

I hear her laugh under her breath and then the sound of her shuffling, grumbling about her ankle until she's sitting back-to-back with me.

"I went up to the village today," she says.

"You did?" The back of her head touches my shoulder. It's unsettling.

"I joined the knitting circle."

"You joined the what now?" I say, surprised.

"The knitting circle." I feel her laugh against my back when she moves. "Do you mind if I pretend you're the actual wall? I can't lean against nothing for long."

"Okay," I say, closing my eyes when she rests her weight against me. I relax too, and we jostle until we find the natural point where we're propping each other up.

"You're a comfortable wall," she says.

I don't know how to respond. I'm struggling to respond at all, because this is the closest I've been to any woman other than Susie for longer than I can remember, and even though we aren't together, it feels like I'm crossing a line. I'm not. Literally, I'm on my side of the line and Cleo is on hers, and up to now we haven't had a flirty kind of relationship. But now that she's leaning on me, I'm suddenly hyperaware of the warmth of her body and the smell of her hair when she tips her head back. It makes me realize how crushingly lonely I am, how much I miss physical closeness.

"Why the big sigh?"

I didn't realize my thoughts were seeping from my body. "Just stuff," I say. "Leo sounded upset tonight."

"Must be tough to comfort him, being so far away."

"Yeah," I say. "He'll be okay, though. He's got Susie." **And I don't**, I think.

"Want to talk about things?" Cleo asks. "I'll listen if you need to."

"This back-to-back thing is starting to feel more like confession," I say, stalling while I decide whether talking about Susie would be a good or a bad thing. "There isn't much to say, to be honest." That's a bottomless lie, but I just don't know where to start and where to end. Does Susie miss me, miss us? She blows hot and cold toward me these days, arctic mostly, but every now and then she texts, usually late at night when she's had a couple glasses of wine. These occasional mixed messages are just enough to keep me in the waiting room of her life, or maybe it's the waiting room of mine. I know one thing. The seats are hard and too damn cold, and I can't stay there indefinitely.

"We're on a break?" I trot out the tired **Friends** line rather than face all the things I'm not ready to articulate.

"Okay," Cleo says quietly.

We fall silent for a few beats. I slow my breathing to match hers—easy in, easy out. It's comforting.

"We're the talk of the island, you know," she says jokingly, probably switching subjects for my benefit.

"I doubt that takes much, to be fair."

"I guess not," she says. "Although it took me by surprise today. I met a pretty cool group of women. I had fun."

Fun. There's something my life's been short on in recent years. Any fun I've had has been geared around the boys. Jeez, I'm throwing myself a big old pity party back here and Cleo doesn't even realize.

"How's your ankle?"

She leans forward, away from me, and I feel better, and worse.

"Do you think they'll call the boat if it's broken?"

"Only if it needs to be amputated."

"I think it might."

I twist around and find she's just kidding, leaning her weight on one hand, her wineglass in the other.

"It's not hurting much anymore," she says. "The wine solved it."

"And there was me thinking it was my good company."

She pulls a face. "You're not bad, for a wall."

"Well, you make a terrible wall," I say. "Too fidgety, and your hair was in my face."

"Sorry," she says. "I'll make sure it doesn't stray over the boundary in future."

"You could always shave your head," I say. "You said you wanted to do something to mark turning thirty."

She screws her nose up. "It'd be a statement."

"Worked out okay for Sigourney Weaver."

"Someone paid her millions to do it, though," she says. "Besides, I like my hair."

From my observations, Cleo's hair is a useful barometer for her mood. When she's lost in her work, with her laptop on her knees and a notebook propped open beside her, she twists her hair on top of her head with a pencil shoved through the knot. Sometimes when she's at the top of the hill, sitting on the Boulder of Reception, it streams out around her head Medusa-like, antennae searching for a signal. It's a curtain she steps behind whenever she feels like opting out and a theater of crazy waves on the rare occasions I've seen her truly let her guard down.

"My bum's gone numb," Cleo says.

I get to my feet and offer her a hand up. "Thanks," she says, dusting chalk off her jeans.

"No, thank **you**," I say. "For the ridiculous distraction. I really needed it."

"Any time," she says. "Maybe that should be my new dating profile—I'm your woman if you ever find yourself in need of ridiculous distraction."

As a man, I see flaws in that immediately. "Can I suggest caution? Other people's idea of ridiculous distraction and yours might be wildly different. Especially on a dating website."

She looks mock offended. "You mean standing on one leg until you fall over isn't everyone's idea of fun?"

"Not with your clothes on, no." I regret it as soon as it's out of my mouth.

Cleo smiles into her glass. I'm not sure, but I think she might be blushing.

"Don't let the image inside your head, it doesn't go away easily." She drains her wine. "Time for bed, I think, before I do myself any more injuries."

"Look, why don't you take the bed tonight? I'll have a stint on the sofa."

She frowns, laying her hand on the back of the sofa. "No, I'm good. I'm used to this beast now, I know how to bend myself around its lumps."

"Are you sure?"

"I'm sure."

"Okay then."

"Okay.

We're stuck in an awkward loop. "You hang up."

She laughs, rounding the sofa to make her bed up. "I will, because I'm knackered."

"Must be all that knitting."

"Don't knock it till you've tried it," she says.

I don't think I will, somehow.

I think of my sons as I lie in the dark: Leo's bony fingers, Nate's scraped knees.

"One, being a dad is the most important thing I am," I say into the silence. "Two, my relationship with my own dad is pretty complicated. A story for another time. And three . . ." I cast around for a third thing to add to my list. I'm not really sure how our conversations in the dark became a ritual, but they're strangely soothing. I've found myself thinking about them during the day, the things Cleo has told me, the things I've chosen to reveal about myself, the small puzzle pieces that add up to a whole person. "I don't like peanut butter." Yeah, I'm aware it's a lame finish, but I really couldn't think of anything else.

"Me neither," Cleo says. "Crunchy, lumpy sandwich spread is weird."

Left to his own devices, Nate would stand in the kitchen and eat an entire jar with a spoon. There are people with a sweet tooth, and then there's my youngest son, who would mainline sugar until his eyeballs spin if no one stopped him. He's the kind of kid who goes at everything full speed, the kind of kid I probably was until life handed me a few sharp lessons on the benefits of staying cautious.

Cleo picks up her three-things cue. "My first-ever job was in a fish and chip shop on weekends. I spent my Saturday nights battering haddock while my mates were trying to get served in the pub." She pauses. "Two, I'm the only woman in my family with dark hair, the others are all blond." I hear her breathe out in the darkness. "Three, I lost my virginity when I was seventeen . . . to the English teacher."

"You know I need to hear the rest of that story."

"He was temporary, a stand-in while our regular teacher had surgery. I walked in to his lecture and felt as if someone had set me on fire. God, did I bust a gut to impress him that summer. I agonized over every word of my essays, imagining him reading them and falling in love with me through the pages."

"And did he?"

"Oh, he noticed me all right. Within a fortnight we were steaming up the windows of his bashed Mini and doing things in school store cupboards that they definitely weren't designed for." She laughs. "It's not as terribly predatory as it sounds; he was twenty-three and wet behind the ears, and I was almost eighteen and no wallflower waiting to be picked."

"At least you didn't lose your virginity to the hot tub salesman," I say, to make her laugh. "Did you and the teacher get found out and run away together like Bonnie and Clyde?"

She sighs. "Nothing so romantic. His stint at the school came to an end after a few weeks, and our affair ended with it."

"Your poor teenage broken heart," I say.

She shifts on the sofa and sighs into her pillow. "He didn't break it really. Someone else did that. A story for another time."

Cleo, October 14, Salvation Island

Single ladies, I'm Beyoncé

Heya," Delta says, looking up from her magazine as I approach the café counter. She's wearing denim dungarees over a white T-shirt, and her dark hair is held off her face with a sequined cherry-red hair pin, her baby bump up front and central.

I pull off my woolen gloves and flex my cold fingers. "Hello yourself," I say, pleased to see her again. "I'm badly in need of hot coffee."

"And cake?" She nods toward a glass cake stand. "Erin made it. She's Salvation's answer to Nigella Lawson."

I pull Erin up in my head: tall, freckles, athletic doctor's wife with a sweet tooth. The kind of woman who looks as if she'd be good at anything she tries her hand at, whether it's baking or brain surgery.

"It's coconut and raspberry jam," Delta says. "You'd be doing me a favor. The baby has insisted on way too many slices." She pats her belly.

"Go on then," I say.

"Two slices?" She eyes me slyly. "Take one back for Han Solo?"

"Just the one will do nicely." I soften my eye roll with a smile. "You're wasted here, you could make your fortune as a saleswoman over on the mainland."

Delta screws her nose up as she pushes coffee and a huge slab of cake toward me. "Nah. Been there, done that. Give me the quiet life any day, especially now this one's on the way."

"Really?" I say. I'd assumed that she'd come back to the island as a temporary measure. She has a cartwheeling kind of energy about her, something in her startling green eyes that suggests wanderlust and adventure.

Delta glances around the warm, quiet café. "I came in here with my mother every Saturday when I was a kid. The woman who used to own it was a terrible cook, only ever baked jam tarts. Burned them sometimes as well." Delta shrugs. "It was the coming here that counted. Me and Mam always walked the long way to collect shells."

I find it hard to imagine Dolores as a carefree young woman beachcombing with her small daughter.

"So is it yours now, this place?" There's an ambience to the café that speaks of Delta's influence: Ibiza chill-out background music, whitewashed walls, a panel of stained-glass art hung in a high window splashing slices of colored light across the pale floorboards.

"Kind of," she says. "It belongs to my uncle Raff, officially, but he doesn't like being tied to running it." There's something in the way she says it that suggests indulgence, that Uncle Raff is someone she adores. "He owns the pub too," she says. "Not that he works there much either. You'll run into him soon enough, for sure. Come to the pub one of the evenings, he's always on the wrong side of the bar."

I find myself wondering how it feels to belong to a community like this, to be part of its story. "I'll do that," I say. "God, this cake is good."

"I know, right?"

"Brianne mentioned that there's a reliable internet connection in here?" I say.

Delta nods. "The Wi-Fi password this week is 'vodka,'" she says, glancing at her bump. "It was 'Pinot' last week. Wishful thinking."

I laugh as I pull my phone out. "Cake is almost as good."

Delta doesn't look convinced as she nods toward the back corner of the cafe. "There's a computer set up behind the partition if you fancy a proper keyboard," she says. "It's not booked until four if you want to use it. You can have it for free, just don't tell Mr. Four O'Clock."

Her easy friendship warms me. "Fab. I will, thanks," I say, ridiculously thrilled by the idea of an hour of decent connection rather than sitting on top of Wailing Hill at the mercy of the weather and the temperamental reception gods. I managed to send my first piece in to Ali on a wing and a prayer; this feels like a luxury in comparison.

"I'll bring some fresh coffee over," Delta says.

I hold my breath as I wait to see if Ali's available to chat, and let it out when her face pops up on the screen, squinting until she slides her glasses on.

"It **is** you," she half shouts, grinning. "How's life out there on that godforsaken rock?"

I glance over my shoulder, hoping no one else heard her. There are a couple of elderly ladies eating cake at a table by the doors and a guy lounging against the counter talking to Delta. I think I'm safe.

"You don't need to shout," I say, leaning in. "Things are getting more and more complicated here. I've just emailed you this week's piece."

She claps like an excited five-year-old. "The first one went down like a bomb," she says. "People have totally bought into the idea of your self-coupling experiment, and the addition of the American is unexpected gold dust."

"He is?"

"Yes with a capital Y, my friend," she says, high-fiving the air. "The fucking irony of marooning yourself on a deserted island and still having to bunk up with some random guy, it's hilarious!"

"But not really in the spirit of the journey," I whisper-shout, scanning for the volume button to turn her down because she's really booming. "It's a damn sight harder to self-couple when I'm not alone. I'm worried, Ali. It feels as if the whole reason for me coming here is compromised."

"I'll bet," she says, not the least bit sympathetic. "Chalk, though? Chalk? I couldn't make this stuff up, and I have a good imagination. You're the talk of the office. Practically of the whole UK. You're a sensation, darling."

I'm used to Ali's "big-sky thinking," as she calls it. Others might call it wild exaggeration. The truth usually lies somewhere in between. "It's just . . . the boat comes in a couple of days, weather permitting, and I don't know whether to get on it."

"Won't he?"

"Not a chance."

"And do you want to?"

I don't say anything, because I don't know the honest answer. I could ask her to try to find me a different place, another remote lodge on another remote island. But I'm here now, and it was such a huge effort to make the leap, and, Mack aside, there's undefinable magic to this place I don't feel able to give up yet. I feel a fragile but definite connection to Salvation, unexpected but unshakable.

"Let me help you out," Ali says, forthright as always. "Stay where you are, at least until after your birthday ceremony. If you come home before then, I hate to say it, but it's all been a big old waste of time. We've told our readers you're going to fucking marry yourself, Cleo. **Marry yourself.** You can't jilt yourself at the metaphorical altar—what kind of message would that send out to everyone in a similar position looking to you for validation about their own life choices?"

"Jeez, Ali, that's putting it a bit strong," I mutter, feeling railroaded. "I'm not the Dalai Lama."

She laughs, delighted. "You are, though! Right now you're the patron saint of single ladies. You're Beyoncé."

"If you do the dance, I'm logging off," I say.

She glances at her watch. "I need to dash anyway. Team meeting at two. I'll tell them you've checked in and to hold off on booking your neck tattoo, because you're going to stick it out like a trooper." She blows me a kiss and then disappears.

Right. So that was an unambiguous order. I log in to social media and find Ali wasn't exaggerating all that much: there's loads of buzz around our "social experiment," as she's billed it. My column and the photos from last week are splashed across the magazine's official account. I can't deny the ripple of professional pride that passes through me at being the most viewed and liked post, or the wave of pressure that follows right behind it. I read the comments for a couple of minutes and then click away from the page, because the blood is starting to pound in my ears. This isn't just my spiritual journey anymore. Responsibility settles heavy on my shoulders. This isn't a flighty experiment for column inches. It's hopes and dreams, mine and a whole load of other people's too.

My idle fingers tap the keys, and without really planning to I've typed in "Mack Sullivan," and "photographer," and "Boston." Oh, shit. Okay. I'd kind of imagined there'd be dozens of hits that weren't connected to the man staying in Otter Lodge, but there he is, top of the list. His website. His work. Sweet Mary, mother of God. He's actually amazing. I scroll through his latest exhibition images. I've never been to Boston, but through the medium of film and Mack's imagination, I feel as if I'm there now. I can smell the clam chowder and hear the roar of the Red Sox fans, and I can imagine taking a duckboat tour on the Charles River. I click on his portrait gallery, and the images staring out at me stir my soul. Some are casual, his subjects caught in a moment, not even aware of his lens. Others are posed with props or close-up studies, explosions of character caught in the slightest of glances toward the camera. Emotion radiates from every pixel. He is a true artist. I realize that, in a way, we're kind of alike—he moves people with pictures the way I strive to with words.

"Five to," Delta says, appearing around the edge of the partition. "Next customer's waiting."

Her eyes wander to the screen and I quickly close Mack's website. I half wish I hadn't logged on at all. Mack . . . the more I know of him, the more connected I feel to him, and that's the last thing I need or want at this juncture. I'm adult enough to admit, privately and to no one else, that he's an attractive man. He has shoulders made for carrying sandbags, and his odd eyes cast magic when he looks at me. Even his clothes fit his body in a way that suggests they're trying to contain dynamite. You know how deeply unsexy Simon Cowell's jeans are? Pressed, boot-leg, like he puts a brand-new pair on every day? Mack's are the opposite: lived in and loved in, and they do that distracting low-rider thing on his hips. I kind of hate myself for acknowledging this stuff. I've tumbled into connections with unsuitable men for most of my life, and this one I know up front to be married and still in love with his estranged wife. Maybe, if I'm painfully honest, the transparent way he loves is part of his appeal, even if it's someone else. It's demoralizing to know that if I wasn't being so actively solo and self-focused just now, Mack might be another failed flamingo to add to my list. What bird would he be? I wonder. Eagles are the only American birds I can think of. I don't need an eagle. They're too grand and attention-seeking.

I sigh, wishing I hadn't looked at his website and found more to admire in him. Right. I have to take Ali's advice and keep my attention where it needs to be. I need to step away from searching for someone else in favor of searching for myself. God, that sounds wanky even to my own ears. And seeing all the social media coverage and interest has added a new layer of stress to everything. I have to get this right for more than just me now. Single ladies, I'm Beyoncé. Temporarily.

Mack is Mr. Four O'Clock. I find him halfway through a slab of Erin's cake, his camera on the table beside his plate. He looks surprised to see me, and I resist the urge to run back to the computer to double-check I closed his website.

"Hi," I say. "It's good, right?"

"I'm not generally a coconut fan, but this could change my mind." He glances across at the counter. "Delta suggested I bring some back for you," he says.

"She did?" I fix her with a **you're busted** look. She just laughs and shrugs her shoulders.

Mack pushes his chair back as he stands and gathers his stuff. "Better make the most of my hour," he says, heading for the computer station. "Video call with the boys."

"How much do I owe you for the cake?" I say, shrugging my coat on as I approach the counter, digging through my pockets for my purse.

"Depends," Delta says, then leans in to whisper. "Nothing, if you give me the low-down on what's going on between you and Han Solo." Her knowing eyes tell me she caught me googling him.

"Honestly, there's nothing to tell," I say, turning to casually check he's out of earshot. "He's technically married, and I'm working on myself. It's just a weird situation we've found ourselves in. We're trying to stay out of each other's way and make the best of it."

"My idea of making the best of being stuck in a remote lodge with a hot man is different from yours, for sure," Delta says.

I glance down at her enormous baby bump, and we both laugh quietly.

"Point taken," she says.

"I'm just not going there," I say. It's not a lie. It's too complicated and my heart isn't up for a kicking from a married man.

"You know what I think is a real shame?" She pauses, her face serious, as if she's about to pass on some sage life advice. "That you don't wear your hair in Princess Leia buns. Honestly, you two could pure clean up on the look-alike circuit."

I really like Delta, but she's a massive wind-up. She laughs, pushing my money back across the counter, her green eyes brimming with trouble as I leave.

Roast chicken is the most comforting smell in the world; I'm prepared to die on that hill. I've just pulled a crispy-skinned golden bird from the oven, and its scent is powerful enough to send me hurtling back twenty years to my mum doing the same thing and gathering us all round the table to eat.

"Smells good." Mack appears, damp-haired and barefoot, fresh out of the bath. We've planned to eat together tonight, a tactical move on my part because I need to talk to him.

"Doesn't it just?" I say, placing bowls of roast potatoes and green beans in the middle of the table.

He opens a bottle of wine and grabs glasses, setting them down alongside the knives and forks.

"Looks like Cleo's Bistro is open for business," he says. "Want me to carve?"

We busy ourselves: the clink of plates as we load them up, the satisfying glug of wine into glasses, the scrape of our chairs when we sit.

"Yorkshire pudding?" I say, adding one to my plate. My mum makes the best Yorkshire pudding in the world, a skill she's ensured all her children have mastered to a satisfactory degree too. Mack looks skeptical.

"You've never tried it?" I say. "Oh, Mack Sullivan, where have you been?"

He places one at the very edge of his plate as if he's hoping it might fall on the floor.

"Tastes kind of like a pancake?" he asks after his first bite.

"What do you think?"

He drinks a little wine, nodding slowly. "I think it's . . . good," he says, going in again to double-check.

"Good." I flush with quiet pride. "I'm not sure I could spend time under the same roof with someone who said no to my mum's Yorkshire pudding."

He pauses, then adds another onto his plate.

"Actually, I need to talk to you about that," I say, following my own clumsy lead-in. "About you and me spending time under the same roof, I mean."

Neither of us has mentioned the fact that the boat comes in a couple of days, because

I honestly don't think either of us knows what to say. "I spoke to my editor today, and she made it pretty clear that I have to stay here until my birthday, at the very least. It'd be unprofessional to bail on our readers."

He doesn't meet my eye as he eats. "Remind me when that is?"

"October twenty-fourth," I say. "Ten days away."

"Okay."

I pick up my wine. "Okay?"

He lays his cutlery down. "You know I'm not going anywhere. This chalk line thing"—he nods toward it—"it's working well. I can handle it if you can."

It's not just that Ali has told me I should stay. My intuition is telling me that Salvation is the right place for me just now, and isn't it a part of my mission to try to trust myself more, to believe in my gut feelings and go with them?

"Okay then," I say, a little disconcerted to have the obstacle between us so easily taken away. I swallow a mouthful of wine, trying to work out how I feel. Relieved, I think? In spite of Mack, or because of him? A question that sidles into the very back of my mind and hides itself away.

• • •

"Thirty's only a big thing if you make it one," Mack tells me.

It's a clear, crisp night, so we've taken what's left of the wine outside to finish on the front steps, blankets slung around our shoulders. Nights like this are an absolute gift here. The stars are all up there doing their thing. I've spent countless hours trying to capture them in my memory bank for when I'm back in star-less London. It isn't always starless in London, of course, but here, it's different. It's effortless, an astral theater of light against endless dark. It reminds me of a concert, when everyone holds up their mobiles, millions of pinprick torches. The low full moon throws a mellow silver glow across the rippled water out near the horizon. I can hear the waves rushing over the pebbles down on the shore.

I think about what Mack just said and I get that he's trying to be helpful.

"I wasn't planning to make a thing of it really," I say, reflective. "It's just . . ." I break off, rolling the stem of my glass. Most people would interrupt at this point, guess at what I'm about to say and offer a platitude. Or suggest I'm worried about being single, mention that I've got a good few childbearing years left in me, if I decide I want kids. Mack doesn't interrupt; he just sits alongside me watching

the beach and waits until I'm ready. I appreciate his silence and drink a little more wine,
because some things are harder to say than
others.

"My dad didn't make it to thirty. He was
twenty-nine when he died."

Beside me, Mack sighs heavily and places
his wineglass down. "Oh man, Cleo. That's so
young."

I nod, dully aware that this is the deeply
embedded crux of everything going on inside
me, the driver behind my need for change,
and exposing it hurts like pulling a scab. "I
don't have any precious memories of him
to remember back on, and I don't know the
sound of his voice to conjure him in my head
when I need his advice," I say. "He was the
great big love of my mum's life. They were so
young when they met, little more than kids really, but it was the real deal. Tom was born just
before Mum's twenty-first birthday, my sisters
not long after." I can't fathom three babies in
three years at any age, let alone back in my
early twenties when I could barely take care
of myself, never mind anyone else. "They just
hit the love jackpot early, I guess. Mum always
calls it her magical decade. And then she lost
him, twenty-eight and on her own with four
kids." I have boundless admiration for my

mum. I was just a baby when it happened, all of us too young to appreciate the burden she carried. "Dad was killed in an accident on the way to work. Left as usual one Wednesday morning with the lunch Mum had made for him in his bag and never came home again. I know it probably sounds crazy, but being thirty, being older than my dad, kind of breaks my heart."

I can't keep the crack from my voice, and Mack scoots in closer to put his arm around me. I lean my head against his shoulder, glad of his warmth.

"I get it now, it makes sense," he says. "The thirty thing."

"I've never said it out loud to anyone else. Easier to let people think I'm scared of being 'left on the shelf.'" I sigh as I enclose the trite, outdated phrase in air quotes.

He squeezes my shoulder softly. "I can't see that happening."

"It might. I don't have the best track record when it comes to love," I say.

"Hey, that hot tub salesman sounded like a dude."

"You reckon?" I half laugh, half huff. "He was just the first on the list of bad boyfriends."

"Who was the last?" Mack asks, looking down at me. "The one who really broke your heart?"

Wow. He sees through me as if I'm made of glass. I don't usually talk about my father, and I don't talk about George Portman either. Until now, it seems.

"George." My failed flamingo. The last guy I let truly close. Just saying his name stirs old wounds. "We lived three doors apart as kids. He was an only child, spent more time in our house than his own growing up. Mum used to joke she was going to have to charge him rent." I close my eyes and I'm eight again and racing around the garden, hiding behind the old shed ready to jump out at him. Again at thirteen, watchfully guarding his school bag full of spray paints while he graffitied the railway arches. "We were friends. Best friends, really. It was never romantic between us at school—he had girlfriends, and I had . . ."

"The hot tub salesman?"

"And the English teacher," I say, wry. "Everything changed when we went to uni. I missed him so much, and we were both home for Christmas, and . . . we just climbed into my single bed, natural as breathing. Me and George Portman. I was blindsided, him as well I think."

"Sounds a lot like love," Mack says, his thumb rubbing back and forth over my shoulder.

"Yeah," I say. "It felt a lot like it too. For a while, anyway."

"What happened?"

I knot my fingers in front of me, my eyes on the ocean. "He was a complicated person. A really brilliant artist." I allow myself to remember the poky studio George rented after we graduated, the cloy of oil paint in my nose, the stifling summer heat, the sagging mattress in the corner surrounded by empty shot glasses. "He turned from a self-centered kid into a narcissistic man, always jealous of other people's success, taking the edge off his resentment with vodka."

Mack doesn't say anything when I stop and take a breath, just waits for the rest of the story.

"I fancied myself a bohemian artist's muse and budding writer, furiously pitching articles to magazines and papers. Gosh, did I take myself seriously," I say. "Any flicker of interest made George spiral." I pause. "To give him his dues, his paintings were incredible; it must be hard having such talent and no one take notice." I mentally close the door on the un-settling memories, not wanting to think about it anymore. "Long story short, my brother turned up early one Sunday morning after I'd called him especially upset at George's behav-ior. He put all of my belongings in the back of his Mini and told me enough was enough. An intervention, really, because I hadn't realized quite how toxic things had become until my brother repeated my words back to me. **I'm worried what he might do,** I'd said. He left an envelope for George, money to get himself cleaned up."

"Did he?"

"I don't know," I say. "I really hope so. He moved up north not long after and lost touch with his family. And I moved to London. Letting go of him was painful, but it was the push I needed to finally pursue my dreams, I guess. Such as they were then. I always hope I'll spot his paintings in an exhibition one day, see his name in the paper maybe." I shrug. "But I haven't."

"Letting go isn't easy," Mack says quietly, and for a couple of minutes we just drink in the silence and watch the water.

As we sit there, I let all thoughts of the past roll back where they belong and focus on the here and now. I slowly become aware of the heat of Mack's neck against the top of my head, the security of his arm across my shoulders, the clean moss and citrus scent of his skin.

"Did you manage to get through to your kids today?"

I feel his sigh slide across my hair. "Yeah. Man, seeing their faces and hearing their voices . . ." He falters. "Makes me want to climb inside the screen to get to them, you know?"

I don't, and I can only hope that my father would have felt the same kind of love for me.

"You're a really good dad," I say. "Your kids are lucky."

We fall silent again, my head on his shoulder.

We've circled a long way from hating each other, something closer to friends. Friends with opposing needs: he wants his family back; I'm working on unearthing myself from beneath a pile of pink flamingo feathers, dusting myself down, and inspecting myself for damage.

"We're like two jumbled-up jigsaw puzzles," I say. "A piece of you has turned up on my board and I can't work out where you fit."

"It's the odd eyes," he says. "You'll never fit me in."

"You don't fit in my puzzle either," he says after a few seconds. "I don't have space for a stubborn English girl who stands on one leg and eats pudding with dinner."

I laugh softly. "You liked it."

His huff warms my hair. "Surprisingly, I did."

"Let's add that to my description." I lift my head from his shoulder and glance up at him. "The stubborn, **surprising** English girl makes me sound more interesting."

Moonlight slants across the planes of his face, a few inches from mine. "Cleo, you've surprised me from the first moment I saw you."

Time grinds to a slow stop here on the wooden steps of the lodge as we really look into each other's eyes, and even though Mack doesn't fit into my jigsaw puzzle and there's no place for me in his, I don't think I've ever felt a moment of absolute connection like this one. I see the shimmer of his fear, and I'm sure he can sense my deep-seated confusion. He smooths my hair, gentle, and my breath catches as I watch the apprehension in his eyes slide toward longing. He swallows, nervous, lowering his head, our lips barely touching. It's agonizingly hot, this melancholy-sexy ache in my bones, the heat of him against me, the way his fingers cradle the back of my head. And then there's no space between us. My hand moves to the warmth of his neck as we share the slowest, deepest of kisses, the low sound in his throat letting me know this has caught him as unaware as it has me. I don't give a thought to how this flies in the face of everything I've come to Salvation for, and he clearly isn't thinking about the whole heap of unresolved issues that brought him to Otter Lodge either. Something has drawn us together for this perfect moonlit moment on these worn wooden steps, to this tender kiss that feels like it's been here all along, waiting patiently for us to find it. Have we stepped around it every day, argued over it, almost sent it flying beneath the soles of our boots? I close my eyes and lean into the feeling, to the pressure of Mack's mouth on mine.

"Cleo." He whispers my name, his fingers massaging the base of my skull, the sexy suggestion of his tongue against my lips. It's like being slowly, pleasurably electrocuted; I hope there are no passing ships, because I think we might be lighting up the shore like a beacon. I slide my tongue inside his mouth, and he meets my needs with his own, dragging me in against him, breathing hard as our kiss slips from slow to searching, from searching to searing, my quiet gasps, his banging heart. I open my eyes and look at his closed ones, his magic eyes hidden from me, as lost in this as I am. His eyelids lift when my fingers find the smooth strip of skin at the base of his T-shirt. His pulse races beneath my palm. For a moment, our mouths still against each other, his eyes locked on mine, a million questions racing through them and my mind, until he snaps and presses me back against the steps with the weight of his body, his hands inside my jumper, the kiss of a desperate man. I want him in a sudden, undeniable way I've never experienced, and his body tells me he wants me just as badly. He drags his T-shirt over his head, the gleam of moonlight silvering his exposed broad shoulders. The wooden steps press into my back when he covers me with the weight of his chest, his mouth over my neck, and I arch into him, giddy. His lips find mine again as his fingers move to the catch of my bra, a sigh of relief when he opens it, a sharp intake of breath when his hand covers the fullness of my breast. He sinks his teeth into my bottom lip, and I gasp, my fingernails digging into his shoulders. I'm not sure I could actually withstand sex with Mack Sullivan, but I'm willing to chance it, because this is already the most primal, sexual moment of my life. I'm sorry for my temporary lapse, Emma Watson, but the only thing I want right now is to have blistering sex right here on these steps.

"Let's go inside," I whisper, breathless and bold in a way I'm usually not, because this feels so right.

Mack looks at me with those magic eyes, staring deep inside my soul again, and I pinpoint the exact moment reality seeps in and the shutters roll down. He covers his face with his hands.

"Fuck. Cleo," he says. "I don't know what the hell I'm doing. I'm sorry."

I stroke his hair because he looks like an anguished man, but he reaches up and catches hold of my wrist. "Don't," he says, his breath still uneven from our kiss. "I don't want this . . . you. It all feels wrong."

It feels harsh, and it feels like a lie, because his body is telling me different. I'm aware suddenly of the late-night chill. I feel like a fool as I clamber away from him, struggling to work my clothes straight. I give up, heading for the door with as much dignity as I can muster. I bang it closed and then lean my back against it, my fists clenched. Part of me wants to open it and drag him inside, but a bigger part of me feels like locking him outside and letting him freeze.

Mack, October 14, Salvation Island

We're basically a couple of burgers

It's more than an hour before I calm down enough to head back inside the lodge. Jeez, I'm a prize idiot. We'd just agreed to lay down our swords, and I had to go and lose my head after a couple glasses of wine and the warmth of her body beside mine. Cleo's in bed with all the lights out, so I move quietly, frustrated and still raw. I know the sane thing to do here is to go to sleep, but after a few ramrod tense minutes in bed, I find myself trying to say something, anything, to explain myself.

"Susie is the only woman I've kissed in more than fifteen years. She was my photography professor's daughter. I spent days studying her face from every angle, in every light."

Cleo doesn't speak, but she shifts just enough for me to know she's awake and listening.

"It matters to me to be an honorable man, Cleo. I need to be able to look myself in the eyes in the mirror when I brush my teeth. My dad cheated on my mother more times than I can count. I'm not him. I'm not anything like him, but still, it scares me that I might fuck up, that the apple might not have fallen far enough from the tree."

I don't need a therapist to tell me I've got daddy issues. I've tied myself up in so many knots about fatherhood, in his failures and my fears of repeating them, that it's a wonder I can stand up straight.

"What just happened out there scared me. You scared me. I scared me. I'd forgotten fire like that even existed. Truth be told, I don't know if I've ever felt heat like it. It kind of blindsided me."

She sighs, and I wait.

"Look, I appreciate your attempts to explain, and maybe by morning I'll feel calm and more accommodating of your feelings, but right now I'm still too wound up to be as grown-up as I'd like to be about this, so could we please just go to sleep?"

"Okay," I say, because she's right. I knew it before I even opened my mouth.

"You know what annoys me, Mack?" she says, and I really wish I'd taken my own advice to let things lie until morning, because now her voice is rising like a simmering pot about to boil over. "That we'd finally reached this paper-thin, fragile truce. It was actually starting to feel as if we could salvage this stupid, ridiculous situation, and then just like that, it's blown sky-high. And I know, we're both consenting adults, but I don't like how you made me feel like such a bloody fool out there, that's all."

"You're not a fool, Cleo, far from it."

"I'm disappointed with myself," she cuts in. "Disappointed that I lowered my guard enough to make yet another shortsighted decision as far as men are concerned. I sat there and told you how I have a knack for letting the wrong guys close, and it's depressing that even when I'm fully aware that I'm stuck in a cycle, I let it happen again tonight. Just keep your sodding shirt on in future, will you? It was too much to come at me with all that . . . skin and muscle and heat."

I don't know what to say. Do I tell her that I couldn't help myself, that the warmth of her body next to mine reminded me of how damn lonely I am, that something about the scent of her skin slides beneath my defenses, that the intimate gleam in her eyes out there on the porch tonight unraveled me?

"Most importantly—and listen to me very

carefully, Mack—I won't shoulder misplaced guilt over kissing a married man. You've been separated for almost a year now, and I'm sorry that your heart didn't get the fucking memo, but cheating is a choice, not a genetic disposition. You're not your father." She jostles on the sofa, irritated. "Fuck, that was harsh. Too much wine. No, I'm not going to apologize because maybe you need to hear it. I'm definitely going to shut up now, though."

"Good night, Cleo." I say. She's damn right that was harsh. Did I deserve it? Does she have a point? I close my eyes and try not to remember how her lips tasted.

"And one more thing," she says. My eyes snap open. "There's a damn good reason that kind of heat doesn't generally occur. It's dangerous. People get burned, then they have to walk around for the rest of their lives feeling as if their internal organs have been sizzled."

I let the analogy sink into my tired, spinning brain for a while. "So we're basically a couple of burgers. Is that what you're saying?"

She sighs loudly. "You stay on your side of the barbecue and I'll stay on mine. That's all I'm saying."

It's late and we've strayed a long way off track here. I try to reel us back in, do a little damage control.

"For the record, the only fool out there tonight was me, okay? You were upset, I was lonely, and we both mistook that for something it isn't. Can we just agree to wipe the slate clean and never mention it again? We make the rules in this place. If we want to press the rewind button and erase what happened, then we can."

It's an appealing thought to be able to pick and choose which parts of your story get to stay.

"Fine." She sounds bone-tired, and I'm dead beat. "Let's do that then."

Cleo, October 15, Salvation Island

Sorry

Fragments of last night parade themselves behind my eyelids as I surface through the layers from sleep to awake. When I risk a glance over the back of the sofa, I'm relieved to find the bed neatly made and empty. Glad of the chance to sink a bucket of coffee alone and reorder my thoughts, I brew up and head out to let the chilled sea wind blow away the remnants of last night. Birds wheel overhead as if in greeting; I like to think they're growing accustomed to my presence here. I walk the beach, scouring the waves in search of the pod of dolphins I've come to think of as belonging to the lodge. Some days they churn the sea silver, but they've evidently found somewhere else to be this morning. The otters have abandoned me too, their cluster of rocks damp and empty in the morning bluster. Gosh, it's really bracing out here this morning. I dip my head against the wind as it buffets me. There's an ancient, mystical feeling to Salvation, as if the island gives something back to those who give themselves to it. The ground feels like a living, breathing thing beneath my feet; I'm convinced there's a beating heart somewhere deep beneath the bedrock. If you tune your ear in you can almost hear the thrum backed by the music of the ocean.

I take a warming slug of coffee and let my eyes rove across the beach, and that's when I notice something different about the swath of damp sand. I squint, and then huff quietly under my breath, trying to decide if I'm impressed by the five large capital letters etched deeply in the sand. SORRY. I look away, wrapping my blanket closer around my shoulders.

Mack, October 18, Salvation Island

I didn't see this coming

I feel as if Salvation Island has permeated my bones. I'd heard so much about this place as a kid that I thought I had a good idea of how it was going to look, but all the photos and folk tales in the world hadn't prepared me for the reality of actually being here. The land undulates beneath the soles of my boots: rolling green hills sliced through by low, stark hand-built walls; earthy peat bogs and the occasional frill of salt-crystal white sand. It's an unforgiving place, but wildly beautiful too, somewhere that feels entirely separate from the rest of the world. It must be something else to see it bathed in summer light. My head is full of its scents, of salt and damp earth and purity; Cleo said the air tastes of diamonds. It's an accurate description. Exclusive and rare.

I've never been anywhere that made my fingers itch for the shutter of my camera quite so much as here, the remarkable lights and moods as weather fronts roll in. It would make a perfect movie backdrop for a tense whodunit or a melancholy gothic. Things at Otter Lodge are a little tense and melancholy too. It was a massive mistake to let things get so out of hand Wednesday night; it's Sunday now, and the atmosphere between us is wearing on me. I behaved like a dick, but the things Cleo said afterward about me not getting the memo that my marriage has ended felt like a knife tip pressed against a taut balloon. I'm furious that she felt she had the right to pass judgment on my personal life. She doesn't know me well enough, or Susie at all, or what we have together back in Boston. What we **had** together. I don't need anyone else to tell me that it's time to let go. I might be in the waiting room of my life, but I decide when it's time to walk out that door. As far as I'm concerned, you don't give up on family. Ever.

Welcoming lights from village windows loom in the distance. It's only just past noon, but it's one of those dark gray days that never seems to get properly light, a close-the-doors-and-build-up-the-fire kind of day. Not that I could do that at Otter Lodge; Cleo and I have taken to prowling around each other like wary animals since the other night. It's a relief to be out of there.

I lose track of time filling my eyes and my camera with countless shots around the village, my imagination caught by foundation stones with dates running back hundreds of years, by the sureness that my ancestors walked these same streets, touched these same stones. But now I'm suddenly aware that it's two in the afternoon and I haven't eaten, and the illuminated windows of The Salvation Arms beckon to me like a siren to a sailor. I don't try to resist. The warm welcome of strangers beats a frosty reception from Cleo. Sometimes a man needs a drink.

I nudge the pub's heavy old black door open and find it packed, as if most of the island's residents have taken refuge from the weather here too. I've already been in once or twice for a beer on quiet weekday afternoons, lucky enough both times to take a stool at the bar and bend the ear of the owner Rafferty, or Raff, as everyone calls him, about the island's history. He's a man of indeterminate age; the lines on his features suggest seventies, but he's

quick to laugh and has a lively glint in his eye
that lends him an air of youth.

"Mack, my man! Come on in and take a
load off, why don't you?" Raff stands up from
a table in the corner by the fire and gestures
his hand toward me. "Over here. Budge up,
people, we've a guest."

"Leave your stuff by the door, Mack. You'll
have someone's eye out if you don't."

I follow the voice and find its source: Ailsa
with her wife, Julia, working their way through
heaping roast beef dinners. Ailsa raises her
glass at me as I unzip my admittedly massive
jacket. She's right; there isn't room to navigate
the pub in it without sending pints flying. I
leave everything but my camera by the door
and thread my way across to Raff.

"Hungry?" Raff says, his hand on my
shoulder as I sit down. Out of nowhere it
touches me, a more fatherly gesture than I can
ever recall from my own dad.

"You read my mind," I say.

"It's beef or beef," Raff says. "Or there's
beef, if you prefer."

A bubble of laughter slides up my windpipe. "Beef sounds good."

Raff catches the eye of the girl behind the
bar. "Bring Mack a plate of food over, Tara,
will you?"

I appreciate the simplicity of not having a choice, the way he's drawn me in and made a place for me among the locals. He makes it look effortless, but beneath his natural bonhomie I sense a person who's spent his life putting others at ease. It's not a skill you can learn.

A pint of Guinness and a plate of good roast beef arrive in short order, and I find myself relaxing into the ebb and flow of chatter as people speak across tables to one another and Raff introduces me to people I haven't yet met on my travels around the island.

"So you're a photographer, then," Julia says, eyeing my camera. "I take a few pictures myself. You'll have to call in."

"I'd like that," I say. I warm to Julia straightaway, just as I did to Ailsa. She has a splatter of pale green paint in her dark hair and traces of different colors on her hands, as if she just put down her brushes and wandered over to the pub for food. I like that kind of casual.

"Watch her, she'll have you on her homemade wine," Ailsa warns.

"Hell, I'd like that too." I grin.

"You won't," Raff says. "It's like boiled goat piss."

Julia doesn't look particularly offended. "It all goes down the same way, eh?"

"Careful, Mack. I only had her stuff once. I couldn't feel my legs for two days afterward." Delta leans in from the far end of the table— a feat, given the size of her bump. "And I was only sixteen or so. I don't know what they were thinking, giving that kind of rocket fuel to a kid."

"You helped yourself, as I recall. My niece was the most badly behaved teenager this island has ever seen," Raff says to me, nodding toward Delta. "Julia's moonshine was the least of your stunts, child. You ran poor Dolores ragged."

The look on his face tells me that he didn't actually feel the slightest bit sorry for his sister, and the laughter in Delta's eyes suggests that she and Raff are probably even more trouble together than apart. I've met Dolores only in passing, but Cleo tells me she's a tough nut to crack. I'm reserving judgment. I know from experience that there needs to be a few straight men around: the designated driver, the safe pair of hands. It's not always a choice to be cast in that role. It's much easier to be the one who skips through life responsibility-free, right? My father strolls into my head and I willfully shove him to the back, because he's been getting way too much airtime lately.

"Do you do headshots, Mack?" Raff taps my camera and then poses rakishly. "I need some new ones for my agent."

"You're an actor?"

He frowns and lays a hand on his heart, suddenly serious. "You don't recognize me?"

Everyone falls silent for a second and stares at me, and darts of panic shoot behind my ribs. I don't want to offend these people just when I was starting to feel accepted.

"I . . ."

And then they burst out laughing, and I realize the joke is on me.

"You had me there for a minute," I say, shaking my head.

An old guy a couple of stools away eyes my plate. "You want that Yorkshire, lad?"

I look at it too. I do kind of want it. "I tried them for the first time last week," I say. "Cleo made some." The one on my plate doesn't look anywhere near as good, so I nod for my neighbor to help himself.

"Where is she?" Delta asks. "She needs to wriggle her bum up here, I told her so."

"Back at the lodge, I think," I say, aiming for nonchalance. "We do our own thing."

I don't miss the way people flick glances at one another and not at me.

"Pretty lass," Julia says.

"Great hair." Delta slides me a look. "Bit Princess Leia."

I frown a little, confused by the comparison.

My empty plate is whisked away and my empty glass replaced with a fresh pint, even though I haven't ordered one. Guinness is the island lifeblood. I tried to order a bottle of beer my first time in here, and Raff ignored my request and slid a pint of the black stuff across the bar at me. "It's Guinness, Guinness, or Guinness in here, fella," he'd said, and a quick glance around at the other drinkers proved his point.

"Delta!" The girl behind the bar laughs and swishes her hands around like she's holding a sword. "Don't."

I have the feeling I'm missing an inside joke.

"The girls are wondering if you've been using the Force over at Otter Lodge," Raff says, attempting to enlighten me, but it's too cryptic. "Waving your lightsaber around, perhaps?"

"Pay these eejits no heed," Ailsa jumps in. "Pick up that camera and take some photographs now, why don't you? I expect you're itching to catch this crazed bunch on film."

Thankfully, the conversation soon moves on from what may or may not be happening at Otter Lodge, and I quietly fire off my camera, attempting to capture the warmth of community: Raff laughing with abandon, his head thrown back; Delta with a protective arm curved around her belly; Ailsa leaning in close to laugh at something Julia said, the blue tips of her hair brushing her wife's cheek. These people are the descendants of my people, our history is entwined. I feel a sense of belonging, invisible roots snaking around my ankles. It's kind of cool, but strange too, because I know where my place is—in Boston, with my family. I don't see how you can truly belong to more than one place.

The journey back to the lodge is windy, my face battered by the cold even when I dip my head against it. I don't usually struggle with the hill, but man, it's tough going this time. I think back over the afternoon of Guinness and good company, or good craic, as they say here. They're solid people, tight-knit, a real family. I've taken some images I'm pleased with today, and I'm excited to get them on my laptop for a proper look. I can feel the foundations of something special taking shape here; every time I upload my daily shots I feel flickers of anticipation. They're good. Better than good. I'm practiced enough by now to know when a project is going well.

The inhospitable land has somehow opened its arms to me, and its strong people make fascinating subjects. I've honed my craft well over the years, and it feels as if it has all been leading up to this time, this island, the professional highlight of my life. It's a source of huge sadness that my home life needed to fall apart in order to send me here. Light and shade, as always in my life, personal and professional. I'm about to push on when my cell vibrates in my pocket; the wonders of Wailing Hill reception trumps the weather again. I reach for it, focusing my eyes on the bright screen in the darkness. My stomach lurches when I see the name on the screen. **Susie.** My fingers fumble for the message. Susie never messages me. We agreed not to, unless it was urgent. My heart hammering, I tap to read the message.

Hi Mack, can you call me when you get this please? I need to talk to you. x

My eyes scan the message, then I force myself to read it again, slower. What does it mean? She'd say, surely, if something had happened to one of the boys. If it's not about the boys, then what? Oh God. I wish I were at home, that I could be there right now and see my sons, see her. This is killing me. **X**? I study the message again, wondering if this is another of Susie's low moments when she needs to check that I'm still waiting around for her. I can't stop my heart from jumping in my chest as I press to return the call and pray for the connection to hold.

"Mack?"

Her voice makes me instantly homesick. "Hey, Susie."

"I wasn't sure you'd get the message," she says. I can hear nerves in her voice and it only makes me more worried.

"Is everything okay with the kids?"

She pauses, and for a second I know pure fear.

"They're fine, don't worry." She falters. "This isn't about them . . . not directly, anyway."

Now I'm confused. "I don't follow," I say.

"Have you noticed Leo gets upset lately whenever he speaks to you?" she says.

I go clammy. Is she about to ask me not to call my sons? Because she may as well ask me to stop breathing.

"Yes, I've noticed," I say, as calm as I can manage. "I was going to talk to you, see if you know of anything on his mind."

The line goes silent long enough for me to worry we've been cut off.

"This is so difficult." Her voice is soft against my ear.

"It's difficult for me too," I say, "being so far away from you all."

I've traveled a hell of a long way to give Susie the space she needs, but I'd walk another thousand miles if it makes her see what's right for our family. Is this it? Is she going to ask me to come home? Apprehension gnaws low in my gut. It's hard to pinpoint why, exactly. This could be the call I've been waiting for, the words I've been wanting her to say.

"I'm seeing someone else, Mack. It's . . . it's pretty serious."

I actually feel the bottom fall out of my world. Twelve months of push me, pull me, waiting and waiting, and still I didn't see this coming. Does that make me an idiot? I sure feel like one right now.

"Leo found out. It's been eating him up not telling you."

My poor sweet boy. "How long?"

She falls silent again, but I can hear her breathing. I've slept beside this woman for more than a decade, listened for her breath in the dead of night. That's how I know she's breathing faster than usual, that her heart is racing. Mine is too. I can hear it roaring in my ears.

"Four months. Five, maybe? I don't know, Mack. A while, but Leo only found out last week."

"Five months?" I say. She's been sleeping with someone else for five months. It hits me like a hammer, doubling me over on the rock. I can't wrap my head around it. I've been gone only a few weeks, so there's been a considerable goddamn window for her to bother mentioning this to me.

"Who is he?"

"Mack, please. That doesn't matter right now."

"Do I know him?"

Her resigned sigh rattles down the line. "It's Robert."

For a second I can't place the name, and then it clicks. "Robert? Your boss, Robert?"

Robert, man of many vests, zany ties, and an annoying habit of calling my wife Susie Sausage. Fuck. I want to smash his jaw in. My kid's heart is breaking over **Robert**?

"Put Leo on."

"Mack, I don't think—"

"Just get my fucking son, Susie."

I can hear she's crying. I don't think there's been even once in our lives when the sound of her tears hasn't bruised my soul. There's a first for everything, it seems.

After a few moments, I hear Leo.

"Dad?"

Honestly, the shake in his voice almost breaks me.

"Hey, buddy," I say, forcing my words out clear and cool. "Listen, your mom and I were just talking about what's been going on over there."

"I know," he says. He sounds about five years old. I'd give my right arm to be able to pull him into a bear hug right now.

"Okay. I need you to listen to me. Will you do that?"

"Uh-huh," he says.

"Where are you?"

"My room."

"On your own?"

"Yeah."

I can picture him clearly. He had a fascination with outer space a few years back, so we decorated his room with astral wallpaper and bedsheets, lamps, the works. On his ninth birthday, I picked up a model of the planets and attached them to his ceiling, all while he slept, his pale hair spilled across his pillow. I wanted him to open his eyes on the morning of his birthday and see Jupiter, Mars, the moon.

"You see the moon I hung up?" I say.

"Yeah," he says.

"I'm looking at the moon here too," I say.

"I'm sitting on top of a hill on an island in the middle of the sea, looking at the moon."

"I wish you were here, Dad."

"I know, bud. Me too. More than I can say."

"I should have told you about him, shouldn't I?"

I dash my hand over my eyes. "No. You did the right thing, son. Some things are just too grown-up for you to have to deal with, and this is one of those things, okay? I'm so sorry you had to worry about this on your own."

"It's not your fault," he says quickly, fury shaking his voice up an octave. "It's Mom's. And Robert's."

"Hey now, listen. I know you're mad, and trust me, it's okay to feel mad, but don't go making your mom feel like a bad person. You know how much she loves you. We both do, more than anything or anyone."

"They were kissing in the kitchen," he says, spilling his secret out hot and fast. "I came in to grab some juice and saw them."

It's rusty nails through my heart. I built that kitchen. Danced Susie around the island when she told me she was pregnant with Nate. Dunked the kids' knees in the sink when they were tiny and hurt them playing.

"I know your mom wouldn't have wanted you to find out that way," I say as low and soothing as I can manage from thousands of miles away. "Talk to her, she's probably feeling even worse about things than you are."

"But, Dad . . ." His voice catches. "I don't want Robert. I want you."

Sometimes being a parent is the best job in the world, and sometimes it's the hardest. "Bud, you don't have to choose between anyone. You'll always have me and you'll always have your mom, regardless of who else is in the picture too."

"Promise?"

"I absolutely promise," I say. "I'll see you really soon."

"Remember we're going to the lake tomorrow," Leo says. "If you can't get me, that's why."

"I remember," I say. Susie's folks are heading to the lake for a couple weeks of family time, a tradition I've always been part of. Is Robert tagging along? The question slides under my skin like grease, even though my rational brain knows the answer. Susie's a good mom and I'm pretty tight with her family; there's no way she'd have her parents meet Robert at the family vacation. The selfish part of my heart is glad they're being forced apart for a while.

"No more worrying, okay?" I say. "It's all going to be fine."

I don't think I've ever told a bigger lie in my life.

"Love you, Dad," he says. I can hear from his relieved voice that he's more settled, the weight has lifted from his shoulders. I'm glad to carry it.

"Have fun at the lake," I say. "Be careful. Tell your brother the same."

"I will," he says.

"Say hi to your grandma and Walt for me." Susie's father is known to everyone as Walt, even to Susie.

"Okay," he says.

The temptation to keep him on the line for as long as I can is strong. "Listen, it's nighttime here and I'm so cold I can't feel my nose, so I better scoot."

"Me too," he says. "Mom's nagging me to find my swim shorts."

"You're sure gonna need them at the lake," I say.

"Love you, Dad," he says again.

"Love you more," I say.

I hear his soft laugh through the phone, and I laugh back, devastated.

Cleo, October 19, Salvation Island

I feel like Winona Ryder

I'm thinking of a beach birth." Delta nudges her elbow into my ribs and sends me a sly wink. "Like a mermaid."

Across from the sofa we're lounging on, Dolores lifts her eyes slowly from her knitting needles and stares at her daughter. "You'll do no such thing, Delta Sweeney."

"I wonder how mermaids give birth." Brianne grins, a completed pink pom-pom hat in her hands. "Through their belly button?"

Delta raises her eyebrows. "Maybe the more important question here, Bree, is how did the baby get in there in the first place? A merman?"

"Girls, please." Dolores binds off the apple-green square she's just knitted and adds it to the communal box. "That's quite enough of that kind of talk."

"I saw **Aquaman** at the cinema," I say, comfortable enough now to join in. "He was colossal, and he had a really shiny trident."

Brianne catches my eye across the coffee table, trying not to laugh.

"I gored someone to death with a trident in one of my books once," Carmen says, tiny but mighty in her chintz armchair. She's knitting a large sweater from her own gray wool.

"I think I've read that one," Ailsa chips in. "One of your filthiest."

"So many complaints." Carmen shrugs. "What did they expect in a book about a psychopathic sex addict? It was right there on the jacket."

"You'll get no complaints from me." Ailsa pats the older woman's arm.

"Ladies, enough already." Dolores presses the back of her fingers against her forehead like a character straight out of a Jane Austen adaptation. "Delta, you'll give birth on your back on a bed like every other Salvation woman before you."

"Actually, there's good evidence that it helps to give birth standing up," Erin says. "Gravity gets the baby out."

Dolores looks at Erin in a way that suggests she'd really like to contradict her but dare not, given that she's the doctor's wife.

"Let's just hope the midwife is a good catch, then," Delta says.

"Bit like catching a wet rugby ball, I shouldn't wonder," Erin says.

"Coffee anyone?" Brianne springs up out of her seat, keen to move the conversation along. It works, and for a while everyone settles to the soft clack of needles and the cozy scent of the homemade carrot cake Brianne has cleared space for in the middle of the table.

"So, Cleo." Ailsa lays her knitting down in favor of a slice of cake. "How's Mack going along with his photography?"

I study the four inches of battleship-gray scarf on my needles. "To be honest I don't really know," I say. "We don't talk all that much."

"Ah," she says. "He said similar about you in the pub yesterday."

"He did?"

Brianne passes me a plate. "He just said you do your thing and he does his."

"Told everyone you'd introduced him to Yorkshire pudding, though," Delta adds.

"There's no secrets round here, is there?" I shove a forkful of cake into my mouth to avoid answering any more questions.

"None at all," Delta says, rolling her eyes. "I wasn't planning to tell anyone who the baby's da is when I came back from the mainland. Turns out I didn't have any choice, his ma is the second cousin of Ted Murphy, who owns the village bakery. She was on the phone blabbing before I'd even climbed off the boat." She pats her bump. "Insert your own bun-in-the-oven joke—everyone else does."

Dolores sniffs. "Not so much as a discount on the soda bread from Ted."

I don't think she intends it to be funny, so I swallow down my laugh.

"Ah, Mam, don't." Delta sighs. "It was no love match. Ryan Murphy might be easy on the eye, but he spends all his days playing computer games and riding round town on a scooter. Honestly, can you see me in a sidecar?"

There's a moment of charged silence as mother and daughter eye each other across the knitting table. I get the feeling this conversation has been rolling around for quite some time.

"No one tell Julia this, but, Cleo, I think I'm carrying a bit of a torch for your man," Ailsa says, probably to change the subject. "It's the broad shoulders."

Brianne turns pink and studies her cake.

"Join the queue, Ailsa," Delta says, glad of the diversion. "Come on, Clee, spill the goss."

I falter, caught off guard. "Um . . ."

Delta looks at me closely, too emotionally astute by far. "Is everything okay over there?"

And then everyone else is studying me closely too, even Dolores.

"Yes, of course," I say, aware that my cheeks are burning. "It's just . . . a bit difficult sometimes, you know?"

"Honestly no, but I'm dying to," Delta says, sensing a story and letting her imagination fill in the gaps. "Oh my God! Have you two been hitting the sheets?"

I cover my face with my hands and groan. "No, of course not. He's still hung up on his ex-wife, and I came here in search of solitude." It doesn't escape me that between the villagers and Mack, I'm a long way from that at the moment.

"But . . . ?" Erin leans in, her clear blue eyes riveted on me as if I'm about to deliver an **EastEnders**-style cliff-hanger. Back home, I've become accustomed to playing my feelings close to my chest, but here in this cozy space, there's a heightened sense of camaraderie and female kinship. I feel like Winona Ryder in that American quilting movie where the women all go to unburden themselves and dish out sage life advice.

"He . . . I mean, we . . ." I pause, struggling

with whether I should continue. Do I really want to do this? It seems I do. "We were both feeling low the other night for different reasons, and a hug turned into something else . . . We kissed. It was an accident, we both felt horrible about it afterward, and now everything is awkward."

Delta whistles under her breath. "Accidentally kissed? As in a brush on the lips, or a full-on accidental snog?"

They all openly stare at me. I don't think any of them are breathing. I place my fork down next to my half-eaten cake. "Full-on accidental snog."

"And?"

"I didn't know kisses like that even existed."

A quiet gasp ripples around the group. Carmen opens the gold catches of her stiff black leather handbag. "I'll just write that down for my next book."

Ailsa reaches across and closes Carmen's handbag softly. "First rule of knitting club: no one talks about what they hear at knitting club," she says, making Salvation's oldest resident huff.

"I just knew he'd kiss like that," Brianne says, then claps her hand over her mouth.

Delta looks at me. "The man is an absolute ride. And if that's how he kisses, imagine how he—"

"We've agreed not to talk about what happened," I interrupt. "We're going to be like burgers on opposite sides of a barbecue, or something else confusing like that."

Erin laughs sharply and looks down at her plate, then glances up again trying to keep a straight face.

"What's tickled you?" Delta asks.

Erin tries hard not to laugh, her shoulders shaking silently with the effort. In the end, the words burst from her. "Big Mack!" She shakes her head. "Burgers." She gulps and looks at me. "Sorry."

It's so out of character for calm, gentle Erin that everyone else laughs too, the mood lightened.

"But the man has a wife, you say." Dolores's words are a cold bucket of water.

"An ex-wife," Ailsa corrects, ever Mack's ally.

"She's still his wife," I say. "They're separated, but I don't think he wants to be."

Carmen lays her handbag slowly on the floor. I notice the way she massages her ringless wedding finger when she studies me.

"Watch yourself, wain. Unless you want your heart broken, my advice is to steer well clear of a man who loves another woman."

No one knows what to say after that. I don't blame them. I pick up my needles and hope the rhythm of knitting will calm my troubled mind.

The boulder on top of Wailing Hill is possibly my favorite place on the island. For reception, obviously, but most of all for the view. It reminds me of a scene from one of my childhood snow globes.

A few hours of female company were a much-needed balm for my tattered nerves this afternoon. Salvation women are made of strong stuff. They're as different as night and day, but solidarity and kinship are instilled in their bones. I envy their shorthand connection that has nothing to do with texts or GIFs. On cue, my phone buzzes with a message.

I open the picture message from Ruby and see my blue top with all the buttons now missing down the back, and aubergine emojis beside the picture telling me Damien was an absolute animal in the bedroom and ripped it off her body caveman-style.

You may as well stick it in the bin, I text back, because honestly, I don't know what else to say. Was I supposed to laugh? Ruby replies almost straightaway; the girl is never knowingly seen without her phone in her hand.

Who pickled your onions? Don't
take it out on me because my sex
life is better than yours. Or is it?
Have you shagged that American
yet? Yes, I've read your updates. Me
and the rest of the UK!

I read the message, then reread it. No
"sorry I wrecked your favorite top" or "how's
everything going, I miss you." Maybe it's because I've so recently left the warmth of the
Salvation women, but the lack of compassion
in Ruby's words cut me.

I didn't come here for sex, Rubes.
You know that perfectly well.

I see that she's read it, and it takes a few
minutes for her reply to come back.

Yeah, right! Declare you're going to
self-couple and all the other grand
eat pray love shit, then shack up
with a married man soon as you get
there. Hilare!

She's chucked a heart-eye emoji and a
laughing face at the end, her way of adding
that she loves me really and is kidding around.

Hilare? It's a bloody long way from hilare, actually, Rubes. It's hurtful.

I know she's waiting for my reply, but I don't respond. After a couple of minutes, she messages me again.

You know what I'm saying though, right, Clee? I just mean you ran away from your problems but found the exact same shit waiting for you at the other end. Same shit, different day! Classic you!

She's added a poop and a sunshine emoji this time.

It's becoming horribly clear to me that however much I think of Ruby as my close friend, time apart is exposing huge holes in our friendship. In a few short texts she's managed to reduce my achievements to nothing and it feels unkind. It's an uncomfortable thought to wonder if we're friends out of convenience rather than genuine feelings. Same address, same age, same city. When I don't reply, she tries again.

At least it's rich pickings for work, a spectacular failed flamingo story! And then as I squint at the screen, trying to work out what the emoji is, she adds, **Sorry! Hit the**

wrong bird looking for flamingo! But this one works too! Crying-with-laughter emoji.

On close inspection, it's a chicken. **Oh, sod off, Ruby,** I think. I'm not chicken. I've come here alone to do something that feels personally important; it isn't my fault Mack's here too. I know her well enough to know she didn't intend to cause offense, but I'm not sure she'd be that fussed to know she'd caused it either.

I came here to learn lessons, and perhaps this is one of them. That realizing when to let go of a relationship is just as important as knowing when to hang on to one.

I don't reply to Ruby. For as long as I'm here, I'm one of the island's women, someone who communicates with an arm around your shoulders, not stupid emojis and exclamation marks.

I'm relieved to find Otter Lodge deserted when I make it down the hill. There's something I want to do, and I'd really like the place to myself for it. Inside, I stick the kettle on and then break the rules, crossing into Mack's half of the room for just long enough to recover my almost empty suitcase from its storage place under the bed.

Flinging it open on the rug by the fireplace, I lift out the only thing left inside: a dress I've owned for quite a few years yet never found occasion to wear. Vintage snow-white cotton, tiny capped sleeves with frills, a froth of lace around the knees—an impulse buy that has always felt a bit too **BBC costume drama** to actually leave the house in. I don't know why it seems appropriate for my thirtieth birthday ceremony, but it does. Emma Watson could so pull it off. I hope I can. It's less than a week until the big day now. In some ways it will be the culmination of my experience here, but in another way it's lost some of its significance, because every moment here feels transformative. I've been thinking about my dad almost every day, about the indelible mark he left on the world in his short life. What legacy would I leave behind if something happened to me tomorrow? Magazine articles are chip paper, online columns soon swamped by millions of other clicks and soundbites. Being part of the knitting circle has reminded me of the value of creating something tangible, a physical reminder I was here. I don't know who, if anyone, will wear the scarf, but I'm making it in the hope of it bringing someone else comfort. It's reminded me how much joy writing has always brought me too. Not the Flamingo column so much these days, but my laptop is littered with half-finished novels, beginnings and middles with no ends. A couple of friends have made the leap from journalism to fiction, and I've attended their launch parties with a secret pang of green-eyed envy. Here in Salvation, I finally have the time and the space, a persistent voice whispering, **If not now, when?**

I thread the dress onto the padded hanger I brought with me in anticipation of hanging it in the lodge to look at in the days running up to my birthday. Obviously, with Mack around, I haven't felt able to do that. I trace the tiny shell buttons down the bodice with my fingertip. It's intricate enough to have been part of a bridal trousseau. Who else has worn it? I wonder. I imagine it lying brand-new and starched among other such pretty garments in a drawer, another girl fastening these buttons, the thoughts that must have raced through her head. The fanciful notion appeals to my romantic heart.

And then I sigh, because my aforementioned romantic heart is giving me quite a lot of unexpected grief. I lay awake for a long time last night, and if I'm honest, much of it was spent resisting the urge to crawl into bed with Mack. Before our kiss, I was able to rationalize our odd couple situation. I'd even started to enjoy the whole staying-on-our-respective-sides-of-the-chalk-line thing. I've come to know Mack Sullivan better in a few weeks than I would have in a few years back in the real world. I've shared more with him about myself than I have with any other person, I think, ever. Our three-things conversations in the dark had become a form of therapy for both of us, sometimes big things, sometimes small things, the things that have made us the people we are. But then we kissed, and it's as if someone picked up a snow globe with Otter Lodge inside it and gave it the most almighty shake. He's royally screwed up my self-coupling project—no, I have. I've screwed it up. I can't even begin to think how I'm going to write my Flamingo column for the next few weeks. I know one thing for sure: we have no future together. He will go home to Boston, and I will go back to London. Those are undisputable facts.

I hang my dress from the bookshelf, and although it's only five-thirty in the afternoon, I abandon coffee in favor of a glass of wine.

Mack, October 19, Salvation Island

She's no mermaid, that's for sure

I'm going down to the beach in a while to try to catch some decent shots of the bay," I say, glancing out the window as I dry the dishes after dinner.

The clouds are racing fast across the sky, playing celestial hide-and-seek with the low moon. There's no rain, and the wind has dropped to something the forecast referred to as "fresh" rather than "gale force." Still bracingly cold, of course, but in Salvation terms at least, relatively calm.

"Mind if I come with you?"

Cleo hands me a saucepan as she speaks. She seemed subdued at dinner, pushing her food around as if she has stuff on her mind. Makes two of us.

"Sure?" I say, surprised she wants to venture out. It's pitch dark beyond the windows.

She nods. "Walk dinner off a bit."

"You didn't seem all that hungry."

She holds my gaze for a second, as if she's about to say something, then changes her mind and just shrugs. "I'll grab my jumper."

"It's freezing!"

Cleo's hopping around barefoot on the shoreline with her jeans rolled up above her ankles. She's been collecting shells for the last half hour, gathering them in the raised hem of her oversize sweater. She looks about sixteen, her hair flying around her face as she screams and runs toward me from the freezing foam.

"Come on in," she calls, laughing and beckoning with her hand. Moonlight catches her face, silvering her cheekbones, dancing through her eyes. I turn my camera, unable to stop myself. I know instinctively it's going to be one of the most stunning photographs I've taken on Salvation.

"Can't risk getting this wet," I say, raising my camera on its neck strap as an excuse.

"Leave it on the sand then," she says, waving

an arm toward the drier sand by the lodge. "There's no one but us here, it'll be safe."

I know she's right. I wasn't really worried for my camera. "You'll get hypothermia if you stay out there much longer," I call.

"Not me," she says, dancing carefree from foot to foot. She doesn't notice the extra-strong wave behind her until it crashes into the backs of her calves, catching her unaware because she's looking at me instead of the water. She shouts out with surprise, eyes wide as she loses her footing and stumbles backward. I can't get to her fast enough, and she goes back on her ass in the freezing water, screaming like she's been shot when a second wave washes clean over her head.

She's scrambling, swearing, coughing out seawater, and I toss my camera aside, grabbing her hands and hauling her sharply up.

"You're soaked," I say. It's an understatement; her clothes are plastered to her body and her hair hangs in ropes around her wax-pale face.

"It's so cold, Mack," she says, teeth chattering, clinging tight to my hands.

"We need to get you inside." I scoop her up as instinctively as I would one of the boys. She resists for the briefest moment, but it's halfhearted, because she's gone from having fun to being on the verge of painful tears.

"I lost my shells," she says, her voice small.

"Yeah, you kind of did," I say, struggling up the sand toward Otter Lodge, grabbing my camera and resting it awkwardly on top of her.

"You're warm," she says, curling into me like an animal in need of shelter.

"You're really not." I take the steps up to the front door, two at a time, and set her down inside the lodge before shrugging out of my coat. I don't like the look of her, she's ghostly pale. "Sit by the fire while I start you a bath, you need to get warmed up."

She nods, shivering. "Okay."

In the bathroom, I throw bubble bath under the fast flow of the water, filling the tub as I pull a couple of fresh towels down from the rack. When I head back to the living room, she's still standing close to the fire, wincing as she tries to flex her stiff red fingers.

"I feel like such an idiot," she says.

"I only wish I'd raised my camera in time," I say, trying to make her smile.

"My fingers really hurt."

"They'll warm up in the bath," I say. "Go on, it's ready."

She's been in the bathroom a couple

minutes when a thought occurs to me. "Cleo?" I say, tapping the closed door. "Can you manage your clothes?"

She doesn't answer straightaway.

She's managed to drag her wet sweater off and fling it in a heap outside the door.

After a second, she replies. "I can't get the buttons on my jeans," she mumbles. "Stupid fingers."

"Do you need me to help?" I say, trying to sound normal.

The door clicks open. I swallow hard as she stands in front of me, and I try my best not to look down because she's naked from the waist up except for a black mesh bra. Has this bathroom always been this small? It feels as if the walls are closing in. My fingers find the top button of her jeans and undo it, then the next, and the next, then the last. I know it's completely inappropriate to be turned on in the circumstances, but there's something undeniably intimate about unbuttoning a girl's jeans for her. I feel like a teenager who can't quite get a grip of himself.

"I'll just help you with them quickly?" I say, my breath uneven.

She nods, her eyes fastened on mine.

I hold either side of her waistband and tug her jeans down as efficiently as I can manage, bending my knees to peel them down her thighs, trying to be quick without being rough. I have to close my eyes because my face is almost level with her underwear.

"Mack, I think I can take it from here," she says, and backs up to sit on the toilet seat and wrestles her jeans down her calves.

So much pale skin, so many curves. "Good idea," I say, reversing out the door. "Shout if you need anything."

I rush outside for a blast of cold air.

"Better?"

Cleo emerged damp-haired from the bathroom a few minutes ago and curled herself into the other end of the sofa, pouring herself a glass of red from the open bottle on the coffee table.

"I feel humiliated," she says, rubbing her hair. "I can't believe I bloody did that."

"It was a pretty spectacular fall," I say, trying not to laugh. "You're no mermaid, that's for sure."

"Agreed," she says.

"I got some good shots out there tonight before you went rogue," I say. I glanced through them while Cleo was in the bathroom; there are some really strong contenders in them for the exhibition. The sheltered bay takes on an

even more last-post-on-earth aura at night—
I wasn't sure I'd be able to capture the unique
feel. Tonight's moon was a real gift, better
natural lighting than any camera flash could
hope to achieve. Mellow, vintage, timeless.
I have a feeling they're going to be some of
the photos I'm most proud of from my time
here. They're the first real pictures I've taken
of Cleo. She has an understated charisma she's
absolutely unaware of, a bright-eyed way of
looking at the lens that feels almost like a dare.

"Can I see sometime?" she says, tucking
her legs underneath her.

"Maybe," I say. I don't usually share my
work with people until it's ready.

"It's okay if you'd rather not," she says per-
ceptively. "I'm like that with my stuff too."

I lean over and throw another log on the fire.
"What's with the dress?"

She stares at the white dress hanging from
the bookshelf, her wineglass in her hands. "It's
my turning-thirty dress. I've owned it for ages
but never worn it," she says, still looking at it.
"Never seemed like the right time. And then
when I found out I was coming here to be
significantly alone"—she breaks off and looks
at me pointedly—"it felt like the entirely appropriate thing to marry myself in."

"Marry yourself?"

"It's how my boss refers to it," she says. "Obviously not actual marriage. More symbolic, an acceptance of myself as whole rather than someone waiting for my other half to show up." She takes a mouthful of wine. "I know it sounds hippie."

"Do you have a ring?"

"No. Balls. I wish I'd thought of that. I could have bought myself a ring on expenses." She smiles ruefully, but I can tell this means a lot to her on complicated levels.

"You know what, Cleo, you don't need a ring or any other outward symbol of commitment. Marriage is in here." I touch my chest.

"Now who's the hippie?" she says.

I roll my eyes.

"I'm sorry if I spoke out of turn the other night," she says. "About you not getting the memo about your marriage."

Her words riled me at the time, but Susie's recent revelations have made me realize Cleo was more right than wrong.

"Don't apologize. I can see it must look pretty pathetic to you, as if I'm trying to hang on to something that isn't mine anymore." I sigh grimly. "Especially now."

She frowns. "Why especially now?"

I don't even want to say the words out loud.

"I spoke to Susie. She's . . . she's seeing some-one else. Her boss. For the last five months."

Cleo stares at me, wide-eyed.

"I know, right?"

"Her boss." She nods slowly, her eyes full of compassion. "Unimaginative."

"Fucking cliché. I guess I should have seen it coming," I say, staring into the fire. "He's always been overly friendly. I mean, the man calls her Susie Sausage."

"Well, that'll never last." Cleo rolls her eyes. "Cutesy nicknames are top of the poll for reasons to break up. And I know that for a fact, because I wrote the poll."

"He wears cartoon cuff links too," I say.

"Scrap unimaginative and change it to dull," she says.

"Let's keep both and add . . ."

"Cockwomble?" she suggests.

It makes me laugh. "Cockwomble? So British, Cleo."

She laughs too. "It sounds even funnier when you say it."

"Okay. So he's a dull, unimaginative cock-womble," I say. "I'll be sure to tell him next time I see him." In all honesty, I'd rather never lay eyes on the guy again. I roll my head back against the sofa and look her way. "I've never met anyone like you before, Cleo. You have a way of making things seem better." I sigh. "I'll miss you when I leave."

She stares at me, her dark eyes serious now. "You're leaving?"

I knew the second I heard Leo's voice that I need to be there when they get back from the lake. "In eight days. I booked a flight this afternoon. It was one thing for my boys to handle me not living with them anymore, but this . . . this **Robert** thing . . . I need to be around for them, let them see everything's still okay, that I'm there as their dad, even if there's another man in their lives."

She holds my gaze. "Yeah. I think you need to be there too," she says.

It surprises me. I didn't expect her to say that.

"I didn't have my dad around when I was growing up," she says. "And there have been so many times over the years when I've wished he was there for me to talk to, you know?" Her eyes shine with tears. "He's become a sort of absent superhero in my eyes."

"That's some billing."

"But you don't have to be absent, Mack. You can just be their superhero."

My God, this woman. I swallow painfully.

"Words are **your** superpower, Cleo. I'm not surprised you're a writer."

She slides her wineglass onto the table and

runs her hands down her face, a gesture I've come to realize means she's working herself up to say something.

"You know what? You're right. Words are my thing, but the right ones are deserting me now at the very time I need them the most."

I'm not sure what she means. "You're struggling with your column?"

"No, it's not that." She glances at the ceiling for a second, as if she's hoping to find the words she's looking for printed on the old wooden beams. "Okay. It's this . . . It's you. And me," she says, and turns to face me. "I need to say something, and I'd really like it if you let me get to the end without interrupting me."

The look in her eyes tells me that whatever it is might be more difficult to hear than I anticipate, but I nod anyway.

"I know we agreed to never mention our kiss again, but I've been thinking about it. A lot, actually. And if you take all the reasons why we shouldn't have kissed out of the equation and just think about the actual kiss itself, it was, for me at least, a heat-of-a-thousand-suns kind of kiss. If all the kisses in my life were a list, ours would be in flashing lights at the top." She mimes flashing lightbulbs in the air with her hands. "I know we both have complicated, busy lives away from this place, Mack, and I'm under no illusion that we're not going to go back to them. I'm fully aware that we'll never see each other again after we leave Salvation, but we're here now, and I'm adult enough to sit here and say I want you. Not forever. I know you're not my forever. And I'm not asking you to be. I don't need you to love me, Mack. But I want you. For one burn bright then burn out beautiful week." She pauses, breathless. "I came here to be alone. But now, what I think I need—what I know I need—is the best no-holds-barred holiday romance ever. No guilt from you. No expectations from me."

She stops speaking and fixes me with those dark, glittering eyes. I can see how nervous she is, and I know how much it must have cost her to put her feelings on the line like that. Jeez, she's ballsy. But still I say nothing, because I'm not like her. I don't have all the right words. The seconds stretch out into a silent minute. I put my wine down and stand up.

"I need some air," I say.

And then I head for the door and leave her sitting there alone.

Cleo, October 19, Salvation Island

Two hundred hours of us

I've never felt like more of an idiot. I'd leave, but there's nowhere to go. **A no-holds-barred holiday romance?** What was I thinking? I sounded seventeen instead of thirty. I was aiming for sophisticated and undershot by about a decade. He leaves in eight days. Why couldn't I have just got through this week and parted as friends? **Are** we even friends? We almost were, I think, before the kiss. And now I don't know how we're going to get through the next eight days. I don't even know how we're going to get through tonight. Mack's been outside for almost half an hour, and I'm wondering if I should . . . Oh, shit. He's coming back in.

I look up as the door swings wide. He stands framed in the doorway for a second and stares at me, and I've no clue what's going on behind his mismatched eyes. I think he's about to say something, but then he doesn't. He slams the door, drags his T-shirt over his head, and drops onto his knees. It takes me a few seconds to realize what he's doing. He's using his T-shirt to scrub out the chalk line.

I don't move a muscle. He makes sure every last speck of chalk is gone, and then he stands up and chucks his T-shirt on the floor.

"The line . . ." I say, swallowing hard.

"We already crossed it," he says. "Come here."

A low thrill runs through me at the husk in his voice. I get up and move round the sofa, clammy-nervous.

"I've never had a holiday romance," he says, when I stand in front of him.

"Me neither," I say quietly.

"Americans don't go on holiday."

"Vacation romance?"

"Never had one of those either."

He reaches out and cups my cheek; I kiss his thumb when he runs it across my mouth.

"I don't know how to be with you, Cleo," he says. "But I want to."

If there was ever a time to be bold, this is mine. I reach for the belt of my robe and tug the knot, letting it fall open. Mack follows my hands with his eyes, then lifts his gaze up to mine, letting me see the effect I'm having on him.

"Take it off," he says, low, halfway between a question and a demand.

You know in movies when people shrug their shoulders and their robe falls off? I attempt a shimmy, and by some fluke it falls in exactly that starlet way, slithering to pool around my ankles.

"That was some damn move," he says, the edges of his mouth twitching.

"I'm pretty proud of it," I say, running my palm down his chest, all the way to the button of his jeans.

"I was wrong when I said you're not a mermaid," he says, winding a length of my hair around his fingers. He traces his other hand down my throat, between my breasts, over my stomach. "Sleep in my bed tonight?"

Like he needs to ask.

I pull him close enough for our bodies to touch. He moans low in his throat and lowers his head to mine. I gasp when his palms skim down the length of my spine to cup my backside.

"Cleo," he says, lifting his face away just enough to look at me with his beautiful eyes. "Are you sure?"

I trace the bunched muscles of his shoulders, then hold his face between my hands. "I'm so sure, Mack."

"I can't offer you anything but this week," he says tenderly.

I don't have anything more to give him either. "Then you better make it memorable," I say.

"I can do that." He dips his head and takes my nipple into the heat of his mouth, and I gasp and push my fingers into his hair, because it feels like he's doing actual magic with his tongue.

The fur throw on the bed brushes my back when he lowers me onto it, his eyes hot on mine, the shallow rise and fall of his chest telling me this is a lot for him too. For a moment it's feral—his lips find mine, hungry and searching. He tastes of sea salt and red wine and of pent-up longing, his tongue in my mouth, his hands over my body. My breath catches in my throat because I want the weight of his body against mine so much it hurts.

"I've tried not to think about this," he says, lying down alongside me naked. "I've tried not to imagine how it would be with us."

"I haven't thought about anything else since we kissed," I admit. He angles his body toward mine and I turn myself into him. We both gasp at the kick-up in intimacy when our stomachs press together.

"Just since we kissed, huh?" he says. "Longer for me."

He reaches for my hands and raises them over my head against the pillow, the look in his eyes somewhere close to drugged as he slides his knee between mine.

"Cleo." The edge to his voice is everything.

I curl my fingers into his palms above my head, his mouth against mine as he moves over me and settles himself between my legs.

His parted lips graze my forehead, my cheek, along my jaw. He looks in my eyes when he lowers his hips, slow and deep, biting his bottom lip as if he's in actual pain. I paint the moment in the sketchbook of my most precious memories in my head.

"Beautiful you," he murmurs, liquid sexy, moving against me, inside me. His mouth drags down my throat. The roughness of his jaw, his hands gripping mine, the arch of my body, the steady thrust of his hips. I'm drenched in him, so hot inside I think I might actually explode. And then I do, and the intensity makes me cry out, unexpected tears on my cheeks. Mack kisses my tears, clutching my hands so tight it almost hurts as he lets go of control, my thighs clamped around his body. It's powerful.

It wasn't making love, because we don't love each other, but it wasn't just sex either. It was another level of intimate, fire hot, a whole new emotion I don't have the words for yet.

"Holy fuck, Cleo," he gasps, his heart banging against mine.

A shaky laugh rattles through me, because it's still an understatement. "I thought I was going to actually die for a minute there," I say.

He rests his forehead against mine, catching his breath, kissing me slowly. "I'm glad you didn't."

"At least they'd have sent the bloody boat," I mutter, making him laugh.

I let my hands learn the angles and curves of his shoulders, the indentations of his spine. I close my eyes. Some kisses have an end. This one doesn't. It goes on, our new way to communicate. My tongue slides over his, his hands move in my hair, we roll onto our sides. He breathes my name like a spell, I move so I'm comfortable in his arms, and still we kiss. He reaches down and pulls the blanket over our bodies, my legs intertwined with his, and still we kiss.

For a woman who finds her way through the world with words, this is a whole new language.

• • •

I'm more asleep than awake when Mack speaks, his breath warm against the top of my head.

"One, I came here scared that Susie would get over me, and right now I'm more scared that I might get over her."

I feel his turmoil in the rise and fall of his chest.

"Two, I drank my first beer at ten years old. I stole it from my dad's fridge after I walked in and caught him having sex with his dental assistant. Right there in his patient chair. He didn't see me. She did, but I don't think she ever told him.

"And three . . ." He runs his hand lightly down my arm from shoulder to elbow. "I don't regret you."

I cover his hand with mine. "And I'm supposed to be the one who has a way with words," I whisper, pressing my lips against his chest.

"One, I'm worried about going back to London. I didn't even want to come here, but leaving feels somehow scarier than staying now. I came for one thing and it's become about something else, and I'm trying to work out what that means for me."

That's the way it is sometimes, isn't it? Life is the stuff that happens in the cracks between your plans and expectations. I cast around for something random to throw in as my number two.

"Two, I didn't hate the ending of **Lost**, although I wish Kate and Sawyer had been together at the end." As usual, I was a sucker for the bad boy. "And I still don't understand where those polar bears came from either."

Mack laughs at that. Wind howls around outside and rattles the windows of the lodge, but here in bed it's warm and blissful.

"Three," I say, "I don't regret you either."

Gray fingers of shadowed dawn slide over Mack's features as I lie awake and study him. He's peaceful in a way he usually isn't, not around me at least. Does he look this untroubled every night when he sleeps? Or has our night together released a tension in him, as it has in me? True to my word, I don't regret what has happened between us. I hope he feels the same when he wakes, that shame doesn't diminish the star-bright burn of last night. There was an inevitability and a trueness to what happened between us, and in the quiet hours afterward, a soul-deep calmness.

I knew it was a gamble, asking him to be with me this week. There was no plan B, no backup place to go if he rebuffed me. I realize also that it was probably a harder decision for him than for me. My love life has been a spluttering series of stops and starts. Mack's spent over a decade as someone's husband, held the same woman in his arms every night. We are at opposite ends, but there's something about this island, this lodge—a fairy-tale edge-of-the-world feel I can't easily explain. It's as if a passing bubble snagged on the chimney last night and settled, snow-globing us inside. I hope it will linger, a suspended iridescent gossamer, protecting us until a brisk northerly blows in and whips it out to sea, taking Mack with it, leaving me behind. Eight days and seven nights. How many hours will that give us together? I move closer into his warmth and his arm settles around my shoulders, his fingers splayed flat against my hair. I close my eyes as I turn my face into his chest.

"Two hundred hours of us," I whisper. I can hear the clock ticking down already.

Mack, October 20, Salvation Island

Part of not drowning is swimming

What are you doing out here?" I say. It's early afternoon, and she's been sitting on the porch steps for a good while now, her dark hair whipping around her face in the wind. I want to tell her she reminds me of an ethereal sea goddess, but I don't, because even inside my head it sounds clichéd.

"Thinking," Cleo says, a million miles away.

"Penny for your thoughts?" I say, hunkering down beside her. Jeez, it's cold out here without a sweater.

"I was wondering whether we need a new rules sheet." She smiles, bumping her shoulder against mine.

"Or we could just have no rules at all," I say.

"I was quite fond of that chalk line," she says.

"Okay," I say. "How about no stalking each other on social media?"

"Afterward?"

I nod. I meant at all, but especially not afterward.

She twists her head to stare at me in silence for a few seconds. "Still no regrets today?"

I don't blame her for rechecking. I left her sleeping this morning, needing to walk and clear my head. "It's pretty hard to regret something that felt so damn good," I say.

She half smiles. "It did feel pretty amazing."

I pull her blanket around my shoulders too so we're huddled together. "I don't mean this in the way it's probably going to sound," I say, but I don't censor myself, because if I do it'll probably come out worse. "I needed last night. I needed to be with someone who wasn't Susie."

"And I just happened to be there?" she says neutrally.

"No, no. It's not that you just happened to be there at all," I say. "It's that you happened to be you. My head has been stuck in a place where I couldn't imagine ever wanting anyone else like that." An image of myself on the morning of my wedding surfaces in my head: the churn of nerves threatening to bring my breakfast back up, my mother carefully straightening my tie. "My marriage. I made vows, I promised to love one person forever. It meant something to me—everything at the time—and it's hard work letting go of all of that, you know?"

Of course she doesn't know. How could she? But I do hope that she'll at least see that my life is complicated. Although actually, right here and now, this doesn't feel complicated at all. She laid her expectations out clearly: let's share everything we are for eight days and then never see each other again. It's cut and dried.

"Are you sure you want to let go?"

"Am I sure?" I shake my head, unwilling to lie to Cleo even a little. "I've defined myself by my position as a husband and a father for a long time now. I guess I'm trying to work out how to be one without the other. I've drifted through the last year like a man clinging to a life raft hoping to be brought aboard again, even though I could see the lights of the ship moving slowly away from me, and . . . and this is a crappy analogy, I know, but coming to Salvation was the only way I could see to not drown. Does that make any sense?"

"Yes," she says. "More than you know. I've been drowning in London too, in meaningless connections and unrealized dreams. Coming here is like a system reset for me."

"A system reset, huh?" I say. I kind of like that way of looking at it.

There's something else I need to say. "I want you to know I didn't sleep with you as a way to get even with Susie. For Robert, I mean."

"No?"

I shake my head. "Part of not drowning is swimming. I guess you could say you're proof I should keep kicking."

She's quiet as she absorbs my clunky attempt to explain what's happening in my head and my heart. That for the next week **she** is what's happening in my head and my heart. My system reset.

"I'm a strong swimmer," she says, leaning her head on my shoulder. "I've got you."

I'm accustomed to needing to be the strong one in life—for the boys, for my mother, for Susie. There is extraordinary comfort in someone saying **I've got you**. It brings a lump to my throat, so we sit for a while and watch the dolphins out in the bay.

Cleo, October 21, Salvation Island

They don't do it like that in Starbucks

I've been to more than my fair share of wedding ceremonies in recent years, a good handful every summer since I turned twenty-five, so you'd think I'd have an idea where to start with the vows for my own. And I probably would, if it were a regular ceremony, but it's tricky to know what to say when there's no one else to say it to. The usual "in sickness and in health" and "for richer, for poorer" don't apply. Do I even need vows, really? Maybe not, but I do rather like the idea of making myself some promises. I've written a list to whittle down. Some sit firmly toward the frivolous end of the scale: I promise not to watch more than three back-to-back episodes of **Say Yes to the Dress** while eating ice cream from the tub and yelling, "It looks like net curtains!" at the screen. Others hover around the middle serious: I promise not to make myself finish books if I'm not invested by page fifty-nine. Don't ask me why page fifty-nine, it just feels far enough in to know. And then there's the big, top-line promises, the ones that will be the most meaningful and probably the hardest not to break. This one, for instance: I promise to rethink my working life, to take the idea of leaving London seriously. I'm giving myself until Christmas to make the break. It's the right thing to do. I know it is, because even just writing the intention down felt like someone had given me a really great massage, that feeling of sweet relief when knots unravel and you can finally unclench your teeth.

"Coffee?"

Mack slides a mug on the table beside my laptop, his hand warm on my shoulder as he stands behind me. I close my eyes and lean into him, sighing when he moves my hair aside to trace his lips slowly over the back of my neck. It's shockingly sensual: intimate, a prelude. His fingers curl around my upper arms and I dip my head forward, blown away by how easily he can steal my breath. He laughs low against my ear, holding me still in my seat, knowing full well what he's doing to me when my shirt slips down my shoulder and he follows the material with the graze of his teeth. He brushes my breast when he slides his hand up to hold my jaw, turning my face to his. We kiss, openmouthed and breathless, and then he pulls away and smiles down at me.

"Get on with your work," he says.

"You distracted me," I say.

"I only brought you coffee." He shrugs.

"They don't do it like that in Starbucks."

"They better not," he says.

I roll my shoulders. "Have you ever been foraging?"

If my sudden change of subject surprises him, he doesn't say. "Nothing beyond picking blackberries with the kids. What are you thinking of?"

"I have this list," I say. "Of things to achieve while I'm here. Foraging is on it."

"What else is on there?"

I click the list up on my screen. "Build a fire on the beach. Write a poem."

"Spend twenty-four hours naked," he reads over my shoulder, raising his eyebrows.

"That was when I thought I was going to be alone," I say quickly.

He grins. "I'm totally into that idea."

"Do you think there's anything to forage on the island?"

He frowns. "You'd rather forage than get naked?"

"I don't think they go together very well," I say. "Because, you know, thorns."

He pulls a face. "You just totally killed that for me."

I reach for my coffee as he scans my list.

"I think you can check swim in the sea off after your dip the other night."

I shudder at the memory.

"I don't think I've seen too much edible stuff around. It's too wet here for most things," he says. "Seaweed?"

I think of the thick, oily strands that snaked around me when I fell in the sea and shake my head. "Maybe I was being optimistic."

"Never stop," he says, gentle. "It's a skill I lost awhile ago."

Sometimes he lets me see the gaping hole in his happiness; it's as if someone fired a cannonball through his chest. I want to curl myself into that space and make him feel whole again. It isn't a selfless act; I'm taking as much as I'm giving. When he rubbed that chalk line out, maybe a little of my resilience seeped into him, a little of his bravery into me. Mutually beneficial osmosis. I hope, anyway.

I made a fire. A tick for my list. Well, strictly speaking, I made a fire with Mack instructing me how, but either way there are actual flames and light from kindling I've gathered, and I feel bountiful and at one with nature.

Mack is sitting on the sand alongside me, our bums saved from the damp by an old checked picnic rug, warm blankets around our shoulders. It's a clear, see-your-breath kind of night, a sky full of stars and a low half-moon over the gently undulating ocean. It looks alive, and I feel more alive for being here. I hope I never forget how beautiful it is tonight. Mack's camera is slung around his neck as always, as much a part of him as his limbs.

"How's the ceremony planning going?" he asks, turning his serious eyes to me. I like that he doesn't make light of my self-coupling project. I hope I never fall out with myself, because consciously uncoupling à la Gwyneth and Chris is not going to be an option.

I nod. "Getting there, I think. I've made notes, but I'll probably just wing it. It's not as if anyone is going to be there listening."

"You mean I'm not invited?" he says, half smiling. "I was gonna put my best shirt on for you."

I roll my eyes. "You're absolutely not invited," I say.

"I could officiate?"

"Could you pull off a decent Elvis impersonation?"

He clears his throat and delivers an alarmingly gravel-sexy couple of lines of "Are You Lonesome Tonight?" and then cracks into a grin.

"Stop, I'm swooning." I laugh and lean against him. "You're still not coming."

"Okay," he says. "But I can come to the reception, right?"

"I'm having a reception?"

"Of course." He rolls his eyes, pure teenager. "Sketchy DJ, cake, speeches. You name it, it's happening."

"Idiot," I say, wrapping my arms around my knees.

"At least let me be your official photographer?"

I think about it. "If I say yes, can we ditch the reception?"

"If you insist."

"Okay. Deal."

"I'll use a long lens, stay out of the way. You won't even see me."

"Paparazzi," I say, aware that Ali will be thrilled to have professional shots.

He mirrors my position beside me on the rug, his chin resting on his forearms.

"My father didn't come to my wedding," he says. "He was speaking at a dental conference."

"I don't like your dad very much," I say.

"He's a difficult man to like."

"And yet his son is pretty damn cool," I say, bumping my shoulder against his.

"My mother raised me," he says. "She's the cool one."

I know that feeling well. "My mum made every single costume for my class's Nativity play when I was five. Mary, Joseph, baby Jesus, wisemen, shepherds. She even made the donkey, took her weeks."

"She does sound pretty cool," he says. "What part did you play?"

I sigh. "The innkeeper. My mother is a great seamstress, but I'm a terrible actress."

"Yeah, maybe so, but I'll bet you're an incredible writer."

Mack has a way of flipping from kidding to serious that makes me catch my breath every time. I stop laughing and swallow hard, watching the firelight on his face, burning him into my memory so he never fades.

"Remind me. Was 'Have wild sex on the beach' on your to-do list?" he asks, sliding his hand inside the back of my jumper.

"No," I say, wriggling my arms out of it awkwardly under the blanket. "But it is now."

• • •

Sometime after one in the morning, Mack presses his lips against my forehead. The bed has reached that optimum comfort level—you know, when the bedding is the same temperature as your body and you're totally blissed out? We're there, cocooned, my leg over his thigh, his hand on my hip, the mists of sleep gathering us in. It doesn't feel as if we've been this close for only three days. Or three weeks. Or three months, even. It feels as if we've been this close forever, as if we know everything there is to know about each other. How can that be? We stayed in this lodge without touching each other for several weeks, but perhaps even then we were touching each other in a different way, with shared secrets in the dark and shared glances across the room. Mack and I have connected in a way I've never known, a way I don't know what to do with, if I'm honest.

"One, my first car was a used Chevy Camaro, a silver dream machine with white leatherette seats," he says. "Which is, not coincidentally, where I lost my virginity. A pact with Alison Green: we were both sixteen and wanted it over with. That car was my portal to manhood."

"Boys and their cars," I murmur.

"Two," he says, "I've seen Springsteen seven

times. Never gets old. My mom is a die-hard fan, rocked me to sleep every night listening to 'Thunder Road.'"

"Could you be any more American?"

"And three," he says with a sigh. "I still don't regret you."

There's something about the late-night gravel of his voice that sends a shudder of awareness through my body. We're too tired and too near to sleep for sex again tonight, but I enjoy our closeness, the brush of his fingertips over my skin. Sex has always been an act that begins with a kiss and ends with a loo dash, a cigarette, or a turned shoulder. But it's endless with Mack, a fire that burns down to embers but never goes out. "Just so you know," I say, "I don't plan on **ever** regretting you."

His arms close around me and he breathes me in deeply.

"Is that number one?" He rolls me on top of him under the covers.

"It's one, two, and three tonight," I say.

And just like that, we go from embers to burn-the-lodge-down inferno.

Mack, October 22, Salvation Island

Temporarily perfect

Well, it's definitely open," I say, looking at the lit pub windows farther down the main street. Cleo and I have taken advantage of today's dry weather and spent the afternoon out and about on the island, a failed attempt at foraging on her part, a spectacular afternoon of photography on mine. I found myself turning my lens toward her often; she lights up my viewfinder like fireworks on the Fourth of July. I don't know yet if I'll look back fondly at shots of her when I'm back in Boston or if it'll feel like a book I shouldn't open, a sealed chapter that only we ever know was written. It'd be a shame, creatively; the pictures I've taken of her are some of my very best. She turns to me now, clapping her gloved hands together for warmth.

"Thank bloody God," she says. "I'm starving."

We've made our slow way across the island with the intention of dinner in the pub, but when I push the door open I see that we might have been overly optimistic. It's New Year's Eve packed.

"Standing room only," Cleo murmurs, pulling her red beanie off as she squeezes in behind me and closes the door.

"Cleo." The girl behind the bar raises her hand to greet us, a checked bar towel over her shoulder. "You two in for the quiz, are you?"

I turn to look at Cleo, and we share a **how do we get out of this one?** glance.

"Cleo, Mack, we're saved," someone else calls. Delta waves her arms above her head as if she's landing a plane from her seat. "Join our team, will you? Give us a fighting chance? Ailsa and Julia can't make it."

Raff puts his thumbs up, and a large glass of red wine and a pint of Guinness are passed our way even though we haven't ordered anything yet.

"Looks like we're doing a quiz," Cleo says, unzipping her jacket. "I don't think food's going to be an option either."

"I think I'm going to die of hunger," I say close to her ear.

"I'm already hangry," she says.

"Is that the same as horny?" I whisper.

"Yes," she says, laughing as she picks her way through the tables with her glass held aloft. I feel a sense of camaraderie as I follow her, greeted like an old friend by locals I've met and photographed on my daily travels around the island. People have been almost entirely welcoming to me, maybe in part because of my family connection, but also because they're justifiably proud of their homeland and want to contribute to the exhibition, to make sure their family and their island's rich history are properly documented. They've given me the unhurried gift of their time, sharing stories and folklore that will bring my images to life when I show them to people thousands of miles away. I'll leave here with a better sense of who I am and where I came from. I've always felt a strong sense of family, thanks to my mother and grandmother, but spending actual time here has imbued my childhood bedtime stories with the salted tang of the sea and the roughened feel of the local stone beneath my hands. I'll bring my boys here one day, my grandkids too if I'm fortunate enough to have them. It's grounded my soul to feel part of a place like this.

Delta squeezes along the bench seat to make

space for Cleo beside her, and Raff magics a chair out of nowhere for me next to him. My legs jostle for space with Cleo's beneath the small table, and she laughs and puts her knee between mine. It's purely practical, but it isn't something you'd do with someone you weren't close to. I don't move away, but all the same, I almost feel I should, as if I'm doing something wrong. It's not that I'm ashamed—certainly not of Cleo, in any case. Of myself, maybe a little. I imagine what my mother would say if she looked through the steamed-up windows right now. She's no prude, but she has a strong sense of right and wrong—where I get it from, I guess. I certainly didn't get my moral compass from my father.

"Hey, Mack," Delta says. "What's your go-to karaoke choice?"

I meet Cleo's eye quickly across the table. "You're not expecting me to sing, are you?"

Delta couldn't look more up to no good if she tried. "The night's young, that's all I'm saying, right?"

"I don't sing, I'm afraid." I laugh to change the subject. I sing all the time at home, but mostly because I consider it my fatherly duty to embarrass the boys.

"Er, hello, Elvis." Cleo grins. "I beg to differ."

"What's this?" Delta leans in, glancing

keenly between us. "Have you been serenading Cleo, Mack?"

"I do a rousing version of 'All Shook Up,'" Raff says. "Got me out of more than one sticky situation, so it has."

"And into a fair few too," Delta says, for once acting more like Raff's sister than his niece.

The conversation moves on from singing, and I scratch my head and look down to avoid Cleo's eye. I'm starting to feel as if coming here together was a mistake.

"I hope there's not too many sport questions," Cleo says. "Swimming is the only sport I'm any good at."

"Have you been to the grotto?" Raff says. "I've not been down there for a good many years."

Cleo and I turn to look at him. "The grotto?"

Delta sighs. "I used to love it down there when I was a kid."

"There's a cave at the far end of the beach around the headland from Otter Lodge," Raff says. "You can walk inside at low tide. There's a pool in there that never empties. You'll not find purer water anywhere in the world."

"Nor colder," Delta says. "I'd come and show you, but you know, the baby." She waves in the direction of her bump. "It doesn't like the hill anymore. Or freezing cold water."

Raff shivers despite the fire in the hearth. "Follow the rocks round at low tide, you'll come to it."

I nod, my interest piqued at the idea of a new, secret place to photograph. "I'll do that, man, thanks."

"How about it yourself, Cleo?" Delta says. "Bit of skinny-dipping is roaring good for your health. No one here ever goes down there unless it's the height of summer, so you'll be safe from prying eyes." She glances at me, laughing. "Irish ones, in any case."

It happens again—the discomfort at any suggestion that people know there's something happening between me and Cleo. I swallow it down but can't help running a hand around the back of my neck and rolling my shoulders awkwardly. Cleo smiles when I glance her way, and I turn quickly to Raff in the hope of rescue.

"'Heartbreak Hotel,'" he says. "And 'Wooden Heart.' That man sure knew how to woo the girls, I'll give him that."

And we're back to Elvis.

"Nothing like a man in uniform," Delta says.

"How's your mom?" I ask. I'm clutching

at straws; I don't expect Delta to have startling news to impart about Dolores. "I took some great photographs of her working in the library a couple of weeks ago. I hope she'll approve." Of all the residents on the island, Dolores was one of the most reluctant to be caught on camera.

"She's grand," Delta says. "Although you wouldn't know it from the way she gives out about her legs."

"Leave her be. She's always liked a grumble, it's just her way," Raff says. "My sister's a fine woman."

"You don't live with her," Delta says.

"And you're lucky to." Raff peers at her over his glasses, flipping the relationship back to uncle and niece. I like these two. They clearly love each other and aren't afraid to say what they think.

"Women." Raff looks at me with a resigned expression. "A mystery to me."

I highly doubt that's held him back; he has **lovable rogue** pretty much written on his forehead.

Cleo smiles and reaches for her drink at the same time as I do, brushing my hand. I pull mine away quickly, too fast, spilling the last of my beer on the table by mistake. It's no big deal, it's mopped up and quickly refilled, but I sense Cleo has picked up on my unease. God,

I wish we were back at the lodge. I'm starving and short-tempered from stress. Cleo catches my eye across the table as the conversation flows around us, and beneath the table she lays her hand on my knee. I can't help it; I move my leg away and shoot her an apologetic half smile, half grimace.

She sits back on the bench and looks at me, her head slightly to one side, then drains what's left of her wine without taking her eyes off me.

"I'm really sorry, I think I'm going to have to leave you guys to it," she says, gathering her jacket up as she gets to her feet. "I'm feeling a bit rough, might be the start of a migraine."

Raff jumps out of his chair. "It's all these people and that fire—I said not to light it. I'll douse it, will I, and you can stay?"

She smiles and rubs his arm. "Honestly, it's not the fire, it's me," she says. "I'll be right as rain after a couple of pills and a snooze."

I pick up my fresh beer and down half of it. "Hang on, I'll come," I say.

"No, you stay," she says, avoiding my eyes. "I'll be better on my own."

No way am I letting her cross the island alone; it's a different beast in the dark. I manage to get most of the Guinness down as she bends to kiss Delta goodbye.

She doesn't glance back as she picks her way quickly across the pub, disappearing even as someone waylays me and shakes my hand. I love the easy conversational skills most of the islanders seem to have been born with, but they don't make for a quick escape when you need one. By the time I'm outside with my coat in my hands, Cleo is almost at the far end of the road. I catch up with her beneath the last lamp-post before the road becomes an unlit path.

"Cleo," I say, putting my hand on her shoulder. "Wait up."

She pauses and turns to look at me. "What was going on back there, Mack?"

I take the coward's way out and pretend I don't understand. "What do you mean?"

She stares at me for a couple of seconds, waiting for my honesty.

"Look, I'm sorry, okay?" I try.

The pale light from the wrought-iron streetlamp illuminates her face.

"You were ashamed," she says.

It's not the word I'd choose. "Not of you," I say, struggling to put my feelings into words.

"Of us, then," she says.

I rub my hand over my face. "Cleo, please. I'm not ashamed of us. It's more . . . when it's just you and me, it's easy. I know people here won't judge us, but—"

"Judge us for what, exactly?" she cuts me off, scathing. "This island may be off the beaten track, but it's not stuck in the eighteen hundreds, Mack. I don't think anyone here really gives a damn whether we're having a holiday fling or not."

"I give a damn," I say defensively. "I'm still a married man."

She raises her eyes to the sky, her breath leaving her body in a slow huff that hangs in the cold night air. "You know what, Mack? Have it your way. You carry on being a married man, even though you separated from your wife more than a year ago and she's clearly moved on. You carry on being a married man until you have a piece of paper that tells you different. And you know what? You'll probably **still** feel like a married man even after then, because splitting up wasn't your choice. And you know where that will leave you? Bitter and lonely, watching life happen from the sidelines."

We stare at each other. She's breathing hard, and I'm torn up inside by the unexpected harshness of her words.

"You know something, Cleo? Maybe you should save your rookie romance advice for your readers, because I'm a fucking grown-up."

"Bloody act like one then," she throws back, her chin rising.

We stare each other down, her eyes brimming with dark, swirling fury, her chest heaving, and Christ, I want her with a suddenness I can't control. I see it happen to her too—the overflow of anger into something else—and I reach out and drag her into my arms, her mouth searching for mine, gasping, clashing, our kissing fierce, our breath ragged.

"I could never be ashamed of this," I whisper, my eyes closed.

"I didn't mean to say all that stuff," she says, stroking the back of my head.

"Let's go home." I smooth my thumb over her mouth.

Much later, I try again, winding a curl of her hair around my finger.

"Being married is a hard habit to break, Cleo. I'm a monogamous kind of guy," I say quietly. "I like the certainty, the finality, of the us-against-the-world thing. Losing those things from my life has been like losing who I am. And lonely, so unbelievably lonely. And then I came here and you blew into my arms, with your crazy curls and your clever wit and a heart the size of Jupiter. But then tonight, being seen out in public with you . . . I felt as if I was doing something illicit, something wrong. The kind of wrong that took me right back to being that kid who walked into his father's office and found him banging his dental assistant. The unsettling feeling in my bones—it's not about you, or us, but about infidelity, how much it screws families up."

Cleo moves slightly, her body a warm weight alongside mine in bed. She's quiet for a little while, and I know she's processing the things I've said.

"You won't screw your kids up," she says. "What's happening here, between us, it's temporary. Temporarily perfect. You're not doing anything wrong, and you're not breaking any promises. And afterward, when you go home again . . . Mack, it's up to you whether you decide to tell anyone, not because it's a dirty indiscretion you need to keep to yourself, but because it isn't. It's here and now and ours alone."

I appreciate her understanding more than she knows. "I like that. Temporarily perfect."

She traces slow circles on my chest. "If you really need things to stay just between you and me, even here on the island, then I can do that. I can absolutely do that. The lodge can be our personal snow globe."

The compassion and understanding— honestly, she slays me. In my head I lower a protective dome over the lodge, the bay, the hill. "You're probably the coolest woman on the planet, you know that?"

"Yeah, I know that," she says.

I feel her eyelids drift down, butterfly wings against my chest, and I close my eyes, tired too. I feel as if I'm walking a tightrope between two stages of my life, and right now Cleo is my safety net. I'll tell her that tomorrow, if I can think of a way to say it without sounding like a dick.

Cleo, October 23, Salvation Island

Am I brave enough?

It's my last day of my twenties today. Goodbye to the girl I've been, hello to the woman I'm going to be. I don't know quite who she is yet, what she's going to do, or where she's going to go, but I do know she'll steer her own ship, calm waters or high seas. No icebergs, hopefully.

I'm ready, I think, for my ceremony tomorrow. Ready as I can be, anyway. I've drafted some words, the creases have fallen from my dress, and I'm sitting in the café with Delta and Dolores having just tried to explain self-coupling to them. Delta gets it, but Dolores has a look on her face that suggests she's trying not to check my forehead for a fever.

"But you don't have a ring?" Delta frowns. "You totally missed a trick there. You could have put it on expenses, right? A whacking great emerald or something."

"I know," I say. "Mack said the same. I don't know how I didn't think of it myself."

"There's a lot more to marriage than jewelry, Delta," Dolores says, folding her napkin.

"Like a groom?" I say, because it's written all over her face.

"It's all very unusual." Dolores chooses her words carefully, but it's obvious that what she actually thinks is that I've lost my marbles. I'm not offended.

"I think it's romantic." Delta sighs. "I don't love myself enough to marry myself."

"Delta, you should." I cover her hand with my own, taken aback by her unexpected despondency. She oozes confidence and positivity; I don't like the thought that she doesn't feel on the inside the way she looks on the outside.

She bats my hand away and laughs, but I see uncertainty on Dolores's face too at her daughter's lack of self-love. I think about the father of Delta's child, the hapless computer gamer who rides a scooter, and I find myself admiring her all the more for having the strength not to settle. Coming home pregnant and alone can't have been easy.

"Will you have a veil?" Dolores eyes me, still unconvinced.

Delta shoots her mother a withering look. "Who's going to lift it, Ma?"

Dolores runs a hand over her perfect chignon, clearly unimpressed. "I had a veil," she says. "In fact, I still have it. Would you like to wear it?" She looks at me again and then pointedly at Delta. "Because I doubt anyone else is going to use it before I die."

"Look now, Ma, that's not very nice. Would you rather I marry Ryan Murphy just so you can get your discount on your soda bread? Tell you what, why don't I have it for one of those nuddy pregnancy shoots all the celebs do. I'd look pure fabulous." Her green eyes flash. "I can use the veil to cover my lady bits, save Mack's blushes."

"Mack?" I say.

"Who else is better with a camera?" Delta laughs.

"You'll do no such thing with my beautiful veil," Dolores says. "Twelve feet of pure white Donegal lace, I'll have you know, made by the best craftswomen there at the time. I felt like a princess, sure I did."

"Ah, Ma. You looked like a proper film star."

Delta and her mum might appear to clash, but scratch the surface and it's obvious how much they love each other.

"I better get going," I say. "I only came for cake."

"Wedding cake?" Dolores says, hopeful to the last.

"Just **cake** cake." I shrug. "It's really not that kind of wedding."

"Evidently," Dolores says. Her smile is watery, as if she's disappointed in me on behalf of my own mother, who, for the record, thinks this whole thing is one of Ali's PR stunts and hasn't really paid it much attention. That's not her fault; I've told her the promo lines, but nothing really of the emotion or sentiment behind it for me. I don't know if she'd understand how my feelings about turning thirty are wrapped up with my feelings about outliving my dad. We find it difficult to talk about him: she knew him inside out and I didn't know him at all. We have no fond memories of him in common to look back on together, to say nothing of the fond ones we never got to make. He'll never walk me down the aisle, and she'll never get to watch him make his father-of-the-bride speech. I say my goodbyes and leave the café, pulling my hood up against the rain. I'm going to be soaked by the time I get back over Wailing Hill.

"You're wet," Mack says, looking up from his laptop when I head back into the lodge.

I laugh and start to shrug out of my dripping coat, but he stands up and extends his hands out to stall me.

"How do you feel about going on an adventure?"

It's an odd question. "Depends. What kind of an adventure?"

"One that involves cave hunting and swimming?"

It's the last day of my decade, I may as well see it out in style. I shrug. "Why not?"

The cave isn't all that difficult to find when you know it's there. The tide has gone out just enough to reveal the entrance; we should have a few hours of safe passage. There's something soothing about the reliable ebb and flow of the sea. You have no choice but to move with the rhythm of the island, so different from London, where there are a million beats and you can choose which to follow at any given time. I've loved my time as a Londoner, but stepping away has shone a light on the fact that I'm ready to leave it. More than ready, actually—I need to leave it. I need the sanctuary of quiet, of calm, of clarity. I need water in my glass for a while rather than tequila.

"Watch your step," Mack says, reaching back for my hand. "It's slippery here."

We pick our way over rocks, slick with sea-weed, as we head deeper inside the wide mouth of the cave, away from the daylight. As my eyes adjust to the shadows, I realize there are paintings on the surrounding walls. Nothing ancient—islander doodles, faded children's splashes, with some more sophisticated works interspersed. There are names painted too, a few I recognize, most I don't. Someone has painted SLÁNÚ, each letter of the island's name decorated with twines and flowers. I step closer to look at a really beautiful image of a galleon with its sails billowing in the wind. I'm near enough to see it's signed.

"Julia painted this," I say, tracing the bow of the ship with my fingertip. "Ailsa's wife."

Mack runs his hand over the colors on the rock face. "It looks like it's moving," he says. He's right, the undulations of the cave wall bring the image to life. I step away as he raises his camera.

"You wouldn't think it'd be easy to hide something the size of a swimming pool down here, would you?" I say, glancing up ahead where the cave splits off in two directions. "You try that side, I'll try this side. Shout if you find it first."

"Just don't go too far or take any crazy risks," he says.

"Do I strike you as a crazy risk-taker?"

He shrugs. "You came to a remote island to marry yourself."

"Touché. Better than dull, though."

"A whole lot better," he says, then pulls his head torch out of his pocket and puts the band around my head, clicking it on. "There. Be careful."

I roll my eyes. "I could already see."

"And now you can see better," he says.

I don't argue because he's right. I stand on tiptoe and kiss him instead, gripping the collars of his coat.

"Cleo, you're blinding me," he says, laughing against my lips.

"I'll see you back here in ten if neither of us finds the pool before."

He looks at his watch. "It's a plan."

• • •

I find the pool first. The path twists narrowly to the right and then opens up to reveal its secret, but something in me stops me from yelling to Mack. Almost every place on Salvation has an element of magic about it, but the ethereal quality in here is off the scale. A narrow shaft of daylight from somewhere overhead dapples the water with stars, and I'm struck momentarily silent by the tranquility of the cavern. It feels unreal. I watch the water, an idea already forming in my head. It's like an icebox in here, but I really would love to look back on the last day of my twenties and remember how daring I was.

I jiggle from foot to foot, aware I don't have much time before Mack comes searching for me. Briskly, I unzip my coat. I know it's going to be freezing, but this very second I don't feel it because adrenaline is coursing through my blood, warming me from the inside as I begin to undress. Coat, sweater, boots, jeans, until I'm down to just my underwear. I pause, unsure for a second. Am I brave enough? I think of Julia's majestic galleon turned toward unknown shores, and it gives me just enough courage to step out of the last of my clothes. I feel exhilarated and alive; this is the most freeing thing I've ever done. I stretch out one leg and dip my toes into the water. Jesus God, it's polar cold.

"Cleo, are you . . ."

I startle at the sound of Mack's voice and turn to see him round the corner into the cavern.

"Oh." He opens his mouth to speak and then closes it again, obviously taken by surprise. "You found it already."

"I did," I say.

"And you took all your clothes off," he says.

"I did that too," I say, the sides of my mouth twitching, because the big, confident American is as surprised and dumbstruck as a teenager.

He glances behind him. "Do you want me to leave you alone?" he says. "You looked like you were having a moment."

I consider his offer. He's right, I **was** in the moment. I push my shoulders back and let the frigid air harden my nipples. I don't think I've ever felt more womanly as I take the clip from my hair and shake it out around my shoulders. "Mack, I'm twenty-nine years, three hundred and sixty-four days old today. I feel magnificent, and I'm going to get in this pool now, and I'd really like it if you'd stay and photograph me while I do it."

I hear him swallow, loud in the quiet space.

"I can do that for you," he says, kind of sexy, but also in a tone that suggests he's genuinely touched I've asked him to document this moment of my life. "You probably shouldn't stay in there too long, though. I don't want to make a habit of rescuing you from cold water."

I smile, holding his gaze for a blazing second, and then I close my eyes and draw in a deep, fortifying breath. I can feel the air settling on my skin like glitter. I'm a beam of pure magic. I psyche myself up and jump into the water, immersing all at once because I know from experience it's the only sane way to do it.

"Oh my God!" I yell, opening my eyes wide to blink away the water droplets on my lashes. "Mack, it's like actual ice! I think I might die!"

He's on his haunches, camera raised, and he gives me the thumbs-up as I gasp and laugh with pure shock, chilled to my bones as I swim across the surface of the water and then turn on my back, floating, thrilled, turned on, alive. I want him to catch every stroke with his lens, to see the woman who has shed her clothes like a snakeskin on the rock, to somehow record this intoxicating feeling so I can look back on it when I'm home again and remember who I was in this very moment, because I want to be this version of me forever.

"I don't think I've ever been that cold," I say, curled up in the corner of the sofa with hot chocolate.

"Not even when you fell in the ocean?" Mack is in the armchair beside me, his laptop on his knees. He lit a fire while I took a long hot bath, and I'm finally feeling as if my inner temperature is somewhere close to normal again.

"That was more shock than cold," I say. "Today took it to a whole new level."

He's been quiet, looking through the images from the cavern. I haven't seen them yet. I don't know if the feelings inside me translated to film or if I just look like a crazy woman drowning in a gloomy pond. And then he turns his screen toward me.

"This one is my favorite," he says.

I don't speak for a while. It's probably the best photograph anyone will ever take of me—I'm suspended on my back in the water, my hair floating around me on the surface, eyes closed, arms flung wide. I'm smiling, lost in the moment. I'm a cavewoman, I'm a sea queen, I'm a force of nature.

"Thank you," I say. "I'm glad you were there."

He closes his laptop and moves to sit on the sofa with me. "Me too," he says. "I've never seen anything like you today."

I put my empty mug on the floor and we lie down together, warmed by the flames in the hearth. Whenever I look back on the final day of my twenties, I'll remember the fire and the ice, Julia's galleon on the cave wall, and the woman I became as I swam in that pool.

Cleo, October 24, Salvation Island

Dearly beloved me

The weather gods have decided to blow away the rain clouds in honor of my thirtieth birthday. I've been awake for about ten minutes, lingering in the comfort of the warm bed, in the buffer zone between sleep and the nervous anxiety about the day ahead. Mack wasn't here when I opened my eyes, but I can smell coffee on the stove and there's a fresh fire in the hearth. "Happy birthday, Cleo," I say into the quietness of the lodge. "Love you." It feels weird. It sounds weird. But today is about self-acceptance, and that means it's about love, so I'm starting the day as I mean to go on.

My dress hangs ready, a froth of off-white vintage cotton. As I lie here in my pajamas, I feel the slow roll of pleasurable anticipation in my gut. What would it be like to wake up on your actual wedding day? I wonder. How would it feel to know that in a few short hours, you were going to vow to spend forever with someone? Would I be a bag of nerves, or serene and full of joyful certainty? I guess it'd depend on whom I was marrying. At least I know one thing for certain: I'm not going to stand myself up at the altar. I went to a wedding once where the bride stood the groom up; it was a proper circus. Not someone I knew all that well, thankfully, but toe-curling all the same. It seemed unnecessarily cruel to allow things to get to that stage before bailing. The poor guy was in bits. But then even the best marriages sometimes end sooner than you'd expect. My mum must have woken full of wonder on her wedding day, unaware she would get only a few precious years with the man she adored. And Mack—he obviously expected his love story to last longer. Would they still have gone through with it if they'd known what lay down the road for them? Or would they have chosen to be alone, avoid the heartache? Maybe I'm doing the right thing after all; I can just about trust myself not to break my own heart.

I wonder where Mack has got to as I cross to the kitchen to grab coffee. We fell asleep on the sofa last night, and he woke me just after midnight, murmured birthday wishes as he carried me to bed. As ways go to start a new decade, it was up there. Grabbing a blanket to wrap around my shoulders, I push my feet into some wellies and head out onto the porch to fill my lungs with fresh Salvation air. Leaning on the railings with my mug between my hands to warm them, I see that someone—Mack, of course—has written the number thirty with shells on the beach, two huge numbers that will stay there until the sea plucks them from the sand later. It touches me. In London, my birthday would be a flurry of texts, calls, streamers on my desk, cocktails in a noisy bar later. I'm freshly glad of my decision not to check my phone anymore while I'm here; I don't want that kind of normal life intrusion today. I'm keeping Ali up to date via email, and I've chatted with Mum on FaceTime from the café a few times. I have her card and birthday gift with me already; she mailed them to me before I left. Here, I'm greeted by dolphins, as if they know it's my birthday and have come to offer their best wishes. I watch them for a while, the wind chilling my cheeks, and it's profoundly peaceful. This is my thirty.

"Morning," someone calls, and I turn and see Brianne approaching with something in her hands. "Happy birthday. I made this for you."

I smile, surprised to see her. She pushes a tin toward me. "Brianne, that's so kind, thank you," I say, lifting the lid to see she's baked me a birthday cake, egg-yolk-yellow icing decorated with flowers and my name. There are a couple of candles in there too. My mum will be pleased when I tell her; she's always said it's bad luck not to blow out a candle on your birthday. I gaze at the cake, choked by the gesture.

Brianne smiles, almost shy. "Come to knitting on Monday, tell us how everything goes?" she says.

I nod. "'Course."

"Good luck today," she says. "I better run, I'm late opening the shop."

I pull her into a quick hug. "You've made my morning," I say, and she flushes with pleasure as she waves goodbye, already heading back toward the track.

What a kind person she is; the cake is so pretty, it must have taken her ages. I hadn't really thought about the usual birthday things today, since I've been solely focused on the ceremony.

I pick up my coffee and take in the stillness for a few more minutes, leaning on the railing around the porch as I gather my thoughts.

"Good morning, Cleo."

Another voice. I turn to the path again and see Dolores.

I try to hide my surprise as I smile and step down from the porch to greet her. "Dolores," I say, unsure whether a hug is appropriate. "What brings you out this way?"

"That child of mine wanted to come herself," she says. "I had to promise to bring these over. She'd have had that baby on the hill otherwise, you mark my words."

She opens a neat jute bag hanging over her arm. I sigh softly as Dolores lays a circlet of wildflowers in my hands.

"She thought the colors would look grand against your hair."

"Tell her it's the prettiest thing I've ever seen," I say. Delta has wound laurel leaves and wildflowers around fine copper, whimsical and bohemian, perfectly her, and somehow absolutely me too. "I really love it."

Dolores nods. She looks at me, uncharacteristically uncertain as I place the circlet on my head, and then she reaches back into the bag.

"This belonged to my eldest sister." She hands me a small blue cotton pouch. "She never stuck to the rules either, always off getting herself in some sort of trouble."

It's kind of a compliment, kind of not, but I don't think Dolores intended it cruelly.

"This is so kind," I say, opening the pouch. "I didn't expect anything from anyone. Brianne was just here with a cake . . ." I stop at the sight of the rose gold claddagh ring I've just tipped into my palm. I lift my gaze back to Dolores.

"It might not fit you," she says. "My sister was quite a fat woman."

I choke down a shocked laugh laced with tears, because it's so Dolores to be generous but vicious at the same time.

"Dolores, I don't know what to say . . . Are you sure? Is it an heirloom? It's so generous of you."

"Bernadette had more jewelry than the queen of England, always bringing things back from her fancy travels. Ants in her pants, that one, always looking for the next adventure," she says brusquely. "Now come on with you, left hand for romance, right hand for friendship."

I fight the urge to wrap my arms around

her because she's absolutely not a hugger. I quite like the sound of Bernadette; I make a mental note to ask Delta more about her when I have the chance.

"Right hand it is then," I say, and we both hold our breath as I try the ring on. It's too big for my ring finger but sits just right on the middle.

"There," I say, holding out my hand with my fingers splayed. "I have a ring after all."

She blinks, looking at it, and then at the flower circlet on my head. "And flowers too."

I smile. "Quite like a bride in my pajamas and a blanket? Don't worry, I do at least have a proper dress."

She looks at me in a way that conjures thoughts of my mum again, a mix of exasperation and something edging toward fondness. Perhaps she does feel an element of in loco parentis while I'm here on her island. "Take care, Cleo," she says softly.

I look at the ring on my finger again, welling up. "I will."

I watch her make her way up the track from the lodge, straight-backed with a clear plastic headscarf to protect her Jackie O bouffe from the wind. This island delivers surprise after surprise, the people most of all.

I find the last dregs of my coffee have gone

cold and tip it over the railing, then head back inside, laying the flowers and ring down carefully on the table beside the cake. All the accoutrements of a traditional wedding, minus a partner. I won't let any melancholy thoughts push their way in, though. This is a day of celebration. There's a hot bath with my name on it and then a wedding for one to prepare for.

"Birthday breakfast?"

I heard Mack come back in while I was in the bath, and I've just emerged from the bathroom to see he's laid the table with flowers, fresh coffee and croissants, a jug of orange juice and toast. There's salmon too. Mack pulls out a seat for me, bowing slightly.

I look up at him and smile, and he holds my gaze, smiling too. "Happy birthday, Cleo," he says. He smells of sea breeze and warm spices when he bends to kiss me, and I breathe him in deep.

"This is a treat, thank you," I say, watching him head back to the small stove.

"It's a special day," he says, glancing at me over his shoulder. He's wearing a white long-sleeved T-shirt, the thermal kind you might pull on as a second skin, something that could belong in the 1930s as easily as today. For a second I imagine we are islanders from yesteryear, a young couple sitting at a simple table with a simple jar of flowers between them.

"Did you pick these?" I say, touching the pale pink petals of a flower I recognize from the edges of the beach.

"This morning," he says, sliding an egg onto my plate. "I caught the fish too," he adds, miming reeling it in as he sits.

I look down at the smoked salmon. "Fresh from Brianne's shop?"

He raises his camera for shots of the table before he grins and picks up his cutlery. "Something like that."

We talk loosely about my plans for the day as we eat, passing the salt, sharing the last slice of toast, refilling coffee cups, the radio on low in the background. Every now and then, I wish I could press pause on life and stay longer in a moment. This is one of those moments.

Mack has taken himself out on the porch with his tripod and camera. He said he wants to get himself organized, but I expect he's really giving me some space to get ready. I appreciate the privacy. I'm bathed and have dried my hair into loose curls. I've applied a little makeup

too, because this girl isn't getting wed without
mascara, even to herself.

I'm nervous, which I know sounds crazy,
but this, today . . . this is why I'm here. When
Ali and I talked about how this day might go,
in every scenario I was always alone. There
was no American making me breakfast, no
islanders bringing me surprise gifts. Just me
here alone to shape the day however I saw fit.
It isn't that I don't appreciate the kindness of
others today, because I truly do, but there's
an unexpected element of performance anxiety now that other people here are aware of
what I'm doing. I don't want to feel foolish
or gimmicky, because the more I've thought
about this, the more emotionally invested I've
become. It's important to me. Yesterday at the
cave was a perfect way to send my twenties
off. I want today to feel as perfect, to welcome
my thirties with open arms. I've mulled over
where to hold my ceremony, and again, Mack
being here alters things. I might have chosen
the porch, but it doesn't feel quite right, more
ours than mine after the countless hours we've
spent out there together, drinking coffee and
talking about nothing and everything. The
same applies to our beach. The boulder at the
top of Wailing Hill feels exhibitionist. I was
undecided even up to our visit to the hidden

cave yesterday, when the perfect spot revealed itself to me. Beyond the cave entrance, there's a tiny corner of the beach sheltered by a guard of weathered boulders. Not quite a stone circle, but pleasingly symbolic nonetheless. I saw Mack's photographer's brain going into overdrive too.

"Coffee?" Mack says, coming in from outside. He hasn't let the fire in the hearth go out for days now, and even the stone walls of the lodge are warm to the touch. "Or birth-day champagne?"

"Let's wait until afterward," I say. We're finally going to drink the champagne we found in the fridge, the bottle that was awaiting the honeymooners when we first arrived. I'm look-ing forward to this afternoon with nervous, swooping jitters, but I'm also looking forward to coming back here later and spending the eve-ning in this warm, peaceful place. And I'm glad I'm not going to be alone tonight. I'm trying not to think more than a day in front of myself at the moment, trying not to count down the days until I'm finally alone. It's funny; I burned up so much furious energy wanting Mack to leave, and now I'm burying my head in the sand about the fact he's going to go soon. Another fact that is apropos of nothing: flamingos bury their heads in the sand.

• • •

"Who are you, beautiful creature, and what have you done with Cleo?" Mack grins when I emerge a little later from the bathroom almost ready to go.

Truthfully, I feel special. I've treated myself with extra care today, taking the time to enjoy the rituals of preparation. It's easy here to bundle up and go makeup-free, but it's been a pleasure to remind myself of the joy I draw from applying eyeliner just so and from taking time to paint my nails, oil my skin. It feels like a luxury to wear my hair down. It's 100 percent going to stick to my lip gloss when the wind catches it, but that's okay.

"Is it too much?" I say, plucking at the frothy hem of my dress. It's so very pretty, I felt instantly romantic as soon as it settled over my body. The tiny shell buttons running down the seamed bodice do that period drama hoick to my boobs. It's womanly-demure and nostalgic, entirely perfect for the occasion.

Mack picks up the flower circlet between his hands as I walk toward him.

"It's not too much," he says, placing the flowers on my head and then stepping back. "Let me look at you."

I do a slow twirl on my bare feet, and when

I'm facing him again, he reaches out and holds both of my hands.

"You look . . . you look sensational, Cleo. Strong and soft, a true island woman. Now go out there and do yourself proud."

It's the rallying speech I didn't know I needed. I don't lean in to kiss him, because this afternoon is so much about me that it feels almost like a betrayal to make it about us. I slide my arms into my oversize midnight-blue cardigan. It's scattered with silver stars and almost as long as my dress, and at the door I pause to put on the yellow-striped Wellington boots.

"I don't know how, but you're pulling that look off," Mack says. "It's kinda woodland princess meets warrior queen."

It's a good description; I'd feared the wellies had pushed me from boho to hobo. I pick up the basket I've packed with the things I might want with me: my mother's birthday card and gift, the speech I've been working on, the ring from Dolores, a few other bits and pieces. It's a clear, blustery pale blue day, one of the best we've experienced since we arrived here. The fanciful part of me hopes my dad blew away the rain clouds. I decide I'm allowed to give my absent father superpowers on my wedding day.

"I'm ready now," I say.

"Want me to walk with you awhile?" Mack says.

I shake my head. "No. I've got it," I say. "Will you be here when I come back?"

"Do you want me to be?"

He isn't asking me to need him. He's asking me what I need.

"I'd like that," I say. "Unless you're busy?"

He lays his hand over mine on the railing. "I'm not busy."

"Okay then." I nod. I look at him, noticing the way the sunlight catches his mismatched eyes and warms his sandy hair. He seems taller and broader somehow, stoic and sure beside me. I get that déjà vu feeling again, that we could be standing in the footprints of islanders from years gone by. If I glance back at him as I walk away, will he be in shirtsleeves and braces, his hands grimy from working the land? I push my shoulders back and walk tall across the beach, reassured by the knowledge he'll be there waiting for me when I get back.

I can feel my elevated heart rate as I make my way over the uneven rock pools, placing my feet carefully to avoid slipping or crushing delicate sea snails clinging to the slick surfaces, my basket swinging in the breeze. I was right about my hair sticking to my lip gloss, but I don't mind, because the skies are blue, my wellies have primrose-yellow stripes, and I'm buoyed by the unexpected kindness of people who were strangers to me before I came here. This is the moment, the afternoon I've waited for. I'm here for this, and it's not lashing down with rain or doomed to fail, it's going to be magnificent and all the things I dreamed it would be, because how could it not? Quiet exhilaration blooms in my chest as I slide between the rocks and place my basket down on the sand in the sheltered alcove. "I'm here," I whisper. "I'm here."

I've shown up for myself. I haven't stood myself up at the altar. Like every other single woman I know, I have a playlist on my laptop of inspiring songs for those moments when I need to feel powerful, and snippets of it merge together now as a soundtrack in my head. My alternative wedding march. Yes, Lady Gaga, I am on the edge of glory, and yes, Alicia Keys, this girl **is** on fire.

I leave my boots beside the basket and walk barefoot to the shoreline, the damp, compacted sand cold beneath the soles of my feet. For a few moments, I stand there and let the lace-edged foam chase over the very tips of my toes, my eyes closed, counting as I breathe in, counting my breath back out again, centering myself. There's no rush.

When I open my eyes, I take the time to notice the physical sensations around me: the chilled breeze on my face, the whimsical movement of my dress around my knees, the shock of the ice-cold water covering my toes. I plant my feet a little wider and rest my balled fists on my hips, shoulders back, chin up. It's a superhero pose I learned from an old episode of **Grey's Anatomy**; one of the doctors used to do it right before going into surgery to save someone's life. It's overly dramatic to say I've come to Salvation Island to save my own life, but I've realized during my time here that I need to release myself from my gilded London cage. This is me pulling up a chair, making myself a cup of tea, and asking myself a really crucial question . . . "What do you want to do with the rest of your life? Or if that's too much, what do you want to do next? Here's a blank sheet of paper, write your story, Cleo. Write your next chapter," I say out loud, still Superwoman at the shore edge. "Make yourself some promises. Tell the wind your secrets and the ocean your dreams."

In any other place at any other time, I might have felt self-conscious talking to myself, but not today. I feel pure and emptied out, as if I'm letting all the negative pressures and feelings pass out through the soles of my feet, and every time the sea washes in, it takes away more of the things holding me back. I'm not someone who follows organized religion, but it's close to a religious experience to feel so renewed, so held by nature.

There isn't a boat on the horizon or a person in the distance. Mack mentioned finding a vantage point up on the cliff for photos, but as promised, I can't see him. I could have the planet to myself right now. I head back to the clearing and pick up a driftwood stick. I use it to draw a large circle in the sand, then add the cushion I've brought with me to save my back-side getting damp. Sitting down cross-legged, I straighten my spine, vertebra by vertebra. My yoga teacher would be impressed if she could see me right now. I must look next-level spiritual. Reaching into my basket, I lay out the contents around me in the circle. A card and gift from my mum. The cotton pouch from Dolores. I'm surprised to find a silver hip flask in there too—whiskey from Mack to warm me. Finally, I unfold the sheet of paper with my notes on it, smoothing it on my knee, holding tight to the corners so the wind doesn't carry it out to sea.

"Dearly beloved me," I say clearly and assur-edly. Just saying those words out loud makes me smile. In my mind, this is my Donna from **Mamma Mia!** moment, preferably the Lily James version. I love Meryl and I actually own a similar pair of dungarees, but all the same, I'm channeling my inner Lily. "I've brought myself here today, in front of Mother Nature, Neptune, and all the mermaids, to acknowledge that I, Cleo Wilder, do take myself, Cleo Wilder, to be my strongest advocate and my most loyal friend, my loudest cheerleader, and my most trusted confidante."

I pause and gaze out to sea, my palms resting on my knees, my hair swirling around my shoulders in the wind. I acknowledge I haven't always been my own best friend, and I certainly haven't always been my own strongest advocate. I've lingered too long in toxic relationships, and I've told myself to put up with things I'd tell a friend not to tolerate.

"I promise to listen to myself, to take the time to hear the voice in my gut, because I know myself better than anyone and I always have my own best interests at heart. I'm wise enough to know when someone is disingenuous, and I know when enough is enough. I also know that I am enough, and I'm brave, and I will succeed. I won't judge myself too harshly when I get things wrong, because everyone gets things wrong sometimes, but I won't let myself off the hook without learning lessons either."

That's quite a thorny one for me. Only a fool keeps doing the same thing and expects a different outcome, but nevertheless it's been the general trajectory of my romantic life. I've hitched my wagon to unsuitable men and then been newly surprised every time the wheels come off. I've tossed this pattern around in my head quite a lot lately, especially because Mack is, for all intents and purposes, yet another unsuitable man. He loves someone else, which is as big and unsuitable as it gets. But then Mack is different, because we're not actually dating with the intention of it heading anywhere. We agreed to our rules up front—when our time is up, we'll close the door on it and throw away the key. I sigh. No, I don't want to sidetrack myself with thoughts about what's happening in my love life right now. This is about what happens next, what happens after Salvation.

"The search for my flamingo is over. I am the flamingo."

You know, I think I might get that tattoo Ali bangs on about when I go home, a tiny flamingo somewhere only I will see it. My inner thigh, or in my armpit. A flamingo in my armpit. God, that's not very appealing, is it? If I ever write my memoirs, I'll call it that.

I laugh to myself because it's absurd, and then I look again at the vows in my hand. I'm quite near to the end now.

"I'll trust myself," I say. "I won't be afraid to turn my ship around and sail in a different direction if the waters get choppy, even if it seemed like the right trajectory when I embarked."

In my head, I conjure Julia's majestic ship from the cave wall and place it on the distant horizon, sure enough of herself to plow through fathomless waters. I see myself at the helm, one hand on the wheel, the wind streaming my hair out behind me as I set a course by starlight. That's the woman I'm becoming, I tell myself, imagining the warm, smooth, worn wooden wheel beneath my hands, seeing the map of the planets and constellations I've laid out to plot my route.

I hang on to the image for a while, embedding it firmly in my brain, because I love it and because I know it's time to turn the wheel and head in a different direction. Everything about coming here has led me to this point, to this vision of myself as skipper of my own galleon. I reach for the blue pouch Dolores gave me and tip the rose gold claddagh ring onto my palm. I touch my fingertip against it the next time I speak.

"I give myself this ring as a symbol of my intention, and of my self-respect, and of hope." I find my fingers are shaking as I slip it onto my right hand. Gosh. I'm so glad Dolores gave it to me; it feels as if it has always been a necessary part of the ceremony. It looks perfect, and the symbolism of the hands holding the heart feels entirely appropriate as I cup my own heart in my own hands today. It's okay to be reckless with your internal organs in your twenties, but I'm thirty now and need more careful curation.

I feel subtly different once the ring is on my finger. Not married, obviously, but committed. It's a good feeling. Grounding. For a couple of minutes I sit in silence, unhurried, concentrating on my breath, embracing the sea-salt diamonds in my lungs. I've never been this close to myself before. A seabird wheels overhead, one of the orange-beaked ones I see regularly. I imagine it returning to the roost with news of my wedding for one, and them all shaking their oil-black feathered heads, mystified.

My mum was mystified by the whole thing too, but then she knows only gilt-edged save-the-date cards and tiered cakes and top hats. All my siblings had frighteningly organized grand weddings; I know it's in her heart that I'll follow suit. I reach for her birthday card now, setting the accompanying gift aside to open afterward. My eyes mist a little when I open it to find messages from my siblings as well as from Mum. Both of my sisters have similar beautiful, sloping handwriting, their messages heartfelt and kind, making me smile as I think of them. Their kids have got in on the act too, bright crayoned hearts and kisses filling any empty spaces. It's harder to decipher Tom's doctor-like scrawl, and I laugh out loud when I work it out: **Happy wedding birthday, you fucking insane weirdo! Guinness is on you when you get back.** I can almost hear our mother scolding him for swearing from here. I swipe a tear from my cheek and read the final message from her.

Happy 30th, my darling youngest child. How terribly modern to marry one's self, but then you always were the pioneer of the family! Hope it all goes swimmingly. Love, Mum x

Her familiar handwriting makes me wish desperately that she were here, so much so that I can smell the perfume she's always worn and hear the rattle of her glasses chain around her neck. "Love you too, Mum," I whisper. I blow a kiss into my hands and release it, hoping the wind will catch it and carry it home to her, that it will slip in through an open window and she'll feel it settle around her shoulders like a scarf.

"**Pioneer**." The word vibrates around me on the sand as I speak it aloud. It is an unexpected choice from my mother about me; I've always thought my family sees me as indulged and fanciful, a scattergun rather than a directional bullet. The word has an air of daring, a sense of danger, a devil-may-care element of bravery. I look out toward my imaginary ship again and paint the word **pioneer** on her starboard bow in looping white letters, and then I open my mother's gift.

It's quite a chunky box that fills my hands. I haven't seen it before, but the worn-at-the-edges tan leather tells me it's a fair age. I lever the lid up on its hinge and find a wristwatch inside, again something I'm sure I've never seen before. The size tells me it's a gent's watch, edged in gold, the strap in plain black leather. I lay the box down, turning the watch over in my hands. On the back, it is engraved with my paternal grandfather's name, Abraham Wilder, letters worn smooth by wear. I trace my thumb over them, and then I spot a note pressed into the lid of the box.

This belonged to your grandfather and then to your father, who wore it every day until he died. It was one of his most treasured possessions. I think he'd like you to have it now. x

I put the note back and close the box, the watch still in my hands. I'm not mystical enough to believe in messages from beyond, but there is something undeniably prescient about my mother's gift. I fasten the age-softened leather around my wrist, and I let myself imagine that my father is giving me a **come on now, love** nudge. I reckon he'd have sat alongside me here on the sand and handed me the watch, and then he'd have told me he was proud of me every day of my life and to always keep my eyes on the horizon. So I do. I look out as far as my eyes can see, and I lift my hand and wave farewell as the **Pioneer** turns slowly and sets sail in a new direction.

Mack, October 24, Salvation Island

Springsteen, a beautiful girl, and a low, gold moon

Cleo should be back anytime now. I raced to be in place to capture shots of her return across the beach and to make sure everything's perfect for her makeshift reception. I know she said not to bother, but it's a special day for her. I can't claim to absolutely understand the whole marriage-for-one thing, but watching her down there on the shore today was an experience I wasn't prepared for. She looked self-contained and complete, strong and radiant. I hope the camera caught something of the mood, the shimmer of anticipation displacing the air around her. I found myself deeply impressed, a lump in my throat when she stood at the water's edge.

I sit on the porch steps with a beer and my camera to watch dusk descend. Three days. I have just three more days until I have to leave. On the one hand, I'm counting the seconds until I see the boys, but on the other, I'm hoarding every minute I still have on Salvation Island. At Otter Lodge. With Cleo. If I'm lucky, I might see the island and the lodge again in years to come, bring the kids here even, but Cleo . . . I know I won't see her again. We are not meant to exist beyond this place. I can't shake the feeling that it was selfish of me to take her up on her "holiday romance" offer, to allow myself to find solace in her laughter, to find oblivion in her body and joy in her easy company. I've wrapped her around me like a shield, letting the arrows bounce off her so they don't pierce my heart. I truly hope they haven't hurt her in the process. My life will be waiting for me when I get home, and there will be no shield. No Cleo. I've spent this last year alone, but always with the hope and expectation that it was a passing measure, that if I could just be patient enough and unobtrusive enough, I'd get to go home again at the end of it. And I **was** patient. And truly, I **was** unobtrusive. And it was hellish most days, the daily battle with myself not to drive over and see the kids, see Susie, to beg to be allowed to stay for dinner. To be included. It makes my skin crawl and my heart palpitate when

I think back to my lowest ebbs, to the long days and dark nights when it just felt like too much. I roll my shoulders and knock back a good slug of beer, washing the bitter thoughts away so I can concentrate on the good things, on my here and now.

It's been a spectacular day, weather-wise—Cleo couldn't have wished for brighter. I'm glad; this whole ceremony obviously means a lot to her. It sounded like a crazy idea when she first told me, but the more I've gotten to understand her, the more I've come to see that her time here isn't really about her work. She seems disenchanted with her life in London, almost as if she was running away from the chaos toward anything that resembled calm. I know her just well enough now to find it out of character for her to shy away from something, and having been only recently on the receiving end of her stubbornness, I know she's got an iron seam running through her core. I'm not sure she's even aware of it.

A white flash appears in my peripheral vision—Cleo. White dress whipping around her knees, pennant of dark hair streaming out behind her, the basket she's carrying swinging in the breeze. She looks like freedom, striding back across the beach, framed by a golden-streaked sunset. A photographer's dream. I raise my beer in greeting and she speeds up, laughing in wonder when she's a few feet from the lodge steps. She pauses, her head to one side, taking in the colored glow of the bulbs I've hung around the lodge's porch.

"You came back at just the right moment to appreciate them." I smile, reaching for her hand as I stand up.

"How?" she says. "I mean . . ."

"Raff loaned them to me." I headed up to the village yesterday to scout out party supplies and hid them beneath the porch. "They're the pub's Christmas lights."

Vintage fairground colors wash her face as she gazes up at me: rose pink, sunbeam gold, apple green. "You did this for me?" she says.

"Hey, a girl only marries herself once, right?" I say. "How did it go?"

She nods slowly, her dark eyes triumphant. "Mack, it was amazing," she says. The words bubble from her like champagne. "Even walking over there I wasn't sure how I was going to feel really, but the minute I got to the clearing, this feeling of utter calmness came over me, and rightness, and oh, I don't know, I just . . . I needed it more than I realized."

I pick up her right hand. "And now you're married," I say, looking at Bernadette's ring on her finger.

She grins. "And I don't even need to change my surname."

"Easier for paperwork," I say. "Hungry?"

She nods. "Starving."

"In that case, welcome to your wedding reception."

She looks at me quizzically. "My what now?"

I hold my hand up to stall her while I duck inside the lodge for a second. I pull out the plaid rug and flick it out onto the porch floor with one hand; I don't tell her I killed ten minutes earlier perfecting that move. I add a couple of cushions and then hold out the softest blanket for her shoulders.

"Your table."

I see it on her face, the gladness, and it warms me. Stepping back inside, I pull out the picnic basket Brianne found for me and place it down on the rug between us.

"Mack," she says softly. "I really didn't expect any of this."

"I know that," I say, twisting the wire from the champagne cork. "I wanted to add to your memories."

She smiles, accepting the glass I offer her. "Well, you've certainly done that," she says. "The ring from Dolores, Delta's flowers, Brianne's cake, and now this. It's been a day full of surprises."

"And the night is young."

Her eyes open wider.

"I'm joking," I say. "This is kind of the pinnacle." I touch the rim of my glass to hers. "To you, Cleo Wilder."

She grins. "Cheers."

She puts on her pre-prepared wedding day playlist, some stuff I recognize and some I don't, and she shares snippets about her afternoon as we eat the food I've picked up. It isn't flashy, just things I could lay my hands on: chicken salad sandwiches, potato salad from Brianne's store, olives fiery with chili oil, a couple of slices of quiche from the café.

"I didn't get dessert," I say. "I saw Brianne had that covered."

"Can you believe that?" she says, shaking her head. "I haven't had a birthday cake made for me since I was a kid."

"You've certainly thrown yourself a birthday to remember," I say.

A laurel leaf falls from her hair wreath when she shakes her head. "Team effort," she says.

"Team Cleo," I say. "You'll have it trending when you post your next piece."

She huffs. "My boss would so love that."

I refill her glass. "Would you?"

"Would I love it?" She pauses, thinking. "I'm proud of how I felt today, and if it helps other people to read about it and maybe feel the same way, then I'd love that, yes. But the whole social media trending thing? Being here, so unplugged from that world . . . I like it. I much prefer it." She sighs. "I'm not going back."

"To London?" I say, surprised.

"I mean, I'll go back, but only to wind things down so I can leave again." She looks out toward the beach. "It's time for me to do something else. I'm just not exactly sure what that something else is yet."

She tells me about imagining Julia's galleon painting from the cave out on the horizon, herself at the wheel. I follow the track of her eyes now and see it too: white sails, anchor dropped, waiting for her to take the helm.

"I envy you," I say. "Nothing tying you down."

"And I envy your ties," she says simply.

"I guess everyone always thinks the grass is greener," I say. "It rarely is, in my experience."

"Better to water your own grass than roll on someone else's," she says, then laughs wryly. "I'm a walking, talking Pinterest quote queen."

"You don't need other people's words," I say. "You have your own way with them."

"Thank you." She drains her glass, absorbing the compliment. "Your photographs are incredible."

I try to absorb the compliment. "It's all I know how to do," I say. I sometimes wonder what I'd be doing if I hadn't found photography. It's been the one unchangeable thing in my life since Susie and I separated; my sure-footing thanks to years of practice, my camera a familiar comfort in my hands. It makes me hope my kids discover passions that lead their lives in interesting directions too.

"I've gotten so used to you raising your camera, I don't even flinch now," she says, drinking quickly from her glass to stop the fizz from foaming over when she refills it. I raise my camera and capture it, including the eye roll she gives me after. I watch her for a few moments, enjoying the unguarded way she laughs, the light in her eyes that seems to come from somewhere deep inside her bones.

"You make a pretty photogenic bride," I say. "I think you'll love the pictures."

She smiles down into her glass. "Thank you. They'll be a fitting way to bow out of the column."

"What will your boss say?"

"About the idea of me leaving?" She sighs. "I think she'll want me to stay, but I also think she'll know if it's genuinely time for me to go. We've become pretty good friends over the years."

"Any ideas what you'll do?"

Her mouth twists to the side as she considers my question. "I'm not sure yet. I've got enough saved up to not work for a few months, so—"

"So you'll finally write a novel," I finish her sentence for her. "And it'll be a huge success."

She looks at me and slowly treats me to that full-beam smile—the one that makes my fingers itch for my camera and my mouth ache to kiss her.

"If you say it, it might come true."

"I should get your autograph now while I don't have to stand in line," I say.

"You'll never be at the back of my queue." She holds my gaze, clear and bold, and I realize how much I'm going to miss her when she isn't in my life anymore.

"You've been so good for me," I say. I hold her hand now, and tears dot her lashes as she looks at me. "Don't cry, it's your birthday."

"All brides cry," she says, and half laughs. "It's an emotional day."

"Okay." I sigh. "Drastic measures." I get to my feet and hold my hand out to her. "Dance with me?"

She blinks up at me, surprised, and then slips her hand in mine. "I guess I should have a first dance."

I pull the picnic rug to the side of the porch, clearing some space. "The floor's ours."

"Okay, but hang on, let me find the right track."

I don't know what she'll choose, and I feel something suspiciously like prom night nerves as I wait for her to come join me in the middle of the porch. She glances over her shoulder at me, barefoot with flowers in her hair, and my God, she's glorious. Then familiar harmonica strains drift on the air, and she turns, laughing as she walks toward me.

"Springsteen, huh?" I say, failing to keep the smoke of emotion from my voice.

"You mentioned it sometime," she says. "I added it to my list the last time I was up at the café. Feels like a little piece of you I can hold on to."

"Come here." I pull her close. "Let me hold on to you tonight."

And so we dance on the porch to "Thunder Road," and although it's cold I don't feel it, because the girl in my arms warms me. She's like holding fire.

"I've seen him sing this live a fair few times," I tell her, my mouth against her hair. "The roar of the crowd at those first notes from his harmonica, thousands of people singing every line back at him." I know every word, every chord.

This song is part of the fabric of my life, and now Cleo will be forever stitched in among its notes and melody too. Bruce sings of Mary dancing across the porch, and I lift Cleo's arm over her head and spin her into a slow pirouette, her white dress swirling out around her thighs as she throws her head back and laughs. Oh, for my camera to catch the colors the Christmas lights throw across her face, the movement of her hair as she dances, the joy in her eyes when she laughs. I catch her close and bend her back over my arm, laughing with her. Springsteen, a beautiful girl in my arms, the low gold moon suspended over the ocean. We dance, and we kiss, and we laugh like teenagers. We're the only people in the entire fuckin' world tonight.

"Happy birthday," I say, as the track comes to an end.

"I love being thirty," she says.

I touch my fingers to my head in salute. "Then my job here is done, pretty lady."

She leans back to study me, her face serious, and then she pulls me in and winds her arms around my neck.

"Oh, no, it isn't."

Her legs wrap around my waist when I lift her up, and I can only agree that maybe the night isn't over just yet.

• • •

We're lying face-to-face, the sheet draped over her hip, her hair all around her on the white pillows. She looks like a painting, shadows and light, hollows and curves, too intimate for any lens to do her justice. Her white dress is flung somewhere over by the sofa, the flowers from her hair ring the brass bedpost.

"One," she says, "that was the best sex I've had in my entire thirties."

I wind her hair around my fingers. "Funny girl."

"Three, I love you a little bit," she says, propping herself up on one elbow. "Not so much that you're going to break my heart. Just enough for you to take a sliver of it home with you, and every now and then, if you press your fingers in **just** the right place"— she touches her fingertips against my heart to show me where—"I think I'll feel it and think of you too."

I look into her eyes, and I swear I feel that sliver slide under my skin.

"You didn't do two," I say, curling my fingers around hers on my chest.

"I didn't need to. Three was kind of big."

"It really was," I say, and I smile because she's lionheart brave to be so honest when she knows there's no future for us. "One, I promise to take extra special care of this sliver of your heart," I say. "Mine was kind of bashed, so your donation is very welcome." I tap my chest. "Consider me patched up."

"I'm practically a doctor," she says with a low laugh.

I run the back of my fingers down her jaw, her collar bone, the curve of her breast.

"Two."

"You're doing two?" She frowns. "Now I feel like a lazy cow."

"Two, I was proud to know you today."

"Mack . . ." She leans in and touches her mouth to mine. "Thank you for tonight. You made me feel special."

"Well, I hope so," I say, because I really do.

She flops back on her pillows, her arm flung over her head.

"Three," I say, when she turns her face to look at me again. "It was the best sex I can remember of my thirties too." It's a difficult confession to face. In the early days of me and Susie, I'd never have been able to imagine us running out of steam, in bed or out of it. This time with Cleo has shown me different; I've remembered how it feels to be wanted and it's heady.

"And four," I say, breaking our rule because

it's her wedding day. "You're the most spec-tacular person I've ever met." I raise her hand to my lips. "And this, right here, is the best damn holiday romance ever."

Cleo smiles, her eyes already closing. I lie awake and watch her sleep, thinking about the sliver of her heart now patched onto mine. I'm going to need it.

Cleo, October 27, Salvation Island

I've stolen Jennifer Grey's best line

I wake before Mack does. There are no storms gathering on the horizon; the forecast for the next couple of days is clear and calm, as if the weather gods agree that it's time for Mack to leave. I look at him now, passed out and peaceful, and I can't imagine being here without him. He fills my days and my nights, my thoughts and my arms. I came here on a self-love mission, and the other night I told Mack that I love him a little bit. I didn't plan on saying it, but I don't regret it either, because it's true. I had no expectation of him saying it back, and that's okay too.

"It's a little stalkerish to watch me sleeping," Mack says, his eyes still closed.

"I'm not watching you," I say. "You just happen to be in front of my eyes."

"You were totally watching me." He grins, opening his eyes, and I look from one to the other, enjoying their irregularity.

"Your eyes are just so you," I say. "Un-expected. Startling."

He turns my hand to his face and kisses my palm. "**Startling?**"

I nod. "You've startled me."

He pulls me close and settles the blankets over my shoulders.

"Will you be okay?" he asks, pressing a kiss against the top of my head.

"I think so," I say after a pause. "Will you?"

He holds me closer still and breathes a sigh into my hair. "I think so."

"I'll miss you," I say, even though I'm deter-mined not to let melancholic shadows darken the time we have left together.

I feel his nod. "I'll miss you too," he says. "These last few weeks have been some of the best of my life."

I lift my face to look at him. "I know you mean finally coming to Salvation as much as meeting me," I say to lighten the mood, "but . . . more me, right?"

He laughs. "More you. Definitely more you."

• • •

Time is an unequal thing. A minute waiting on a cold train platform feels like an hour; other times an hour passes in a blink. These last days and hours with Mack have raced by at warp speed—every time I look at the kitchen clock it's as if the hands are a tag team dashing around the face with more speed than they're entitled to. We were walking on the beach after breakfast, and then I blinked and we were on the sofa by the fire at dusk. We clutched steaming mugs of coffee outside on the steps at daybreak, and I blinked and it was whiskey in my hands under a sky full of stars.

I have something that feels much like a hangover, post-birthday blues mixed with post-ceremony relief shot through with anxiety about the changed landscape ahead.

We sit side by side on the low seawall, our eyes watchful for the boat that's going to take him away. It's only Tuesday; the boat is making a rare out-of-sequence visit to deliver a haul of pumpkins, one for every household in the village, a long-standing annual tradition courtesy of Raff. They could probably have been sent over last Friday, but I get the impression Raff made the arrangements for Mack's benefit. Trust Raff to be the only one important enough to mess around with the schedule. Mack's bags are stuffed to the seams on the damp sand at our feet. Only his camera remains unpacked, around his neck on its frayed leather strap as always. He has a slice of pale skin just there; I shouldn't imagine it ever sees enough sunlight to match in. It will no doubt be the same when, if, he removes his wedding band. His skin is crisscrossed with tracks that tell his story.

"I'm not going to cry," I say, knowing I probably am.

"Man, I hate goodbyes," he says.

"Everyone does," I say.

There are a million things I want to say, but all the words feel trapped in my chest. It was written into the terms and conditions of our agreement that this has to end. There will be no Facebook friend requests or drunken late-night **miss you** texts. These words right now matter more because they're our last ones to each other.

"Should we shake hands?" he jokes, his smile too distressed.

I hold my hand out. "Why not?"

"I was a broken, sad guy when I got here," he says, taking my hand and not letting go. "I don't feel like that anymore." He rubs his thumb back and forth over my knuckles as he speaks. "You fixed me."

"Jesus, Mack," I say, swiping the heel of my palm over my eyes. "Not yet." I'm so perilously close to crying it's actually hurting my throat to speak. "What if I never feel like this again?"

I know. I sound as if I've stolen Jennifer Grey's best line, telling Patrick Swayze that she's scared of walking out of that room and never feeling the same way for anyone else again. She delivered hers with far more passion and far less snotty tears, though.

"You told me the other night that you love me a little bit," he says. "I didn't say it back at the time, and I should have, because your honesty deserved mine. I love you a little bit too." He kisses my forehead. "You are so entirely fucking lovable, Cleo Wilder."

It's such a Mack thing to say.

"And you know something else?" he adds, saving me from having to pull myself together enough to reply. "A little bit might be better than a lot, because this way we get to walk away remembering only the best of each other."

"Maybe a lifetime of micro–love affairs is the way forward." I smile, trying to put a brave face on it. "I might put that in my final piece, a bit of sign-off advice."

"It could be the next big thing in dating," he says forlornly. "You could start a micro-love movement."

"You'll be a legend in my head forever," I say.

He looks away, and the sound he makes in his chest tells me he's finding this every bit as difficult as I am. I squeeze his hand. It feels as if we're passing the **I'll be the strong one now** baton between us.

"I borrowed you from Boston, and you borrowed me from London. And now, there are two little boys in Boston who need their superhero back."

His kids' faces come to me, Susie's too—the image from Mack's wallet he showed me on the very first day we met, in a misguided effort to prove it was safe for us to spend the night under the same roof. I can't imagine that a man who wears novelty ties and calls her schmaltzy names could hold his own for long against a man with magic eyes, whose kiss feels as if he's giving you a piece of his soul. He's going home, and if the woman doesn't have rocks in her head, or, like the Tin Man, is missing a heart, she'll take one look at Mack and realize she made the biggest mistake of her entire life. In my head, I see his kids running to meet him at the airport, and Susie meeting his eyes over their shining heads as he hugs them. It's a love story. But it isn't my love story. Mack and I have held on to each other, and now it's time to let go.

"I think I see the boat," he says, standing.

I see it in the distance too, and it all feels horribly, lurchingly real. "Oh, Mack," I say, getting to my feet. "You're really leaving."

He turns and pulls me into his arms, the tightest of hugs, the hardest of goodbyes.

He holds my tear-streaked face in his hands. "You're the micro–love of my life."

I look into those wonderful mismatched eyes and find them brimming with another time, another place longing. "I micro-love you too," I say.

Our kiss is tear-salty and endless, bittersweet beautiful. I hear the boat's engine idle as it draws near to the beach, and I have to stop myself from clinging on, from begging him to stay, because I know he can't. I even know that being alone is the right thing for me right now, but none of that matters, because the thought of never seeing his face again is killing me.

"I won't call," he says against my hair.

"And I won't call. Oh, I have something for you," I say, remembering. I dig in my jeans pocket and press something small into his hand.

"Chalk," he says, laughing and crying as he looks at it. "I'll keep it forever."

"I'll think of you whenever I hear

Springsteen," I say. **And every other day of my life,** I don't say.

"I'll think of you too, often," he says.

We turn to look at the skipper of the boat as he trudges up the sand and calls out to us, a huge net of orange pumpkins leaving drag marks in the sand behind him. "Just the one of you, is it?"

Mack nods. "Just me."

"I'll take your bags down, will I?" If he can see that we're both a mess, he has the good grace not to mention it, leaving just one bag behind on the sand for Mack to pick up.

"Right then," I say, breathing deeply through my nose. "You best get going."

He takes my cue, nodding briskly. "Can't miss that connection."

He looks over his shoulder at the waiting boat and then into my eyes. "I'll be seeing you then," he says, even though we both know he won't. He cradles my face between his hands, one last moment of connection.

I pull my jacket tighter around my ribs, even though it's a warm day by Salvation standards. "Just go," I say. "Go, and don't look back." I aim for brave, but the truth is I don't want him to see me fall to pieces.

He stares at me, long and so full of meaning that it speaks a million words, and then he turns and walks away, his bag slung over his shoulder. I watch him all the way to the shoreline, see him hand his bag to the skipper, and then he hesitates. He hesitates, and my heart goes into weightless free fall behind my rib cage, because he's running back up the beach toward me.

"I told you not to look back," I say, trembling.

"One," he says, breathing hard, clutching my hands. "Promise me you'll write that damn book, Cleo."

I nod and I cry, because this is all so hard on my heart.

"Two," he says, "you're in here forever." He touches one hand to his chest, choked up.

"And three . . ." he says.

"Don't say it." I put my fingertips against his lips, and he closes his eyes and kisses them. "Just go."

This time he doesn't hesitate. I watch him clamber aboard the boat, and I rest my backside against the seawall and raise my hand. A farewell, a salute, a thank-you.

He stands at the bow of the boat as the engines power up, and as it begins to reverse, he cups his hands around his mouth and shouts something to me. The wind catches his words, delivering them to me just as the boat turns away toward open waters.

"Three, I don't regret you."

I stand there sobbing as I yell it back at the top of my lungs, bent forward with the effort, hoping the wind will be as reliable a messenger to him as it was to me. And I don't. I don't regret a single second of us, but right now it feels as if in mending him, I've broken a part of myself.

It's been eight hours now since Mack left. I'm not ashamed to say I cried like a lost child as soon as I walked back into the safe haven of Otter Lodge. He'd laid a fire before he left to make sure there was a warm welcome waiting for me, but there wasn't, because he wasn't there anymore. For such a small space, it feels cavernous without his belongings. No huge red coat hanging on the back of the door, no camera parts littering the table, no unfamiliar toiletries mixed with mine in the bathroom.

I sat outside on the porch steps first thing this morning while he packed, dolphin-watching with my morning coffee rather than witness him extricate himself piece by piece. You might suppose it would be easier because I always knew that it was going to end so abruptly. You'd be wrong. I think back to the moment I was bold enough to suggest we throw caution to the wind, and I wonder if I'd do the same again if I knew then how I'd feel now. Probably. Definitely. Of course I would, because my time with Mack has been magnificent. There's a price to pay for full immersion in a warm bath of beautiful, sudden love, though. You know that moment when you step out of the bath and snatch for your towel to get dry and warm again? There's no towel. I'm shivering. I'm exposed and alone, and I have to stand here like this until the sun dries me off itself, eventually. I realize I've unintentionally broken one of my vows: to protect myself from harm. Because make no bones about it—this feels like harm. As if I'm injured, as if a piece of me has been amputated. It's shocking to me that I didn't know him a month ago. It's such an insignificant amount of time, too short, surely, for someone to impact my life so much. Am I being foolish to attach such weight to our short affair? No. I've been in relationships before where I've gotten to know someone in hops and catches, a couple of hours at the cinema, an afternoon at the Tate, home again alone for days in between. Those relationships lasted weeks or months or even years, but they were never emotionally as long and definitely not as intense. We've rowed, we've laughed, we've cried, and we've loved. And now we've said goodbye. Our snow globe romance, a perfectly encased beginning, middle, and an end. I drag the quilt from the bed to the sofa and stare into the fire, remembering, even though it would be more beneficial to forget. I don't want to forget Mack Sullivan. Will he fade from my mind no matter how hard I try to hold on? I don't have his photographs to look back on. I don't have anything to remember him by. At least while I'm here on the island, I can see him everywhere I look: down by the shore as I stand at the kitchen window, across the table from me at breakfast, beside me in bed if I wake in the middle of the night. But I won't have those familiar comforts when I leave Salvation. When I leave the island, I'll leave the last traces of us behind me on the sand. I don't want to go.

Mack, October 29, Boston

I know what endings feel like

I haven't let anyone know I'm coming home today. I've moved through the last couple of days on autopilot, away from Cleo, closer to the kids. I dragged my bags through arrivals at Logan, acutely aware in a way I've never been before of the sheer scale of the place, the noise, the volume of people. In some ways, the anonymity of the city is welcome; in other ways, I ache for the rhythmic sound of the ocean, the peaty, salted taste of Salvation air, the smell of Cleo's hair.

I miss her violently. I swing between feeling like a fool for allowing things to spiral out of control and justifying it to myself as unavoidable. Damn, she was brave to lay it on the line, not knowing how I'd react. Truth is, the minute she lowered her defenses, mine washed away like Salvation sand at high tide. It does her a great disservice to suggest that it was just a right place, right time thing. If anything, it was a right person, wrong time thing—for both of us. I have too much going on in my life, too many unresolved feelings here to contemplate moving on with a woman who lives half a world away. Besides, Cleo has too complicated a relationship with herself at the moment to be in the right place for a romantic partner. She's craving a period of self-reliance, and she needs to focus her love inward before she can afford to give any away. Somewhere down the line, though, it's inevitable that she'll meet someone new, and he'll be the luckiest guy on the planet. I have no right to feel kicked in the teeth at the idea of her with someone else, but I do. I feel like I've crash-landed back on the unforgiving gray sofa in the furnished apartment I call home these days, and it's horrendous. I chose it purely because it's ten minutes from the kids. I have no clue who lives next door. I don't want to become part of the community or sign for packages for the neighbors. Photographs of the boys are the only personal items I've bothered to put up. It would take me less than half an hour to clear my stuff out of here, intentionally ready at a moment's notice to go home. Home. How much more complicated that is, now that there's Robert. And Cleo too, I guess. I'm going to have to tell Susie about her. Not that I feel as if I did anything wrong, but how can we discuss Robert without me being up front too? Not that it's the same thing. Cleo isn't going to be part of the boys' lives. She won't help them with their homework or read them stories at night. They'll never even know her name. The thought of Robert doing any of those things flattens me, a hard shove on my solar plexus that has me lying back on the sofa with a hand on my chest. I close my eyes and visualize myself back on Salvation Island. I'm standing on top of Wailing Hill; down below I can see lights in the windows of Otter Lodge and smoke rising from the chimney. It's a little after five in the afternoon here in Boston, which makes it just after ten at night in Ireland. Cleo might be curled up on the sofa with her laptop, or perhaps she's having trouble sleeping and is out on the porch steps looking at the stars with a shot of whiskey in her hands. God, if only I could snap my fingers and be next to her in a heartbeat. I press against my chest, feeling for the beating shard she embedded there, and in my head I walk down the hill to wrap a blanket around her shoulders. I hope she was right about the connection. I hope that wherever she is right now, she's just paused and unexpectedly thought of me.

"Mom?"

"Mack!" Her voice is shot through with surprised pleasure.

"It's good to hear you," I say, closing my eyes, because I feel about thirteen again. I can see her settling onto the bench seat in the hallway, a mental throwback to the old land-line phone that used to be there. She could sit anywhere she wants to answer calls these days, but she's never gotten out of the habit of sitting at that hallway table.

"The line is so clear," she says, pleased.

"I'm not surprised," I say. "I'm in Boston."

"You're home?" she says, caught off guard. "Already?"

I hear concern slide into her tone at my early return. She knows how much going to Salvation meant to me, and that I wouldn't be home early unless it was necessary.

"Is everything okay with the boys?"

"They're fine, I'm fine. It just felt like the right time to come home," I say. She's been a rock-solid support to me, gathering me in when I turned up on her porch and broke down not long after the separation happened, choking out my words because I just couldn't figure out what I'd done so damn wrong. I don't want to tell her about Robert over the phone, and I wouldn't know where to start about Cleo. If I'll ever tell her, even. What would I say? **Hey, Mom, guess what happened, I had myself some good old vacation sex!** How immature does that make me sound? Besides, it doesn't do justice to what happened in Otter Lodge. Should I tell her I fell in micro-love instead, and so it follows that I now have micro-heartbreak? If I had to find words for how I feel since leaving Salvation, I'd say I feel as if I lost something. Not like when you've misplaced your keys or your wallet. More like, say, if the Red Sox disappeared tomorrow, or if I couldn't hold the familiar lines of my Leica in my hands. They're foundation stones of who I am. I'd be less of a person without them in my life. So, yeah. I'll probably never tell my mom about Cleo, because I don't have the right kind of words to convey her importance, or her absence. And here's the thing—I have something to compare it against, because this isn't my first brush with the end of a love affair. The white-hot panic and brain-numbing shock of separation from Susie is an all-too-recent experience. I've had to get used to living without all the best parts of my life, the desolation of not being with my kids all the time, the twisted-knife pain of rejection by my wife, the profound loneliness of this condo, and, in a way, the shame.

So yeah. I know what endings feel like—messy and complicated and terrible. The end of my stay with Cleo wasn't any of those things. We didn't hurt each other or break any promises. It just was, until it wasn't anymore, but dammit, I miss her. I miss the simplicity of Otter Lodge, the beauty of Salvation, the pleasure of being with someone who expected nothing from me. Cleo's company was a spark of pure joy in an otherwise bleak year.

"Will you come over soon?" Mom says. "I'd love to see you. Or I can come to you, see the boys?"

I'd love her to visit, but not here in this condo. She always stayed in the yellow spare room at home, but that hasn't happened since everything blew up. I hate that her relationship with the kids has had to take a hit because mine has; she shouldn't have to be collateral damage. Better that I go see her for now. Besides, I think the next few days might be a bumpy ride between me and Susie—better that my mom isn't in the mix.

"Let me just get settled back down here and I'll head up. The boys get back from the lake tomorrow. I'll tell them to FaceTime you and fill you in, okay?"

She pauses, and I know she knows I'm not okay. "Sure, son," she says. "I can't wait to see your photos. Your grandma is excited too."

"How's she doing?"

"Oh, about the same," Mom says in that careful, bland tone she always uses when talking about Grandma. It's tough for my mother, watching dementia begin to scramble her mother's precious memories. It's not too bad yet a lot of the time, but I know it takes its toll on them both. Grandma's going to love seeing my photographs of the island; they might even spark insights and recollections that will mean so much more to me, now that I've spent time there myself. If you looked at images of Boston eighty years back, it would be unrecognizable as the place it is today, but I doubt Salvation has changed very much at all. "I'll come soon," I say. "I promise."

Cleo, October 30, Salvation Island

Chicken soup for the soul

T op of the morning to you, Cleopatra!" I've called my mum for some chicken soup for the soul, but it's my brother's jokey tone I hear when the call connects.

"Hey, Tom," I say, smiling into the fierce wind whipping around the top of Wailing Hill. They'd issue a stay-at-home weather warning for this back in London, but here it's just a regular Friday. "What's new with you, big brother?"

"Ah, same old, same old. Work's shite, Eve wants to divorce me, the kids have destroyed the house, and the dog stinks. I'm hiding at Mum's for an hour of tea and sympathy. I'd much rather hear about your honeymoon. Is it all romantic dinners for one and long walks on the beach?"

I process his complaints, knowing full well he's disgustingly happy in his domestic chaos. Eve adores him, and his house is straight out of **Country Interiors**.

"Something like that, yeah."

"Hmm, you don't sound ecstatic," he says, suspicious. "I could always come over and stay with you for a week, if you like? I seriously doubt anyone would miss me here. They wouldn't even realize I'd gone until no one put the bins out."

"Yeah, because the only thing odder than a honeymoon for one is a honeymoon with your brother," I say, laughing at the idea of it. Dolores would rip her sister's ring right off my finger.

I hear Mum demanding her mobile in the background as Tom makes gagging noises down the line.

"Cleo darling!" she says after a moment, amplified because Tom has switched her on to speakerphone. "Happy belated birthday!"

"Mum." I close my eyes and pull her comforting face up in my mind.

"How was it?"

"Yeah, it was . . . honestly, it was kind of profound. Thank you for the watch, it was timely."

We both laugh a little at my rubbish joke.

"You okay, love? You don't sound yourself."

Ah, mums. They just know, don't they? I scrunch my nose up and burrow deeper inside my hood, so the cold doesn't freeze the tears on my lashes.

"I'm all right," I say, trying not to sound as if I'm lying.

She pauses for a beat. "Why don't you come up here for a few days when you get back? It's been too long since I last saw you. I could do coffee cake. Shall I make your bed up?"

I picture my childhood bedroom: pink fairies on the wallpaper and curtains Mum sewed herself. It's been redecorated since, but I still feel eight years old again whenever I sleep in there.

"You do make the best coffee cake in the world," I say.

"Yes, then?"

In my head, I curl up in the armchair by Mum's fire with a huge slice of cake and a cup of tea, Mum in the other chair with the same. Her book is open on her knees, and there's an afternoon game show on in the background, **Countdown** or something similarly benign. The pull is powerful.

"Can we say maybe for now? I'm not sure when I'm heading back yet, and then there's work and everything." I grimace, because I know it sounds as if I'm putting her off.

"Have I got to come over there to fetch you, young lady?" she says.

"Not you as well." I smile. "Tom's already booking his ticket."

"Road trip," Tom shouts loudly in the background.

"We just worry about you, Cleo," Mum says, gentle in her reproach.

"I know. And I appreciate it, but I'm a big girl now. Thirty."

"You'll always be the baby to me," she says.

"The annoying baby," Tom calls.

I laugh with them, clinging to their familiarity, wanting to pull them close. My time here has helped me see the parts of my life I need to jettison and the parts I need to hold tight. "I better go," I say. "I'm in danger of freezing solid."

They hang up in a flurry of goodbyes, and I shove my hands in my pockets to warm them up. The weather up here is extra harsh today, the wind feels as if it could take my skin off.

I get to my feet and jiggle my numb bum, my guts full of pent-up, nowhere-to-go frustration that escapes my body in a long, loud growl. It feels unexpectedly good to let it out. I glance around; there's no other human for miles, so I do it again, a louder and longer animal howl this time, and then again, and then again and again, until I'm hoarse and exhausted by the effort but strangely exhilarated too.

Mack, October 30, Boston

There will be other places and other times

I stop my truck a little way down the street from the house, in need of a couple minutes to get myself together before I walk up the familiar driveway and ring the bell. I have a key, of course, but I don't use it these days when I go over. I feel in my pockets for my cell. I should call, maybe, let Susie know I'm coming rather than dropping in, as I often have in the past. It's never been an issue, but now that there's Robert, it feels like it could be. I don't know if I have it in me to make nice with him, especially not after too much coffee to stave off the jet lag. I'd rather not be put to the test anytime soon.

It's such a beautiful house. Not the biggest or grandest on the street, but Susie cried the first time we saw it, and I knew I'd move heaven and earth to make it ours. I look at it now, remembering the hours spent comparing similar shades of blue to paint the clapboard exterior, the graceful curve of the ivory wrap-around porch, the turret room at the far end that made this house the one Susie had to have. Our bedroom is up there, a rocking chair still in the window where Susie used to sit when she nursed the boys. The house was sold to us as a fixer-upper, and man, did it need a whole lot of work. I've replaced pretty much every board on that front porch. I didn't need a hobby for the first couple of years after we bought it; I acquired several new ones when the realtor handed the keys over. Floor sander, kitchen builder, rudimentary plumber—you name it, I learned it, and without the benefit of my father's experience to lean on. It was okay, though, because I had Susie's dad instead. My gut twists at the thought of Walt and Marie, Susie's tiny, hilarious mother. I miss them all; I wonder sometimes if Susie realizes how much, and how hard it is for me when they've been my family too for so many years. The fallout from a separation ripples out across every area of your life, and you lose a damn lot more than one person. Friends are forced out to the edges, relationships you counted on struggle; people feel compromised and forced to pick sides. Marie won't bring my favorite apple cinnamon muffins over at Christmas; my mother won't stay in the yellow bedroom for Thanksgiving. Change after change. It's bleak.

I finally pull up and park at the curb. Susie's car is in the driveway, telling me they're home. No other cars around. That's good too. I wonder how often Robert visits, if my kids' hearts sink or leap when his car pulls in. Objectively, I know he's no threat to my boys, that he's a decent enough man. Dull, but decent. I huff, pushing him out of my head, and then I forget him completely because Nate comes flying out the front door and runs down the driveway, waving his arms at me.

"Dad!" he yells, high-pitched, blond hair flying, all flailing limbs as he runs along the sidewalk. I'm out of my truck, laughing, arms outstretched, and he flings himself at me. I haul him up; God, I've missed him. I close my eyes, relieved, and his skinny arms grip tight around my neck. The smell of his shampoo. The slightness of his body. The childish sound of his voice. I blink away the tears and laugh instead, pulling my head back to drink his face in.

"Hey, you," I say, ruffling his hair. "How're you doing?"

"I caught the biggest fish this year," he says, bouncing in my arms.

"Wow, you did?" Walt is an avid fisherman, there's always a competition to see who can land the biggest catch.

"I took a photo." He wriggles down, still clutching my hand. "It's on my iPad, come on."

"I definitely need to see this," I say, letting him tug me along. "Is Leo home too?"

Nate nods. "He hurt his leg at the lake."

I frown, hating that I don't already know this. Nate runs back through the door he left open, and I hang back, tapping on the vintage stained glass. Homesickness kicks in hard as I stand and look at the wide central hallway: the floorboards I sanded, the rug we brought back from a long weekend in Nantucket.

"Hello?" I call, my hand still half raised. I swallow hard when Susie appears in the kitchen doorway at the end of the hall, a half-carved pumpkin in her hands. Familiar longing kicks me in the teeth.

"Mack," she says, coming toward me, surprised. "I thought you were still in Ireland?"

I shrug, aim for nonchalant. "It just felt like time to come back," I say. "How was the lake?"

She blinks, still flustered by my unexpected appearance. "Oh, you know. Good. Mom said to say thanks for the flowers." She pauses. "It was a nice thought."

I sent flowers for Marie's birthday, aware

my name was probably missing from her cards and gifts.

"Is that supposed to be a spiderweb?" I nod at the mess of lines on the pumpkin.

She looks down at it. We both know I'm the chief pumpkin carver.

"We're late putting stuff out this year, with the trip and all. I almost didn't bother, but you know." She shrugs. "The kids love it, so . . ."

Anything that makes things feel normal for the kids is a good thing in my book. "Need a hand?"

She half smiles, uncertain, and for a moment she reminds me of the college student who used to pose for her father's photography class, apprehension in her clear blue eyes. I can almost hear her running my offer through the scanner in her brain to check for inflections of tone, analyzing my word choice, assessing any hidden meaning. There isn't a hidden meaning. I just thought it would be better to have something to actively do, rather than sip coffee and make awkward conversation in the kitchen I used to cook pancakes in on Sunday mornings.

"Sure," she says. "The boys would really like that."

I run her words through my own internal scanner, and it spits out a note suggesting that Susie emphasized the boys would like my help, which perhaps implies that she wouldn't. I scout around inside my head and yank the plug out of my internal scanner as I follow Susie down the hallway to the kitchen.

"Is Leo around?"

Susie places the pumpkin down on the central island. "Up in his room, I think."

I hate having to wait for permission to go upstairs. "Okay if I . . . ?" I say, looking toward the sweep of the staircase.

"He's on crutches for a few days," she says quickly. "Went over awkward on his ankle at the lake. Just a ligament strain, the doctor said."

"You didn't let me know," I say. It's not intentionally accusatory. I just feel cut out of the need-to-know loop.

"Mack, you were in Ireland. I can't tell you every little thing that happens," she says defensively. "I dealt with it, he's fine."

"Maybe we could make injuries one of those things you tell me about at the time," I say, equally defensive, because I'm damn sure she'd want to know straightaway if anything happened on my watch.

She sighs, and I wish things weren't always this tense between us these days. "Go on up," she says. "See if he wants to come down and help carve, he usually likes to."

I leave her opening a cardboard box marked HALLOWEEN on the side, my handwriting surrounded by childish ghosts Nate added for special effect.

Leo's door is closed, so I tap and push it open. He doesn't look up straightaway, engrossed in the game console in his hands.

"No hi for your old dad, kiddo?" I say, leaning against the doorframe.

He looks up instinctively at the sound of my voice, and I see the second he realizes I'm not his mom come to get his dirty clothes or Nate here to annoy him. It's like the flick of a light switch, dim to full beam.

"Dad!" he yells, throwing his console aside, forgetting his ankle injury as he scrambles to get up. He stumbles, winces, and I shoot over and sit on the bed, pulling him into a hug.

"You've grown," I say, because I say it every time I see him. I swear he puts an inch or two on whenever I leave the room. "War injury?" I nod at his ankle.

He screws his nose up. "It doesn't hurt much unless I walk on it."

Shadows dull his eyes. I know he's remembering our last conversation about Robert.

"Did you have fun at the lake?" I say. "Nate tells me he won the fishing competition."

Leo grins. "Gramps was so mad."

I can imagine. Walt is a wonderful grandfather, but he struggles to keep a lid on his competitive streak, even with the kids.

"Why are you back already?" Nate frowns. "I mean, I'm glad you are, but I thought you said you were staying there longer?"

I hear what he's really asking. He thinks I cut the trip short because of Robert. This kid is too perceptive for his own good sometimes. I look at him, trying to decide the appropriate level of truth for a twelve-year-old.

"I missed you guys too much," I say. "Kind of figured you'd be glad to have me around."

Leo lets go of a deep breath, the kind you do when you're deeply relieved, but his eyes are still troubled. "You didn't come back because of me, did you?"

"I came because I wanted to be here." I give his shoulders a squeeze. "I can, you know, go back again, if you've had enough of me already?"

He rolls his eyes and grins his adorable grin. He's at that goofy stage when his grown-up teeth look too big for his still childish face. So much growing to do; he's going to need me, and I'm determined to be here.

"Will you stay for dinner?"

"Well, first someone needs to carve those pumpkins," I say, avoiding the question. "Because we all know your mom isn't the best at it, right?" Susie is many things, but art isn't her forte. "Come on, I'll help you get down the stairs."

I bear his weight as he stands, and for a second when he leans into me I gather him close.

"Love you, Dad," he says. "I'm really glad you're home."

My heart expands. "Me too, kiddo."

Coming home was 100 percent the right thing to do. I hope Leo learned today that whenever he needs me, even if I'm halfway around the world, he only has to say the word and I'll be there.

For the next couple of hours, anyone watching us might have been fooled into believing this was just any Halloween, that we were your regular American family, carving pumpkins and decorating the front porch like the rest of the neighborhood. I've always been a Halloween fan, but this year the macabre undertone feels particularly matched for the dark unease between me and Susie. We've both tried our best to make this time feel like a slice of normality for the boys, but scratch the surface and they were fraught with tension. Every time she glanced at the clock, I wondered if it was because Robert was due soon. If I made a comment, she automatically narrowed her eyes, searching for the double meaning. I hope the boys at least know that our family foundation hasn't crumbled, that we will always be able to be together like this regardless of what's happening between me and Susie. I read somewhere that if you put the kids first, everything else falls into place behind it. I'll go on record now and say that advice was much easier to swallow when there was no one else in the picture, but I guess it's even more crucial when things get complicated. I think we've more or less pulled it off. So far, anyway.

Now they're over in a neighbor's backyard with a bunch of other kids, and we're sitting out on the porch the way we often used to. It's the first time we've been alone for a while.

"I'm sorry you found out about Robert the way you did," Susie says, her eyes trained ahead on the street rather than me.

"I'm more sorry Leo found out that way," I say. I could be kinder, but it cuts deep to know Leo now lives with the same kind of memory of his mom as I do of walking in on my dad. I almost say as much; she knows, after all, how much that particular discovery has eaten at me over the years. I bite my tongue, though. It'd be a low blow, especially as she's probably already connected the dots.

She rubs her hands down her face. "It was so awful, Mack. He cried, I cried." She sighs. "I really wish it had happened differently, that I could rewind time and make it not happen."

My father didn't experience any guilt, or even know I saw him that day. What happened to Leo is a world away from what happened to me, Susie will make sure of that. Me coming back here today will make sure of that.

"How've you been?" I ask. New shadows hang under her eyes, and there's brittleness to the set of her shoulders as she sits on the porch swing. I've seen her curled into that spot reading more times than I could count, one eye on the kids playing out in the street. She's anything but relaxed today. Her blue eyes are bright with unshed tears when she turns them on me now.

"I haven't been sleeping too well. Just, you know"—she knots her fingers in her lap, fidgeting—"worrying about everything."

Every part of me wants to put my arm around her and reassure her that everything will be okay. That's always been my role in our relationship—the strong shoulder, the rock everyone can lean on. But I don't put my arm around her today. I can't, because I don't know what my role is in Susie's life anymore. It's clear-cut with the boys—I'm their dad, it's carved in stone that I'll love them forever, no matter what. I look at Susie now, and it's hard to think the day will ever come when I don't love her too. She's the mother of my children, the woman I married, the love of my young life. If we were a Venn diagram, the boys would be the center, Susie on one side and me on the other, always overlapping. Different circles might overlap Susie's on her other side, and other circles will overlap mine too, but the original three must stay connected or the whole thing falls apart. My parents let their circles drift apart. I won't. With those circles in mind, I reach out and put my hand over Susie's.

"This is going to feel really messed up for a long time," I say. "But we'll work it out, because we have to, for the kids." I nod toward the ghoulish Halloween display we made together. "The kids needed to see that we were okay, and doing that together showed that whatever happens, we are."

"I didn't want you to find out about Robert the way you did. I really am so sorry. I wanted to tell you properly, myself, face-to-face. And I was going to—remember the day you came over and told us you were going away? I'd decided to tell you that day, but it felt wrong once you said you were leaving."

I can't lie—I wish she'd found the words. There's no easy way to hear the person you love is with someone else, but three thousand miles away on a hill in the pouring rain was definitely the worst way. But if she had told me about Robert then, there's every possibility I wouldn't have gone to Salvation at all. And if I hadn't been to Salvation, a whole chunk of who I am now would be missing.

"Robert wasn't the reason, you know," Susie says. "He wasn't the reason why. It happened months later. I didn't even see it coming, it just . . ." She shrugs. "I was low, and he was kind, and it just happened."

I look at the floor. "I believe you." I do. I'd like to think there was enough honesty in our marriage for neither of us to have cheated.

"I don't even know if it's anything yet," she says. "I know I said it was serious. I thought it was. Got caught up in it, I guess. Too soon, I think."

I can't help but wonder what caused the setback for them. I'm pretty sure they didn't play happy family the whole time at the lake, but maybe he headed down there for a day. I find myself hoping that he's a terrible fisherman.

"Too soon to know?"

She looks at me then, and a tear spills down her cheek. "Too soon after you, Mack Sullivan."

I have to tell her about Cleo. It isn't fair that she's laying it on the line and I'm not.

"Listen, Susie," I say, trying to pick the words that will hurt the least.

We both look up as a car eases to a stop just down the street. "Shit." Susie dashes her hands over her damp cheeks. "It's Robert. I didn't know he was coming."

Ugh. I pinch the bridge of my nose as she jumps to her feet. I watch Robert get out of his sensible sedan, glad the kids aren't here to watch this. Button-down vest? Check. Goofy tie? Check. Wary expression? Check. Sudden fury burning through my gut like acid? Check.

"I should go," I mutter.

Susie turns to me. "Mack, you don't have to . . ."

I can't tell if she's asking me to stay or to go. Way I see it, if I stay I might hit him, which would undo all the good work we've done here this afternoon. I know I kind of forfeited the right to such indignation when

I rubbed out that chalk line in Otter Lodge, but there's no applying logic to the emotions running through my veins right now. I've known Robert for more than seven years. Has he always had a crush on Susie? Has he been hanging around in the wings, waiting for a crack to worm himself into? I'm angry with him in a way I'm not with Susie. I could pay a psychologist a small fortune to offer me a whole host of enlightened theories as to why this burns, or I could just listen to the wounded lion in my chest telling me this dude moved in on my pride when my back was turned and I should rip his fucking face off. I'm not proud of my feelings, but there they are.

"I'm gonna head out," I say. "Tell the kids I'll call them later."

Robert slides back into his car in an almost comical reverse move as I take the porch steps two at a time. I don't even look his way, just keep on going until I'm back in my truck, gunning the engine, getting myself out of there before I do anything stupid.

Later, I sit at the dining table, three beers in, photos of Salvation Island on my laptop in front of me. I'm framing it as work in my head, but what I'm really doing is looking for a way to ease the ache inside me. I'm reminding myself that life won't always feel this hard, that there will be other places and other times, that I can slow dance to "Thunder Road" under the stars and still be a good dad. I've picked at my scabs over the last hour or so, scrolled through old photos of the kids when they were little, of Susie looking exhausted and beautiful in her hospital gown a couple of hours after Leo was born, of homemade birthday cakes and wobbly first steps. It's so much to let go of, this love. Baby teeth and first curls tucked away in envelopes in a house I no longer live in; the tie I wore on the day I married Susie, folded into the box with her wedding dress in the attic. The romance of us tangled with the hot mess of parenting, diluting us and strengthening our bond all at the same time. I can't shake the depressing weight of failure off my shoulders. Other people make it—why not us? I've spent long, sleepless nights turning that question over in my head, walking through the places when I didn't do enough, when I didn't say the right thing, and it's futile. It's hard work falling out of love when you don't want to.

I click through the images of Salvation, letting the island seep slowly into my head, beauty to balance the bitterness. Moody skies, rolling gray seas, rain-lashed beaches, the warmth of

Raff's smile behind the bar in The Salvation Arms. Man, I wish he were here to share a beer with right now; I could use some company to save me from drinking alone. Delta fills my screen, her green eyes full of trouble. The granite crosses at the church on the headland, a lone islander stooped to tend to the flowers. It brings me a great deal of comfort knowing Salvation is still out there living and breathing: the welcome of the people, the hostility of the weather, the sanctuary of Otter Lodge.

I click again and Cleo's image fills my screen, laughing over her shoulder into my lens as the wind whips her hair across her mouth on the beach. They say the camera never lies for good reason. Every now and then, in just the right light at just the right nanosecond, you can capture the entire essence of a person in a single frame. This is one of those magic moments. I can hear her carefree laugh; I can see her innate goodness. If you didn't know the person in this photograph, you'd want to. You'd look into her eyes for a while and you'd know that she's someone who leaves a bright trail of starlight behind her, guiding lights for lost souls on the darkest of nights. That's me, Cleo. I could really use your guiding lights tonight.

Cleo, November 2, Salvation Island

Message received, universe

K aren Carpenter was bang on the money about rainy days and Mondays. It's Monday morning **and** it's rainy, a double whammy, but I'm not complaining because it suits my mood. I've already been up once and gone back to bed—the weather can do whatever the hell it wants.

Mack's been gone for six days now. It feels like six hundred years and then it feels like six seconds, as if I blinked him away. How I wish I could blink him back. I won't even try to deny how much I'd love to look out the kitchen window and see him walking down on the beach, or to roll over and find him sleeping in bed beside me. It's excruciating. Micro-love, we called it, but this feels like a major-love hangover. I've gone full-on

mope—"Thunder Road" on repeat, can't face
food, haven't brushed my hair. I hate feeling
this rough; I feel as if I'm letting myself down.
I stood on the porch at first light this morning and squinted out to sea, wondering if
the **Pioneer** has lifted anchor and sailed without me, bitterly disappointed by my lack of
gumption. **I didn't expect to feel this bloody
terrible,** I shouted, leaning forward over the
railing. **It's not my sodding fault I miss him
this much,** I yelled, full of fury, shocked by
the actual physical pain of heartsickness. I
need Mack to post me back that sliver of my
heart, I think it might have been arterial. Is
that a good enough reason to get in touch,
even though we promised we wouldn't? We
have each other's numbers; we scrawled them
on the rules sheet on the fridge, for emergency
contact only. I could sit on top of Wailing Hill
and call him right now, listen to the clicks and
silences of my desperation beam out across the
miles to wherever he is. I won't. Of course I
won't. But the fact that I could almost makes
me feel worse. It'll get easier. It has to. I won't
die of heart malaise. This isn't a Shakespearean
play. I'll pull myself together soon, honestly I
will. I'll brush my hair, eat something. Delete
"Thunder Road" from my playlist. Even as I
think it, I press play one more time. Bruce

plays his soulful harmonica and I curl up in a ball in the middle of the bed and cry.

There's a note shoved under the door when I open my eyes. I see it from across the room, a flash of white on the floorboards, and I jump out of bed and scrabble for it in case it's from Mack. Oh God! Did he come back? I straighten and lean against the door to open the folded piece of paper. It isn't from Mack.

Hey Cleo, don't miss group today, we have something for you. D xx

Delta. I sigh as I balance the kettle on the stove. I don't think I can muster myself enough to walk over to the village this afternoon. I'm still wearing yesterday's jeans and crumpled red-and-black-checked shirt, and my hair is more knot than not. I'm not going to go.

I take my coffee out onto the porch to think about it some more. I danced on this very spot on my birthday, spun round by Mack, my dress twirling out around my knees. I close my eyes and try to summon the joyful girl I was in that exact moment, but she's beyond me. I take a sip of coffee, a hot scald in the cold wind, and I sit down because standing is suddenly too much effort. I sit cross-legged and cradle my cup for warmth, my eyes fixed on the bay. He's out there somewhere, across fathoms of water and several time zones, back to being a father and a son, brilliant photographer and discarded husband. Only maybe he's not discarded anymore. I had no idea it was possible to miss someone this much. I keep reminding myself that we had such a brief affair, it's unreasonable to allow myself to fall this shockingly low. I put my half-full mug down on the sandy boards, sick of coffee on an empty stomach.

Don't miss group. I expect Delta knew that any phrase that allowed me a choice would fall on deaf ears, whereas I feel less able to ignore such a direct order. **Don't miss group today.** I circle my thumb over the crystal face of my father's watch. I've worn it constantly since my birthday, pressing my cheek against the cool glass sometimes for comfort. Midday, it tells me. **Get up off the floor, child,** he tells me. **Brush your hair and walk your bum over that hill. Don't miss group.** I sigh as I pick up my mug and head inside in search of a hairbrush.

Brianne notices me first and fires herself across the room.

"You came," she says. "Come in, let's get

you out of that wet coat. I'll hang it over the radiator to dry." Her eyes brim with motherly concern, even though she can't be more than a few years older than me. She hurries me across to the group, where the women are already shifting seats to make space for me on the sofa beside Delta.

"Come on, love," Delta says, patting the cushion. "Sit yourself down and get warm here now."

I lower myself in between Delta and Erin, who rubs my knee and hands me a cup of coffee. "Delta was sure you'd come, we made you one ready. There's cake too. You can take some back to the lodge if you don't feel able for it now."

I realize my hands are shaking only when I grip the blue-and-white-striped mug.

"Hey." Delta puts her arm around my shoulders. "It's okay. You can let it all out."

And I do. Someone takes the precarious coffee from my hands as my body heaves with sobs, and I tell them how terribly I miss Mack in jerky sentences, and they say all the right things and gather in close around me as I cry it out. They know; I can see it on all of their faces. They know that there's no such thing as micro-love. There's just love.

"A man like that's going to take some

getting over," Ailsa says, and they all nod in grim agreement.

"Could I write that line down for a future book?" Carmen asks after a beat, and I half laugh because I know that's exactly why she said it.

"Thank you for the note. I'm glad I came," I say, when I feel calmer.

Dolores adds a nip of whiskey to my coffee as Delta squeezes my knee. "We were coming to you if you didn't. I'd already asked Cam to barrow me over the hill. He was on for it."

I don't for a minute think she's joking. I can easily imagine Brianne's huge husband pushing Delta over Wailing Hill in a wheelbarrow. I shudder out a deep sigh, relieved that these women have folded me into their flock like a lost lamb. I've many friends in London, but there's an unavoidable transiency, people come and go. Here, people grow and stay. I've spent more time with Delta than with most of my colleagues, and I've worked at the magazine for almost four years now. And so it was with Mack too. We jumped straight into each other, feetfirst.

I feel my shoulders slowly slide down from my ears as conversation ebbs around me, replaced by the click of knitting needles and the clatter of plates, the sound of the radio low in the background. An orchestra of comfort. The women's accents rise and fall, musical as they pass me a slice of cake or a ball of wool, a reassuring hand on my shoulder as someone gets up. They instinctively pitch it at just the right level of compassion and comfort, letting me settle down after my initial outpouring.

"I feel like such a bloody weakling," I say, when Delta arches back to stretch her shoulders and asks if I'm okay now.

"Today maybe," she says. "It'll make you stronger in the long run, mind."

"You think?" I look at the half-made scarf on my needles.

She nods. "For sure."

Dolores glances up at me. "Not too strong, though," she warns. "Don't go building your wall so high you can't climb over it."

It would probably displease Dolores a great deal to know how much I like her. It's good advice. Right now I'd build those walls good and tall from Salvation rock, double thickness for good measure.

"It takes a tough woman to weather something like this," Carmen says.

"She's tough enough," Erin says with no hesitation.

"Can I just stay here forever?" I sigh.

"Not at Otter Lodge, I'm afraid." Brianne

bites her lip, her eyes full of apology. "I heard from Barney this morning. He's coming back to stay in the lodge in a few weeks, told me to hold off any more bookings for a while."

"Oh," I say, crestfallen. It's such unwelcome news. I know I have to leave the island sometime, of course, but this feels like yet another ticking clock, as if the decision has been taken out of my hands. Otter Lodge has become my sanctuary. I don't like to think of anyone else sitting out on the porch, watching the beach or greeting the dolphins in the morning. My temporarily buoyed spirits nosedive, and I find myself ready to head back over the hill. The women fuss, holding out my warmed jacket for me to shrug my arms into, loading my bag with tinfoiled parcels of cake and what's left in the whiskey bottle. Delta follows me to the door and adds another parcel wrapped in brown paper.

"Open it later," she says, hugging me over her ridiculously huge baby bump.

"Go back inside," I say. "You'll make the baby cold."

She laughs. "A bad mother already. This poor one has no chance."

I leave her there and head off, thinking how wrong Delta was just now. That baby is one of the luckiest kids on the planet to be born on Salvation among these people.

• • •

Dusk gathers as I make my way back up Wailing Hill. I'm wearing Mack's deeply unflattering but hugely practical head torch, which he left in my coat pocket and made me promise to use. I'm glad of it this evening, but also glad no one can see me.

It's almost dark when I reach the summit of the hill, and I drop my bum down on the now familiar slope of the boulder. I know exactly how to position myself on it now, there's a particular spot that's been molded into a gentle curve by countless backsides across the years. I'd like to think mine has added a little to the groove too.

I click the head torch off to better appreciate the view. I left the porch light on for myself at Otter Lodge—I couldn't bear the thought of returning to a cold, dark place. For a moment, I imagine Mack is in there now building a fire, and it's so sweet I could set myself off again. But he isn't. Solitude awaits me, and actually, after an afternoon of such bolstering company, I find I don't mind the thought of some time alone.

A noise in my pocket startles me—my phone connecting to the network. I switched it back on after Mack left, just in case. A message from my mum; she has a coffee cake cooling on the side and wishes I were there to eat it. She wants to get a visit arranged as soon as I'm back in England. I haven't told her much about what's been happening here, but she's my mum. I know she reads my work and finds all the invisible words between the lines, that she's deciphered secret SOS messages I didn't even know I'd sent. Another message, this time from Ali, to let me know she's approved my request to take the chunk of annual leave I'm owed and tag it on to my time here. I sag with relief. It's a tiny window of breathing space, more Salvation days before the sand runs through the timer.

Another message arrives, and I almost don't look because there's something incongruous about the glare of the screen against the timeless dark skies. But I do look, and I breathe in sharp when I see the name on the screen.

Mack.

I stored his number in my phone when I took the rules sheet down. I intended to keep the list as a memento, but I've misplaced it, probably swept up with the clear-out after Mack left. Is he in trouble? Did he not make it safely home? I'd have heard by now, surely, if not. Hardly breathing, I click his message open.

One—Springsteen just came on the
radio and I thought of you.

Two—I fucking miss you, and the
island, and the lodge. But you most
of all.

Three—You know what three is.

Oh, Mack. I read and reread his words.
Of the two of us, I thought I'd be the one
to break our pact, the one who ended up a
little drunk and a lot lonely with my phone
in my hand. What do I do with this? Reply?
I think of him, about his long journey home,
the stress he will have been under returning to
Boston, the roller coaster of emotions he'll be
going through with Susie and seeing his boys
again. I can't even begin to imagine how you
process building a life, a family, with someone
and then having the rug pulled unceremoniously from beneath your feet. I saw how cut
up he was about Robert, and I'm sure Susie
will feel the same boot in her gut when, **if**,
Mack tells her about us. He's flown home to
face a truckload of agonizing conversations
and decisions. I expect messaging me was a
desperate, alcohol-related escape route back to

Salvation. I hate to think of him alone in that condo he detests, beer in one hand, phone in the other.

I study his words again, thinking about my options. I could just not reply, stick to our agreement. It would send a clear message: **This isn't a good idea, Mack. One text leads to another, and before you know it we're friends on Facebook and torturing ourselves looking at photos that break our hearts.** He may well have woken up regretful about even sending it. Not replying would solve that. But then, he might also wonder if I ever even received it, if it got lost somewhere along its three-thousand-mile journey, if a passing mermaid plucked it from the air in an act of female solidarity to protect me from further harm. I feel certain he wouldn't contact me a second time, and that would be that.

I think all these commendable thoughts, knowing all the time that I'm going to reply. Of course I am. I just don't know what to say. I try out various options before I strike what I hope is the right note.

One—I'm sitting on top of Wailing Hill wearing your deeply unfashionable cyclops torch.

Two—I miss you frantically.
The lodge feels too big without
your ridiculous coat taking
up all the space.

Three—I went to the knitting
group today and cried like an idiot,
but I still don't regret you.
Not now, not ever.

Three A (because I know you don't
approve of a fourth)—Don't feel the
need to reply. I get that you
probably drunk texted, or you
were at a low ebb or struggling
to readjust. I've replied,
so we're even again now. x

I press send, then slide my phone into my pocket. I could sit here and wait awhile, see if he replies even though I told him not to. He might; he's hours behind me, so it's early afternoon in Boston. I wait for just enough time to be sure my words have fired themselves off in search of him, then I click on the head torch and set my sights on Otter Lodge. It's still mine for now; I have to make the most of it.

I'm pleased to see the fire I left in the hearth hasn't completely died out, and I feel a sense of accomplishment when I'm able to revive it.

Fire means light and heat, cavewoman neces-
sities I can provide for myself. I mean, I put
the lamps on too, because I'm not an **actual**
cavewoman, but the sense of satisfaction in my
own capabilities is real. I can do things to make
myself feel strong. Heat up some soup, light
some candles, layer on my favorite cardigan. I
remember feeling apprehensive before I came
to Salvation at the thought of being alone at the
lodge. I worried I'd feel too remote, too alone,
exposed. A little afraid, even. If anything, I feel
the absolute opposite of all those things tonight.
I'm in need of this silence, and I feel held and
supported by the thick stone walls around me.
When Mack was here, it was a nest for two;
now it is a nook for one. My eyes come to rest
on the brown-papered parcel Delta gave me. It's
tied with simple string, and there's a note.

**Most of Salvation's women have had
need of one of these at some point in
their lives. You know where we are if
you need us. X**

I pause, the package resting on my knees.
I'll take good care of that note, it will always be
precious to me. Pulling the string, I fold back
the paper, and then I gather up the contents
and press my face into it with a soft, grateful

sigh. I didn't think I had any tears left in me today, but it seems I've got a backup well. It's a blanket. A blanket made up of knitted squares, stitched together to make a patchwork quilt of color and comfort. I shake it out and wrap it around my shoulders, squeezing my eyes tightly shut. It's as if the island women have wrapped their arms around me, an intentional show of sisterhood, of feminine solidarity. I sit for a few minutes and let the layer of warmth sink into my skin, and then I open my eyes and examine it. I recognize the yellow wool Ailsa used recently and Carmen's unmistakable battleship gray, **the warmest on the island.** I smile at the thought of Dolores's lemon-sucking expression every time Carmen says it. There're other colors too: moss green, bubble-gum pink, cherry red, turquoise blue. Offshoots of projects I've seen growing on their needles. God, what a phenomenal group of women. I feel honored to count myself even temporarily among their number. I wonder if they realize how special what they have is, or if they're lucky enough to be able to take their good fortune for granted, an accepted part of islander life. They look after their own, and every now and then, they sweep a lost lamb into their fold. "I'm a lucky lamb," I whisper. It's the exact right gift at the exact right moment. I'm reminded of the first time

I laid eyes on my lime-green clamshell laptop, the feeling of being understood, the swell of intention behind my ribs. I feel it again now, a cosmic nudge to listen to my gut. "Okay," I whisper. And then I say it again, louder, more resolute. "**Okay.**"

I get up and make myself a den on the sofa with pillows and my beloved patchwork blanket, then I fire up my laptop and open a blank document. **Message received, universe,** I think, flexing my fingers. It's time to write.

Mack, November 6, Boston

It's over now

I became a depressing single-dad cliché tonight. I ordered a pizza rather than cook a decent meal, let the kids drink soda at the movies even though we've always been careful about their teeth. It wasn't done to score cool-parent points against Susie; I just wanted to give the boys all the stuff I could give them, because I couldn't give them the one thing they asked for when I picked them up from school this afternoon: for their mom to come with us too. I tortured myself in the dark movie theater, imagining them getting their heads together, deciding which of them would be brave enough to ask me, trying to pick out the right words to get their parents together for a few hours. I've been that kid, the one who thinks if he can just force his folks to spend time together they'll remember how good things used to be. I haven't forgotten our good times either. I didn't tell them that, of course, just glossed over it and sold them on fizzy soda and as much popcorn as they could handle. Distraction, the oldest trick in the parenting handbook. Hey, Nate, look at my stupid elephant impersonation, not the cut I'm cleaning up on your knee. Hey, Leo, let's go to the skate park instead of thinking about that kid's party you didn't get invited to. It's easy when they're small; they look at you and they absolutely know you're going to make their world better. I hate that I can't do that for them this time. Soda and popcorn are a poor substitute for their mother, but it's the best I could come up with at the time. And now they're late for bed and nodding off on either side of me on the couch, my arms around them as we watch the sports headlines on the eleven o'clock news. I hate having them stay here in this condo, even though their presence transforms it into a home for a few hours for me. They pretend they think it's cool, but they're terrible liars. Maybe after Christmas I'll look around for somewhere better. I pull the boys closer on both sides of me, my feet propped on the glass coffee table.

"You're the peanut butter," Nate says, glancing up.

I look down at him. "I am?"

"In the sandwich," he says. "We're the bread, and you're the peanut butter in the middle."

"Can I be ham instead?" I say. He knows I don't like peanut butter. "Or stretchy cheese, the kind you get on pizza?"

He shakes his head and grins, closing his eyes as he settles deeper into the crook of my shoulder. "Crunchy peanut butter is my favorite thing in a sandwich."

I press a kiss against his citrus-scented hair. "I know. Okay. I'll be peanut butter."

He opens one Susie-blue eye and looks up at me. "Crunchy?"

"Crunchy," I say. He closes his eye again, satisfied, and I wonder how something as crazy as peanut butter can make my chest ache with emotion, as I think of Cleo, of how a shared dislike of peanut butter was one of our secrets in the dark.

Leo's more asleep than awake on my other side, his fingers clutching a handful of my T-shirt. His hair smells of the same shampoo as Nate's. Mine used to smell the same too. It's the smallest of insignificant details, a tiny wedge between us because I couldn't remember the exact brand of shampoo, even though I sniffed every damn bottle in the store. On the one hand, it's really not important, but on the other hand, separation is made up of a million tiny disassociations that eventually add up to passing someone on the street and barely recognizing them.

There are two breakfast plates in the kitchen sink, two coffee cups on the table, when I run the boys home midmorning, as agreed. Susie sees me notice, and I know she wishes she'd cleared them away. It messes with my head to think of Robert sleeping here in my bed. Do I have any right to the anger that simmers my blood when I imagine his head on my pillow, his hands on my wife? I correct myself. **Ex-wife**. Is that the right term I should use, since we've been apart for a year? We're in this weird limbo, still officially married. There's this huge schism down the middle of us, like we're a landmass splintered in two by an earthquake. There must have been a hairline crack there for a long time, one I didn't notice. Even when it widened, I didn't pay enough attention. I didn't see that damn crack until it was a canyon, too wide to safely jump, and Susie was on the other side, drifting away. And now Robert is standing over there beside her in an eye-wateringly awful vest, and I'm over here feeling like a stranger in my own house. It's a lot.

"I was thinking about Thanksgiving," I say.

Susie busies herself loading the dishwasher, tense. For as long as we've been together, we've hosted our parents here for Thanksgiving.

"I thought I'd spend it with my mom this year," I say. "See Grandma, show her the photos of Salvation."

I see the relief on her face as she straightens, a fight avoided.

"I'd like to see your photos sometime too," she says. "Was it everything you've always hoped?"

I haven't found the right time to tell Susie about Cleo yet. She's just handed me an in. The kids are in the den, Robert can't be heading over seeing as he's evidently just left, and I have nowhere else I need to be.

"Yeah," I say. "It's a special place." **Jeez, Mack. Find the words.** "Suze, I met someone there."

She's making coffee, tipping beans into the machine her folks gave us as an anniversary gift a few years back, reaching for mugs. I see my words settle, her movements falter.

"As in . . . ?" She lets the question hang incomplete as she unscrews the lid from the sugar, and then slowly raises her blue eyes to mine. I looked into those eyes at the altar at our wedding, over the heads of our newborn sons, across crowded parties in silent agreement to sneak out early. Right now, those eyes are watchful, guarded in anticipation of incoming peril.

"As in a woman," I say softly.

She stands stone-still, spoon in hand. Blinks a few times. "Oh," she says. A tiny word, just a sound, really, but she fills it with a hundred unspoken other words. **Oh, I'm blindsided. Oh, I'm sorry, I feel like you just punched me in the heart. Oh, I'm tired. Oh, I love you, I hate you, I miss you, I'm furious, please stay, just go.** Believe me, I know exactly how she's feeling right now. It's like looking in a mirror, so familiar I have to look away.

"Is it serious?" Her hand starts to shake. "What will you do? Move to Ireland? FaceTime the kids on their birthdays and Christmases, send for them in the summer? Take them to see Buckingham Palace?" The pitch of her voice gets slowly higher as she speaks, shocked, painting pictures of things she knows will never happen. We'd always daydreamed of taking the kids to Europe, to the Eiffel Tower, to England. Letting go of long-held dreams is hard, even more painful when your brain inserts someone else into the picture in your place. Susie has just erased herself from our family trip to London and inserted a faceless woman beside me.

"Of course not. You know me better than that," I say quietly. "It's over now."

She frowns. "So what, you're telling me just to hurt me?" she says. "Revenge for Robert?"

Now I'm frowning too. "This has nothing to do with Robert," I say, keeping my voice down so the kids don't hear. "This is me being honest, because I don't want it to sit between us as a secret. Because we all know where that gets us, don't we?" It's spiteful and I'm not proud of myself, but all I can remember is that night on Wailing Hill, Susie's panicked confession, Leo's pain. I've tried to make this easier on her than she made it on me, and still she's throwing it back in my face.

"Forget the coffee," I say, standing up. I need to get out of here before this erupts into a fight the boys don't need to hear. "I'm gonna go."

"You know where the door is," she says. And then she turns her back on me and stands at the kitchen sink, gripping the edge. For a second I want to cross the room and hold her, but I don't. I walk out, feeling as if I've just pulled the pin from a grenade and lobbed it over my shoulder into the hallway.

• • •

One of the only good things about the condo is the bar a couple blocks away. I find myself in there, half an hour later, rubbing shoulders with serious morning drinkers and a barman wearing a been-there-done-that expression. It takes two beers to get the fire in my gut under control; the third has me reaching for my phone.

One—The weather tower downtown is steady red today, incoming storm, and the bedroom window in the condo lets the rain in.

Two—I looked at the stars last night and thought of you.

Three—Everything is messed up. I miss you. I don't know what the right thing to do is anymore.

Three A—I didn't drunk text you last time. This time I'm three beers down, but I still know what I'm doing and I still don't regret you. I don't regret telling Susie about us either, but man, being an adult is hard work.

Three B—The photos. My God, Cleo, looking at the photos of Salvation breaks my fucking heart.

I send the message without reading it back or giving myself a chance to think better of it. I don't know if she's still in Salvation or if she's been swallowed up by London again, if she'll read and delete or if she'll reply.

"Don't send it, fella," the guy on the next stool says, bleary-eyed as he nods toward my phone.

"Too late." I shrug.

He throws his hands up. "Don't say I didn't warn you."

I settle my tab and walk out onto the blustery street. I can't stomach listening to some stranger's woes, I've got enough of my own. I wasn't exaggerating when I said looking at the photographs is hellish. Objectively, they're my best work by a mile. The Salvation exhibition will be my strongest yet, if I can just find a way to work on it without falling into a self-indulgent pit of longing and reaching for the Irish whiskey I brought home with me.

Cleo, November 13, Salvation Island

Diamonds in, fool's gold out

I go home exactly one week from today—weather permitting, as always. I don't want to leave, especially not now when I'm galvanized by the need to write. I feel unstoppered, as if someone popped a cork and words are spilling from my fingers. It's a huge release of energy, therapy of a kind to pour everything from my head to my fingers to the page. I didn't pause to outline a plot or toss ideas around. There wasn't time. My jumbled emotions spiraled around me, a tornado hovering over the roof of Otter Lodge, and I am sitting cross-legged in the eye, trying to harness it onto paper before it blows away. It's a love story, but not a girl-meets-boy kind. I mean, she **does,** and it's all kinds of spectacular, but that's not the essence of her story. She's me but she isn't; he's Mack but he isn't; it's Salvation Island but it isn't. It's an expression of womanhood and an exploration of sisterhood, and yes, I know I sound like an absolute twat, but oh my GOD, this book is consuming me. I tell the dolphins the latest plot twists at dawn, confide my heroine's secrets up on Wailing Hill boulder at lunchtime, and Jupiter awaits my midnight word count update. I jump in the bath and then climb straight out again because I need to record something before I forget it, and I fall asleep on the sofa beneath the patchwork blanket with my laptop balanced on my thighs. I eat for fuel and I drink for inspiration, and when I look in the mirror, this dazed, crazy-eyed person chucks me the **keep going** thumbs-up. I don't care that I'm talking to myself as I work, I'll take manic euphoria over last week's misery any day. I don't even know if this thing I'm writing has any form or structure or beauty, if anyone will ever read it besides me, but I'm bleeding out into this manuscript in a way that feels so wholly transformative that I have no choice but to continue.

Mack texted me again today; it came through as I ate my sandwich on the boulder on Wailing Hill. I go up there most days now, sandwich and a flask of coffee in hand. I guess you could say I'm communing with the island, grounding myself in a way that feels, I don't know, spiritual? I make noises too, deep exhales that turn into moans or chants, and I get louder until I eventually stand up and scream. And you know what? It feels amazing. Like a purge. I mean, I always double- and triple-check there's no one else around, because I'm self-aware enough to know I look as if I've completely lost the plot, but I haven't. I've found it.

He did the three things again. Or five, in actual fact, which I'm taking as an indication of how rubbish he's feeling. I texted him back, hoping it will be a bright spot, even though his days are so different from mine it's as if he skipped planets rather than countries.

One—I saw the dolphins at dawn this morning. The sea was a proper witches' cauldron.

Two—I'm writing like a crazy woman. Words are seeping out of me as if I'm one of those pink sea sponges in the rock pools down on the beach.

Three—I'm sitting on Wailing Hill (of course)! Don't tell anyone, but I've started to actually wail when I'm up here. I'm turning into a regular old hippie, Mack. ☺

Three A (don't blame me, you went over too)—I don't regret you. How could I? You unlocked something in me, or maybe something in me unlocked because of you. Either way, you were the key, and I'm a freer woman because of it. Told you—hippie. Take care of you, and special care of that sliver of my heart. x

I thought more about what I'd said after pressing send. What I actually think is that he unlocked something **around** me, an invisible cage constructed of all the props I thought necessary in my life. London. My job. My friend Ruby, even. Sitting on top of Wailing Hill this afternoon, I breathed fresh air in all the way to the pit of my stomach. Diamonds in, fool's gold out.

Mack, November 16, Boston

The dad who wasn't there

The too-small wooden school chairs force Susie and me to sit closer than we've been in months, sardines in the middle of a sea of smiling parents at Nate's class assembly. Everyone knows we're not together anymore. We're last year's gossip, no doubt superseded by some other poor souls whose lives took an unexpected nosedive. Susie knows them all by name; I'm such an infrequent visitor that the teacher almost handed me the wrong kid a couple of months back. I laughed it off, but it's the kind of incident that perfectly illustrates Susie's point, I guess. Thank God she wasn't there to witness it and record it for future reference. Things between us are a little glacial right now, to say the least. We haven't spoken properly since I told her about

Cleo. She's ramrod straight beside me, making herself as small as possible in an attempt to not touch me.

"Good morning, parents!"

Nate's teacher is singsong happy as she greets us, the kids cross-legged on the floor behind her in various costumes and states of fidgety anticipation. They each got to pick what they wanted to be today; for reasons known only to himself, Nate's inside a full fish suit, a lurid, blue-padded onesie, with just his blue-painted face and skinny arms poking out the sides. He catches sight of us and leans around the teacher to wave, his fin poking the kid beside him in the eye. There's something different about his face, besides the fact it's blue.

I lean in and whisper to Susie. "Did he lose a tooth?"

She sighs without looking at me, her hands tight in her lap. "Last night. He's a kid, Mack, it happens."

"Right."

I get that. He is a kid, it does happen, and I don't expect Susie to let me know every little thing. It's just hard to get used to not being there to put the dollar under his pillow.

"You missed a lot of teeth over the years," she hisses out the side of her mouth.

A woman in front throws us a look over her shoulder, probably not wanting our argument as the backdrop to the recording of her Harry Potter son.

"I guess it didn't cut so deep when I knew there'd be a next time," I say, trying to explain, probably making it worse. Definitely worse for the snarky woman in front of us.

We're saved from making any more of a scene by Nate standing up, a wriggly blue fish, trying to hold a piece of paper between his too-far-apart hands. My heart melts for this kid, even more so when he shoots us a quick, nervous glance before he reads his speech.

"I'm a fish today because I caught the biggest fish at the lake this year. My grandpa Walt was very proud, although I think he was mad too, because he always catches the biggest one. Except for last year when my dad did, but he wasn't there this year, which made me sad. My brother hurt his ankle too, but he's all right now."

I know for a fact that every last person in this room is either looking at me or wants to but is too polite. I'm the dad who wasn't there. I avoid eye contact with everyone but Nate and give him the thumbs-up, feeling like every dad in the room is mentally giving me the thumbs-down.

• • •

I don't stick around for coffee. Susie follows me out to my truck.

"Mack, I'm sorry. I promise you I didn't know he was going to say that."

I lean back against the driver's door, feeling like I've just been in a barroom brawl. "Okay." I don't have enough in the tank to offer anything else.

"He's just . . . he's just a kid trying childish manipulation tactics to guilt his parents into getting back together."

I know she's right. I'm not mad at Nate, I'm just all-round mad at the world right now. I'm not mad at Susie either, because despite our current differences, I know she wouldn't have okayed that speech.

"I'm sorry for what I said in there," she says. "About the teeth. You're a really great dad."

We fall silent as a group of moms passes by on the sidewalk, all doing a bad job of pretending not to stare at us.

"It means everything," I say. "What Leo and Nate think of me means everything."

She looks at the ground, too late for me to miss the damp tears that pool on her lashes. "It used to be my opinion that mattered," she says.

I'm struck by this. Even though she's the one who no longer needs me, she still wants me to need her. I know she's still getting used to the idea of me with someone else, but the revelation is eye-opening to me.

"Your opinion will always matter to me, Susie."

She swallows and lifts her head, eyes as blue as my mood. "Come back to the house for coffee?"

Cleo, November 20, Salvation Island

Have I failed you, Emma Watson?

Fifty days. I landed on this island fifty days ago, a fish out of water, an out-of-sorts girl in stiff new walking boots. I leave today, finally, and it's no exaggeration to say I feel like a different woman will step aboard that boat back. How can it possibly have been only fifty days? I hope I've bathed in enough bracing Salvation air for it to have left a permanent seal of protection on my skin. So much inside me has changed. The sea conditions are fair out there today; it's no millpond, but calm enough for safe passage.

My bags are packed and the lodge is spick and span. There's just time for one last coffee on the front steps before Brianne's husband comes to lug my bags over the hill for me. Yesterday was a barrage of tearful goodbyes, raised glasses at The Salvation Arms, and promises to stay in touch. I feel as if I'm leaving home, which is bizarre really, because I'm going home.

I can't begin to put into words how much I'm going to miss Otter Lodge. I take endless photographs on my phone, nothing like Mack quality, but I want to capture it all today, so that when I'm back in my own bed tonight I can look at it and see it again. Maybe I'll send the photos to Mack too, once I have the kind of real-world data that allows for picture messages. I'm sure he'd love to see it again. He's been texting me on and off, three things as always, snippets of his days that reveal how much he's struggling. I've been replying with a list sometimes too. It feels like bending the rules of our pact rather than breaking them. Holiday romances burn bright and then burn out—my own words. I guess I didn't realize how slowly the heat dies down.

I tip my too-cold coffee on the sand beside the steps and sigh. Oh, Emma Watson, is this even slightly what you meant? Have I failed you? I didn't self-couple in the way I planned when I arrived here, and I definitely didn't self-couple at all for eight cataclysmic days in the middle, but actually, since then, I think I've self-coupled in a wildly effective manner. Me, my squares blanket, and my beloved laptop full of words. We are as one; if the boat gets into any trouble out on the ocean later, I'm hanging on tight to those two things until I get rescued.

Cameron appeared bang on time with the barrow for my bags just now. I'm much fitter than I was when I arrived here, but even so, I was almost bent double with the effort of trying to keep up with him over the hill. When he glanced back and caught me almost dry-heaving, he suggested I do as Brianne often does and hop on his back. I didn't need to be asked twice—I clambered up that man like a kid on an apple tree.

"You make a most excellent taxi." I grin as he deposits me by the seawall. "What's the fare?"

He piles my bags up. The boat is already here, moored just off the bay, and I'm suddenly full of panicky **I'm not ready yet** emotion, because this is it.

"On the house," he says, and then he swings around when someone yells his name, sharp and cut through with alarm. I follow his gaze, and we both see Brianne running down the dirt track from the shop toward us. She's gasping for breath by the time she draws close, visibly distressed.

"Cam," she rasps, red-eyed. "It's Raff. Tara went to the pub for her shift and couldn't get any answer when she knocked."

My stomach does a sickly dip.

Cam shakes his head, because Brianne's face already tells us the next part of the story.

"Dolores had the spare key. She went in and found him stone cold in bed." Brianne closes her eyes and tears spill from her lashes. "He went to sleep and didn't wake up, the silly old goat."

"Oh no," I whisper, sitting down heavily on the seawall, aware my fingers are shaking when I press them against my mouth. Cam holds Brianne as she cries, and I look away when I see he's in tears too. He steers his wife across to sit beside me on the wall, then sandwiches her between us, his elbows on his knees, his head in his hands.

I put my arm around Brianne's shoulders and squeeze her tight. "I'm so sorry," I say.

Brianne shakes her head. "Dolores is in bits. Delta too."

My heart hurts for them. Dolores and her brother were chalk and cheese but still each other's biggest fans, and Delta adored him like a father. Raff was too big a personality for such a small community to lose; it's going to devastate them.

Brianne pulls a folded blue note from her pocket. "She asked me to give you this, if I caught you."

I dab my eyes dry and smooth the paper open on my knee.

Cleo, can you stay awhile longer? I know the answer is probably no, but if you can, I could really use a friend. Delta x

Sometimes in life you're asked to go out on a limb and do something, even when you know it will have repercussions on other areas of your life. You step up, or you don't. I know Delta would understand if Brianne goes back without me, but I think of the patchwork blanket and everything it represents. Friendship. Sisterhood. Love. The boat sails without me today.

I'd say every living soul on the island is packed into The Salvation Arms tonight. I've been behind the bar most of the afternoon, with Delta on a stool close by. She cried buckets when I walked into the pub earlier, and poor Dolores looks glassy-eyed, a radio that's lost its signal. People have turned up with plates of sandwiches and all kinds of other stuff, and we've set it out on a hastily erected trestle table over on the far side of the room. Carmen made her way from her house at the far end of the village with a huge Guinness cake balanced on top of the bars of her walking frame, and it really touched me when she quietly took off her gunmetal-gray shawl and wrapped it around Dolores's shoulders. The warmest wool on the island had never been more needed.

"No one's money is any good in here today," I say, when someone tries to pay me for their drinks. It was the only instruction I was given when I stepped behind the bar. Dolores issued strict orders to unlock the doors for the islanders and not let anyone pay a cent.

"You okay?" I say, heading around to the other side of the bar with a cup of tea for Delta just after nine. She's held up heroically all afternoon, but she must be dead on her feet. "You look knackered."

It's noisy in the bar, so many people eager to share their stories and anecdotes about Raff. I've heard outrageous tales, all true no doubt. He was a man who burst at the seams with life. There's music too. A couple of Raff's oldest friends have set up in one corner with an accordion and a tin whistle, joined at some point by Ailsa on guitar and Erin's tall husband,

Luke, island doctor and dubious fiddle player. If you were to look through the steamed-up pub windows, you could easily mistake it for a New Year's Eve celebration, entirely fitting for a man who danced through life like a party streamer. **Such joy,** people have said to me. **Such a rogue,** others have said. And then there are those who've told me quieter stories about a man who turned up with school shoes for their kids when money was tight, who sent Sunday lunch to people who were alone or under the weather. It feels very much as if Salvation has lost its father tonight.

"He's been toasted to the rafters," Delta says, even as someone behind her raises his glass. "I'd kill you for a whiskey." She reaches out and grips my arm to steady herself as she slithers awkwardly off the stool. "Need to pee again."

I smile as she hangs on to me, and then I pause, disconcerted because my foot is suddenly warm. When I look down, I see why, and when I look back up again slowly, Delta grips my hands hard enough to cut the blood supply.

"Ah, shite," she says quietly. "My water's just broke."

• • •

"Raff would have pissed himself laughing at this, wouldn't he?" Delta says, cradling her newborn son in her arms a few hours later. We're in Raff's cozy sitting room behind the pub, where she's propped on the big green sofa Raff sometimes used to catch forty winks on between the afternoon and evening shift. Everything kind of changed gears out in the bar once word went round that Delta's water had broken. Dr. Luke calmly laid down his fiddle, to everyone's relief, and guided his patient out of the busy bar, accompanied by Erin to give him a hand and Dolores for moral support. In London, it would have been a mad panic of hospital bags and running red lights. Here on Salvation, it's, **Hold my pint, I'll be back through shortly to toast the baby.**

"No swearing in front of my grandson, now," Dolores says. She sparked to life the moment she realized her daughter needed her. I wouldn't put it past Raff to have looked down at his sister in trouble and given his niece a bit of a nudge.

Dolores studies the tiny boy in her daughter's arms and then places her hand tenderly on Delta's cheek. Delta meets her mother's eyes and nods—silent, bittersweet acknowledgment that their family has experienced profound loss and bottomless joy today. I feel a sudden jolt of longing for my own mum. It's been too long since I last saw her, last shared a cup of tea and basked in her calming company. Dolores twists to glance behind her for a second, searching, and then she reaches across the back of the sofa for Carmen's gray shawl. She discarded it earlier in the heat of the moment, sweat on her brow, and now she carefully lifts her infant grandson and wraps him up.

"There you go." She perches beside Delta, her eyes on Salvation's brand-new resident. "The warmest wool on the island."

I smile and look away, caught between a laugh and choking back tears. Brianne passes Delta tea and toast, and Erin sits beside me, bum resting against the table, whiskey in her hand.

"Your husband was amazing," I say to Erin, full of admiration. Duty done, Dr. Luke has headed upstairs to the bathroom, because in truth he looks a bit like James Herriot after a rough day in a drafty barn on the dales.

"He is that." Erin nods, proud. "Feckin' terrible at the fiddle, though."

And just like that, everyone in the room starts to laugh. I bloody love this island.

• • •

It's past three in the morning when I finally head up Wailing Hill. Otter Lodge is empty for another week yet. I didn't put up a fight when Brianne said to hang on to it for now, and Cam brought my bags back from the dock. It's all in darkness down there when I reach the boulder, the outline of the building picked out only by moonlight. It's not expecting me back. I wonder if it will be pleased to see me, or if the old stone walls will sigh with resignation at the sight of me trudging up the front steps. **Not you again, drama queen. We were hoping for a bird-watcher or a professor.**

Reaching for my phone, I tap open a new message to Mack, heavyhearted to be the bearer of such unexpected news.

One—It's been a hell of a day for Salvation, Mack. I can't tell you how many times I've wished you were still here. I was supposed to go home today, but stuff happened and I didn't.

Two—I've some sad news to tell you. Raff died. He went to sleep and just didn't wake up. Dolores found him in

bed wearing a "Frankie Says Relax" T-shirt, which is just so bizarrely appropriate for him, isn't it? I honestly don't know how Salvation is going to cope without him.

Three—Some brighter news: Delta had her baby a couple of hours ago, a boy. I expect the stress of the day had something to do with it. She went into labor in the pub—as only she would! It's certainly been an unforgettable twenty-four hours. I'm so tired, Mack. I'm looking at Otter Lodge now from the boulder on top of the hill, and . . . well, you know how it looks. Like home. x

I press send, shuttling life and death news across the ocean. It's about half past ten at night in Boston; there's a good chance he'll be awake and see it come in. The wind here is bitterly cold tonight. My cheeks are freezing, but still I sit awhile and stargaze, mapping out the few constellations I can identify. Ursa Major. The Plow. Jupiter, as always. I'll head up to the café in the morning and contact Ali, I decide. I'm expected in the office on Monday morning and I'm obviously not going to be there. I've no clue what I'm going to say to her yet. I'll sleep on it.

My phone vibrates, letting me know a message has arrived.

One—You sound in need of someone to hold you tonight. I wish it could be me.

Two—Raff, man. Devastating. I've just poured myself a whiskey in his honor.

Three—Good for Delta, a new baby always raises spirits. A toast to the new boy too, then. To beginnings, and to inevitable ends.

Three A—And lastly, a toast to you. Be happy always, Cleo. Dance to "Thunder Road" and scatter your beautiful words across the pages. x

I read his words and then click my phone off and look out to sea. **To beginnings, and to inevitable ends.** I can't shake the feeling that I'll never hear from him again.

Cleo, November 23, Salvation Island

If found, return to Slánú

So, the boat is coming back today, out of sequence because someone actually died. My fingers itch to text Mack, but I don't, because our last texts were loaded with full-circle finality. A birth, a death, final advice. I'm not sure where you go from there.

Bruised clouds have hung over the island since Raff's death, a mournful dimming of the lights by the weather gods. Delta's baby is a spark, though. I called round to see her this morning, and between terrifying me with TMI post-birth stories and wrangling the baby into a suitable breastfeeding position aided by a pile of pillows and a printed-out diagram, she made a proposition that set all the cogs and wheels in my head awhirl in unison. I held the baby and listened to what Delta had to say, and then I left her to head down to the café. It's closed today, but she's given me the keys to let myself in.

Coffee in hand, I fire up the computer and wait for it to connect. I already texted Ali over the weekend to let her know about the emergency change to my plans, so she knows enough to understand why I'm not back at my desk in London this morning. She also knows the boat is coming back this lunchtime, weather permitting, so I should be in the office by Wednesday. Barney Doyle is over on the mainland waiting to come across, and special supplies have been ordered in for Raff's funeral next week. Barney Doyle, owner of Otter Lodge, Mack's mystery relative. I'm harboring unreasonable resentfulness toward Barney; I hope he loves the lodge enough. I feel as protective toward it as it has been of me. I dithered over leaving him a note this morning with instructions about how to light the temperamental stove and the special knack to closing the kitchen window so it doesn't rattle in the wind. I didn't, of course. It's his place, I'm sure he knows its foibles.

My stomach flips as I wait for Ali to appear on the screen, the ringing tone amplified in the silent café. My bags are ready to go, but I am not.

"Come in, my roving reporter, are you receiving me? Is this thing on?" She taps on the screen as she looms in close to the webcam.

I grin and take a sip of coffee. "It's good to see you too," I say.

"So much hair," she says, making big air motions around my face with her hands. "Spa day on the cards asap, you've earned it, girl. The wedding ceremony column has lit up social media. Those photos, just wow." She crosses her hands over her heart and nods, priestlike.

Sometimes it's best to just come out with things, to say what you need to say quick and fast before you can back down. This, I know, is one of those sometimes.

"Ali, I want to resign with immediate effect. I'm working on one last piece, and then it has to be over."

She blinks, craning her immaculately made-up face toward the screen, her hands still over her heart. "You can't resign. Put your red pom-pom hat on and get back here, we need you."

"Ali, I'd really like to get this off my chest in one go."

"Cleo," she says, but stops when I shake my head.

"Please?" I say. "The last thing I'd ever want to do is leave you in the lurch after you took a chance on me. You've done more for me than you could possibly know, and I'm forever grateful." I pause. "You saw that I needed some time out, so you sent me here on this mission almost against my will, and I'm so glad, Ali, because it's been absolutely life changing. Cataclysmic. I've fallen in love with Salvation Island, and with a man, and then with myself, in that order. I don't care if I'm having a bad hair day, Ali." Of all the things I've just said, I know that last bit will land. "I've been writing like I'm possessed, words spilling out, and if I come back to London now that will stop. I'm not asking you for more time off. I know you need a bum in my seat. But it won't be my bum. My place is here for a while yet. The boat is coming today and I'm not getting on it. If I do, I'll lose the impetus—being here is an essential part of the magic equation." I stop speaking, breathless.

"You fell in love with him?" she says. "You found your flamingo?" For a cynical business-woman, she's just swooned like a teenager in her bedroom.

"Oh, Ali," I say. "Yes, I fell in love with him, and no, he's not my flamingo. This isn't really about him, it's about me. I mean, he's part of the story, of course he is. We had this major micro–love affair, and a man like that takes some getting over," I explain, stealing Ailsa's line about Mack. "And I don't really want to get over him anyway. I've internalized all the brilliance of us and now it's part of me. I don't have him, but I don't regret him."

She sucks down a sharp intake of air. "Fucking hell, Cleo, behave. You sound like you're reciting lines from a Hollywood rom-com."

"I feel as if I **am** living my own movie," I say. "I don't know if it's a rom-com, though. More one of those finding-yourself dramas."

"Can we get Emma Watson to play you?"

"Hell yes." I grin. "That girl knows how to rock a bad hair day."

Ali falls silent, and serious. "You're really not coming back?"

I shake my head. "No."

"We can't keep paying you, you know that, right?"

"I know," I say. "I'll be okay for a while."

She narrows her eyes at me. "You better dedicate that fucking book to me."

And then in true Ali style, she blows me a kiss and slams her laptop shut. No lingering goodbyes for that woman. She'd get on well with the seabirds at the lodge.

I sit in the quiet of the closed-up café, con-templative. Delta made me an offer I couldn't refuse this morning. Raff owned this café and the pub too. Both places now belong to Dolores, who in turn has handed them straight to her daughter—Delta laughingly said it was to make sure she'd stick around, and there's probably some truth in that. Closer to the truth, though, is that she was never planning to leave anyway, and this small new property portfolio has set her up for the future.

"Stay at the pub," she said. "The flat up there is empty now. Raff's staff are going to manage the place between them, but I could really use some help in the café, just a few hours a day. My hands are kind of full of this baby."

I look around the simple whitewashed café, remembering back to the first day I came in here. I loved how the light streamed in through the stained-glass art on the window, casting rainbows across the stripped wooden floor, the radio in the background. It only opens from eleven till two in these darkest months, but it should be just enough of an income if I'm frugal. I don't need much, especially here. So I'm staying awhile. The relief of not having to leave feels as if someone has taken their hands off my shoulders. I turn back to the computer, not looking forward to telling Mum I won't be home for Christmas after all.

Barney isn't at all like his distant relative; he's whippet-wiry with a mop of white-blond curls, a perpetual traveler's tan, and wooden beads around his tattooed wrist. He trudged into the pub just now, dragging his battered rucksack behind him with one hand, his other arm bandaged against his chest.

"Shark bite," he says, grinning as he pulls up a stool at the bar beside Delta. "I remember you. Wicked Witch in **The Wizard of Oz**, school production, mid-nineties."

She moves the sleeping baby from one arm to the other. "I remember you too. Glinda the Good Witch."

He shrugs his good shoulder. "There were no little blond girls, what can I say?" He downs a good third of the Guinness I've poured him. "I heard about old Raff over on the mainland."

Delta sighs and raises her glass—tonic in a G&T glass—to the photo of Raff tucked into the mirror behind the bar. I doubt a man has ever been more toasted.

"Funeral's on Thursday," she says.

"I can pull a decent pint if you need

someone behind the bar," Barney says, looking at his glass. I feel slightly put out; I know my Guinness pouring skills aren't top notch, but I'm getting there.

"With one arm?" Delta says, doubtful.

Barney slides off his stool and nips behind the bar, reaching down a glass from the overhead rack and flicking the tap with an air of confidence that only comes from experience. We watch in silence until he places the admittedly perfect pint on the bar and then bows with a small flourish of his good arm.

"Barman of the world," he says. "Santorini, Sydney, Sweden. You name it, I've probably mixed a mojito there."

"Anywhere that doesn't begin with S?" I laugh because he's infectious.

"Salvation?" he says, crossing his fingers. His pale blue-gray eyes dance with trouble; I think he'll fit right in behind this bar, if Delta sees fit.

"Not much call for mojitos round these parts," Delta says testily.

"You haven't had a mojito until you've had one of mine," he says. "Where's your mint?"

"In a jar in the fridge with all the other condiments." She's putting him through his paces, but I can hear amusement behind her dry tone.

"I'm Cleo," I say.

"She's a writer," Delta says.

"Is she now?" Barney says, looking at me. "And what do you write?"

"Um, magazine articles in London, until this morning. I just jacked my job in." His eyes widen, interested. "I was supposed to go back home on the boat you came over on, but I've decided to stay instead."

"To finish her novel," Delta adds.

"Well, that's a story I need to hear more of," Barney says. "And who's this fella?" He nods toward Delta's baby.

Her face softens as she looks down. He really is the most angelic child, peaches for cheeks and a shock of his mama's black hair.

"He doesn't have a name yet," Delta says. "He's new. Born in Raff's sitting room through there three days ago."

"And you're propping the bar up already," Barney says. "Good on ya, I like your style."

"It's my pub," she says, shades of Peggy Mitchell.

Barney contemplates the baby. "Quite the forelock he's got going on there. Call him Elvis?"

Delta breaks into a laugh. "How much would Raff love that?" she says.

"Almost as much as your mother would

hate it," I say. Delta's already told me she's most likely going to call him Rafferty; it seems only right.

"Oh," I say, digging in my pocket reluctantly. "The key to your lodge."

"You've been staying there?"

"For the last couple of months." I nod, putting the key on the bar. "I love it, you're very lucky."

He rubs his chin, thinking. "Crossed wires? You stayed there with my cousin, right? I heard bits of the story from my sister."

"Something like that," I say.

"Do you know Mack well?" Delta asks. I frown; she knows perfectly well that Barney and Mack are pretty much strangers.

Barney shakes his head, oblivious. "Not at all, really."

"You're nothing alike," she says. "He's a lot like Han Solo, and you're more like the wimpy one. Luke Skywalker."

"You're really holding this blond thing against me, aren't you?" he says.

She puts the baby on her shoulder. "I'm suspicious of newcomers, what can I say?"

"Ah, but I'm not a newcomer, now, am I?" he says. "Look, I'll prove my allegiance."

He drags his T-shirt up the unbroken side of his body to show us a faded tattoo on his chest, a postage stamp with IF FOUND, RETURN TO SLÁNÚ written across it.

Delta looks at it, assessing, and then at him. "How are you going to cope over at Otter Lodge on your own with one arm?" she says.

"Badly," he says, and laughs.

"You can stay here if you like, seeing as you're going to be working behind the bar. The flat upstairs is empty."

I stare at her. "I thought I was moving in here?"

The baby grumbles when she shrugs. "You were, but wouldn't it be easier for you to stay at the lodge and Barney to stay here?"

I look at Barney, and he looks at me.

"If it suits you, it suits me," he says easily. "I'm more of a middle-of-the-action guy anyway."

We all take a moment to look around the empty pub.

"But the flat was part of my payment," I say quietly to Delta, a little embarrassed. "I can't afford to rent Otter Lodge."

Barney speaks before Delta can. "Hey, it's cool," he says, pushing the key back toward me. "You stay there, I'll stay here, same plan. It'll save me having to get over that infernal hill, and I'll be able to roll downstairs to work. Win-win."

Otter Lodge keeps coming back to me like a lucky talisman.

"Thank you," I say.

I catch Delta's eye, and she just raises her eyebrows at me in a **well, I sorted that one, didn't I?** way. She's a funny one. On the surface she's devil-may-care, but in the space of one morning she's just employed two people and organized their living arrangements, all with a newborn snoozing in her arms.

"Was it really a shark bite?" She nods toward Barney's shoulder.

He puts his head to one side, and for a second they stare at each other, two wanderers who've both felt the pull of home.

"A great white. I was surfing off the east coast of Australia."

Delta huffs, grudgingly impressed. It's fanciful, but I imagine Raff standing beside me, watching this encounter and rubbing his hands together with glee.

Mack, December 23, Boston

Let her be

This is the shot to lead with," Phil Henderson says, decisive as always. We're upstairs in the Henderson Gallery, the place he owns and where I've shown my work for the last few years, where I'll display the Salvation exhibition in February. Older than me by a couple of decades, he's a sharp businessman and something close to a friend.

He twists his monitor on the desk so I can see the photograph he's enlarged on the screen. Raff stares back at me, fedora at a sharp angle, his silver hip flask raised to the camera. I came across him sitting on the seawall one afternoon, having a shot of whiskey while he waited for the supply boat to get to shore.

"Why this one?"

Phil throws his hands up. "People automatically expect a place like that to be cold and inhospitable. Unlivable. This guy makes it look like the coolest place in the world."

I can't argue with that. Salvation is an almost invisible mark on a map, but it's left an indelible imprint on me.

There's a package waiting for me when I get back to the condo, battered brown paper wrapping and airmail stickers that track its journey across the globe. I recognize Cleo's handwriting straightaway from her rules list on the fridge—I brought it home with me tucked inside the pages of a book. Placing the parcel on the table, I make coffee and load the dishwasher, side-eyeing it every now and then.

Did I leave something behind that she's sent back? She hasn't mentioned anything in our texts, but then they aren't that kind of day-to-day conversation. They're more . . . I don't even know how to put it. More abstract. She tells me things about herself. That she had her one and only fight at thirteen with a girl who insulted her brother, and I tell her that as a teenager I sometimes wore one brown contact lens to make my eyes match. It's cathartic for both of us, I think, a silvered arc of connection from Salvation to my condo.

I don't regret it. I don't. But now that I'm here in the reality of my Boston life, I know it isn't fair of me to use her as a crutch every time I feel low. I'm a father, first and foremost. I'm in the middle of a messy separation, and I know my judgment is sometimes clouded by resentment and old hang-ups. I don't know how to do the right thing by the boys and be happy myself too. If it's their happiness or mine, they'll always win. I watched Cleo bloom like a sunflower turning its face toward the light. And then she turned to me and asked me to turn with her, and for a while I did. We did. It was dazzling, a true privilege, and then it ended, and I was left feeling like you do when you step off a breakneck roller coaster and your legs turn to spaghetti. Her too, I expect, so it's only natural that we're finding the connection hard to sever.

My eyes come to rest on the parcel in front of me. I'm going to open it now, because it feels like a ticking bomb. There's a layer of white tissue paper inside the brown paper with a note pinned to it.

I heard your weather tower is flashing red. C x

I rip the tissue and find a battleship-gray knitted scarf. **Oh, Cleo,** I think, holding it in my hands. It's chunky and uneven, a little wider in places than others, as if the person who made it wasn't 100 percent sure what she was doing. There's snow in the Christmas forecast here in Boston. Is Cleo heading back to London soon? Will she be sucked back into the vortex of her old city life? I look across the room at my cellphone and then at the scarf, and I sigh and hold my head in my hands. **Let her be, Mack. Just let the woman be.**

Mack, December 24, Boston

Everyone has seen **Gremlins**

D ad!"
Leo shoots outside when I pull into the drive.

"Be careful on the ice," I say, kissing the top of his head. "You don't want to go down on that ankle again."

There's been a blast of suitably festive arctic weather this week, constant mutterings of potential snow. I push my chin into the gray scarf around my neck as I grab my duffel from the back seat. Susie has invited me to spend tonight at home rather than juggle the boys between two places, which is a relief on many fronts. I don't want to wake up on Christmas morning alone at the condo, and I definitely don't want the boys to have to spend even a second of it there either. I haven't bothered with any decorations there because it would be like pimping a jail cell. Mom asked me to join the friends and family who fill her home every year, but that would have meant not seeing the boys, which is a dangerous precedent I'm not prepared to set. It was difficult enough not being with them for Thanksgiving. Mom did her best to paper over the cracks, of course, turkey and all the trimmings, and it was a real moment to share my photographs of the island with my gran. We took our time, the three of us poring over the images and our memories around the table. I managed to hunt down some Irish folk music on my phone too, worth the effort when Gran closed her eyes to listen, a faraway smile lifting the corners of her lips. I love them for their efforts, but the holidays are for kids and I need to be with mine, so here I am, about to spend the first night under my own Christmas-lit roof in almost a year. We may have gone small on Halloween this fall, but I came over a couple weeks ago to help Susie make sure we made up for it by going all out on holiday decorations. It's a competitive kind of neighborhood when it comes to decking the halls, but we're more than holding our own. White lights pick out the roofline, and candy cane garlands wrap around the porch pillars. Light nets throw diamond dust over the shrubbery, and a family of glittering reindeer frolic on the lawn. There's a fir tree up on the porch too, with lights and bells that turn the chill wind into music. It's walking the fine line between enough and too much, an extra bit of effort to ensure the boys don't feel deprived. I'm dully aware that all the lights in Boston can't make up for having their family back together, but we're doing our best and that has to count for something.

"Hey." Susie appears at the doorway as Leo dashes back inside to tell Nate I've arrived, a huge fresh Christmas wreath in her hands. Silver ornaments on her sweater, lipstick as red as the candy cane garlands around the porch.

"I don't know which is more festive, you or the house." I smile. She's let her hair grow long enough to wear it in a ponytail, and I feel a lump in my throat when she turns around to hang the wreath, because she reminds me of the cute college student I fell hard for. I watch her for a long second, clearing my throat as I pull myself together.

"Here, let me do that," I say, because she's struggling to get it on the hook.

I lift the mistletoe wreath from her and hang it carefully on the hook I banged in a few years ago. Susie and I stand alongside each other and survey the wide, picture-perfect fire-engine-red front door. A solid family home. A family together for the holidays.

"I'm glad you're here," she says.

I look down at her. "Me too."

The kids are in bed, the gifts are wrapped beneath the tree, and Susie and I are at either end of the couch with an empty bottle of red between us on the coffee table. It's been a bittersweet kind of day: food prep for tomorrow's lunch with a soundtrack of nostalgic Christmas music, a movie in the den before bed with the kids in new Christmas pj's, bowls of popcorn balanced on our knees. It's as if we've made a silent agreement to sweep the fact that we're separated under the table. The boys' eyes were overbright and their voices unnaturally pitched around the dinner table earlier, hope painfully high as their watchful eyes flicked constantly between us. Is this the wrong thing to do? Are we setting them up for post-Christmas heartache? God, I hope not. I'm already dreading leaving them again tomorrow evening when Walt and Marie arrive for a few days. Back to the condo of doom. I've made myself a Christmas promise: whatever else happens, that place has to go.

"I've seen this movie a million times," Susie says, stretching.

"Everyone has seen **Gremlins** a million times," I say. "That's kind of its charm."

Onscreen, the evil gremlin ringleader is locked in a deadly kitchen battle with the mother of the house.

"You know what? I think we watched this on our first Christmas Eve in this house," she says.

I remember. "We had that hand-me-down TV with the line down the center of the screen and couldn't afford to replace it." We'd spent every dollar we could scrape together on the down payment for the house.

She smiles, looking down into her wineglass. "It was worth the stretch to buy this place."

"No arguments there," I say. "This is a great house for the boys to grow up in."

She nods, thoughtful. "They miss you."

"I miss them too," I say. "Every day."

"I know you do." She sighs, bending forward to slide her glass onto the table. Her sweater rides up, revealing the familiar small brown birthmark at the base of her spine. I swallow a mouthful of wine and look away.

"I got you something," she says, pulling a gift-wrapped box from behind a cushion.

"Susie, I didn't—"

"It's nothing big," she says quickly, scooting closer to hand it to me.

I haven't bought Susie a gift. Not because I didn't consider it, but I just couldn't get my head around the gift-buying etiquette for your ex who's currently dating her boss. There's no handbook for that, is there? Robert has a pronounced gray streak in his hair; it's an effort not to compare him to the gremlin currently tearing things up on the TV.

I put my glass down and accept Susie's gift. "Thank you."

I open it: it's a photograph in a black frame. I look at it for a few quiet seconds, and then I look back at Susie.

"One of my favorite days ever," she says.

Taken the summer before last, it's a black-and-white shot of the four of us by the lake. Walt took it one warm evening; I remember the day so vividly I can almost smell the BBQ and feel the burn of the old rope swing on my palms. Nate is gangly on my hip, his head dropped on my shoulder. Leo's arms are wrapped around Susie's waist beside me. We're all laughing at some off-screen joke.

"We used to laugh like that a lot," I say, remembering.

When I look at her again, fat tears gather in

her eyes. "I don't know how to not love you, Mack," she says.

I've sensed a thaw in Susie in recent weeks: invitations to stay for coffee when I come over to collect the boys, an occasional hand on my shoulder, a fresh batch of lemon cookies she knows I like. It's more than gestures too—her gaze holds mine over the kids' heads sometimes, reminding me of times when that lingering look told me she couldn't wait to be alone later.

I don't know what it all means, whether it marks a step toward friendship, or if hearing about Cleo came as a jolt to her.

"Hey." I put my arm around her shoulders. "Don't. You can't cry on Christmas Eve, it's against the rules."

She crumples into me, snaking her arm across my body. I lower my head—her hair smells of the same shampoo that the boys use—and for a few minutes we stay that way, Susie's shoulders heaving.

"I don't want to not love you either." I smooth my hand down the slippery silk of her hair and press a kiss against the top of her head. "It's okay for us to still love each other."

She inches back and lifts her face, tear-spiked lashes around her cornflower-blue eyes.

"I don't think I can love Robert, not enough, anyway." I can feel the warmth of her breath on my lips, see the pain in her eyes. "Do you love her, Mack? Is it the same?"

The shake in her voice breaks me. "Of course it's not the same," I say gently. "Suze, we've spent years building our love. Our home, our kids. Nothing will ever be the same as that."

"It scares me that I don't think I'll ever love anyone else as much as you."

I've laid awake countless nights and burned for Susie to want me back. Our lives have been entwined every day since I was eighteen years old. She raises her head to mine now, our lips touch, still, tender, and I close my eyes and see a kaleidoscope of us. Our first tremulous kiss against her parents' back wall. Our wedding day kiss, the promise of forever on our lips. The relieved press of my mouth to her exhausted one after the safe arrival of our first son. And a million other kisses in between, some lustful, others needful, each one a new sentence in the story. She's been my love for almost half of my life, but we've never shared a kiss this meaningful, or sorrowful. I ease back and look into her eyes.

"I know you're going to think it's just

nostalgia and wine and the holidays talking, but it isn't. I'm so sorry for what I did to you, Mack. To us."

"Susie," I whisper in the warmth of our familiar living room on the comfort of our familiar couch. Everything about this situation is right. I'm home again, and it's Christmas Eve. The tree lights glow in the corner, and on TV something unbelievably sweet unexpectedly morphs into something so vicious it could rip your heart out.

Cleo, December 31, Salvation Island

I haven't missed London at all

You made it," Delta says, when I push through the door of The Salvation Arms at lunchtime.

"It's so cold, I can't feel my face," I say, stamping my feet as I unwind my scarf and hang my coat on the stand.

Carmen looks over at me from her armchair by the fireplace and raises her hand, queenlike, to get my attention. "I'll knit you a balaclava for coming over that hill," she says. "My wool—"

"Is famously the warmest on the island," I say, and then laugh because both Delta and Erin said it with me. It's pretty busy in the pub this afternoon; it looks as if I'm not the only one who fancied some last-day-of-the-year company. There's a fire in the hearth and a sense of camaraderie among the islanders, more a family get-together than a pub. But then I guess that's kind of what this is—the community here come together as an extended family, no one a stranger for long on Salvation. I'm easily the newest person on the island, not counting Barney because he grew up here, and everyone knows my name and my business, thanks in most part to Delta. People regularly ask me how the book's coming on—I think I might just put a blackboard out on the porch at Otter Lodge and update it with my daily word count. Not that people would see it; I rarely get visitors over there now that the weather has turned so cold. I honestly don't mind; the solitude suits my mood just now. I open the café for a few hours on weekdays, and that's enough social interaction to make me brush my hair. Monday to Friday, at least.

"Old Cuban, madam? It's similar to a mojito, only better." Barney is so at home behind the bar it feels like he's always been there. Everyone misses Raff terribly, of course, but it's almost as if the universe knew he was going to be taken from us and convinced a passing shark to sink its teeth into the effervescent Barney Doyle.

"Don't mind if I do," I say. "Although you

should know I've propped up many of London's finest cocktail bars, so I'm judgy."

Barney lifts his eyebrows, enjoying the challenge. He's completely ignored Delta's reticence and is slowly but surely educating the residents of Salvation on the delights of a good Tom Collins and the iconic cosmopolitan. I don't think any of us are likely to forget Dolores releasing her inner Barbra Streisand after a couple of gimlets on Christmas Eve. She isn't embarrassed because she can't remember, and none of us have the balls to remind her.

I watch Barney in his element behind the bar, making it look effortless in a Breton T-shirt with the baby strapped to his front in a papoose. "We're having some boy time, aren't we, Elvis?" He hands me my drink, rubbing the baby's foot with his other hand.

Delta rolls her eyes. "I'm just glad of someone else taking him for a while," she says. "He spends ninety percent of his life with his face shoved in my bloody boobs."

I glance down laughing, because the unguarded look on Barney's face suggests he thinks baby Raff is one lucky kid on that score. Or Rafferty Elvis, as Delta has officially called him, a nod to her uncle and a shock for her mother rolled into one.

"Not bad," I say, sipping the Old Cuban.

"World class," Barney corrects me. I don't admit it, but he's right. He could give Tom Cruise a run for his money.

Delta touches the rim of her glass against mine. "To you, Cleo," she says. "I feel as if you've lived here forever. Never leave me."

"And to you," I say, swallowing back tears out of nowhere, because she's my kindred spirit and coolest friend, the reason I was brave enough to stay.

She taps the claddagh ring on my right hand. "It's good to see Aunt Bernadette's ring get a fresh airing," she says. "She was the island's original wild child. Pure crazy, she was. I used to nag my ma something rotten to be more like her when I was a kid, more adventurous." She laughs softly. "I stuck her postcards from exotic places around the rim of my bedroom mirror, determined to follow in her footsteps as soon as I was old enough to escape this place." She glances across the bar toward Barney and her sleeping son. "I guess I've finally grown up and realized what matters."

"You should tell your mum that," I say, knowing Dolores would love to hear it.

Delta barks out a sharp laugh. "You're kidding me, right? Those words will never pass my lips to my mother's ears!"

I hide my smile in my glass. Delta has her aunt's thirst for adventure, Raff's loyal streak, and a good dose of her mother's iron will. I look across the bar as the baby starts to cry and wonder what kind of child he'll grow into, if he'll give his mum much trouble as he grows. Probably, if he's half as spirited as Delta.

The door opens and Brianne comes in, a flurry of fur and sheepskin boots, followed by Cameron, who has to duck his head under the doorframe. She makes a beeline for me as soon as she's hung her coat.

"I've something for you," she says quietly, so no one overhears. "A **package**." She leans in so close she's practically kissing my ear. "From America."

She slips it from her pocket into my hands as if it's class A drugs. It's about the size of a chunky letter, an inch or two deep. Okay. I know only one person in America.

"Thanks," I say, my eyes lingering on it, wondering what's inside. Mack and I haven't been in touch since before Christmas. I sat for a while on Wailing Hill on Christmas Eve in case he was lonely and got in touch, but nothing. I wonder if he sat alone and waited to see if I would make contact too, or if he's making a good fist of putting us behind him. Maybe he felt obliged to send me something because I sent the scarf. I hope not. I'm glad Brianne had the sensitivity to go low-key; I know Delta would be gagging to know what's inside. I am too, in all honesty. I have another Old Cuban and a hold of the baby, but all the time my hand keeps sliding back to touch the package I've shoved into my bag. Did he take something of mine back to Boston by mistake? I haven't missed anything, except for the sliver of my heart. I have a little rum-induced laugh to myself at the idea of opening the gift to find a pulsing piece of flesh inside it.

"God, these cocktails are strong," I say, finishing my second.

Delta sighs into her cup of tea. "I wouldn't know."

"At least you won't have a headache in the morning."

"Yes, I will, from lack of sleep. And sore boobs and a butchered lady garden."

I hug her, patting her back. "You wouldn't have it any other way."

She rolls her eyes, because I'm right. She may be battling the physical effects of being a new mum, but she's head over heels in love with the Elvis-haired child.

"Time for me to go home," I say. "I need to get back over the hill before dark."

She squeezes me hard. "Happy New Year, Clee," she says. "I'm so glad you stayed."

"Thank God I can knit," I say. "Your mother wouldn't have let me otherwise."

"Don't big yourself up too much there now," she says. "I saw that scarf, remember."

We laugh, and I kiss and **happy New Year** hug my way slowly out of the busy pub, shrugging into my coat, meeting Brianne's eyes last. She gives me the briefest of nods, her job done.

"Hello, beautiful lodge," I say, pleased to see the glow of the fire still alive in the hearth. I've a Christmas tree too; Ailsa and Julia lugged it over the hill as a surprise a couple of days before Christmas, along with a box they'd put on the bar in The Salvation Arms for people to donate a decoration or so. I cried, of course. Being decent human beings seems to come easy to these islanders. Dolores sent a spare string of lights, and Carmen wrapped a vintage silver star in newspaper to go on the top.

I haven't missed London at all. The idea of rammed shopping streets and packed bars does nothing for me these days. I missed seeing my family over Christmas, my mum especially, but on the whole it's cathartic spending my days and nights alone here.

I make coffee, standing at the kitchen sink to watch the beach as I wait for the kettle to boil. I add a slosh of New Year's Eve whiskey to my coffee and take it to the sofa with my squares blanket and the brown paper package from America.

I haven't moved a muscle for the last hour. My coffee has gone cold and my face is damp with tears. Mack has sent me an album of our time together, an intimate record of us. The table set for breakfast for two, a jar of wildflowers beside the milk jug. Empty whiskey glasses on the coffee table by the dwindling fire. Our boots lined up beside the door. The infamous chalk line, his bag on one side, my suitcase on the other. The roofline of the porch picked out by borrowed vintage rainbow bulbs on my birthday. My white dress hung ready to wear. And me. Image after image of me, some of them too personal to ever show anyone else. On the porch steps with a blanket wrapped around my shoulders, coffee cradled between my hands. A black-and-white shot of me sitting up naked in bed, the sheet around my hips. I don't think of myself as beautiful, but he's made me beautiful in these photos. I linger over them all, taking the time to remember the circumstances of each one, the things we said to each other. He turned his lens on me so often I grew used to it, unselfconscious. I knew, probably, that I'd get to see the pictures one day, that I'd look back and remember him, remember us. It's the most precious gift anyone has ever given me.

There are only two pictures of us together. Mack turned his lens toward us once in bed, his arm outstretched. My head is resting on his shoulder, the white sheet tucked under my armpit, his fingers curved around my upper arm. In one shot we're both looking directly into the lens, sex drenched, and in the other my eyes are closed, his head turned away to press a kiss against my forehead. Love drenched. I put the album back in its padded envelope. I don't know when I'll ever feel able to look at it again.

There's an invitation tucked into the back to his exhibition at the end of February. I trace the bold black letters of his name slowly with my fingertip, thinking.

It's five minutes to midnight on the last day of what has turned out to be the defining year of my life. I'm sitting on the boulder at the top of Wailing Hill, layered up because it's freezing, a hip flask of whiskey in my pocket, but I wouldn't want to be anywhere else in the world. I've come to sit up here with my thoughts, to let the year that's gone by blow away on the wind and catch the scent of the new one as it arrives from the east.

I whisper hello to Jupiter, wondering if Mack can see it too. He's been heavy on my mind this afternoon. Looking through those photographs has brought him so near I can almost see the outline of him walking along the shoreline, his camera loose around his neck.

"You know what?" I speak out loud, because I'm someone who talks to Jupiter now, clearly. "It's okay. It's okay to say it. I loved Mack Sullivan in the most sudden, spectacular, sexual, spiritual, protective, primal way imaginable, and for a little while he loved me back in all the same ways. It was proper human magic."

I take a slug of whiskey, shuddering as it goes down.

"Oh, I know what this island does," I say, conversational in that way whiskey makes you. "I'm onto it. Salvation has its own force field, spinning people in from across the globe to this tiny spit of rock at will. Barney came because Raff left. I arrived on the very same boat as Mack. I mean, come on! What are the odds of **that**?" I sip again from the hip flask, shaking my head. "It's the universe meddling on a grand scale. Audacious." I fall silent, thinking about the unexpected life I've found myself living here as I watch the rise and fall of the sea. One minute to midnight.

It occurs to me that I could end up living on this island forever. I'll be Carmen to Delta's Dolores. It's not the worst scenario I can imagine for myself. I mean, I probably won't, but I'm happy here for now, which is big news. My mum's coming over for a few days in February; I'm hoping a few other visitors might make the journey at some point too. It's an intentionally short-term plan; I'll stay until spring and then see. How freeing, really, to not feel as if I'm striving for the next thing.

I check the time on my phone, and as I stare at the screen it clicks over to midnight. London will be a riot of drunken kisses, the sky a blitz of fireworks. Here, nothing happens. It's just me, Jupiter, and the sea, and I'm okay with that. I don't want to be my own flamingo forever because I kind of liked loving someone else, but I'm content to be my own best friend and staunchest cheerleader for now. I'm my own temporary flamingo. I bump shoulders with the imaginary Emma Watson sitting beside me; I think she'd be proud of how far I've come. Out on the horizon, moonlight picks out the billowing ghost sails of the **Pioneer**.

"Happy New Year!" I didn't plan on shouting, but my words come out at volume when I stand up and raise my arms, flask in one hand, phone in the other. "Here's to you, Salvation, you've made a woman of me!" I thought I might cry nostalgic tears tonight, but I laugh at my keen sense of the melodramatic instead.

Sliding the flask into my coat pocket, I click open a message to Mack.

> **One—The photo album arrived today. Thank you! It made me cry, it's so beautiful. I'm incredibly proud of you. Good luck with the exhibition.**
>
> **Two—Happy New Year! I mean it. Do whatever it takes to be happy, Mack, you deserve it.**
>
> **Three. x**

I don't type that I don't regret him, because sometimes I do. He's set the bar unrealistically high, and I need to believe there are other people out there who can reach it. Maybe in time the universe will cast its love net wide for me again, bring a forever love my way, but I can't see how yet. It set the bar too high the first time around.

I push my phone into my pocket and head down toward the welcome lights of Otter Lodge. A brand-spanking-new year. Anticipation rather than fear bubbles behind my rib cage for what lies in the unshaped months ahead. The **Pioneer** won't sail without me, because I am the pioneer.

Mack, January 17, Boston

I am their forest

"Make a wish, Leo," Susie says, the huge birthday cake ablaze in her hands. Thirteen candles. The world has a brand-new teenager. How the hell do I have a teenage son? I think back to my own teen years and feel a very real fear. I was pretty rebellious back then, hard work for my mom, I realize now. Will Leo constantly push the boundaries too? Maybe, maybe not. He has a lot more people around him to lean on than I did.

"Might be easier if you take the mask off, kid," I say. He's pretty darn pleased with his new baseball gear and couldn't wait to take photos of himself head to toe in the latest Sox uniform and catcher's equipment.

"I can blow between the bars," he says with

a laugh, his chest heaving as he sucks down a deep breath and blasts out the candles in one go.

"Good job," Susie says, placing the cake down on the table as Leo heads off to grab a knife.

"Think he's planning to eat between the bars too?" I say.

"You know it," Susie says, removing the chocolate-encrusted candles from the cake.

"Mom, Dad!" Nate skids across to the window, warp speed as usual. "Grandpa's here!"

Susie glances at me and frowns. Her parents are up in Maine visiting Marie's sister. I shrug, assuming Nate's mistaken, when the doorbell rings. I glance out the window as I get up, but I don't recognize the slick black SUV on the street outside.

"I'll get it," I say, a bad feeling grumbling low in my gut as Nate bounces around me along the hallway. I swing the door wide, braced for the chill wind and bad news.

"Hello, son."

My father, unannounced as usual. "Dad. This is a surprise."

He adjusts his scarf. "In the area on business. Thought I'd drop over and say happy birthday to this guy." He's all smiles and humor as he cuffs Nate's shoulder.

"Wrong kid," I say.

"Just testing." Dad laughs, shrugging his mistake away.

"There's cake," Nate says. "Leo's eating it with his catcher's mask on."

"This I need to see." Dad grins, stepping in from the cold. I hold in my sigh as I move aside to grant him access, hating that I don't feel as if I have any option.

"Susie," he says in that convivial **long time no see** voice he's so good at as he unbuttons his long wool coat and unwinds his scarf. Always a sharp dresser, my father, with an eye for a well-cut suit and the ladies, my mother once said.

"Alvin," Susie says, her smile guarded as her eyes flick over his shoulder toward me. I shrug, nonplussed. "You're just in time for cake."

I watch him as he laughs and charms the boys, a card with money for Leo, a bill from his wallet for Nate's piggy bank. They sit on either side of him, pale against his West Coast tan, basking in his praise.

"The Red Sox, huh?" he says, nodding at Leo's uniform. "My team. You're a chip off the old block, kid."

"Me too, Grandpa," Nate says, lifting his sweater to show my father his favorite Sox

T-shirt. I watch them tumble over themselves to impress him, and it's all I can do not to shove him back into his expensive coat and send him on his way. My kids don't need to try to impress him.

"You guys should all come out to California in the summer," he says, as the boys barrel out of the room at the sight of the neighbors' kids in the street. "They would love the beaches."

"We have beaches," I say.

Susie looks as if her face is aching from fake smiling her way through the last half hour. It speaks volumes about how little my father's in touch that he doesn't know about our marital problems, and volumes about my relationship with him that I've tried to skip over it since he walked in the door.

"More cake?" Susie says, clearing the table.

Dad puts his hand up, a hard no. "More than enough sugar for one day."

He's like that. Has a pious way of making himself seem virtuous at the cost of the people around him. Susie takes the cake back to the kitchen, probably questioning if she'd been a little heavy-handed with the chocolate frosting.

"How's work, son?"

I nod, tell him the bare bones about the

upcoming Salvation exhibition. He narrows his eyes at the mention of the island and then laughs, too long and too loud.

"That the place even exists is news to me," he says, shaking his head. "The way your mom used to talk about it, dragons and pirates and all that kids' stuff." He's amused, enjoying himself. "Tell me, did you find treasure, Captain Mack?"

It's enough. The jovial tone, the ever so slightly superior note. This may not be my home anymore, but it is my house and he's leaving. I pick up his coat and hand it to him.

"I'm just seeing Dad out to his car," I call to Susie.

She pops her head around from the kitchen. "Bye, Alvin. Thanks for dropping by."

My father looks at me for a silent, assessing beat before slowly getting up and following me down the hallway. I don't look back until we're beside his car on the sidewalk.

"Did I do something wrong?" he says, and one could be forgiven for thinking he's clueless. The hint of challenge in his eyes says differently, though.

I look at him, trying to decide if it's worth the effort.

"Today, or for the last twenty-five years?"

His eye roll is so subtle you could easily

miss it, but I didn't. "Come on, Mack, you're a man now, and a father. You know it's no bed of roses."

No bed of roses. His words hammer home how differently we view the role of a father. His permanent sneer is making my fist itch.

"Being a father isn't supposed to be a bed of roses," I say. "It's not just pretty for a while and then disposable when it's useless to you. It's a forest, constantly changing, growing, evolving. It's shelter and roots and branches to climb and leaves to break their fall."

He doesn't come back with anything. Maybe I've gotten through, or maybe he just couldn't give a damn. Either way, this conversation ends on my terms.

"You were right earlier. My kids **are** a chip off the old block," I say. "But my block, not yours."

I watch his taillights until he's out of sight, and then I sit down heavily on the porch steps, winded. Leaning my head against the post, I close my eyes and listen to the high-pitched laughter and yells of the boys over in the neighbors' yard.

I am the canopy over their heads, the ground beneath their feet, the soft pile of leaves to land on. I am their forest. I am their home.

Cleo, February 12, Salvation Island

Kylie Minogue will look eighteen forever

My mum has commanded the high seas to allow her safe passage, and the ocean has obeyed her bidding. I watch her climb from the boat in a far more dignified style than I could ever hope to manage and stride briskly up the sands toward me, waving one arm madly over her head in greeting. I half run toward her, feeling like six-year-old me at the end of the school day, desperate to hurl myself into her reassuring arms.

"Mum," I say, rocking back and forth as I hug her tight enough to cut her circulation off.

"Well," she says, shaking sea spray from her hair when I let go. "That was a bit of a faff."

I laugh, because that's so typically my mother. When I came over on the boat, I thought I was going to die. Mum found it a bit of a faff. Tom always jokes that Mum and Emma Thompson must have been separated at birth because they have that same brisk, no-nonsense way about them that makes you feel comforted and protected and utterly sheepish simultaneously. I don't know anyone who doesn't like my mum. Except maybe the physics teacher who called my eldest sister lazy, one parents' evening, and received a public dressing down for his trouble. Mr. Jenkins aside, she's universally acknowledged as all-round marvelous.

"Come on then," she says, linking her arm through mine, making light work of her backpack. "Show me the sights."

"Sure you wouldn't rather go straight to the lodge?"

She shoots me a look under her salt-and-pepper fringe. "Plenty of time for that later."

I glance at my watch. We can walk up to the village for a while before dusk.

"G&T in the pub?" I suggest.

Her eyes light up. "Lead the way."

"Let me guess," Mum says, unbuttoning her coat. "Delta?"

"What gave it away?" Delta skims a look down at the shock of black hair on the cocooned baby in her arms. His tiny profile is peaceful in sleep, dark lashes and rosebud lips. "This guy?"

"I'd heard he was the cutest baby in all the world." Mum smiles, her eyes on the baby. "And so he is."

Barney surveys us from behind the bar. "My turn to guess now," he says, tapping his fingertips on the edge of the drip tray. "You look like a woman in need of a"—he tips his head to one side, thinking—"French 75."

Most people would be largely unfamiliar with Barney's extensive cocktail repertoire. My mother, however, is not most people.

"Heavy on the gin, easy on the lemon juice," she agrees.

Barney all but punches the air. "Naturally."

And there she goes: Delta immediately on her side, Barney sensing a cocktail ally. She's an effortless pied piper, gathering friends and fans in her wake. It feels strange seeing Mum here on Salvation, as if my two worlds have nudged against each other, overlapping just enough to allow her to cross over.

"Do you knit, Helen?" Delta asks when she brings Mum's drink across to our table beside the fire. It's quiet in here this afternoon, in the post-lunch lull.

"Badly," Mum says, which is a lie, because she knits much better than I do.

"You should bring your ma to group next week." Delta passes me the baby as she flops beside me. "I swear he gets heavier by the hour. Every day's arms day at baby gym."

"Michelle Obama's got nothing on you," I say, clinking glasses with Mum. "Barney's cocktails are the best on the island," I add, watching her take her first sip. Barney does a bad job of pretending not to watch too, and an even worse job of not hanging out to hear her verdict.

"Ooh, isn't that heavenly," Mum says, looking over her shoulder at Barney with a nod.

I'm not certain, but I think Barney Doyle, supercool barman of the world, is blushing.

"Another one to add to my list for when I can ever bloody drink again," Delta says, sighing.

"I had a glass of champagne every day when I was nursing my four," Mum says. "Doctor's orders."

Hope flares bright in Delta's green eyes. "And they turned out all right, didn't they?"

"He was delicensed a few years later, though, so don't put much stock by his advice."

"Ah, shite."

I pat Delta's leg beneath the table as Mum knocks back half of her drink and puts the glass down. "Dutch courage," she announces, and shudders. "Darling, I've got some news."

I go clammy in case it's something terrible, and Delta's hand slips into mine.

"I've got a boyfriend."

Of all the things I thought she might say, that wouldn't have even made the list. I'm so surprised I don't know what to say. Baby Raff covers for me with an impromptu fart, making Delta jump up and take him from me, laughing as she leaves us to it.

"Anthony," Mum says, uncharacteristically flustered as she supplies info I haven't asked her for. "Online, would you believe?"

"Honestly, Mum, no, I wouldn't," I say, blindsided. She doesn't have a computer and barely uses her phone. "I mean . . . how?"

"Tom set his old computer up in my spare room so I could talk to you properly, the screen on my phone is so small. I wanted your head to be life-size."

I half laugh, because this whole conversation is weird.

"Anyway, I had this message ping in from Anthony James, a boy I went to school with. Had a terrible crush on him, truth be told, everyone did. He wanted to plan a school reunion, so I offered to help."

I nod and down my drink. Barney glances at me from behind the bar, always ready to refill an empty glass. I'm grateful. This is going to take more than one gin. It isn't that I mind—I don't. It's just that she's been happy on her own forever. She's Mum. She's Gran. It's easy to forget that she's Helen too.

"And how's it going?" I ask, fumbling my way forward in the conversation. "Has the reunion happened?"

"For two, as it turned out," she says. "He's widowed too. Ten years ago."

"Right," I say, swallowing, smiling gratefully at Barney when he arrives with two French 75s.

"The others already know," Mum says. "I asked them not to tell you. I wanted to do it myself."

Nervousness clouds her gentle eyes, and I hear the yearn for approval in her voice.

"Mum, I don't mind, if that's what you're worried about," I say. "It just surprised me, that's all."

"It surprised me too," she says with a relieved laugh that verges on a girlish giggle.

I raise my glass, a toast. Some things feel as if they're set in stone, don't they? The tide will always come in, Kylie Minogue will look eighteen forever, and Mum will always be single. It jolts me to acknowledge that even things written in stone can change.

"Do you want to talk about him?"

Mum's question comes out of the blue as we sit on the steps of Otter Lodge before turning in. We haven't mentioned Mack all day; it's been a whirl of meeting, greeting, and settling in. We're stuffed with her homemade spag bol, made at home and brought over in Tupperware stashed in her bag. It wasn't the only thing either: my belated birthday coffee cake is on the counter with a couple of slices now missing. I don't have a clue how it made it safely from Mum's kitchen to Otter Lodge, but it doesn't especially surprise me. Her question, on the other hand, does. I've never talked about Mack to her as anything more than the inconvenient American.

"There's not much to say, Mum. He was here for a while, and now he isn't."

She puts her arm around me and tucks the blanket in. "What's he like?"

Oh. "He's . . ."

God, he's so many things.

"He's a brilliant photographer, and an even

more brilliant father. He's a little bit broken, and he smells like the morning sea breeze." I lean my head on her shoulder. "He loves the Red Sox and Springsteen. He has this strip of pale skin across the back of his neck where his camera strap lies." I touch my fingers to the back of my neck in the same place. "He carries a piece of chalk I gave him in his pocket and a sliver of my heart in his chest." I hold up my thumb and finger to demonstrate the small amount of space I inhabit three thousand miles away. "He takes his coffee bitter, and he can't stand on one leg for anywhere near as long as I can. His eyes are two different colors, and cheesecake would be his death row dessert." I close my eyes remembering all of our late-night lists. "And for a little while, he made me feel as if I'd swallowed stars."

Mum rubs my arm, absorbing Mack in sound bites. "Do you remember our neighbor's dog when you were little?"

I nod. "Same kind of eyes."

We sit beside each other in the quiet Salvation night.

"Not many people make you feel as if you've swallowed stars," she says eventually.

I rub my index finger over the face of my watch. "Did Dad?"

She laughs softly, remembering. "It's taken

me all these years to even go for coffee with another man, Cleo. Your father made me feel as if I'd swallowed the sun whole."

I look toward the bright glow of Jupiter. "Twenty-five years is a long time to be lonely," I say.

"It is," Mum says. "Although I didn't really have time to be lonely, not with four kids to take care of."

I can't imagine how hard it was for her in the early days. She's made of stern stuff, my mum; she's going to fit right in at knitting group.

"And Anthony?" I say. "How does he rate on the star-o-meter?"

She glances at me. "I'm not sure yet. A nibble around the edges of the moon, maybe."

I smile. "Does it really taste of cheese?"

She laughs. "Good red wine and Italian meals, so far."

Now that I'm over the shock, I'm glad to hear about Anthony's arrival on the scene. Mum deserves more than to live her life through her children and her grandchildren.

"Mack's invited me to the opening of his exhibition in a couple of weeks," I say. "In Boston."

"I saw it on the fridge," she says. "You should go."

I look at her, surprised by her directness. "You think?"

"Well, why not? You've sent your manuscript off now. The timing fits."

"It's not just about timing," I say. "His whole life is there."

"He wouldn't have sent you an invite if he didn't want you to go," she says reasonably.

"Maybe," I say. "Or maybe it was a moment of weakness he already regrets. He didn't reply to my New Year's text, but then someone has to be the one who hangs up for the last time, don't they? It's a fitting date to underscore the end. Maybe he's happy with his family again and wants us to be friends. Or perhaps he's lonely and it'd be good for him to have me around, but at what cost for me, Mum? I'm in a good place here." I splay my hands out toward the bay. "And I'm in a good place in here." I tap my fingertips against my forehead. "I've stumbled across magic here. I'm not ready to give that up on the off chance of love."

"Cloudy with a chance of love," she says. "Like the film."

"That's meatballs, Mum."

"And suddenly we're back to Anthony again." She shoots me a coquettish look I don't think I've ever seen on her before.

"I'm going to try very hard to forget you said that." I laugh, pulling a face.

"Think hard about Boston," she says. "Regrets get heavier as you get older."

I nod. I've been thinking about it on and off since the invitation arrived.

"Come on," I say. "Time we called it a night."

I stand and give her a hand up, pulling her into a hug. "I'm so glad you came," I tell her.

"I'm glad you came here too," she says.

I'm gratified she can see how much Salvation has changed me. I pick up our glasses and follow her inside, my eyes lingering on the invitation pinned to the fridge before I turn out the lamps.

Mack, February 26, Boston

Opening night

So many of my important people have made the effort to be here tonight. Susie and the boys, Walt and Marie, my mom and my gran, and my best friend, Daryl, and his wife, Charlotte. Their faces are welcome beacons in the gathered crowd, soothing my opening night anxiety.

"I'm really very proud of you today, son."

Walt shakes my hand, his other hand a reassuring weight on my shoulder. He's not a shirt-and-tie guy, but he's made the effort tonight, probably harassed into his navy sports jacket by Marie.

"Well, I had a good teacher," I say.

The glint in his eye tells me he appreciates the compliment. Things between us are mostly good, if a little awkward sometimes. I know how hard it's been for Susie's folks to navigate the breakdown of their only child's marriage; I'm grateful for their presence tonight, for the boys as much as myself. It tells them good things about the fluidity of our family, that even if the shape of things change, the bonds that hold us all together are unbreakable.

"Nate tells me you're on the move," Walt says.

I nod. "Somewhere with a yard for the boys," I say. **Somewhere that doesn't suck my soul,** I think.

"You know where I am if it needs any fixing up," he says.

"I appreciate that," I say, trying not to choke up. Walt's the guy who taught me how to hold a camera, but he's also the guy who taught me how to be a father. He's still teaching me, even now. Susie's parents know about Robert, and she's probably told them there's been someone else for me too, but they haven't taken it upon themselves to judge or offer unsolicited advice. They're just steadfast, which is just about the most valuable thing they could be when everything else is sliding around on a listing ship. Susie appears beside her father, beautiful in a simple black dress.

"Daddy, you're monopolizing the star of the show." She laughs, linking her arm through Walt's as she catches my eye and offers me a fragile smile. We've been in a strange place in our relationship since our kiss on Christmas Eve. She ended things with Robert a while ago, and I know she's disappointed about my move from the condo to somewhere more permanent. We've been out for a few family days since the new year started, trips to the movie theater and the zoo, but I can't define my feelings and I'm not sure about hers. Every decision is skewed by the boys; what's good for me isn't necessarily what's good for them, and it's a difficult puzzle to get right. And I have to get it right. My dad got it very wrong with me as a kid, and it left me feeling like a thrift-store puzzle with missing pieces.

"Mack, I think Phil's looking for you to make your speech." Susie steers Walt away, turning back to look at me over her shoulder. "Good luck." She holds her crossed fingers up and I realize she's wearing her wedding ring again. She sees me notice, and her blue eyes say things she can't voice in this packed room with her father standing beside her.

"Is everyone here?"

Phil nods. "Pretty much. Plus a couple of extras who turned up for the free drinks—always happens."

I scan the room in search of unruly dark curls and find nothing. I don't know why I thought Cleo might be here, she hasn't said she'd come. She hasn't said anything at all, in fact, since her text on New Year's. I've maintained radio silence from my end. It feels like the honorable thing to do.

Daryl stands on my other side as Phil makes the introductions. "Speech ready?"

I feel inside my pocket to double-check, even though I know it's there. I'm reminded of standing beside Daryl on other speech-worthy occasions, my wedding and his. Phil steps aside, and I step up. I thank people, running through a few essential names, and then I stumble over my words when the door opens and someone slides in at the back, their face hidden by a rain-damp umbrella. A woman. My pause makes everyone else turn to look too, a suspended-time moment until she lowers the umbrella. I clear my throat, thrown off. **It's not Cleo.** I shove my hand through my hair and take a drink of water, focusing my eyes on the speech I've written out on the piece of paper in front of me. It doesn't feel like the right words anymore, so I fold it up and slide it back inside my jacket.

"Salvation is a tiny island, an inhospitable rock off the Atlantic coast of Ireland you won't find on any tourist trail," I say. "No one goes there by accident, and that's kind of what makes it special. It's the very definition of community, and it's the land of my ancestors—my mother's family, the place my grandmother told me stories about as a child." I take a moment to acknowledge them both, seated on the side of the room: my mother, straight shouldered and proud; my grandmother, birdlike and serene. "She spoke of patchwork hills and stormy oceans, of shipwrecks and pirate treasure. I expect some of her stories were embroidered for the eager ears of a small boy, but in other ways they were entirely accurate, because I feel as if I found genuine magic there. I've tried to capture the essence of Salvation on film, and I'm incredibly proud of the images around us on the walls here tonight. But it's impossible to capture the salt tang of the clear sea air when it dries on your lips; someone exceptional compared it to drinking diamonds.

"A photo can't convey the smell that rises from the earth as you walk the hills, a unique blend of ozone and peat and history, of heather under your boots, and of soil enriched by the sweat and toil of the generations of islanders who've worked the land. I've never met people with a surer sense of who they are or a stronger sense of kinship. They embody the word **clan,** and they walk between the syllables of **brotherhood**. And **sisterhood**, of course—the women of Salvation are warriors and empresses. You might imagine that people like this would be tribal, exclusive of others; that they'd turn suspicious eyes on a stranger to their shores. But they didn't. They opened their arms wide and welcomed me in. Their music stirred me, their folklore stories even more, and man, did their whiskey fry my brain." I wait for the ripple of laughter to die down. "That guy there." I nod toward the life-size shot of Raff sitting on the seawall, his fedora dropped over one eye. "He embodied everything that's amazing about Salvation. A raconteur, a lionheart, and a family man. Loyalty runs in their blood. And in mine, and in my sons." I raise my chin, proud to be of Salvation stock. The kids preen on either side of Susie.

"My time on the island has changed who I am," I say. "I left Boston in search of my roots, and I found them among the stone crosses in the island churchyard. I discovered the pleasure of stepping off the grid, the simple joy of conversation, the satisfaction of nurturing a live fire. It's a place too small to even warrant mention on most maps, yet it's herculean in the hearts of those lucky enough to know it." I look around the room and raise my glass. "To

Salvation. Never has a place been more aptly named."

"Am I exceptional?" Susie asks, leaning her back against the wall with an almost empty wineglass in her hand. Walt and Marie have taken the kids home with them for a sleepover, and I've just seen my mom and grandmother safely into a cab. The gallery is empty now besides a few stragglers hoping for a last free drink.

I swallow. "You're an exceptional mom."

I regret not being more generous with my words as she rapidly blinks away the sting, pushing herself straight to walk slowly among my images. I watch her pause to study Raff, then move along until she is standing in front of a black-and-white landscape shot of Otter Lodge. Cleo is sitting on the porch steps, coffee in her hands, the beginnings of a smile lifting her mouth. I've purposely not included many pictures of her, just this one and an accompanying shot taken the night she stumbled into the ocean. I shot it as she clowned around on the shoreline, shells gathered in the hem of her sweater, an expression of unguarded joy and daring as she laughed at the lens. I look at it now, at her eyes on mine, and I realize, belatedly, it's a snapshot of the exact moment I fell a little in love. Susie looks at it in silence, her back to me so I can't read her expression. We haven't talked about Cleo again since I told her that it was over. We haven't talked about much of anything, in truth, but it isn't fair on either of us to stay in this holding pattern.

"I can see it in her eyes," she says quietly. "The way she looks at you."

I swallow. "I didn't include them to hurt you."

"We've hurt each other." She turns to me, forlorn. "I pushed you away, but I didn't expect you to go so far that I'd lose you forever."

"I'm here now," I say, wishing we could have this conversation somewhere else. Anywhere but here, where Raff's eyes meet mine from beneath the brim of his fedora and the villagers raise their glasses to me in The Salvation Arms. I can't bear to look at Susie with Cleo dancing around on the beach behind the rigid set of her shoulders. These two worlds cannot overlap.

"But is here where you want to be?"

Sometimes it is, sometimes it isn't. "You know I'll always be here for the kids. And for you."

"That wasn't what I asked," she says, looking again at Cleo. "You met someone exceptional, Mack. Your word. The connection jumps from these photos like live electricity." Tears brim her lashes. "It's undeniable, and painful, and heartbreakingly beautiful."

I can't find any words that won't make the situation worse.

"I love you," she says, choked up. "Too much to hold on to you."

"I love you too." I reach for her hand, emotion thick in my throat. "You **are** exceptional, Susie."

She studies me, then reaches out and brushes her fingers lightly over something on my cheek.

"Chalk dust," she says.

Cleo, March 19, Salvation Island

Officially an island woman

"Are you sitting down?"

"On a boulder on top of a windy hill," I say, jiggling my boot-clad foot with nervous anticipation. I called Abbie, my literary agent as of several weeks back, as soon as her **call me** message beeped in. It's a thrill to say "my agent." I'm dropping it into conversations like a freshly engaged fiancée flashing around a diamond.

"Okay, so as you know, the manuscript went out on submission on Wednesday."

I bite my lip, waiting. I've done a fair amount of shoreline pacing over the last forty-eight hours, imagining London editors reading my book. I've barely held back from sending **please love it** messages in bottles bobbing from the shores of Salvation over to the whale-gray swath of the Thames.

"There's been a brisk amount of interest, Cleo," she says. "I've had several offers already, and I know of at least two other interested houses. It's become an auction situation, best and final offers by close of business on Monday."

"Whoa." I laugh, giddy. "Slow down. You're saying impossible things and I'm struggling to keep up."

"Okay, deep breaths. It's happening, Cleo. You're going to be a published author." Her voice skitters toward excitement at the end. I love that she sounds as thrilled by this turn of events as I am; I feel as if I have someone well and truly in my corner.

"Do you want to know the offers that have come in already, or wait until the bidding is over?"

That's the kind of question my dreams are made of. "I think I'll wait."

"Good choice," she says, and then blurts out, "But just so you know the ballpark, it's a substantial six figures."

I go still. I manage to hold it together long enough for us to have a collective gasp and make plans to speak again on Monday afternoon, and then I end the call and stare out across the bay, my heart racing like a runaway train. My book is selling at auction, and there's a bidding war. Have I even understood this turn of events correctly? I have, I know I have. I slide down off the rock and plant my feet shoulder-width apart, hands on my hips. If ever there was a time for the superhero pose, this is it. I feel bloody magnificent.

Later, I stand on the porch with my usual last-call whiskey, a midnight toast to the stars and my good fortune. I can barely believe I've been here for almost six months now.

I'm officially an island woman, someone who knows the tide times and takes pleasure in watching the seasons unfurl. Do I miss my London life? Every now and then, for about five minutes. The internet here is shit and my Mac eyeliner has run out, but those things aside, Salvation wins hands down. Abbie, **my agent,** thinks my moving here is the craziest, coolest thing she's ever heard, especially since I've written a book about a girl who runs away to a remote island to self-couple and never goes home again. I heard her sharp intake of breath when I told her what inspired it; I could practically hear her pitch letter writing itself.

It's been a fairly clear day, but there's snow in the overnight forecast, so I've stocked up in preparation of hunkering down for a few days. I'm childishly hoping to wake to my first island snowfall.

"Good night, Salvation." I raise my glass. "See you in the morning." I drain the last of my whiskey and head inside.

Something wakes me just before dawn— a noise. Driftwood blowing around on the beach, I think. Feeling for my phone in the semidarkness, I see it's just turned six, and I'm caught in that delicious space between falling back to sleep and getting up to peep out the window to see if it's started to snow yet. I can't fight the urge to let my eyelids drift down; I'm warm and blissfully comfortable, and then I open my eyes abruptly again and lie perfectly still, because someone is knocking on the door. It isn't an emergency kind of knock. More of a light **are you awake?** sort of tap. I sit up and push my feet inside my fur boots, wrapping the patchwork blanket around my shoulders as I cross to the door and pull the bolt back.

"Hang on," I say. "I'm coming."

My money's on Barney, at Delta's behest,

come to insist I wait out the snowstorm at the pub, or Cameron bringing extra supplies at Brianne's insistence. I'm just about to drag the door back, and then I stop and hold my breath, because I can hear music. My fingers pause on the catch. Bruce Springsteen is playing the harmonica. I squeeze my eyes closed for a second and listen, my forehead resting on the door, shaky fingers pressed against the beginnings of my smile. And then I swing the door slowly open, knowing it isn't going to be Barney or Cameron standing on the porch.

"Mack."

"You didn't come to the exhibition." He pulls a large black photograph album from inside his coat and places it in my hands. "So I brought the exhibition to you."

"You came three thousand miles to give me this?"

He smiles, those beautiful, odd eyes of his gentle. "I've been having trouble sleeping."

I'm overwhelmed by the unexpectedness of him, by the wash of pure relief that slides through my veins at being in his orbit again. Narnia snowflakes fall steadily around the lodge, melting on the shoulders of his stupid red coat. "How . . . when . . . ?" I can't formulate the questions queuing up behind my soaring, absolute joy. I want to hurl myself into his arms, pull him inside into the warmth of the bed, but I don't do any of those things because I don't know what's going on here yet. I put the album down and gather the patch-work blanket closer as I lean my shoulder against the doorframe. "What's been keeping you awake?"

"Ah," he says, running his hand over his snow-damp hair. "Well, my watch isn't right. I keep it set to Salvation time so I know what time it is where you are."

I tuck my foot behind my ankle and look down. God, Mack Sullivan, you sure know how to deliver a line.

"Cleo, my life's complicated and messy, but I'm a different man because of our time together. Susie kissed me on Christmas Eve, and I couldn't kiss her back because I wanted it to be you."

I listen, letting his words unlock doors I've closed for the sake of my sanity. I've worked hard to convince myself that I'd never see him again. That he'd found a way back into the life he'd left behind. That my life needs to move forward without him in it.

"Someone exceptional told me a while back that my heart's no good at getting the memo," he says. "But I've got it now."

I nod, drinking in every inch of his face,

because I've missed him more than I thought possible. "And what did it say?"

"It said to travel three thousand miles to ask you to dance to Springsteen on the porch because you deserve that kind of big-gesture romance." He glances over his shoulder. "Hell, I even ordered snow, Cleo. Do you have any idea how hard that shit is?"

He reaches out and holds my hands. "Look. I have to be, I **want** to be, where my kids are until they don't need me around as much. But coming here, meeting you . . . you kind of blew my mind, you know?" He pulls me closer. "Will you come to Boston? Not permanently, but sometimes? And I'll come to you when I can, wherever you are. We can have a hundred holiday romances."

He has no idea how perfect that sounds to me. After everything I've discovered about myself, if he'd asked me to bend myself fully into his complicated world, I don't think I'd have been able to do it. But he hasn't asked that of me, because he isn't that man. He's **this** man, one who understands how much I've come to value my freedom and solitude, that my Salvation story has chapters still unwritten.

"I guess I would like to see that weather tower," I say.

Relief softens the tension in his jaw, and I

realize how nervous he was, that it wasn't easy for him to come here and lay it all on the line. We look at each other for a few silent heartbeats, and then he restarts the Springsteen track and squeezes my fingers.

"Dance with me?"

Tears catch in my throat as he tugs me out onto the porch and folds me inside the warmth of his ridiculous red coat, into the familiarity of his arms. I lay my cheek against his chest as Bruce plays his bluesy harmonica, tears in my eyes as I look out toward the snow-dusted beach and remember the last time we danced like this. I don't know what the future holds for me and my inconvenient American. I don't know if he'll ever be able to stand on one leg long enough to be my flamingo, and I'm okay that there are so many empty pages waiting to be filled. That's a story for another time, though, because right now, this snow globe Salvation moment feels just about as good as life gets.

Eighteen months later

Hello,

Remember me, the flamingo hunter who went away to marry herself on a remote island and never came home again? It's been eighteen months now since my final sign-off, and I feel as if every cell in my body has been reprogrammed. Did I ever find my flamingo? Reader, I found more than that. I found my flock.

During my years as a dating columnist I made finding love my all-consuming mission, each new date a cocktail of hope, expectation, disappointment, and despair. I downed hundreds over the years, and all I ended up with was a purseful of paper umbrellas and a jaded heart. I thought it was a numbers game, that the law of averages meant that if I just kept rolling the romantic dice, eventually I'd win. I was wrong. I was never going to win like that, because although something essential was missing from my life, it wasn't a partner.

They say you have a second brain in your gut, and despite trying to drown it with all those unsuitable cocktails, my gut knew I was living the wrong life. It tried to tell me, but I couldn't hear it over the day-to-day chaos I'd surrounded myself with. And then I came here to this island, and little by little, I listened. A quiet suggestion of change, a nagging surety, a liberating relief. I'm the kid who hung around to help the school librarian unpack the new books, fanning the pages to inhale the smell. I'm the teenager who slept with her lime-green clamshell laptop under her pillow every night. And now I'm all grown up, and I'm a novelist, spinning words into worlds, living exactly the life I was meant for. Still on my island. Still in the lodge. It's mine now, as if it was always here, waiting for me to find it.

What am I going to do now? Drink coffee on the porch and watch the stars. The American (remember him? big red coat and a ridiculous head torch?) is due here in a few days. I'm soaking up the space and the silence before he's sitting beside me on the steps again, no chalk line required.

What am I going to do after he leaves? More of the same, I expect, until it's time to haul anchor and turn my sails in a different direction.

Thank you, Emma Watson. Thank you, Bruce Springsteen. You both changed my life more than you could possibly know.

I let my gut be my compass and it led me home. Listen to yours too.

Cleo x

Cleo Wilder's debut novel, *Dearly Beloved Me*, is out on Thursday in all good bookshops.

Acknowledgments

Thank you to my exceptional editor, Katy Loftus.

Thanks also to Vikki Moynes for your generous support and editorial help. I'm really lucky to be surrounded by brilliant people. Thank you Georgia Taylor, Ellie Hudson, Leah Boulton, Karen Whitlock, and everyone at Penguin UK, especially the formidable Rights Team.

Huge thanks to my dynamo U.S. editor, Hilary Teeman, I've been so bolstered by your help, guidance, and encouragement. Gratitude also to Caroline Weishuhn and everyone at Ballantine, I'm so thrilled to continue this ride with you guys.

Thanks to my agent, Nelle Andrews, for

your steady hand on the wheel. Here's to many more adventures on the publishing high seas.

My family are my everything, love you all forever.

I often turn to my Facebook friends if I get stuck, so thank you all for humoring me and answering my random questions.

Maya and Sally—my writing wing-women and crisps-for-breakfast bezzies—love you both lots.

My Bob-land sisters—almost twenty years together! We're definitely the best internet coven around.

Last but never least, a million thanks to my readers—I'm truly indebted.

ONE NIGHT
on the
ISLAND

Josie Silver

RANDOM HOUSE BOOK
CLUB

A Conversation with Josie Silver

Is Salvation Island based on a real place? From where did you draw inspiration for the island and its inhabitants? What did your research process look like?

So, first of all—no, unfortunately, Salvation is not a real place, or based specifically on one! If it was, I'd be first in the queue to rent Otter Lodge. I knew from the outset that I wanted to create a fictional island to suit the needs of the story, to give Cleo and Mack the perfect backdrop. Removing the limitations imposed by reality allowed for complete freedom, but that definitely didn't mean I was off the hook for research. Covid restrictions prevented me from traveling over to Ireland to get an on-the-ground feel, so I was really reliant on the net, on books, and on chatting with people. I spent quite some time reading up on Ireland's islands, digging out documentaries, scouring YouTube footage, anything I could get my hands and eyes on, really, to bring the islands and the people to life as much as possible in my head. And then it was time to mentally pinpoint Salvation Island among the existing islands on the map, to decide its terrain and size, to paint the landscape in my head. It feels as if it is a real place to me; I've closed my eyes and walked its coastline countless times, and mentally tramped up and down Wailing Hill daily over the course of writing the book. I can feel the worn indent of the boulder at the top of the hill and would love to settle my bum up there and watch the sea for five minutes. I was shooting for complete escapism, for a faraway fantasy feel—my very favorite reads are the ones that whisk me away from my armchair for a few hours. That's very much my hope for my readers with this book.

Belonging is one of the main themes of the book and I wanted the islanders to form the bedrock of that. Cleo and Mack both arrive on Salvation feeling disconnected and lonely, with the sole intention of becoming even more so at Otter Lodge. Neither expects to discover a lodger in-situ or a community that will gather them close, but the islanders see two people in need and do precisely that. I myself grew up in a tight-knit community (not on a remote island, sadly!) where everyone knew each other and family was central, so I tuned in to that when thinking about the inhabitants of Salvation. Every community needs its elders, its tear-aways, its matriarchs, its jokers, its carers, and its children, and Salvation is no different. Carmen, Delores, and Raff are very much the old guard, with Brianne, Delta, and Barney holding their hands out for the the baton as the next generation. The island's young people are shaped by the traditions and remoteness of the island but are thoroughly modern too—they're moving Salvation with the times, albeit at a gentle pace. My ultimate aim was to create the kind of community we all yearn to be part of, meaningful and supportive, rich with laughter, loyalty, and love.

What was it like to write an American character? How did finding Mack's voice compare to writing Cleo's?

I'm a big fan of American TV and there's an embarrassment of riches around these days thanks to the various streaming services. I tell myself my TV habit is research and it makes me feel less guilty about clicking open Netflix when I should be working! And it really is research because it gives me such a goldmine of wonderful American men to draw my characters from. **This Is Us** is a perfect example (I'm OBSESSED!)—Jack's devotion as a husband and a father, Randall's dependability, Kevin's angst, Toby's humor. Going back a little further, Tom from **Desperate Housewives** was so self-assured but honest and vulnerable, he's long been my gold-standard fictional husband. And of course the mighty, beloved **Schitt's Creek**. I am so in love with the entire Rose family! The transparent way they love, the underscore of decency, the wit, the heart, and the humor—I admire it hugely. So I drink in all of these shows, and all of these male characters, and they fill me with inspiration when it comes to creating characters of my own.

I'm also fortunate enough to have a brilliant U.S. editor who diligently ironed the Britishness out of Mack's chapters, for which I am eternally grateful!

Where did you find the inspiration for the self-coupling celebration Cleo has for herself?

Of all the elements of the book, Cleo's self-coupling ceremony felt like one of the most crucial parts to get right. I knew I didn't want it, or her, to feel gimmicky or foolish. I wanted it to cut to the heart of her anxieties around losing her father, and demonstrate her sincerity and sense of self-worth. I was super-keen to include important stuff around the theme of self-acceptance behind the novelty of the "Wedding for One!" headline.

I used the traditional wedding vows as a kick-off point, and then tried to think more widely about the things we'd wish for the women in our lives, for our friends, for our sisters. Isn't it always so much easier to give advice and support to others than to turn that love inward on ourselves? I guess I wanted Cleo to feel strengthened and empowered, and above all, to feel whole.

What does your writing process look like? Has it been affected by lockdown?

I was really lucky to have had a garden office installed six months before the pandemic hit—I honestly don't know what I'd have done without it! Like most other parents around the globe, I suddenly became teacher and full-time mom around my usual workload, so having a space to escape to that was just mine was especially valuable. That said, I found being creative really tough in the early months of Covid—my anxiety and uncertainty seeped onto the page in the form of a half-written, angst-ridden book that was very difficult to write. In the end I abandoned it and switched upbeat to write **One Night on the Island.** The relief of closing that earlier document has stayed with me. There was definitely an element of pandemic escape involved with writing **One Night on the Island.** It was a tonic to head down to my office most afternoons and transport myself mentally to Salvation Island. I really hope that my escape becomes the reader's escape too.

In general I'm not a plotter. I like to have a beginning and a probable end in my head and then start writing the story to see where it leads me. I really enjoy the process of getting to know the characters in that way. They say or do things to make me pause and think "Oh, okay, so **that's** where we're going," or "Are you **sure** you should do that?" I love the element of surprise, although it's definitely a more stressful way of working than plotting everything out beforehand.

What books have you been reading and loving lately?

I'm halfway through **The Ex Hex** by Erin Sterling—a really good witch story is always on my auto-buy list and this one is fabulous! I recently finished and loved **The Confessions of Frannie Langton** by Sara Collins. It's powerful and immersive and being adapted for TV soon. I can't wait to see it. Like many others, I'm a **Bridgerton** devotee. Watching the series has led me to reading Julia Quinn's historical romance series—I'm a few books in and happily addicted.

Questions and Topics for Discussion

1. **One Night on the Island** begins with Cleo in London and Mack in the United States deciding to take some time for themselves to think about their lives and where they want to go next, since life hasn't quite shaped up for either of them the way they thought it would. Have you ever been in a similar situation where you wanted to take a step back and re-evaluate? Did you find it was a good experience? Why or why not?

2. As Cleo and Mack realize that they'll be staying together in Otter Lodge for the foreseeable future, they (begrudgingly) decide to try and make the best of it by setting boundaries so that each can get some of the solitude they seek on Salvation Island. Were they successful in their approach?

3. Sometimes, it can be easier for people to open up to strangers about difficult parts of their lives rather than to people close to them, as Mack and Cleo do throughout the novel. Why do you think they did? Have you ever felt this way?

4. Cleo's mission on Salvation Island is to "self-couple" and provide a fresh perspective for her dating column, and she sets about this task by preparing a ceremony to "marry herself" at the end of her stay. What did you think of her personal journey while she was on the island? Was she successful in finding self-love and self-acceptance? Why or why not?

5. Mack, on the other hand, is on Salvation Island to give his estranged wife the space she needs while also trying to come to terms with the state of their marriage himself. How did you feel about Mack's situation? Did he make the right choice in coming to the island? Why or why not?

6. While on Salvation, both Cleo and Mack are surprised to find themselves truly taken by the islanders and their way of life, especially because of the sharp contrast to their lives in large, bustling cities. Have you ever visited a place or met people that gave you a newfound

appreciation for a way of living different from your own? What was that experience like? Did it change your perspective or priorities in any way?

7. As a result of their respective stays on the island, both Cleo and Mack decide to make rather large changes in their lives. What did you think of those big decisions they made? Would you have done the same in their positions? Why or why not?

8. What did you think of the somewhat unconventional ending of the novel?

About the Author

JOSIE SILVER is an unabashed romantic who met her husband when she stepped on his foot on his twenty-first birthday. She lives with him, their two sons, and their cats in England. She is the #1 **New York Times** bestselling author of **One Day in December** and **The Two Lives of Lydia Bird**.